UNWELCOME VISITORS

"Something fishy," Mike said. "Unless I miss my guess, we've got visitors slipping up on us from the rear."

McLafferty turned, crouched, and moved the length of the long, sandy fracture between slabs of stone. He heard Moon's rifle go off, nodded, and surveyed the area below. Nothing. He scanned the slopes above him, heard noise, and scrambled upward, pistol in hand, toward the sandy trench that led across to Moon and Tallchief.

"Cortez! Don't move!" he called out.

Suddenly Cortez hurled himself to one side, rolled, and fired, the shot singing wide of its mark.

But McLafferty didn't miss. Cortez's body convulsed, his mouth, wide open, sucked in a final breath. . . .

⊘ SIGNET (0451)

ROMANTIC ADVENTURES

- ☐ **THE MCLAFFERTYS by Jude Williams.** A bold man and a brave beauty—in an American wilderness saga of passion and revenge. Mountain man, Michael McLafferty and the beautiful half-Cheyenne, Moon Morning Star, are caught up in a quest for revenge against the man who killed their Indian friend. And nothing could distract them—not even their passion for each other. . . . (146255—$3.50)

- ☐ **DESERT MOON by Jude Williams.** A man's iron strength, a woman's passionate courage—in a rousing American wilderness saga that began with the *MacLaffertys*. Mike MacLafferty and his beautiful and brave wife fight a ruthless gang of killers against murderous odds. (149246—$3.75)

- ☐ **IN THIS SWEET LAND: INGA'S STORY by Aola Vandergriff.** Vowing to make a new life for herself among the ruined dreams of the post-Civil War South, beautiful Inga Johannson struggles to reckon with her two daughters who are beginning to feel the stirrings of womanhood. Meanwhile the two men in her life vie for her love, ignite her passions, divide her heart . . . The first magnificent saga in the DAUGHTERS series.
  (135849—$3.95)

- ☐ **DEVILWIND: JENNY'S STORY by Aola Vandergriff.** The second powerful saga in the DAUGHTERS series . . . a turbulent, romantic novel filled with all the passion and savagery of the wilderness. On a trackless Western plane, proud and passionate Jenny St. Germain searches for her lost lover, and discovers savage terror and untamed ecstacy as captive of the Navajos. . . . (146069—$3.95)

- ☐ **A LAND REMEMBERED by Patrick D. Smith.** An unforgettable family's rise to fortune from the guns of the Civil War to the glitter and greed of the Florida Gold Coast . . . as the MacIveys discover what it takes to turn an American dream into American reality. . . . (140370—$3.95)

Prices slightly higher in Canada.

Buy them at your local bookstore or use this convenient coupon for ordering.

NEW AMERICAN LIBRARY,
P.O. Box 999, Bergenfield, New Jersey 07621

Please send me the books I have checked above. I am enclosing $_____
(please add $1.00 to this order to cover postage and handling). Send check or money order—no cash or C.O.D.'s. Prices and numbers subject to change without notice.

Name_____

Address_____

City_____ State_____ Zip Code_____

Allow 4-6 weeks for delivery.
This offer is subject to withdrawal without notice.

DESERT MOON

Jude Williams

A SIGNET BOOK

NEW AMERICAN LIBRARY

NAL BOOKS ARE AVAILABLE AT QUANTITY DISCOUNTS WHEN USED TO PROMOTE PRODUCTS OR SERVICES. FOR INFORMATION PLEASE WRITE TO PREMIUM MARKETING DIVISION, NEW AMERICAN LIBRARY, 1633 BROADWAY, NEW YORK, NEW YORK 10019.

PUBLISHER'S NOTE

This book is a work of fiction. Names, characters, places, and incidents either are the product of the author's imagination or are used fictitiously, and any resemblance to actual persons, living or dead, events, or locales is entirely coincidental.

Copyright © 1987 by Jude Williams

All rights reserved

SIGNET TRADEMARK REG. U.S. PAT. OFF. AND FOREIGN COUNTRIES
REGISTERED TRADEMARK—MARCA REGISTRADA
HECHO EN CHICAGO, U.S.A.

SIGNET, SIGNET CLASSIC, MENTOR, ONYX, PLUME, MERIDIAN and NAL BOOKS are published by NAL PENGUIN INC., 1633 Broadway, New York, New York 10019

First Printing, October, 1987

1 2 3 4 5 6 7 8 9

PRINTED IN THE UNITED STATES OF AMERICA

1 Heavy gray clouds ran in from the desert, pouring over the high backs of the Ruby Mountains. With temperatures dropping to near zero each night, a good snowfall was likely. Perhaps the white stuff would begin that evening.

"Just the way it's supposed to, off East in the civilized world," McLafferty reflected. "I wonder if anyone's bothered to tell our friends, the damned Shuckers out there, tonight's Christmas Eve of the year of Our Lord, eighteen-hundred and forty-nine? Well, the devils don't do anything—but they just keep hanging around, day after day, until a man's brain starts boiling inside his skull. Rumor has it they're fond of horsemeat. . . ."

He slapped Gray Boy on the rump, clucked his tongue at the big stallion, and slid the corral gate back into place.

Mike glanced towards the oversized, half-completed log cabin, a drift of bluegray smoke rising from the clay and rock chimney he and Moon finished a month earlier, with that damned Fiddlehead Wilson sitting there and smoking his pipe and providing a constant critique of their efforts. Mike's wife, Moon Morning Star, managed to ignore Wilson's banter—or she laughed if the old mountain man actually said something funny—but there were times when Fiddlehead's drollery began to get on McLafferty's nerves. He loved the man, but Wilson affected him that way occasionally.

Anyhow, when Fiddlehead suggested taking the buckboard and mules on a "quick run over to Salt Lake" to purchase supplies and to get "a sackful o' Christmas presents for a honest-to-Gawd potlatch," Mike agreed to it, no questions asked.

Now, however, Christmas was upon them, and no sign of Fiddlehead.

Well, maybe Noel could come a few days late at the base of the high Ruby Mountains. For Moon, Halfbreed French and Iroquois—Cheyenne by adoption and inclination—Christmas wasn't important and never had been. As a matter of fact, little Jacques White Bull, her son, had never in his life known Christmas—though if he were a White boy in the settlements, he'd be waiting for St. Nick to come slipping down the chimney on this particular night. The giving of presents was important to Elizabeth Harrington, however, Mike and Moon's semi-adopted little red-haired sixteen-year-old who was a far piece from her old home in Kentucky. Had things gone well for her, she'd have been in Oregon by now with her brother and their friends, and not with a half-reformed gambler and gunslinger and his Indian warrior—woman of a bride. Instead, there were bodies lying dead and buried out on the Hastings Cutoff where Moon and Mike were obliged to leave them, and Elizabeth was (at least temporarily) a member of the McLafferty family.

Had anyone asked Mike last winter, he'd have said for certain he'd be in California by now, either digging for gold on his own claim or working the monte tables of the goldcamps, plying his acquired trade of professional gambler. Instead, all the unpredictable things happened, naturally, just the way they weren't supposed to. Mike's close friend White Bull of the Cheyennes was dead, and he himself was married, so to speak, to White Bull's widow. In the old days, the boys all insisted Joe Meek's woman, Mountain Lamb, was the most beautiful female the Big Coyote ever created, but in the judgment of many, Moon Morning Star wasn't far behind her.

"No matter how you look at it," McLafferty told Gray Boy, "Moon's no ordinary woman. She scares me at times, and I don't commonly scare easy."

Beautiful Moon—when summertime came to this huge, empty land of peaks and desert, she'd bear McLafferty's child. Boy or girl, it didn't make any difference.

The big stallion nibbled the sleeve fringe of Mike's buckskin jacket, and the man rubbed the horse between the eyes, the way the animal liked. Then Mike turned and walked to the house, eager to be inside next to a roaring fire. He slapped his hands together in an attempt to bring some circulation back into them, rubbed the back of a wrist across his nose, and blew a breath of steam out into twilight.

He reached the steps of the log ranch house, kicked clots of snow from his boots, and was about to enter when he heard a rifle shot echoing from somewhere down the ravine which led out to the desert floor and Humboldt's South Branch. Two additional shots followed, and Mike didn't doubt it any longer—an old Hawken flintlock rifle, its noise seeming to crackle as it bounced upcanyon and reverberated from bare rims beyond high meadows.

He opened the door.

"Moon-Gal!" he called out. "Fiddlehead's on his

way in. We'll have some presents to pass around after all, if the gap-toothed thief didn't get drunk and blow our money on poker."

Moon turned, lithe and utterly feminine, her three-months pregnancy just beginning to show. She walked across the warm room to where Mike stood in the doorway.

"Mac-lafferty, you told me there's no firewater in Mr. Young's city," she said. "We must trust our friend Fiddlehead. If he's come back, then he's brought the the things we need. When has he ever let us down?"

Mike put his arm about his wife's waist, squeezed her through a thickness of finely-tanned white deerskin, and grinned.

"You're right," he said. "And he's probably pushed those poor mules half to death in order to get here on time. Wants Jacques to see just how it ought to be done on Christmas. Best we get some coffee on so Mr. Whiskers feels properly welcome."

Snow began to fall in windless darkness, a few flakes at first and then gradually gaining in intensity. Lantern in hand, Mike came in from rubbing down and feeding the hungry pack mules.

"Fiddlehead, you never cease to amaze me," he mumbled into the night as he opened a leather-hinged door and stepped inside to where Wilson was passing out the various items he'd been able to purchase in Salt Lake City.

For young Jacques there was a snap-case compass ("So's ye don't head off north an' meet yoreself comin' south"), for sixteen-year-old Elizabeth some new clothing and several small blue vials of perfume ("worse than any skonk, by Gawd, but young gals is suppose to like the stuff"), and for Moon some tent-sized dresses (" 'Cause she's got bread in the oven, Michael ye idjit, an' soon'll be bigger than the two of us possum-pounders put together").

"She's bigger than we are now," Mike chuckled, winking at his slim, sinewy wife.

"Damn rights," Wilson went on, directing his attention once again to young Jacques and beginning a long-winded yarn about how he and Hugh Glass once got turned around in a range of mountains "that was all one great big magnet," even though Hugh was carrying a fancy ship's compass Jean Laffitte gave him the day Glass quit being a pirate and started being a mountain man.

A big fire was roaring in the fireplace, and the McLafferty family relaxed. Wilson had driven the mules hard in a race against time and incipient snowfall, and by all rights the old man should have been exhausted. Instead he was in more than usually buoyant spirits.

"I think our friend must have a secret," Moon laughed as she poured whiskey into each of the three coffee cups.

McLafferty nodded, sipped.

"Don't let on that you know, Moon-Gal, or he's likely to tell us about it."

Fiddlehead was just explaining Glass's theory of why pine trees grew upside down in the Magnet Mountains when he caught Moon's comment, broke off his tale, and grinned.

"Matter o' fact," he said, "this child did pick up a leetle gassip. Met Termite Joe Hollinback in the settlements, an' he's jest come up from Taos by way of Pueblo. Michael lad, ye've heard about Queen Vikki, ain't ye? Shore ye have. Ye've been to Pueblo once or twice. Well, for Miz Moon's benefit, she's the bosslady at the whorehouse—was, that is, until jest lately. Well, Sam Tarrango, he done run her an' her

DESERT MOON 11

feelin' on it. By Gawd, when Wilson makes love to a female, she don't never forget it neither. Got this special thing I do with—"

Mike glanced at Elizabeth Harrington, whose attention seemed to have shifted from her blue vials of perfume to what Fiddlehead was in the process of saying.

"Aw hell, the trapper continued, looking sidelong at Elizabeth, "ye know what I mean, lad. Anyhow, I've got me a intuition, ye might say."

Moon Morning Star pressed close to Mike's side, whispering into his ear.

"Mike Mac-lafferty, you must build us a small cabin above the high meadows," she said. "I'm becoming like a white woman—I want to make love, but there are too many people in the house."

"Cabin fever, squaw," he mumbled.

He stood up, walked to the door, opened it, and stared out into a steady snowfall.

"There's no Saint Nicholas, folks, but the sagebrush kingdom's filling up with snow all the same. Merry Christmas. Merry Christmas to all us crazy people. By God, we'll make a prosperous ranch out of this rendezvous site yet. Cattle, Mr. Wilson. We need a good herd of cattle. The time'll come when all this land's settled, and the McLafferty spread's going to be right in the thick of things—with Mormons east of us and hungry miners in California to the west."

Moon looked askance at Fiddlehead Wilson, who wrinkled his nose.

"Shut the door, ye overgrown idjit. Must be close to zero out thar. Why do ye think Miz Moon built us a fire? Ain't even no fool as big as Mike McLafferty would think about raisin' cows out hyar," Wilson said, "unless ye're jest figgering to give them pesky gals out o' town, including leetle Sunshine Hobson—who's, ye might say, a special friend to this old coon dawg. Once spent half a season's wages jest lyin' around in bed with that lass, I did."

"Never had the pleasure of meeting Victoria Queen," Mike said, winking at Moon, "but I'm on her side already."

"Wal, Queen Vikki didn't take kindly to bein' run out o' town that way, an' by Gawd her an' her girls done rode back an' stuck up the bank—Tarrango's own operation. Must of hit 'er jest right, too. Hollingback says they cleaned out near fifty thousand dollars. Ain't that somethin', now? An' then took off—some say for St. Louis, some say for Californy. Hell, could be they'll stop by an' visit. I sort of let it be known in Salt Lake whar I was, jest in case ol' Sunshine ain't forgot me."

"Sure it wasn't five-hundred, not fifty thousand?" Mike asked.

"Fifty thousand, ye pigheaded fool of a swampwater Irishman, an' not a penny less. Damned near cleaned old Sam out, from what Hollingback told me. Only trouble is, what happens if he kotches up with 'em? But that Queen Vikki's a crafty one. She'd been Tarrango's mistress for two, three years. Hell, I even heard rumors she an' Sam meant to tie the knot—sort of make honest thieves out o' each other. Now she's the richest hooker on this side of the Mississip."

"If she's clever as you say," McLafferty suggested, "she's on her way to New Orleans or Richmond or even New York. Tarrango won't be following her to the States, not with half a dozen warrants out on him."

"Sunshine'll talk 'er into coming this hyar way," Fiddlehead insisted. "Ye'll see. Got me a real gut

Shuckers some varmints to kill. But even if we manage to run off the injuns, an' even if ye manage to herd a bunch o' cows out hyar, why whar would ye sell 'em?"

Mike shrugged, pulled the door to. He crossed the room, tousling Jacques' hair as he did so and winking at Elizabeth. He came around behind Moon and placed his hands on her shoulders, squeezing gently.

"Tens of thousands of emigrants'll be stumbling over the California Trail for the next few years. My beautiful wife thinks I'm right, at least."

Moon grabbed his hand and bit softly at his thumb, teasing even though they both knew there wasn't much they could do for what ailed them—not at the present, anyhow.

"I think I would like some more whiskey," she replied. "But just whiskey this time. That terrible coffee ruins the taste."

The storm passed in the night, and Christmas day dawned clear over a world of high white mountains, snow-draped firs and pinyons, and brilliantly glittering sage country spreading off to the Sulphur Springs Range. Hawks and eagles drifted against flawlessly blue sky, intent upon hunting in the snow's aftermath. There were times, Mike had decided some months back, when Ruby Mountain country was the most beautiful spot on earth, and this was one of those times.

Fiddlehead walked out early to tend to and commune with the mules, and took note of crisscrossed jackrabbit tracks and the prints of a large bobcat not far from the house as he himself crunched along through the crusted whiteness.

"Mules," he said, "this old porkypine figgers Mike an' Moon are probably wantin' to spend a few hours alone. It's that way with human critters, ye see. Chances are, they ain't had a chance to do no serious matin' in a spell, if ye get my drift—not with no proper teenaged gal in the house and with Jacques doin' everything but swinging from the rafter poles . . ."

Plan firmly in mind, he returned to the house, grumbled something half-intelligible at McLafferty, walked to where Moon was fixing breakfast for the clan, and announced his intention to make a foray to the woods beyond the high meadows.

"Goin' to need some help, though," he said, nodding. "Guess I'll take the leetle warrior an' miz Bethy redhead with me. They can fetch squaw-wood while this child's using the choppin' axe. Give ye an' Mike some time to yorselves."

Moon stared at the mountain man, then looked like she was furious with herself when blood started coming into her cheeks.

Mike laughed, but she nodded, smiled.

"You'll be gone three or four hours, then?"

Wilson squinted and wrinkled his nose.

"How much time's it take ye two?" he demanded.

Moon and Mike each had a drink for good luck, and then they kissed for a long while. Mike ran his hands all over Moon's body, pausing here and there to do a little squeezing or soft pinching. That was something Moon hadn't much liked when she and Mike first started being not just friends and conspirators and hunters of a wild animal named Laroque, but it was something she'd come to enjoy and even to demand as a prelude to their lovemaking. Mike could always tell when it was working because Moon started having trouble breathing regularly. As for himself, the feel of Moon's breasts and buttocks through her deerskin clothing was enough to make him forget about whatever world was beyond just the two of them. Kissing was another white man's vice she'd become inordinately fond of.

"Mike," she whispered, her voice so low and throaty he could barely make out what she said, "lock . . . the door . . . just in case."

He slid the tip of his tongue into her ear, growled like he wanted to eat her alive, and then stepped across the room to set the wooden slide bolt.

"In here, Mac-lafferty!" Moon called from the bedroom.

He moved toward the doorway, quite conscious of an ache in his britches, an ache no one but Moon had ever been able to elicit in quite the same way.

She was lying on the bed, atop the skin of the big grizzly she'd killed near South Pass the previous summer. Her eyes were closed, and her long hair was draped down over her breasts, coiling between and to either side, though how she managed to undo her braids so quickly Mike wasn't certain. Her knees were pulled up, and the illusion was nearly that of a woman who was still half a child and who'd inexplicably fallen asleep in a very strange position.

"Take your boots off, damn you," she whispered. "We don't have to finish in ten minutes this time."

"You sure you can wait that long?" he chuckled.

"Of course."

"What if I can't?"

"I'm going to make you keep your little toy ready for an hour or so," she replied, sitting up on the grizzly skin and running her tongue over her lips. "I want your whole . . . attention!"

"Bossy female," he muttered as he sat down on the bed's edge and pulled off the boots. "I'll give you some attention, all right."

"I like to look at you when you're naked and excited for me," she laughed.

He crawled onto the bed, and just then she leaned forward and grabbed hold of him—as he was hoping she would.

"I'm going to ride my stallion for a while," she whispered. "Lie down."

McLafferty obeyed, watching Moon through half-closed eyes as she crouched over him and then ... then they were together, clinging to one another, his hands on her breasts, her throat arched back, eyes closed, the storm of her dark hair cascading over her shoulders, mouth open and forming a small, intense zero.

Mike didn't think he could last more than a couple of minutes, not after so long, but Moon sensed what was about to happen and pulled off him.

"Plenty of time today," she said. "I want it all. You cool down, Mike McLafferty, or I'll bite off your ... nose."

"Jesus, Moon," he groaned.

They lost track of time, sensing only that perhaps a couple of hours had gone by. True to her word, Moon LeClaire Morning Star McLafferty was careful not to allow her husband to finish until after the two of them had done just about everything they could think of. Mike felt good when Moon began to moan and sing those little short yelps the first time, and for some reason or other all he could think of was summer thunderclouds and rain lancing down over rolling, dry-grass prairies. Somewhere in the back of his mind there were birds crying out, only he couldn't tell what kind they were, maybe some cross between mockingbirds gone crazy and crows in a Missouri cornfield. All he knew was that he wanted it to happen again, and he slid down on her and stayed there until his mouth was completely numb. Moon was sweating, and so was he, their bodies completely slippery with what they were doing.

Then Moon went limp and whispered, "No more, no more, come back into me."

He covered her, and it was like sage burning on top of a bed of coals.

Afterward they lay together, just holding one another. Moon was crying and smiling at the same time, something Mike had never understood, and she was pressed up against him, one hand lying on his chest. He could feel sleep coming on, knew he couldn't resist it. But Moon started pulling at the hair on his chest. After a moment he realized why. A thumping sound.

Someone was pounding on the damned door.

"Fiddlehead must be back—or something's happened," Moon whispered.

Mike sat bolt upright, instinctively reaching for his Colt and only then realizing it was with the rest of his clothing, heaped in a pile at the foot of their sleeping pallet.

They both rose immediately and began to pull their clothing on, laughing as they did so like a couple of kids caught swiping a fresh-baked apple pie.

"Just a damned minute!" Mike yelled. "Fiddlehead, don't you remember why you went off to cut firewood?"

"Open the door, McLafferty!"

The voice did not belong to Fiddlehead Wilson. Suddenly Mike was completely awake, as though someone had thrown cold water on him. He pulled on his leathers and his boots, told Moon to get into the pantry and wedge something against the door, shook his head, and strode over to the door.

"Who's out there? Identify yourself."

"An old friend," came the reply.

"Don't have any old friends," he grumbled. "They all ran out of tin and starved to death."

"Come on, Big Mike, open the door and act friendly. Benton said you'd stake us to a meal."

"You've seen Aloysius? Who was with him?"

"Weren't nobody with the old coot. Open the door before I kick the damned thing in. Ain't after you, just want some information is all."

Mike drew his Colt Walker, slipped back the slide board, and pushed the door with his foot—half recognizing the voice but still not certain who it was. Then he was face to face with Black Johnny Cortez and two of his cronies—a half-breed Apache named Wolf Mask and scarfaced Pete the Gun, an individual McLafferty had once been obliged to coldcock after Pete accused him of doctoring the dice they were using in a little game of craps at a post out on the Republican River. Cortez had already drawn his revolver, and the two men, guns in hand, glared at one another.

"Gentlemen," Mike said, "welcome to Ruby Dome Ranch. This could make for an interesting shoot-out, damned near point-blank."

"I figured on it, McLafferty. No goddamn hospitality for an old friend. Well, you drill me, an' I drill you. Ain't any way either one of us can miss, as I see it. Listen now, Sam Tarrango sent us after Queen Vikki and her three sluts. They come this way, but we lost their trail—must of cut for the hills before the snow started. Me an' the boys, we guess you've got 'em inside, now ain't that right? Our quarrel's not with you, Big Mike. Just hand over the whores, an' we'll be on our way."

2

Get into the pantry and block the door shut! Is it possible that Michael Red Coyote still doesn't understand me any better than that?

Moon pondered the question briefly as she finished pulling the doeskin dress over her breasts and hips, then took down her gunbelt from the peg on the wall. McLafferty had pulled the bedroom door shut behind him when he went out to talk to the strangers, and so she couldn't hear their words, but she understood the tones of their voices well enough—coarse voices, raised in command, the tone a reckless man uses when he's holding a gun on another. She could feel her heart beating hard against the wall of her chest. She'd heard such voices before.

I must keep my thoughts calm, as Leg-in-the-water, my Cheyenne father would counsel, as White Bull taught me to do when we hunted together. Breathe deeply and think of nothing.

But she couldn't keep vision from turning inward for an instant, in time to the night when Jean Laroque and his men had first come to the Cheyenne camp on the Laramie River, the camp of Leg-in-the-water and the others of her adopted people, the only family and friends she'd known since girlhood—since her white father, a French Canadian trapper, died.

Those white men had been drunk, and their voices were like the ones Moon heard outside the door now. They'd come from a wagon train that had stopped for the night near Fort Laramie, one among many such trains bound in the summer of 1849 for the place called California, where there was said to be a great deal of the yellow metal that made white men go crazy. They had wandered into the village, already red-eyed and reeling with bad whiskey, looking for excitement, for plunder to be taken at gambling or at gunpoint, and especially for women.

Coarse-bearded faces gleaming with the sweat of whiskey and excitement in a flickering glow of campfires, teeth glittering in grimaces of laughter or bullying assertion, a young girl, White Bull's sister, screaming as a drunken stranger dragged her by the wrist into darkness beyond the fireglow, shouts then from the men, White Bull rising to intercept the kidnap, the next moment White Bull, Moon's husband, crumpling slowly, slowly, an expression of astonishment in his eyes as color drained from his face.

"Not Red Coyote too, no, I will not allow that," she whispered as she buckled on the belt, heavy with its holstered revolver on the right side, sheathed skinning knife just in front. Automatically she drew the revolver and checked its cylinder, although she knew it was always loaded, and again her breathing became fast. White Bull's revolver, the weapon with which she'd finally avenged his death before she became Mike McLafferty's woman, even though she had come to love the tall, redhaired white man during the time they rode together on the trail of revenge. All that had happened only a short time ago, really, no-more than half a year, and yet it seemed already as if it had been a different lifetime. Now she carried Red Coyote's child in her belly, and they had built this cabin, this home, this life together, and she knew she would kill these men or die herself before she'd let them take her husband from her.

She stepped quickly to the small window at the rear of the bedroom, opposite the door, pushed aside the piece of blanket that covered it and served as insulation against the keen cold that seeped through an oiled piece of split hide nailed over the opening. She drew her skinning knife, slashed along two sides of the hide covering, climbed upon a table and out through the window.

It was only when her feet touched the partially melted layer of new snow that she remembered she hadn't put on her moccasins. Icy, numbing pain flowed up toward her ankles, but she whispered words learned from eavesdropping in girlhood on certain rituals, words not meant for women but which she had made her own in the time when she became White Bull's avenger.

> Pain, touch my body. My spirit
> Does not fear. My heart welcomes you,
> Gift of the Dreamer.
> Not woman's heart, not child's heart
> But the heart of a strong bull buffalo,
> Let that be mine.

She stepped to the corner of the cabin, slipped along close beside a wall to the second corner.

A dark-haired white man was speaking, revolver in hand, while a second held a rifle loosely in the crook of his elbow. This was a grinning, hard-faced individual with hair down past his shoulders. Indian, she thought, but not Cheyenne, perhaps a half-breed white like herself. A third man was disfigured by a ragged scar that slashed down the side of his face and twisted his mouth into a snarl like that of a trapped ferret. She watched for a moment to "see which way the stick floats," as Fiddlehead would have advised.

"Big Mike claims he ain't hiding nobody," the man holding the revolver said, "so I figure he won't mind if we just have a look inside, eh, Pete?"

The scarfaced one took a step toward Red Coyote as if he would go past him into the cabin.

"Like hell," Michael Red Coyote growled, moving his gun so that it was trained on scarfaced Pete, then shifting it back to the other white man. The Indian laughed.

"Mexican standoff, hey Black Johnny? Don't worry none, amigo. He kills you and Pete the Gun, I'll send him along with you."

"Shut up, Wolf Mask, you ignorant half-breed Apache," Pete snapped. Black Johnny addressed McLafferty in the tone a white trader might use when trying to convince an old Cheyenne woman to give up a half dozen fine buffalo robes in exchange for a handful of glass beads.

"You know you can't win, Big Mike," he said. "We ain't askin' much, you gotta admit that. Just want to check around for them whores. They ain't nothin' to you, not enough to end up dead over. Odds ain't favoring the house now. Card hustler like you ought to know that."

"The odds have changed, gentlemen," Moon said then, stepping into full view now and holding her pistol steadily on Wolf Mask. "You will do as my husband asks."

The men glanced at the woman, startled, all but

Black Johnny, who had the presence of mind to keep his gaze on Mike. The eyes of the other two shifted back and forth rapidly, speculating.

"Moon, for Christ's sake . . ." McLafferty began, but she ignored him, speaking to the scarfaced Pete and the half-breed Wolf Mask.

"You're wondering if perhaps you can jump me and take me hostage. You're thinking that a woman probably will not shoot you. Those are foolish thoughts. I've killed other worthless men, and it gave me only pleasure."

"Wagh! Ye can bet yore ma's cathouse on that one, gents," came a new voice, and Moon laughed inside. Fiddlehead Wilson had appeared, apparently from nowhere, and stood behind the trio, the 50 caliber eye of his big Hawken buffalo gun shifting back and forth from one to the other. "Now," he continued calmly as the strangers whirled to face this new challenge, "ye got about one chance, an' that one's slippin' away from ye. Drop the irons, boys, an' the three of ye clear on out."

Wolf Mask held his rifle trained on Red Coyote for a fraction of a second longer, his eyes glittering. Then he shrugged and dropped it to the ground. Cortez laughed, holstered his pistol, and slapped Michael on the shoulder.

"Hell, Big Mike, we didn't mean nothin' by it," he said. "We was just havin' some fun, thought we'd give you a little scare. Truth is, I mostly just stopped by to see my ol' compañero. How the hell are you, you mangy brush wolf?"

"About the same as the last time you tried to blindside me and steal my poke, I guess. Now that we've had our visit, why don't you climb back on your pony and hit the trail before my wife and my friend get tired of waiting?"

"You always accused me of that, Mike, but you know it ain't so. Look, we just want those gals, all four of them. Think you might of known them once, Big Mike."

Here he winked at Moon. She drew back the hammer of her revolver, watched the garrulous white man wince, then grin and begin babbling again.

"Look, why don't we all go inside where it's a little warmer, have some coffee? Damn, a man could freeze his balls off—beggin' your pardon, ma'am."

Moon stared at him and held her pistol steady until his eyes dropped, and he turned back to McLafferty.

"Not much hospitality in these parts, is there, Big Mike? Well, I'm workin' for Sam Tarrango these days. Might be you've heard of him. Richest son of a bitch in Pueblo, old Sam is, but he's fifty thousand lighter since Queen Vikki and her crew got done with him. He had 'em set up in the finest whorehouse west of St. Lou, was even talk about him marryin' the one bitch, but that wasn't enough for Vikki, I guess. Robbed him blind and took off, and Sam put a thousand on each of those purty little heads. But don't go tryin' to collect it for yourself, McLafferty. Next time I'll catch you when your friends aren't around. You sure you ain't seen 'em, pardner?"

"Damn if he ain't got runs of the mouth," Fiddlehead drawled. "What do ye say, Moon-Gal? My ears is jest about rubbed raw with all that jawin'."

"I'm ready to kill these men," she said, nodding, "Then I can go inside and warm my feet."

Black Johnny Cortez turned, glanced at each of the speakers, spat a stream of tobacco juice near Mike's feet, sneered.

"Come on, boys, let's get the hell out of this hole," he said, and turned to mount.

"I'll remember 'em, Johnny, every damned one of 'em," Scarface said as he swung up onto his sorrel mare. "Especially you, sweetcakes," he finished, staring at the woman. She returned his stare, but the back of her neck felt as if a ghost had breathed on her.

Wolf Mask laughed, gave a war whoop, and the trio rode slowly past the corral and the small lean-to stable, their hunched figures stark against the new whiteness of the meadow and snow-hung boughs of the pinyon stand beyond it.

Fiddlehead watched them until they were out of sight beyond a grove of aspens at the lower end of the meadow, then shouldered his Hawken and sauntered down to his friends. Moon nearly laughed at his peculiar, bandy-legged gait. He pulled his greasy bearskin cap lower on his few strands of silver-white hair, squinted up at Mike, and thoughtfully stroked his straggle of beard.

"Can't say much for yore taste in visitors, Sonny. Moon-Gal, I know ye don't take kindly to advice a-tall, but I got me a feelin' ye'd be a mite more comfortable in by the fire, maybe even with some shoes on, but o' course that ain't none of my nevermind."

Mike looked down at Moon's feet and then roared like a bear and tossed her over his shoulder.

"Hope the two o' ye are done with . . . whatever it were ye was doin'," Wilson grumbled as Mike dumped his burden onto the buffalo rug in front of the fireplace, "cuz me an' them younguns is jest about froze blue up thar. Got enough wood piled up to fill three wagons, an' I had to keep tellin' 'em we needed more."

"What on earth are you going on about, Fiddlehead?" Mike grinned, winking at Moon. "We didn't know what to do here all by ourselves. We got so lonely we had to call in Black Johnny Cortez and friends to keep us company."

Fiddlehead snorted, hitched up his trousers, turned to warm his backside at the fire. The wizened face, nearly invisible between cap and beard, grew thoughtful.

"Don't like the looks of 'er, Michael me lad. Them gals out there alone in this kind o' weather, an' them three bushwhackers after 'em. Cortez an' the scarfaced bastard I know, Pete the Gun. Their favorite trick was gettin' lads drunk an' shootin' 'em. Pretty sure the injun was in Taos some years back. Gunned down a Mexican kid not more'n sixteen, seventeen years old. No reason a-tall. Told somebody the youngun reminded him of his brother, an' he jest happened to remember how his brother used to whip on him when he was little."

"Nice fellas, all right," McLafferty agreed. "Pete the Gun. The other two aren't much better. I've had dealings with the three of them. They've been traveling together for a few years, looks like. They're Sam Tarrango's men, but I guess you heard that part."

"Yep. Well, I reckon this old hawg better get back to the upper meadows an' rescue that pitchpine an' the two whelps. You keep the door bolted an' the guns ready, Moon-Gal. Ain't no guaran-tee them boys is gonna keep on going' once they're out o' sight."

Fiddlehead ambled to the door, and then turned back for a moment, his hand still on the latch.

"Sunshine an' the rest o' the girls. If Cortez has been trailing Queen Vikki an' hers—wal, mebbe I might poke around a bit myself after I get back with yore pups."

Mike laughed.

"The ring-tailed raccoon's in love, Moon. Fiddlehead, just exactly what did that Sunshine gal do to you, anyhow?"

"Shows how much you know, ye wet-behind-the-ears calf. Ye ever seen this child to get all hound-dawg-eyed over any squaw, white or red? It ever occur to ye those gals jest might be in trouble, freezin' or starvin' to death or even kidnapped by the guldanged Shuckers? Or worse yet, maybe them three old friends of yours'll find 'em."

"The four damsels in question somehow seem much more likely to be back in St. Louis. Sunshine's most likely sitting on a potbellied judge's lap, alternately sipping champagne out of a silver goblet and whispering sweet nothings in his ear. Thought you were going to go get our kids?"

Fiddlehead snorted, his special snort denoting infinite contempt, and stomped outside, banging the door behind him.

Michael sat down on the rug beside Moon, leaned back until he was lying stretched out, his hands behind his head.

"Probably be a half hour at least until they return," he said, his eyes gleaming. "Where were we?"

"You were just rolling onto your side and beginning to snore," she laughed.

"That right, Princess Moon?" he grinned, and twined both hands into her hair and pulled her down on top of him.

She nodded, and he slipped a hand up under her skirt. She gasped.

"You're starting something you won't be able to finish, white man," Moon said. "Your manhood will not be ready to stand up for another three days."

"Probably not," he said. "We'll see. Then his hands were moving over her again, and she did not wish to say anything at all for a time.

* * *

"Half dozen or more o' them Te-Moak red divvels, I tell ye, ye cottonheaded idjit—thank ye kindly, ma'am."

Fiddlehead interrupted his excited diatribe to take the tin cup full of steaming coffee Moon held out for him and then resumed pacing maniacally around the room. A haunch of venison was roasting on a spit in the fireplace, yams roasting down in the coals, and cornbread baking in a cast-iron Dutch oven to one side. Elizabeth and Jacques White Bull were curled on the rug in front of the fire, the small boy happily eating sugar candies Fiddlehead had brought back from Salt Lake. Jacques glanced up from time to time with a look of bright but unconcerned interest, his face growing steadily more sticky. But redhaired Elizabeth, the girl who had become, Moon thought, either sister or daughter to her, stroked Jacques' hair and nodded as Fiddlehead spoke, her eyes round with worry.

"What Uncle Fiddlehead says is true, Mike," she put in. "I saw one of them peering at us through the branches of a tree after Fiddlehead left. I didn't know what else to do, so I made Jacques get into the wagon with me and lie down, and then I took the pistol and just held it and prayed. I was so frightened, but the Shuckers didn't really bother us. Just watched. After a while they didn't even try to hide, and I was sure they were going to try something. That was when you came back," she added, looking up at the mountaineer. "I don't know what would have happened if you hadn't."

"I was not afraid," said little warrior, grinning, his mouth rimmed with black, a combination of sugar from the candy and soot from the fireplace.

"Course ye warn't, ye little hell-raiser," Fiddlehead snorted. "Ye ain't afraid o' the divvel hisself. Ye got no more sense than yore ma or that freckle-faced Irishman she hangs around with!"

"I'm not afraid of anything," Jacques nodded, "but that's not what I mean. They're nice. I talked to one of them."

"Ye what?" Fiddlehead exploded, and at the same time, suddenly cold, Moon said "What do you mean?"

Jacques shrugged, and dug into the stocking Elizabeth had insisted upon putting the candies and other trinkets into.

"A man. He talked to me when I went to gather some sticks by myself."

"Why in the name of the blue-balled Jaysus didn't ye tell me, ye little skonk?"

Jacques looked up, shrugged again, popped a hard red object into his mouth.

"What did he say to you?" Mike asked, giving Fiddlehead a warning glance.

"I don't know. He didn't use any words that I know except maybe one or two. But he was nice. He didn't hurt me. When he heard Fiddlehead coming, he ran away."

The three adults stared at one another, silently agreed that they would talk of this later, when the children were asleep. Even Jacques was beginning to look uneasy, and Elizabeth's face had gone absolutely white.

"Well," Moon said, getting up and going to the fireplace, "I'm sure it's nothing to worry about very much. How could anything possibly happen with Mike and Fiddlehead both here to take care of us, eh?"

As she spoke, she tried to smile reassuringly at Elizabeth.

"Not to mention your formidable self," Mike

laughed, rising and putting his arms around Moon from behind. "Isn't this by-God feast about cooked?"

After the feast, Fiddlehead produced yet another surprise, a bag full of candied fruit that he'd also brought from Salt Lake. Even though Jacques had been too full of candy to eat very much roast venison, he found room for the new sweet. After dinner Elizabeth insisted on singing Christmas songs, all of them standing around the little tree McLafferty had cut and Elizabeth had decorated with bits of colored cloth, popcorn, and this and that. She tried to teach Jacques and Moon the words to the carols, but the son learned them much more easily than the mother. The child was obviously very much taken with the whole ritual and would almost certainly insist on celebrating it from now on.

Moon, however, grew a little impatient with the proceedings. She was not entirely unfamiliar with the holiday, for her white father had on occasion made an attempt to explain the Christian religion, and there had been two or three times in her girlhood when for some reason he happened to remember the holiday and kept it in such rudimentary fashion as might be available to a fur trapper in winter camp. But for whatever reason, this slight indoctrination into the mysteries of the white man's god never really took. She'd come to love Elizabeth Harrington in the months since she and Mike found the redhaired girl wandering in the desert, raped and brutalized by Jean Laroque and his men, but Moon was still suspicious of the white religion, of a god who slept with women and left them virgin, who sent his son so the white people could torture him and kill him and then worship him. She doubted whether even Elizabeth, devout Christian though she was, really understood all of it.

Did she pray to this god while Laroque's men were raping her? She believes this creator has time to pay attention to each little human's troubles, to listen to their words. Perhaps that's true, but it does not seem that way. The Cheyennes believe that One Above dreamed the world, and Old Man Coyote built the world according to the dream. The dream was perfect, but Coyote's careless, and so the world didn't turn out exactly as One Above planned. This is probably no more true than the God who answers prayers, but it seems more like the world I see around me, filled with pain, with senseless tragedy as well as great joy, great beauty. One Above doesn't know how Coyote slapped things together, because he's sleeping again, dreaming of other worlds.

Mike, Moon, and Fiddlehead sat by the fire late that night after the two young ones went to bed. They drank coffee, and Fiddlehead poured a few more drops of his whiskey into each of the cups. "To celebrate-like, even if ain't any of us but Liz-beth sartin sure jest what it be we're celebratin'."

"It is important to her, whatever it is," Moon said. "It was the way of her people, and I think she feels a strong need to keep that. So many things are still strange to her, not the way she expected them to be at all when she left Kentucky. Losing her family, and then what Laroque and his men did to her—she isn't over it yet."

" 'Course she ain't," Fiddlehead snorted. "Ye don't get over things o' that sort. Jest live through 'em, like we all do. But I don't like them Shuckers hangin' around the younguns. Put a scare into 'er today, sure."

"You think they had kidnapping in mind?" Mike asked. "Maybe it really is time to shoot a couple Te-Moaks, scare the rest off. I don't have anything personal against them, but . . ."

"But they're only Indians after all, is that right?" Moon snapped.

"Hell, Moon, you know that isn't what I meant. I probably would have killed them already if they were white."

"Careful," she said. "Remember, I'm half white, too."

"Sounds like ye cain't win comin' er goin' to me, Hoss," Fiddlehead laughed. "I don't know. Maybe ye just oughta leave 'em a buck or a bighorn sheep or two. But ye better mind them younguns. Likely if I hadn't of come along when I did, they'd of made off with the leetle warrior, an' then whar would ye be?"

Moon shivered, crossed her arms over her breasts.

"We've got to do something," she said. "Red Coyote . . . ?"

He shrugged.

"Like Fiddlehead says, I guess. Keep a close eye on Jacques and Elizabeth. The Shuckers can't go on hanging around forever. They're bound to lose interest after a while, find something else to amuse themselves."

"If they touch my son, I'll kill them," Moon said fiercely.

McLafferty rolled over on the rug, nuzzled the side of Moon's neck. She pulled back, pretending indignation, then giggled.

"Shee-it," Fiddlehead groaned, getting up and pacing restlessly in front of the fire. "Didn't the two of ye get enough o' that nonsense this afternoon? By Gawd, I ain't gettin' them kids up to go traipsin' off after firewood through the snow again."

He sloshed another measure of whiskey into his cup, held up a nearly empty bottle toward first Mike and then Moon, one eyebrow raised in question. When both shook their heads, he shrugged, poured the last few drops into his cup, drank it down, and wiped his whiskers with the back of his hand.

The room was warm, shadows dancing in the corners away from the red firelight, but outside a wind had come up again, icy currents finding their way in through an occasional chink in log walls. There was just a touch of cold at the side away from the fire, a reminder.

Fiddlehead walked to the door, opened it, and let in a great blast of frigid air and a swirl of snow, the icy particles from the last storm blown up again by the wind.

"Shut the door, ye overgrown idjit!" Mike laughed, echoing Fiddlehead's words of the night before.

Wilson didn't seem to hear him, stood staring out into darkness for a few more seconds before he closed the door.

"By Gawd!" he said suddenly. "I jest cain't stand to think on it, Michael. We gotta find them gals, that's all they is to it."

"What? What are you going on about? You still worried about—what's her name?—Sunshine and Queen Vikki and those other sporting women? Hell, I told you, they're in St. Lou by now."

"Nope. I got me an intuition, lad. They're out thar somewheres, close by, too, and we got to go find 'em."

"My husband is not going out in the middle of the night to find a group of women," Moon said. "I will not allow it."

"Right ye are, Moon-Gal," the old conniver nodded. "It's blacker than the inside of a black ba'r out there right now. So we wait fer daybreak. Glad we're all agreed, then. Reckon I'll be turnin' in, an' so should ye, sonny. Got a long day ahead of us tomorrow."

"Now hold on, you damned mountain lawyer . . ." Mike began, but Fiddlehead only winked at him and disappeared into a curtained-off alcove where his blankets were spread on the floor.

Mike and Moon stared at one another.

"Red Coyote, you're not going to do this thing, are you?" she asked. "Will you leave me alone with Jacques and Elizabeth when the Te-Moaks are hanging around the way they are?"

"Tell the truth, Moon Morning Star . . ."

"McLafferty,'" she corrected him. "You know I'm not Moon Morning Star any longer. My name's Moon McLafferty."

"Moon Whatever. You know you're not afraid of a few half-starved Shuckers. You're not afraid of God and the devil and Old Man Coyote put together. What you're afraid of, Miz Moon, is your poor henpecked captive white man going off to search for a gang of professional ladies. Admit it."

"I will admit no such lie," she replied. "What do you care if the Te-Moaks come and take Jacques and Elizabeth and me, yes, and our unborn son as well? Go after your women of pleasure, then. Perhaps I will find a Te-Moak husband who pleases me better than you."

"You admitted it, then! Moon, I don't think there are any women out there at all, but you know how Fiddlehead is when he gets a burr under his saddle. I doubt if there's any way to talk him out of the notion. I have to go along. What if he's by himself and runs into Tarrango's men?"

Moon stared into the fire, sulking. In a moment,

McLafferty began to tickle her until she was helpless with laughter.

"Perhaps," Moon gasped, "you think because I am laughing that I can no longer be angry, but that isn't true. You know I hate to be tickled."

"Wouldn't do it if you didn't. Do you hate this, too?"

Sullen silence, and then the woman gasped, "Yes, oh yes, Red Coyote, I . . . hate . . . that."

Silence again, or rather many small sounds—the snap of a concealed pocket of pitch catching in the fireplace, occasional keening of the wind at the corners, two people breathing. And then, a few moments later, the cabin was shaken by Fiddlehead's thunderous snores.

3 In truth, McLafferty wasn't in a mood to venture out into a frozen world of basin and range and a foot of snow along the trails to search for four presumably lost ladies of the evening. Fiddlehead was insistent, however, and when old Iron-in-the-Water got his mind set on something, there was no sane man capable of talking him out of it. Not even the offer of a game of twenty-one, penny ante and penny bet, was sufficient to dissuade him.

"You really figure they're out there, then?" Mike demanded. "If they didn't go east and if Queen Vikki's as clever as her reputation suggests, then I'd guess she's gone north into the Snake River country—maybe headed toward Oregon City."

"I told ye, this child's got a powerful intuition."

"How long you gonna be gone, Mike?" Jacques asked.

"Maybe I'll ride along, since you insist on going" Moon said. "I don't wish my husband to be wandering around the desert with women who sell themselves. Do you know this Victoria Queen or not? What you said was . . ."

Mike shrugged.

"Know who she is, that's all."

" 'Fraid you're stuck with the big lout," Fiddlehead chuckled, winking first at Moon and then at Elizabeth. "Bethy, when ya gits hitched, ye goin' to be as all-fired possessive as Moon hyar? Seems like any normal female-woman'd be proud for her man to be rescuing dam-sells in distress."

"Stupid white women," Moon grumbled. "All right, then go ride in the snow."

The day was clear and nippy, but thin winter sunlight still felt good on McLafferty's back as Gray Boy plodded through the white stuff, not so deep down along the sage bottoms as it was close about the ranch house and already turning soft, melting. Jackrabbits were everywhere, and a herd of perhaps a hundred pronghorned antelope went flashing away as Fiddlehead and Mike topped a small rise, surprising the animals as they grazed at tall stubble along the west face of a black rim. Mike had read about some big African cats, cheetahs, that were supposed to be faster than pronghorns, but he never believed it—figured it would be interesting to have a race sometime, if there was a way to do it. In any case, he knew where he'd put his money. A whole conclave of eagles and hawks were perched atop a boulder heap, just looking around and apparently not even interested in hunting. They fanned their wings occasionally and sometimes stopped to groom their feathers.

"Got full bellies, do ye?" Fiddlehead called out. "Good huntin' this morning early? Peace to ye, brothers!"

The big birds ignored the men as Fiddlehead and Mike and their pack animals passed on by, moving northward, where South Branch joined Humboldt's main stream—where Jean Laroque and his cutthroats lay sleeping more peacefully than they ever had in life, two or three in a group under heaps of river stones—and that was where, of course, both Moon Morning Star and Mike McLafferty were also supposedly buried. Such, at least, was the information passed along to Lieutenant Edgeworth and his bluecoats.

With McLafferty's luck working, Mike realized, no doubt he'd one day come face to face with the good officer, and at that point he supposed he'd be obliged to tell the man he was Mike's twin brother, Mack. Edgeworth wouldn't buy the story, of course, but it would at least give him something to chew on.

The Humboldt was running high, nowhere near flood stage, but its water, blue-gray from snowmelt up on the North Fork, Mary's, and Bishop branches, was running swift enough that fording the little river might well prove difficult. Ruts left by wagons full of emigrants headed to California the past year were totally erased from the mudbank near the river. Elsewhere a thin blanket of snow lay over the California Trail—if anyone had passed this way, it would have had to have been before the last storm.

"Wolf Mask an' them, ye figger they kept on headed west, lad? Ain't come this direction, anyhow."

"Not unless they doubled back from Sulphur Springs. We might find a sign on the other side of the river."

"Jest testin' ye is all. I figgered that. Michael, I tell ye, I know them gals is out hyar somewhar. I feel it in me damned bones."

"That's rheumatism, Fiddlehead. A man gets to be your age—"

"Horse-warsh! This prairie dawg can hobble about as well as he ever could, for a fact. Ye guess we might as well ride on upstream a piece? Ain't going to get back tonight nohow, not even if we ride clear into dawn. Moon don't expect us home."

"Possibly that's why she was a little edgy. With those damned Te-Moak Shuckers hanging around. I wish they'd make off with a mule or something and be done with it."

"I'd say leetle Jacques is a more likely target. It's the damnedest thing about injuns an' kids. I remember Joe Walker tellin' me once, back in '29 I think it were . . ."

McLafferty rapped his heels to Gray Boy's sides, urged the horse forward.

"Let's ride until there's no more light," he said. "If you've got one of your long-winded lies coming on, Mr. Wilson, tell it while we move. Moon's all right. All the same, we shouldn't have gone wandering off on a goose chase this way—maybe I should've shot one of those skulking bastards. The rest would have gotten the idea."

"Michael, they ain't done no harm yet. Leave 'em be till there's reason. Fact is, yore ranch may be settin' plumb in the middle of sacred ground or summat—ye thought about that?"

"Good to reflect on," Mike nodded. "Why is it you waited until now to call forth this theory?"

"Ain't no theory, jest a real strong suppose. Hold on, McLafferty, thar it is! I told ye! When Fiddlehead Wilson gets a suspicion, she's damned well true."

"What are you talking about, old friend?"

"Smoke, that's what. Use yore sniffer, ye dung-eatin' dog! Thar's a campfire a mile or so up ahead."

"I don't smell anything."

Fiddlehead was right.

McLafferty was fair at tracking, and he'd spent half his life in the mountains. He could smell bear and deer and beaver; he'd hunted a good deal of meat and fur just that way, with his nose to the wind. But Fiddlehead, he was something different. And it wasn't just him, either, but all the real old-timers—Benton and Hollingback, Bridger and Carson, even Bill Sublette had an uncanny nose, whether the man had turned businessman or not. Mike spent a good deal of time with Billy one season up on the Judith River, and of course it was Sublette who'd hired him on in the first place.

Anyhow, Wilson either smelled smoke or his intuition told him the four prostitutes had to be close by. A half mile upstream Mike caught the scent too, and then they saw it—just barely visible by cold, failing light. If not the women, then it was at least someone who'd holed in beneath a steep bluff at a bend in the Humboldt.

On the off chance there might be a few more of Sam Tarrango's hired guns about, McLafferty and Wilson tethered their animals a couple of hundred yards shy of the camp instead of firing off two or three rounds and just riding on in.

The temperature was dropping toward zero again, and snow crunched beneath their boots. It was crusted just hard enough to hold a man's weight and not much more. They moved slowly, carefully, not speaking at all, and then slipped down to the river's edge. No snow lay under the cottonwoods and willows along the Humboldt, and Mike and Fiddlehead more or less felt their way to a point just beneath where smoke rose from a shelf sheltered by junipers and pinyons.

"Somethin's wrong," Fiddlehead whispered. "It's dinnertime, but ain't no food cookin'. Wah! This child don't even sniff coffee. Hesh, now, an' let's listen close."

Mike grabbed hold of a bent sapling and pulled himself carefully up the frozen bank. Then he was flat on his chest on the snow, hugging the ground, pistol in hand.

"Kin ye see anything, sonny?"

"It's the women, all right," he answered. "At least one's still alive; she's feeding the fire. Others are bundled up close by, but they're not moving."

"Bundlin' is all. Maybeso they're in a bad way, or else jest savin' their strength."

"That your friend by the fire?"

"Naw, never seen this'n afore. Looks like she's half a kid, about Bethy's age, mebbe two-three y'ars older. Cain't ye tell?"

McLafferty nodded, glanced at Fiddlehead, the latter half visible in shadows.

"Could be they're not the ones we're hunting for, old-timer. Perhaps we can help out in any case. One hell of a poor place to be spending a midwinter night on the high desert."

"It's them, all right," Wilson whispered. "See that big spotted pony yonder by the bushes? That's a Nez Perce gelding what Tarrango give Queen Vikki three summers back, when I was in Pueblo an' spending me time with old Sunshine."

"You're certain?"

"Does a b'ar sheet in the woods, ye idjit? O' course this child's sar-tin!"

Mike got to one knee, revolver still ready.

"Hellooo the camp! We're friends, and we're coming in!"

The young woman by the fire started, cursing in Spanish, fumbled about in the heavy coat she wore, and withdrew a short-barreled pistol.

"*Ojo!*" she called out. "*Dios mio!* Vikki, wake up, we got dogs in the bushes, *perros!*"

"Friends!" Mike replied, still not rising to his feet. "We have food with us!"

Those under the pile of blankets struggled to get untangled, confounding themselves in the process. Then three more female faces peered out.

"Leetle Sunshine!" Wilson yelled. "Ye thar, gal? This be Fiddlehead Wilson. Me an' Mike McLafferty has come to pull yore bacon out o' the fire!"

"Who?" a voice asked. "Who is it out there?"

Fiddlehead laughed softly.

"She'll recollect in a moment. Jest wasn't expectin' me to show up, that's all."

"You going to let us come in and warm ourselves or not?" Mike demanded. "Our horses are close by. We've got chow in the saddlebags. If you're not interested, then we'll just be about our business."

"Tarrango!" the Spanish girl hissed. *"Malandrin!"*

"Chauncy Wilson?" a thin, yellow-haired woman said. "Is that really you, Chauncy?"

Fiddlehead laughed again.

"Told ye she'd remember directly. Only that ain't me real name, an' don't forget what I'm sayin'. Jest told her it was. Sounds more dig-nified."

The mountain man let out a whoop.

"O' course it's me, Leetle Sunshine. I come to save ye."

The Spanish girl now retreated from the fire, and the remaining three were on their feet. The tallest of the group stepped forward one or two paces, a revolver in each hand.

"Come on in, then, but come slow. I know how to use these things. Michael McLafferty the gambler, you're out there? You're welcome then, and more than welcome if you've got food. The damned truth is, we've had nothing to eat for three days. Boys, welcome to Queen Vikki's place, even if it's no more than a bare patch of snow in the trackless desert!"

Zero cold on the Humboldt, and Mike dragged in a big pitchy stump to the ladies' fire. With no way to chop the wood into smaller chunks, he gathered an armful of dead sage, built up the blaze with that, and placed the weathered stump astride the flames. In short order some pitch began to burn, throwing off a good deal of welcome heat but a considerable amount of black smoke as well. Under the circumstances, it was a fair compromise. It might make their eyes water, but they weren't about to freeze to death, either.

Fiddlehead fetched in the animals and opened the saddlebags, pulled out his old crusty blue-speckled coffee pot, tossed Mike a slab of venison, and set to crushing a handful of beans.

With meat sizzling over open flames, Wilson's pot beginning to turn its mixture of melted snow, coffee, sage leaves, and willow bark into something that might actually prove drinkable, and a few chunks of Moon's cornbread warming, the *compañeros* and their lady friends were in a fair way to having a small feast. The women, hostility now vanished, stood by expectantly.

"Four rumpled angels," Mike thought, "their wings drooping just a bit—and a damned odd place to run into them too, when you get right down to it. According to Black Johnny Cortez and Joe Hollingback, they've got a wad of purloined bank deposits with them. Chances are they'd have ended up dead, nonetheless, if Wilson hadn't insisted we come look for them."

Along with Victoria Queen, the tall, dark-haired, big bosomed leader of the gang, was Santa Maria de la Cruz y de la Rosa, the Mexican beauty who'd been tending fire when Mike and Fiddlehead showed up. Maria was in her early twenties, as it turned out, but her features were extremely delicate, giving an appearance of a girl several years younger. In boots and denim britches and a sheepskin coat (skinning knife in a sheath on her hip), she gave the impression of one well able to look out for herself, and Mike guessed she'd more than once found reason to use her Abiline toothpick.

Standing beside Maria and holding her hands out tentatively over the flames was a mulatto girl called simply Little Sister. This one was certainly no more than sixteen. It was possible she was a runaway slave, for her soft, almost dulcet voice suggested Louisiana delta country.

"Sister's my right-hand man," Vikki said. "When I get ready to retire from the business, if I ever do, Sister's the one who'll probably take over. She's already a hell of a fine hooker—men like her. Don't let her quietness fool you, McLafferty. She's blessed with common sense, something real uncommon. More than that, she's kept us going out here on the trail—good with a rifle, and she can even mend harness, hunt, and shoe horses if necessary. You keep your mitts off her for right now. We're not taking customers until we get to the goldfields. There's a proper time and place for everything."

The final member of this strange quartet, standing beside Mike but with Fiddlehead Wilson hovering about her like some love-smitten teenage boy and bearded mother hen in buckskins as well, was Sunshine Hobson, a sweet-faced blond girl, a trifle skinny and small-breasted and looking more like a misplaced schoolmarm than a hooker turned bank robber, on the lam and half-starved beside a desert river.

Well, as McLafferty concluded years earlier, a man was well-advised not to go strictly by appearances.

He'd only half believed Fiddlehead's tale about spending most of a season's wages on a professional lady, but now Mike could see clearly that around Sunshine Hobson, Wilson's loquacious reserve and inherently cynical nature were considerably altered. The crazy old bastard was actually in love, or at least pretending quite hard. McLafferty's Sancho Panza had been transformed into either Quixote himself or perhaps even a genuine Lancelot.

Yet a more wonderful paradox was this: It was clear from the beginning that Sunshine Hobson, though she might well be as hard as flint toward most men, nursed genuine fondness for Fiddlehead. A grand courtship, Mike mused, unfinished at some indefinite time in the past, was now underway again.

"Coffee's ready," Little Sister said. "So's bread. Y'all goin' stand around an' wait for it to burn?"

"Sister's right," Victoria Queen nodded. "Mike McLafferty, please to cut up the deer meat—half raw or not. Anticipation's worse than starvation, and that's a fact."

"Chauncy," Mike grinned, "I wonder if you might be so kind as to serve the ladies?"

Fiddlehead cast him a baleful glare, wrinkled forehead and mouth, and reached for the coffee pot.

"Use that name again," he muttered, "an' this child o' the woods'll skulp ye clean."

Mike squatted beside the flames, grasped the willow stub skewering handles he'd stuck into the slab of venison, removed the roast, and placed it atop some juniper boughs cut for the purpose.

Beyond the firelight, several pairs of eyes gleamed an unblinking amber-green—two coyotes and a wolf, the three animals close together. They sat patiently among shadows, hoping the half dozen humans who'd invaded their territory might be thoughtful enough to toss out a few scraps.

Screech owls trilled in the bitingly cold darkness, and Humboldt River murmured in the raw trench of its bed.

The party moved out with first light, heading back to Ruby Dome Ranch. The women were somewhat groggy with aftereffects of the ordeal they'd been through—wandering aimlessly for several days through snowstorm and bone-chilling wind, little or nothing to eat, and the dead cold of nights. Sunshine Hobson suffered from frostbite in the toes of her left foot, and Little Sister's face was burned from freezing wind as she'd attempted without luck to bring down game. Fiddlehead applied bear grease to Sunshine's toes before they left camp, making a great deal out of what didn't appear to be a genuinely serious problem.

They made fairly good time, passing by the forks and turning south toward the ranch. Temperatures were on the rise once more, and again the snow began to melt.

Victoria Queen pulled her spotted gelding alongside Gray Boy and manufactured small talk as they rode along, but finally came to the point.

"Mike McLafferty," she said, "I don't know what you've heard, if you've heard anything. You must have had some reason to come looking for us, though. So I take it you've had word from Sam Tarrango. Am I right?"

He nodded. "Wilson heard rumors in Salt Lake a couple of weeks ago—went there to pick up supplies. Tarrango ran you out of Pueblo, as I gather."

"That's all you heard?"

"Not exactly. Story is you robbed a bank, Vikki, made off with quite a pile of cash. Matter of fact, some of Tarrango's boys are trailing you, but I guess you know that. Otherwise you wouldn't have swung north, away from Hastings Trail. You shook loose of Black Johnny Cortez and his two associates, and damned near starved to death for your trouble. Cortez, Pete the Gun, and an ugly-looking Apache named Wolf Mask showed up at my ranch on Christmas Day."

"Cortez, Pete, and Wolf Mask? Sam doesn't just want his money back, then. He wants me dead, and the girls too. Those three are his executioners. All right, Michael McLafferty. I'll level with you. You've kept my beans from burning once, and that means you're an ally. I may well need your help again, and I'm willing to pay for it—pay you well. The truth is, my girls and I took what was coming to us, and a little more. That sonofabitch Sam offered to buy me out for about a dime to the dollar. When I wouldn't go along, he brought in his gunslingers, and they moved us out, lock, stock, and barrel. Little Sister and I thought things over, and that's when we rode back to Pueblo. Big celebration that night—supply wagons in from both Santa Fe and St. Louis. Maria honeyed up to Sam's banker, and when she left Duggin's saloon with him, we sort of took the man prisoner. To make my story short, we persuaded him to open Tarrango's private vault. Then we tied up clerk Spectacles and gagged him—that's what he wanted anyway, but not under those circumstances, if you know what I mean. And the four of us rode out of Pueblo, laughing like crazy women. So here we are."

"Quite an adventure." Mike nodded. "How much did you take, if you don't mind my asking?"

"Always bad manners to ask a lady about her wages, McLafferty, but Cortez probably told you something or another. To the penny, then. We cleaned the box out—fifty-six thousand, two-hundred and ninety-four dollars and twenty cents—that and some Mexican bonds that probably aren't any good anyway. And this."

Vikki reached into her bodice and withdrew a compact lined with velvet. In it lay an emerald the size of McLafferty's knuckle.

"Jesus Christ!" he said, whistling softly. "You've got a king's ransom, then."

"No," she replied, smiling in ladylike fashion, "let's call it instead the queen's price. Sam wanted to give me a dime to the dollar. As it turns out, he bought me out for a dollar to the dime. What's sauce for the goose is sauce for the gander, as my daddy used to tell me. Of course, it's possible this stone's just green glass. But I don't think so."

They reached Ruby Dome Ranch shortly before sundown, and Moon stood in the doorway with a more than suspicious expression on her face. Mike kissed her properly and then introduced her to the angels.

Mike took care of the animals, and when he came inside, everybody was relaxed and comfortable with one another. Elizabeth was talking with Little Sister, the two girls in a corner by themselves, and Fiddlehead had Sunshine perched atop a couple rolled-up buffalo robes, her naked foot in the air as she held mud-spattered full skirts tightly about her legs. Mike guessed she'd changed into that costume while he was out with the horses and mules, no doubt in deference to Wilson's eager attentions.

The group talked, drank elder tea laced with whiskey (one of Moon's inventions), and kept the fireplace blazing. Moon asked Vikki a number of seemingly innocent questions, but Mike knew what she was up to. Moon had a way of getting to the heart of matters without seeming obvious. There were other times, of course, when she chose to be extremely blunt.

At length Moon asked Elizabeth to put Jacques to bed, and the boy, despite some protests, went good-naturedly with his 'big sister.' A few moments after Elizabeth returned, the child let out a long scream and then bolted back into the main room of the house, wild-eyed and obviously terrified.

"Little Bull! What's the matter?" Moon demanded, leaping from her chair and brushing past Maria and Victoria Queen to take her son into her arms.

"Shuckers ... outside my window," he managed, still gasping for breath. "Looking in ... staring at me ... making strange faces ... one's all painted blue."

"It's all right, Jacques, it's all right," Moon whispered, calming the child both with words and with her physical presence.

McLafferty grabbed his coat, checked the cylinder of his Colt Walker, and motioned to Fiddlehead.

"This thing's gone far enough," Mike said. "Next, you know, they'll move into the house, just like a bunch of damned wood rats. Whatever they're up to, I think it's the showdown hour. Get the lantern lit. Let's see what the hell's afoot."

He was through the door and into the night, Wilson directly behind him.

The Te-Moaks were gone, just as he figured they'd be, the snow crusted over once more as night cold settled in. Other than in an area near the rear window where the Indians had been standing, Mike could detect no footmarks at all.

"Yonder the barn, most likely," Fiddlehead suggested, holding the lantern out before him. "Them boys can run like a prairie wind."

The night was without sound—no, there was one noise. A solitary wolf howled in the canyon, its voice drifting through darkness.

"Ain't no wolf, sonny," Fiddlehead remarked. "Their lookout's caught sight of our lantern, that's all."

"Guess you're right," McLafferty said, holstering his gun. "It's Jacques—no question he's the one they're after."

4 Sharp cold stung Moon's face when she stepped out into silver-gray pre-dawn light to fetch water, a cold so intense she was forced to catch her breath. But she relished the chill after the overheated cabin, enjoyed the few moments' solitude as well, for the house, already too small for the "family" of five, including Fiddlehead, had grown oppressively crowded with the addition of the four women Michael Red Coyote and Fiddlehead had brought in from the snow. Moon enjoyed the company, certainly, for it had been months since she'd had any female companionship besides Elizabeth, and she found the four prostitutes to be remarkable women. McLafferty's obvious apprehension about how she'd receive the guests amused her.

"You have peculiar ideas about me, Red Coyote," she told him when they were alone. "I am a woman, too. Why do you think I would not understand as well as you that we sometimes do what we must to survive in this world? Even if this is what they enjoy, what harm is there? Of course, if I sensed an attraction between my man and one of these ladies, perhaps I would be less hospitable."

Moon thought about the prostitutes: Vikki, stronger

at least in spirit than most men, was clever as well, humorous and sharp-witted, with a stock of stories to rival even Fiddlehead Wilson, although her tales were of a decidedly different nature. Santa Maria de la Cruz y de la Rosa, the small woman with the very long name was no rival to Vikki for intelligence, yet the intensity of her feelings and opinions was in itself a powerful force. Moon's favorite, however, was Little Sister, the dark girl no older than Elizabeth but worldly wise beyond her years, self-sufficient, a survivor who took just what the world dealt her and made the best of it. Satirical, at times, without being cynical, pragmatic without bitterness, she met challenges with quiet competence, loyalty and warmth. She and Elizabeth, in particular, had become fast friends, and Jacques doted on her. It would be hard for these two to say good-bye to Little Sister.

But what Moon enjoyed perhaps most of all was watching Fiddlehead, that grizzled philosopher, acting as foolish as any lovesick boy over the pretty blonde, Sunshine Hobson.

Probably I worry too much about Fiddlehead, she thought. If there was ever one who can take care of himself, in every way, White Whiskers is that man. Perhaps I worry about him because he reminds me of my own father, Jacques LeClaire—a trapper, too, as strong and self-reliant as Fiddlehead, but he always seemed terribly lonely beneath his strength, even to my child's eyes.

The light was growing quickly as Moon stepped away from the house, and streaks of cloud above the Rubies to the east were gathering a hint of rose color. She took her time walking to the spring, watched the clouds glow more and more vividly and an intense point of white light appeared above the shoulder of a peak, radiance suddenly glittering everywhere, blinding in a white, frozen winter world.

Yes, she thought as she chipped out fragments of ice from the shadowed pool, it was good to have unexpected company for a few days.

The previous night everyone had sat late around the fire, drinking coffee and talking. The "angels," as Fiddlehead called them, were excited, making plans for what they would do when they reached the gold country of California.

"With the money we've got now, we can set up in the fanciest house those poor farm boys have ever imagined," Vikki laughed. "We'll be picking gold nuggets like plums at harvest time. Won't even have to stir ourselves, just wait for them to drop in our laps. Sure you don't want to come with us, Big Mike? We can use a good card man. Make yourself enough in a matter of months out there to set up your little empire here with all everything you could want." She glanced at Moon, laughed easily. "I see that look in your eye, Mrs. McLafferty. Just keep that hogsticker there in your girdle or wherever it is. I meant for your man to bring you an' the whole family, what the hell? More the merrier. Don't figure you'd want to go to work for me, but you and the youngsters can go pick nuggets out of the streambeds while your man's pickin' 'em off the miners."

"*Como le va? Por dios*, with the money we got, who needs to work, eh?" Maria asked.

"What else you goin' do with yo'self?" Little Sister drawled.

"Don't know," Maria replied. "Maybe buy some pretty clothes, marry a rich man,"

The mulatto girl smiled, winked.

"I give some consideration, right at first, 'bout how

I was gonna buy me a house maybe an' hire a maid an' just sit in the sun for a while, but then I start thinking, 'What you goin' do with yo'self?' I'd get so damn tired after a while, I prob'ly burn the house down an' start all over. Go off huntin', maybe."

"I don't know. I think all along someday I be Dona Maria something or other, you know, an' have a big hacienda, lots of cows, horses, *servientes*, give big parties, fiestas for all the *dias santas*. I don't think I get bored, no, not one bit."

"More power to you, honey," Vikki laughed. "But for the time being, maybe you better stick with the rest of us working gals. I can tell you from sad experience, with ideas like you've got, it don't take no time at all to go through a few thousand bucks and end up flat. Nobody who hasn't been there would believe how easy it is, ain't that right, Michael?"

"Don't ask me." Mike laughed. "I blew a good part of my poke by going respectable. A wife's a special case. I mean a proper, eastern wife," he added, glancing nervously at Moon. "Damn! I've dug myself a hole again, haven't I, warrior woman?"

He looked instinctively to Fiddlehead for help, but the mountaineer was preoccupied. He and Sunshine were in a corner, talking occasionally in low voices but mostly staring at one another in mournful silence.

"Don't worry, Red Coyote," Moon smiled. "I will not scalp you in front of company. Perhaps if you are very nice to me, I will not scalp you at all."

"Fiddlehead, ye old stump-grinder," Mike called out. "By the blue balls o' Gawd, man, cain't you see when a *compañero*'s got hisself in trouble?"

"Ye never will l'arn it right, will ye? I give up on ye long since, pup. Now let me be for a piece. I got some considerin' to work through."

"Why don't you let us in on it, hoss?"

"Let ye know when the time's right," Wilson said, and lapsed into an unnatural silence again.

The conversation flowed on around the brooding mountain man for a time, and at last he rose, cleared his throat, and began.

"I been chawin' on this for a time, folks, but I can't see no other way around 'er. I know ye needs me here at the ranch an' all, Michael, but dang it, it jest ain't human to let defenseless gals go off on their own again. Look what near happened to 'em already. Now I been tryin' to get around them two contradictory facts. Fact is, you two need me here, but t'other fact is the gals need somebody to look out fer 'em along the trail to Californy. Now puttin' them two facts together, ain't no way I can go an' do what's right in both directions."

"Well, Chaunce," Mike began, grinning as Fiddlehead glared at him, and then went on. "Sorry, my mistake. What I was going to say—I see your point. It's the slow time of the year here, anyway. Not much any of us can do until things thaw out a bit. About the only problem we've got is the Shuckers, and they're nothing Moon and I can't handle. Haven't seen hide nor hair of the devils for several days now, not since they scared Little Bull. Could be they've given up on us. I think Moon would agree that we'd rather have you escort the ladies than think of them out there all helpless as they are."

"Can't recall the last time I was said to be either helpless or a lady," Vikki chuckled, "but I thank you kindly for the sentiment, boys."

"All right, all right," Wilson continued, "now jest hush fer a minute and I'll tell ye the rest o' me plan. I was thinking, 'Now, how can I help the angels an' do somethin' useful fer Mike an' Moon, too?' Then it finally come to me. Ye're goin' to be wantin' cows.

Least I reckon ye needs some cows if ye're goin' to have a proper cattle ranch."

"Planned on something of the sort, yes—"

"Wal, then," Fiddlehead said triumphantly, "hyar's the good part. I go to Californy with the angels here, an' pick ye out a herd of breedin' stock from Vallejo an' Sutter an' whatever other ranchers they be an' get the varmints fattened up through the winter an' ready to go in the spring. Then ye come meet me, an' we escort the critters back home hyar when the snows melt out o' the Sierras an' they's plenty new grass along the trail. What do ye think?"

By the time Moon awakened in the morning, Fiddlehead, obviously impatient to be on his way, had a huge fire roaring in the fireplace and a pot of his sage-tinted coffee bubbling to one side. The women were stirring in their blankets spread across the floor, except for Little Sister, who was already up and slicing salt pork into a pan. With the firelight shining on her smooth forehead as she kept her eyes down on her work, she looked heartbreakingly young. As Moon knelt beside her to pour coffee, the older woman spoke on impulse, not really expecting her next words any more than the girl was.

"Stay with us, Little Sister," Moon said. "Elizabeth loves you, and so does Jacques White Bull. What you have is not a good life for a young girl. You can help us here, and someday, maybe next fall, when we send Elizabeth away to school, we will send you also. You will be able to make something of yourself, that is what Mike says. You will be welcome—"

"Trying to steal my second-in-command, Moon?" Queen Vikki's sleepy drawl came from a pile of blankets.

By now the other women had risen from their

blankets, and Mike, Jacques, and Elizabeth came in. The main room had become crowded, and many voices were talking at once, the women making last minute plans for departure, Mike and Fiddlehead discussing details of the cattle buying and also possible dangers of the trip. That was when Moon noticed the water bucket was nearly empty and gladly took an opportunity to escape outside for a few minutes.

A strange world Old Man Coyote built, where a young girl's best hope for a good life comes by selling her body to strangers. There are many things I will never understand about white people. Perhaps they are all crazy.

The morning sky was flawless, thin blue, and a wind swirled from the east, not exactly a warm wind, but one carrying a tantalizing hint of spring across the land that would be gripped by winter for several months yet.

Fiddlehead and his angels left before the sun was even a quarter way up the sky, and the four left behind watched the party out of sight, waving and calling back and forth with words of good luck, promises to meet again. Jacques struggled manfully to hold back the tears, but Elizabeth's cheeks were wet in early sunlight. Even Moon, who badly wanted her house back, nonetheless felt the peculiar hollowness that departing guests leave.

It was not a day to stay indoors; in the morning Mike and Moon took Elizabeth and Jacques out to exercise the horses, and after noon, while Jacques was napping and Elizabeth was reading again one of her four precious books that Mike had brought back from a trip to Salt Lake earlier in the fall, husband and wife slipped away, telling Elizabeth they intended to ride up into the Rubies to hunt for bighorn.

"No Shuckers for miles, far as I can tell," Mike said. "I was watching for a sign when we rode out this morning. Most likely the Te-Moaks have given up on whatever they had in mind. After all, they've got to make a living, too."

Birds appeared on that midwinter day as if from a shaman's hand, hundreds of birds where none had been in evidence before, small birds scratching at patches of dirt where snow melted, large birds, hawks and ravens and vultures riding air currents high up.

The tall, redhaired man and the dark, slender woman rode to the head of the big meadow, up through pinyons and junipers to a smaller meadow above. Water sang in little rivulets everywhere, released from melting snow. On the ridge beyond the upper meadow Mike and Moon rested their horses, and looked back on the series of mountain valleys below. The trees had lost their burdens of snow, evergreens blue-gray and dark against the whiteness of the meadows. The cabin and the curl of smoke rising from its chimney seemed very small and lonely, huddled there with a few outbuildings against the great, stark emptiness of a winter land. Beyond, far beyond, the desert floor stretched, rolling and pale, to the next range; beyond that was only blue sky.

"Have the whole damn place filled up with cattle in a few years," Mike said. "I figure summer pasture up here, but for next winter maybe we should build the main house down at the foot of the mountains. Have a feeling the critters and the people too would be better off below when snow starts flying. Hell, maybe we ought to start all over, on the east side of the Rubies. Remember that long lake at the foot of the mountains? Desert to the other side, but grasslands around the lake, cottonwoods and willows and God's own number of birds. . . ."

"Of course I remember," Moon said. "That's where Aloysius and his son Big Dog caught up to us. ... Red Coyote?"

"What is it, Moon-Gal?" he asked absently, eyes still fixed on the distance.

"Is this really what we wish to do? Stay here forever? I think you wanted to go with Fiddlehead today."

"Don't talk foolishness, woman," McLafferty grumbled.

"No," she insisted. "I saw a look in your eyes. You wanted to go with them because they were *going*. I don't think you're the kind of man who stays in one place forever. I think you'd rather wander here and there, do one thing and then another. The only real difference between you and Fiddlehead is that he's older. Michael McLafferty, I love you as I have loved no other man, but if you wish to go, then that is what you should do. I wouldn't be angry with you, not really. Leg-in-the-water's people will take me back, and you could come stay with us when you wanted."

"You're outright perverse, Moon. You trying to get rid of me, or what?"

"No. I'm just thinking about things. You were not happy when you tried to settle down before. Maybe I talked you into this. Last summer neither one of us was sure."

"Hush up, Moon, and look. Look, damn it!"

McLafferty swept his arms wide to indicate the whole panorama of mountain ridges and valleys, the singing, empty distance of desert beyond.

"This ain't St. Louis," he continued after a moment, "and you aren't a spoiled city girl with delusions of living like gentry. I want land. I want that little one that's in your belly. What do I have to say? Maybe someday, when the baby's not a baby anymore, and we can leave Fiddlehead in charge of things, you and I'll go off for a spell, have a look at the ocean if you'd like. Will that satisfy your wanderlust?"

"We were talking about your wanderlust, Mac-Lafferty."

They rode through the high country without fixed purpose, merely taking pleasure in the unexpectedly balmy day and in each other's company. They said little, pointing out a bird or a coyote, making plans. The sunlight was beginning to shade into yellow of late afternoon when they returned to the upper meadow, and they were talking of the house, the real house they'd begin building after Mike returned that following summer with cattle.

Suddenly a shot ripped through the air, followed quickly by another. The man and woman then spurred their horses, galloping with reckless speed over stony, inclined ground to the lower meadow and the house and corral.

Jacques, Moon thought frantically, Elizabeth.

The shots came from the cabin, or very near. Black Johnny and his men? Or the Te-moaks. Perhaps this time the Shuckers had succeeded, perhaps this time they'd taken Little Bull.

Please, no . . .

When they reached the cabin, they found Elizabeth just inside, still clutching Moon's revolver, her face stark white, eyes wide. The girl was sobbing with fear.

"I didn't know what else to do." she sobbed. "Dear God, I may have killed him."

"Killed who?" Moon shouted, grasping Elizabeth by the shoulders and shaking her slightly. "Where's Jacques? Where is he?"

"Here I am, Mother," said a small, muffled voice, then asked, "Can I come out now, Liz-beth?"

Without waiting for the girl's reply, Jacques emerged from a pile of blankets, shook hair back out of his eyes.

"It was those people again," he said, "the Shuckers. The blue man was with them. We were outside, and they almost caught us. We didn't see them coming. I wanted to fight them, but Liz-beth made me hide in the blankets."

"They tried to follow us into the cabin," Elizabeth added. "There must have been five or six Indians, I don't know. They started banging on the door, and I got Moon's gun. I didn't know what else to do. I shot through the door. Somebody screamed. I didn't want to kill . . ."

"Can't be far off yet," Mike said, his face grim. "You think you hit one of them?"

"I don't know, don't know. I was afraid to open the door."

Moon comforted Elizabeth, while McLafferty went back outside, looked around.

Blood on the earth, not much—a scratch maybe. Red clipped somebody, all right, but it's probably not fatal. I'm going after the sons of bitches.

He stepped to the door, opened it.

"Moon, I've had enough. This thing has gotten out of hand. You be all right here?"

Moon nodded, one arm around Elizabeth's shoulders, the other holding Jacques tightly to her.

Two hours later, after full dark had settled on the meadow, Mike McLafferty returned, shaking his head.

"Can't understand it," he said. "They couldn't have had more than ten minutes' head start on me, but it's as if they melted back into the rocks. I'm beginning to wonder if we're dealing with real Indians or figments of our imagination, something conjured up out of mirages. Look again tomorrow, I guess, but I don't think we'll find anything."

Moon sat before the fire, Jacques asleep in her lap. She swayed gently back and forth with a rocking motion and hummed something deep in her throat. Firelight gleamed in her eyes as she glanced up at McLafferty, but she didn't reply to his comments. After a time she rose carefully, carried the sleeping child off to bed.

"They'll be back, Michael Red Coyote," she said. "Next time, we must be ready for them."

5 With Fiddlehead Wilson and the angels on their way to California, and with no more appearances of the Te-moaks following Elizabeth's winging of one, the following days at the McLafferty ranch were relatively peaceful. Cold winds whistled down from Ruby Dome's high summit, and on ridges below the peak, ancient bristlecone pines and limber pines shivered in icy blasts. Downed trees, their resin-laden wood resistant to dry rot and incursions of carpenter ants, lay scattered about, rime-cloaked, dissolving with extreme slowness as rushing air hurled particles of sand against them.

Mike McLafferty gazed toward the summit of Ruby Dome, only its pure white top visible above the pinyons and firs along the ridge opposite the ranch. He thought about those strange trees up high and wondered how old they really were. Several months earlier, before winter storms had set in, he'd idly counted rings on one of the downed trees and discovered that a century was contained within just about an inch of wood. Did each band really count a year, as he'd been told? If so, then he gauged what was left of the downed log represented well over a thousand years. One fallen tree had been much larger, and so perhaps that one was—what? Two thousand years old, perhaps three? And how long had the deadwood been lying there on the back of the range, abraded away with infinite slowness?

The biggest of the live trees—alive when Christ was born? Far earlier than that, perhaps when Moses led the Children of Israel out of Egypt?

Such spans of time were stunning to comprehend.

Mike thought about a story he heard once among the Hopis. A leader named Spider Woman long ago led her people in a time when the waters stood up as high as mountains, and she followed a great column of smoke by day and flame by night—details remarkably similar to those in the Book of Exodus. What was the meaning, and how could the same story have come about half a world distant? Might the Hopis have come from Egypt as well?

No, the people said. They had always been here, in North America. This was indeed the land where human beings had been created.

"It's a mystery," Mike told Gray Boy as he cinched the saddle and mounted.

McLafferty rode downcanyon, heading for the South Branch to cut cottonwood poles. When enough of these were skinned and lopped into sections, he'd bring the mule wagon and haul the rails back to the ranch, would use them to extend his corral.

"Maybe that's what happened to the water that used to cover most of this desert," he mused.

Any damned fool could see that the broad basins between mountain ranges were remnants of the bed of a huge, ancient lake or inland sea. Perhaps Salt Lake, two hundred miles or so to the east, was all that remained.

But such speculations didn't cut very many cottonwood poles.

He had a dozen saplings on the ground and had leaned on his axe to rest for a moment when he glanced to the south and saw an approaching caravan of some sort, riders and a couple of wagons heading west on the Hastings Trail. As they drew nearer and details of the party became apparent, he rubbed a hand across his eyes and stared hard. Even as the group approached too near to mistake the nature of the vehicle, McLafferty was certain that he could not be seeing a fancy, citified coach, lacquered in black to a high gloss (dulled only by spatters of mud) and with bright red-and-yellow wheels as well as polished brass lanterns and a team of matched bays drawing it across the rough desert trail. In addition, perhaps a dozen riders flanked the vehicle, and a chuck wagon trailed behind, a large wagon of the sort more commonly seen on the Oregon–California route.

The outfit was two hundred miles from the nearest possible point of origin to the east and perhaps five hundred from Sacramento City or any of the gold camps beyond the snow-choked passes of the Sierra Nevada.

As the apparition drew even with McLafferty, a head emerged through a small curtained window. The head shouted an order and then withdrew. The driver reined in the team, and the riders flanking the coach also pulled up, the chuck wagon also drawing to a halt.

The outriders were a roughly dressed lot, generally unshaven, and the two lead men stared at Mike with cold eyes, hands resting on rifles carried across saddles. McLafferty stared back at them, placed his own hand on the butt of his holstered Colt Walker.

Not good odds if it comes to shooting. Wait and see, Big Mike. Who the hell would be in this place with such an outfit? Maybe I fell asleep over the cottonwood poles, and this is a damned dream.

The coach door swung open, and the passenger emerged, a figure nearly as incongruous to the place and time as his carriage, a rather short, trim man, dark-haired and with a thin mustache, eyebrows waxed into high arches. He was wearing a wide, flat-crowned Mexican hat, black slacks, and a tight-waisted coat with a short cape lined in crimson silk. The costume was complimented by an elaborately ruffled shirt front and completed by a red silk cravat fastened in place by a very large ruby-and-diamond stickpin. His hands flashed with a half dozen rings, some set with stones of onyx, sapphire, and diamond, and others of plain or filigreed gold.

"McLafferty, isn't it?" the apparition said, holding out a heavily jeweled hand. "Big Mike McLafferty, yes. I never forget a face. As I recall, you lightened my purse considerably at the monte table one evening back in Pueblo. Heard you had a place around here somewhere, but I didn't believe it. Didn't think anything but rattlesnakes and sagebrush lived in this god forsaken country. You've turned sod buster, I take it?"

Mike stared at the man for a moment longer, then burst out laughing and shook the offered hand, bearing down harder than was absolutely necessary and grinning ironically.

"Sam Tarrango. By God, Sam, if you don't look more the part of the whoremaster than you did last time I saw you. Business must be going well for you. Sorry about those boys."

"Boys? What's that?" Tarrango asked absently, his eyes moving past Mike as he scanned the surrounding landscape.

"The ones you sent after me—the ones who were

supposed to kill me and take back the gold I won from you. Remember, Sam? I was saying, I hope their loss didn't inconvenience you too badly."

"Oh, that." Tarrango laughed, slapped McLafferty on the back. "No hard feelings, I hope. I was a little short on ready cash right about then. Had to sell some holdings to cover it. Just business, old buddy, nothing personal. Hell, I like you, McLafferty. Did at the time."

"Sure thing, old buddy." Mike grinned, touching at the butt of the revolver again. "So what brings you out this way? If you're still looking to recover your tin, you're looking in the wrong place. Spent that poke a long while back.

"No, no. Water under the bridge. Never figured to find you out here at all, like I said. I would have guessed you'd be fleecing miners in California by now. What the hell do you do to make a dollar here, anyway? Fleece the goddamn coyotes?"

Tarrango found his statement to be very amusing, and McLafferty waited, smiling patiently, for the other's prolonged, braying laughter to subside.

"Why don't you come on up to the house, Sam? Give you a chance to win back what you lost to me before. Think I might have an old, dog-eared pack of cards around someplace."

"That a fact, Big Mike? Well, it sounds real nice, old buddy, but to tell the truth, I'm passing through on business. Don't imagine you've seen anything of Vikki Queen and three other sluts that lit out with her?"

"Matter of fact, I did. They spent a few days at the ranch, but they didn't say anything about you being after them. Just heading west to try their luck. I thought it was kind of funny they'd be heading to Oregon, though."

"Oregon, is it? You're sure about that?"

"For a fact. My foreman rode along with them for a piece to show them the trail. Still with them, I guess. Believe you know the old gent, Sam—Fiddlehead Wilson, by name. I would have figured fancy women like that would be wanting to try their luck in the goldfields. . . . Like I say, thought it was strange."

Tarrango nodded. "Vikki's nobody's fool," he said. "She figures California's the first place I'd look. You've been real helpful, Big Mike. One other thing—I sent out some men after the whores. You might even know them. Black Johnny Cortez, Pete the Gun, the half-breed Wolf Mask? You seen them too?"

McLafferty shrugged. "Nobody's been along the Hastings but those women. If you sent Cortez after the ladies, what are you doing here yourself, Sam? The women beat you out of some money, and you're having second thoughts about Black Johnny . . ."

"Oregon. Up north to the Snake River and over, then?"

"I don't know that I should have told you anything, Tarrango. Just what is it you're after them for? How much did they beat you out of, anyway? I got the idea they had a pretty good stake to start out with."

"Shit, Mike, they robbed my god-damned bank. Vikki took fifty thousand dollars and then some, the bitch. After all I did for her—"

"You own a bank now, Sam? You've come up some since we played cards. At the time you were pretty much a small-time chiseler, owned a couple of whorehouses and gambling halls was all I remember. No offense, old buddy." McLafferty grinned as Tarrango frowned, glanced back at a couple of his men, still mounted and with hands resting on gun butts.

Tarrango stared at McLafferty for a moment longer, then shrugged, smiled expansively.

"I'm doing all right, I guess," he said in a confidential tone. "I own a good bit of real estate and quite a few officers of the law, judges and such. Even got Beckworth's old hotel. I figure on being mayor before too long. After that, who knows? Jefferson Territory's bound to be a state one day, going to need a governor. It's a hell of a fine country, Big Mike, and I mean that. Where else does a kid born the son of immigrant parents get a chance to be governor of a by-God state, I ask you?"

"But Vikki and the girls cleaned you out, eh?" McLafferty said. "Ready cash, anyway. Fifty thousand, you say." McLafferty whistled. "You could run a hell of a campaign for that, eh?" he continued. "Well, if a man's short of ready cash, I can see now why you wouldn't be interested in a friendly poker game. Didn't mean to put you on the spot."

"Oh, hell, I've always got a little something tucked away." Tarrango winked at McLafferty. "No, they didn't run me short, hell no. It's the god-damned principle, Big Mike, you know what I mean? Why, I almost offered to marry the worthless bitch."

"Vikki? Quite a woman. Well, if you don't want to come up to the ranch, I better get back to work. Take a rain check on that game, then?"

"Hell, I guess I'm up to sitting in on a few hands at that, old buddy. Day's still young. Plenty of time, plenty of time."

"Good," McLafferty grinned, slapping the dandified newcomer on the shoulder. "I'll just ride on up and warn Moon—that's my wife—that we've got company for supper. Been a while since you've had a home-cooked meal, I'll bet. Better leave your remuda here, though. The trail upcanyon's not too good. You trust your boys here to keep watch on the outfit?"

"Sure, much as I trust anybody," Tarrango laughed, waving down the rifle that had come up as one bearded individual scowled at McLafferty. "I even trust Addams here and the boys to come looking for me if I'm not back by evening."

"Sure thing. Like I said, you get saddled up, and I'll go on ahead to tell the missus."

Tarrango turned to his driver.

"Addams," he said, "you and the men make camp. Me, I think I'll wash up a bit before dinner."

McLafferty's mind worked rapidly as he mounted and rode up the trail toward Ruby Dome Ranch. If he could keep Tarrango occupied until dark, and hopefully ensure a late start the next morning, that was so much more lead time for Fiddlehead and the angels. If it were possible, he might even provide an escort for the Pueblo magnate for a few miles, to make sure that he found clues to the passing of the women northward, toward Snake River country and beyond.

But at the moment he had to make sure he arrived at the ranch well ahead of his visitor, to make certain Moon and Elizabeth and even little Jacques should have the proper version of the truth, to pass along to Tarrango.

Wilson, ye old Rocky Mountain hawg, Mike thought, I hope to hell you've covered up your trail at least a little bit.

As he rode into the meadow, where the buildings stood dark against remaining patches of snow, there was a sudden motion. Half a dozen figures broke from cover behind a clump of pinyons. Mike pulled his revolver, and fired a volley of shots over the heads of the fleeing Indians, for it was once again a band of Shuckers. The shots had no effect except perhaps to hasten the flight of the Te-Moaks, leaping like deer across the open spaces and into cover once again.

McLafferty thought briefly of pursuing the intruders on horseback, shrugged, and fired off another shot into the air instead before he turned his horse toward the cabin where Moon, gun in hand, was just emerging from the front door.

Sam Tarrango sat down at the wide, hand-hewn table in the main room of the McLafferty ranch house. Moon and Elizabeth set to work preparing a pot of coffee and a meal of venison, boiled roots of wild parsnip, and camas flour bread while Jacques watched the newcomer warily, sensing the obvious tension between the two men.

"So where's Beckwourth now?" McLafferty asked. "I spent some time in St. Louis, and I guess I haven't kept up on frontier news. Four years ago old Jim came into Pueblo with that big herd of horses, sold them at auction, and found out his wife had married—what was his name? Your dude friend, John Brown."

"Ah, yes," Tarrango grinned. "Things did get a bit complicated there for a time. It was right about the time you skinned me alive and headed north with the proceeds, I believe, old buddy."

"With a few of your cutthroats on my trail, as a matter of fact."

"Business, McLafferty, just like I told you. But back to your original question. Luisa Beckwourth Brown was, one might say, not in the least interested that her presumably dead husband had returned. She stayed on with Brown, and they're quite happy to this day, I'm pleased to report. As to the redoubtable Mr. Beckwourth, he found his way to Santa Fe and Taos and was accused of conniving with the Indians to steal army horses. Once a horse thief, always a horse thief, I'm afraid."

"Beckwourth was cleared of the charge," McLafferty said. "You know it as well as I. What I want to know is how'd you happen to acquire Jim's hotel in Pueblo? From what I understand, you've managed to buy out the Bents as well and nearly everyone else."

Tarrango polished the rings on his left hand across the front of his vest.

"Business is like a game, way I see it. Some men win, and some men lose. As for Beckwourth, I heard he and McIntosh headed back to California about two years ago— may have been there when the gold was discovered, in fact. More power to the old liar, I say. Bill Sublette always spoke highly of him—which is odd, when you think about it. World of difference between the two."

"Sublette wasn't always the businessman you've known," McLafferty said. "He and Davy Jackson and Jim Bridger and Kit Carson, Le Blueux, Benton, Harris—Beckwourth too, until he got kidnapped by the Crows and went over to American Fur—all of them rode and trapped together, first for Ashley and then for RMF, and after that Bill grubstaked the boys. Sublette, he's the one who gave me my first break. It was him I first went up country with, but he was with American Fur by then."

"So I understand, old buddy." Tarrango smiled. "Well, I've ridden a few trails myself, whatever you think. But when a man gets to be somebody, if you know what I mean, old buddy, his habits change."

"See they have," Mike grinned. "But now that Queen Vikki's cleaned you out—"

"I'm after Victoria Queen because the rotten bitch

betrayed me. You can understand that, can't you? She'll regret what she did, bet on it, card sharper. But she won't regret it long."

"I understand the boys in Oregon City hang murderers." Mike shrugged. "Well, you up for a little game of cards, old buddy? I'm a bit out of practice, but . . ."

Moon brought a pot of coffee and two tin cups, poured them full. She glanced at Mike, shook her head in warning. She'd seen Cheyenne men exhaust their entire wealth during an extended session of the hand game. What was Michael Red Coyote up to? Why had he made this foolish challenge?

"Don't have much use for a log cabin in the midst of a desert wilderness," Tarrango said, grinning, "but inasmuch as you've gotten your hands into my pocket in the past, I suppose a small game might be in order. You set the game and the stakes, Mr. McLafferty, and I'll be pleased to oblige you."

The men ate quickly, and then Mike cleared the table and got out a deck of cards and a leather pouch full of chips.

Once begun, the game went on for several hours. The early hands were mostly a matter of the two experienced gamblers feeling one another out, almost in the fashion of a pair of professional boxers, but then the wagers began to rise as McLafferty and Tarrango alike determined the time had come for definitive action.

Tarrango took three consecutive hands, and Mike's previous winnings were considerably diminished.

Moon watched nervously, imagining that the dream of a prosperous ranch was now in jeopardy. She overcame an urge to interfere, intuiting that such intervention would do no more good with Red Coyote than it would have with White Bull, her Cheyenne husband. When it came to obsessive behavior, both of her husbands were of a kind. Perhaps that was the primary reason they'd been such close friends, blood brothers, each committed to a defense of the other's honor. And perhaps that was also the reason they both fell in love with her and why the one, McLafferty, had ridden away from the Cheyenne village in deference to a rival who was also his best friend.

But she was edgy, angry even.

In tones more annoyed than she intended, she sent Elizabeth and little Jacques out to tend the animals and to bring in firewood, and then she sat down before the fireplace to do bead work on a pair of moccasins.

The final card of the hand was dealt. Mike had a jack showing, Tarrango a ten.

Moon watched as Mike studied his cards and, grinning, pushed forward a stack of chips valued at a hundred dollars. She closed her eyes, glanced toward the wall where Mike's New Haven Whitney cap and ball .54 caliber rifle rested on a set of pegs. She gave thought to taking the rifle down and using it to order Sam Tarrango out of her house.

Tarrango, oblivious to whatever Moon's intentions may have been, studied Mike's face and nodded.

He matched the bet and raised two hundred.

"I've got him, Moon-Gal!" Mike said, turning to his wife. "You see how this works—the man thinks I'm bluffing, and so he's set to keep calling and raising. A genuinely experienced gambler, not just an owner like Sam here, such a man like that would realize his opponent's undoubtedly got four jacks. Not my old buddy, though. Figures he can push the stakes up on me—run me out o' tin, as the saying goes. Moon, you watch this now. Even though I've flatass told him what I've got, Sam here still think's I'm blowing smoke. Give some people the God's own truth, they still don't believe you."

"You calling, Big Mike, or just talking?" Tarrango asked, visibly annoyed with McLafferty's breach of gambler's decorum.

"Calling. You see, Moon, if I raise, Sam can come back at me with a raise of his own, one I can't really match unless I want to put everything on the line. He's got me outgunned with money, but I'm not buying into that. Besides, Sam's lost enough lately, what with Queen Vikki robbing him blind and all . . ."

"All right," Tarrango said, his eyes narrow, "gentleman's agreement, then. If you've got what you say you have, then you'll go for it. Allow me to double my present bet. Then if you still wish to call, I can't raise. What do you say? How's the stick floating, old buddy?"

"Gentleman's agreement, is it? You double your bet, and I call? Let's see the color of your money, then."

Tarrango pushed out the last of his chips.

"The pot," he said, nodding. "You still want to see me?"

"This man's a fish." Mike grinned at Moon. "Well, there's no accounting. I call."

Tarrango turned over his cards, revealing a full house, three tens and a pair of kings.

"It's like I said," McLafferty grinned.

Four jacks and a lone eight of clubs.

Tarrango stared at the cards.

"You worthless sonofabitch!"

Mike winked at his opponent, stood up. If trouble were going to come, it would come now.

But instead Tarrango broke into a laugh, slid back his chair.

"You've taken me, Big Mike. I'll be back this way after I've handled my other business. Perhaps a little rematch at that time, old buddy?"

"Fair enough," McLafferty agreed. "Moon, bring out that bottle of whiskey Fiddlehead's got tucked away. Sam and I both need a drink."

"All right, McLafferty, you sonofabitch," she replied. "So do I."

In the morning Mike accompanied Sam Tarrango back to his men, shook hands with him, and bade him farewell. He watched as the strange entourage moved off, with the sullen-faced Jack Addams driving Tarrango's fancy shay, heading northward toward the Humboldt Forks and, presumably, the emigrant trail that would take them to the Raft River Cutoff and eventually to the Oregon road.

Home once more, McLafferty was in an ebullient mood. All in all, he'd come out of the card game with 724 additional dollars, hard cash.

Moon, however, berated him for angering the wealthy man.

"What if this Tarrango comes back and burns our ranch? He's got a gang of men, just like Jean Laroque. You don't use your head, Red Coyote!"

But McLafferty was confident they'd seen the last of the man from Pueblo. Even if Tarrango realized he was on a wild goose chase, he'd no doubt proceed south from Oregon country, toward the California goldfields, or else return to Pueblo by way of the Mormon settlements.

In any case, the poker winnings would buy a few more cattle for the Ruby Dome spread. Hell, that much money would cover food and other supplies for six months or more. He'd won a considerable little victory.

"Be nice if our Shucker friends would take to following Tarrango, as a matter of fact," Mike said. "Surely that fancy wagon or something in it must have caught their attention. I saw three or four of the lads up on the rim, just as Sam and his boys were heading off to Oregon City. . . ."

6 Fiddlehead and the angels rode westward under cold, empty desert skies—not so much as a vulture in sight.

"Chauncy," Sunshine Hobson asked, "you going to stay in California with us, or are you really going back to Ruby Dome Ranch?"

"Wagh!" he replied, forgetting himself for a moment. "I'm afraid I got no choice. Mike an' Moon, they cain't hardly get along without me thar to tell 'em when to come in out o' the rain. Like children, they be. In any case, Mike's give me money to buy him some cows, and they's no way he could run the varmints home without help, so I'm obliged to go back with him when he shows up in May. But I got a knack for crossin' deserts an' mountains, if they's a reason for doin' 'er. When ye need this child, he'll be thar, Sunshine."

"Well, I'd like it. But you mustn't be falling in love with me, Chauncy. I've told you that before. I'm a working girl, and you're not one to settle down anyway. You've said so many times."

"Truth, truth." Wilson grinned. "But that don't mean we cain't get together from time to time. O' course, if ye lose interest . . ."

She raised one eyebrow and smiled, her blue eyes twinkling. In Fiddlehead's mind, it were pure perfect the way she done it.

"Working girls have no business being in love—that's what Victoria says. When a working girl falls in love, she's all through as an entertainer of gentlemen. Then she's got to get married, because otherwise she's got no way of supporting herself. I . . . well, I don't know. But you've never settled down, and I don't think you've even considered it. All your life you've just wandered around, Chauncy, trapping animals, fighting with the Indians and driving supply trains."

"True enough, true enough," he agreed, winking at her. "And a good life it's been, too. Ain't over, nuther. Me, I figger to live until I'm a hundert or so. This child o' the mountains is a long way from the boneyard. So I expect I'll come visitin' for as long as ye wants me to."

"How . . . old are you?"

"Truth is, I've done forgot. Let's see, I was born in . . . Guess it were the day before I first laid eyes on ye, Sunshine. An' that makes me younger than leetle Jacques, don't it?"

Sunshine looked away from him, off across a big swale ahead. The present conversation was essentially a repeat of one that had transpired in Pueblo several years earlier.

"You've probably got a favorite . . . lady in every whorehouse in the West. Leave me alone, Chauncy. I don't believe a word you tell me."

"Shore ye do," he replied, still grinning.

The situation Fiddlehead found himself in was unique even with his wide range of experience. He'd ridden many trails over the years, and the world had changed considerably, even if he hadn't. Another trapper, Bully O'Bragh, used to say that men never got old if they just stayed in the mountains—a corollary, so to speak, of Bridger's Law: Meat don't spoil in the mountains. With these bits of wisdom in mind, Wilson reflected, probably the only reason his hair had gone white was because he kept getting itchy feet, and every so often he headed for the settlements.

He'd led trapping parties and even emigrants halfway to Oregon until he got tired of the whole thing, and then he went off 'yondering' and just sort of forgot to come back. No harm done—there were others who could hunt, and he'd never signed on as wagonmaster. A hunter, that's all. The truth was, a man could just take so much responsibility and no more.

But hyar I be, he thought actin' fluff-headed over a female what calls me Chauncey, my honest-to-Gawd Christian name, though I pretend it ain't. An' I'm actually leadin' the filly an' her boss lady an' two companyeros across the desert toward the goldfields in Californy, an' half the time these women are drivin' me crazy.

They were pretty damned things, though, all of them, and it was almost worth it just to be around them, Sunshine Hobson in particular. When he left her four years earlier, he'd apparently neglected to take part of himself back out into the High Shinin'.

The female with real promise, however, was Little Sister—if a man were looking for a permanent mate. The fact that Sister was part black merely added to her down to earth mystery. In any case, west of the Sandhills, all folks were the same color anyhow, and the only difference was which side of a gunfight one was on. Little Sister might have been a run-off slave, just as Mike McLafferty said, but the entire idea of slavery was repugnant to Wilson—whether it was White or Indian doing the slaving. But even the Blacks did it—in Louisiana there were Negro plantation owners with slaves of their own.

Well, Sister, she was something. Not many a woman could shoot and ride the way she could. South of Sulphur Springs Range, the girl had knocked over an antelope when the creature was still a hundred yards off, and that was good shooting for anyone.

The new year of 1850 had come in clear and cold, and Wilson led his strange band of immigrants westward through a desolate, frozen landscape that was mostly basin and range and sagebrush, as he was determined to avoid the California Trail—since that route was the most likely for Wolf Mask, Popgun Pete, and Johnny Cortez to have taken. Probably they'd be sticking to the Humboldt River, clear on over to the Sinks and Truckee River and the Meadows. But this particular desert was all new country to him, since he'd never before taken it into his head to come so far west—except with those Oregon-bound settlers who'd been headed through Snake River country off to the north. Yep, it took a special kind of fool to herd greenhorns across frozen desert, so he guessed he was one.

McLafferty had made Fiddlehead a copy of his map and insisted he take it along, but he knew damned well the only map that might prove valuable was one a man kept in his skull. He'd put Mike's map into his possibles sack and hadn't looked at it since. The numerous notes Mike scribbled onto the paper wouldn't do him any good anyway, since the truth of the matter was that he could barely read, and Mike had a fondness for long words.

Coming through one pass, he stopped to ponder a

blue-gray sandstone and wondered if it were some kind of ore. He'd never been interested in mining, but he couldn't help thinking about possibilities. He broke up some of the rock and let the creek wash it. Sure enough, there were a few speckles of gold, though probably not enough to make the thing worthwhile.

Two weeks out of Ruby Dome, they reached the big bend of what Fiddlehead judged to be Joe Walker's river and could see the peaks of the Sierra Nevada.

Walker River was running a good flow, south to north, and the three women and one man followed upstream, parallel to the big white wall of mountains. But Sierras or no, the problem of getting across didn't look impossible. True, Joe Walker and his men ended up eating their mules before they got across, and the Donners ate each other, but that was before wagon trails really got established.

Still, January wasn't a good time to be heading across. Wilson would have preferred to circle the range northward, but out there somewhere were Black Johnny, Wolf Mask, and Pete the Gun. If push came to shove, Fiddlehead had no qualms about handling the lot of them, but only a tomfool invited problems. Cortez and his mates were probably camped off by Truckee Meadows, just waiting for Queen Vikki to show up.

They were also running short of meat. Game had been extremely scarce for the preceding hundred miles, and Fiddlehead knew he'd best get them supplied with a couple of deer or antelope before they headed across the mountains. Little Sister had taken care of the rabbit situation most of the time; she was good at hunting, and she enjoyed it immensely. Rabbit flesh, along with some flour and water and wild carrots or camas roots when these could be found, was quickly steamed next to the coals, and it wasn't a bad meal. Santa Maria de la Cruz y de la Rosa skinned the creatures and cut them up, while Sunshine did the actual cooking.

"Problem with Maria's name," Fiddlehead chuckled, "it takes a body a day an' a half jest to say it."

At Walker Forks they set up camp. A storm was brewing after days of clear skies, and Fiddlehead had a bad feeling they might end up stuck in one place for a week or more.

"Vikki," he said, "Ma'am, this child figgers to go hunting. We got a long haul ahead, an' only blind fools'd wander this kind o' country without their saddlebags stuffed with jerked venison."

Queen Vikki nodded. "You really think we can get across these mountains ahead? Maybe if we keep on riding south—"

"Farther ye go, the higher they get, ma'am. Might be another two hundert miles to whar we could cross easy. But ain't no pile o' rock an' snow ever stopped Fiddlehead Wilson before."

Vikki continued to look doubtful, but she agreed nonetheless.

"Chauncy, I think perhaps Little Sister would like to go hunting with you. Wouldn't she be a real help? I know she's a good shot."

Hunting wasn't exactly women's work, not as Fiddlehead construed matters, but Vikki could tell poor bull from fat cow. Little Sister wasn't ordinary female, no more than Moon McLafferty was.

"Hell," Fiddlehead recollected, "she done swamped that one antelope for us. Mebbe two hunters is better'n one. Sister, ye up for it?"

The mulatto girl grinned. She'd been waiting for

an invitation. "Yes sir, Mr. Wilson. I'm ready, for true and I'll be pleased to skin antelopes when you shoot 'em. I'll learn from watching you."

Sunshine looked somewhat miffed. She pushed a wisp of yellow hair back under her knit cap and stared straight into Fidddlehead's eyes.

"Sister," she said in a low voice, "you keep your hands off Chauncy, now. He's mine, sort of."

Hearing her say so made Wilson's heart do a half-step, and he flashed a wide, crooked-tooth grin.

"Don' worry, Sunshine," Sister said quickly, her tone as soft as the fuzz on a gosling's hind side, "I respects your rights."

Fiddlehead winked at Sunshine.

"Figger the lass can keep herself under control," he said. "Any case, she'll be busy. Me, I guess I'll jest snooze under a big pinyon an' let her hawg-tie us some antelopes."

Sunshine Hobson stamped her foot and then grabbed hold of Wilson's beard and tugged it, then gave him a small pecking kiss on the cheek.

A faint trail ran along the river and then upslope across a rocky ridge and down to some sage flats beyond. Nothing of the sort was on McLafferty's map. Perhaps it was an Indian trail, though its width gave the appearance of having horses on it from time to time. But no hoof marks showed, partly because of intermittent snow cover and partly because there just weren't any. Nothing at all since the winter storms set in.

"Has to be deers or elk somewhar," the mountain man told Little Sister. "The varmints come down out o' the high country in October, before the first snows. Should be winterin' in one or another of these flats. This child don't figger it. Anyhow, I guess we keep riding."

"Yes sir, Mr. Wilson," the girl replied. "Maybe we head yonder, where the creek feeds in under dem woods? Look like a good place for deer to me. Deer feel safe in swamps."

"Right ye are. Good idee. Wal, let's leave our varmints hyar an' walk on down, one o' us to either side. Jest recollect, afore ye start shootin', this bearskin cap o' mine ain't no jackarabbit."

"I promise. Jes you don't shoot Little Sister, neither."

"It's a bargain," he snorted.

The gall o' some people, Fiddlehead thought, talkin' that way to an old high shinin' *cahuna* like me. O' course, mebbe that's Sister's way of sorta lettin' me know I hadn't no call to be questioning her ability to tell the difference between a Fiddlehead an' a wombat.

At length they split up, Sister tramping the south side of the ooze and Wilson to the north. He came downslope on the low end, just where the creek gathered itself before dropping into a steep, rocky gully with dense forest all about. Then he sat down to wait, knowing the girl would make enough noise in the undergrowth to flush out whatever game might be hiding in under the willows and aspen brush.

After a few minutes an old cow elk came picking her way upslope, and Wilson tapped the priming pan on Old Blunderbuss, his Hawken buffalo rifle, set the triggers, and waited until the animal was no more than thirty yards off. His shot made more noise than he was expecting, because of some boulders just behind him. The elk dropped—a clean pass, right under the ear. A man ran a risk with head shots but not at close range, and not if he knew what he was about. The cow settled to her haunches and appeared to go to sleep.

Fiddlehead Wilson thanked Big Coyote and made a prayer for the elk's spirit so that it could find its way to the spirit world. It was a habit he'd picked up when he was with Termite Joe Hollingback and the Pawnees years earlier, and the ritual made sense. The animals kept people from starving, and so people were obliged to assist the animals' spirits into the next world, partly so they might come back and be elk again, or deer, or jackrabbits, for that matter. Things stayed in balance that way, and everyone was happier than they would otherwise have been.

Fiddlehead nodded, immediately reloaded his rifle, a habit so ingrained it was automatic.

Little Sister walked up from the marshy area, saw the cow elk lying dead, and waved Fiddlehead a salute.

"Nice gal," Fiddlehead thought, but he didn't mention how she'd set the whole thing up for him, though he guessed she knew anyhow.

The mountain man cut in through the elk's belly, careful not to rupture the spleen or gall bladder, and took out the liver. Sister made a terrible face when he suddenly took a bite.

"Good for what ails ye." He grinned and then offered her a bite. "Big Woods medicine."

Sister was doubtful, but then she tried some and admitted it wasn't half bad.

Fiddlehead was beginning to see why Queen Vikki had so much faith in the lady. He helped with butchering, and the two of them cut up the meat and tied it up into sections, intending to wrap it in slings formed out of the hide. What they couldn't use, coyotes, wolves, and vultures would have a good time with.

Fiddlehead fetched the animals, and while Little Sister was busy loading the mules, he followed the trail a short distance, then climbed onto a rocky hogback and looked out over the country.

What he saw didn't much please him. No more than a mile or two off, and it looked as if the three men had already camped for the night.

Three fellars, an' they is somethin' damnably familiar about 'em. This child ain't positive sure, but almost. Johnny Cortez, Wolf Mask, an' Pete . . .

Wilson hightailed it back to Little Sister, told her what was up, and together they rode toward their camp.

Fiddlehead considered a night foray, just as he and Hollingback had done once against a Kiowa hunting party. With a little luck, he'd be able to put Tarrango's bounty hunters under. Or he and the angels could slip off and outrun the pursuers. If Sam Tarrango had put a thousand dollar price on the women's heads, a scalp price conditional on the return of his money, then it was certain Cortez and his friends intended murder, pure and simple. The women's hair was the proof Tarrango would demand, even if he did get his money.

As he rode, Wilson attempted to put himself into Tarrango's place. Without question, Cortez, Wolf Mask, and Pete the Gun had worked for Sam for years, off and on. But if Vikki had all that money, what was to keep the boys from stealing it, having their way with the women, blowing their brains out, and leaving then where the bodies would never be found? In point of fact, there was no reason.

"Wal, mebbe Tarrango don't actually have good sense. Rich men jest sort of assume they can pay for whatever they want, an' their lackey will naturally do 'er."

That was another matter.

Right now Black Johnny was on their trail, even if

he didn't know it yet. The boys had ridden south along the edge of the mountains when Victoria Queen and her girls didn't show up at Truckee Meadows. Or else Cortez heard something somewhere, but how could he have?

"Don't make no never mind."

Chances were the boys had heard the Hawken go off, unless they were blind drunk.

7 Sunshine hugged him when he and Sister returned to camp, but then she saw he wasn't grinning like a schoolboy.

"What's wrong, Chauncy? You look as though you've seen a ghost."

"Three of 'em," he said. "Whar's Queen Vikki?"

Victoria Queen came out of the lean-to Wilson had put up for the women, hands on hips, ready to take charge of whatever the situation was.

"Tarrango's gunhands," he said. "They're camped no more than five, six miles downcanyon. Victoria, I don't think we can outrun 'em, an' that's a fact. But they'll be up hyar in the morning to check us out. We can wait nearby an' try to ambush 'em, or we can be long gone, whichever ye think best."

She studied him coolly and carefully before she said anything. "If we can't outrun them, Chauncy, then what are you suggesting? I don't like the idea of ambushing anybody. Turning bank robber was one thing, because I had money owing me. But murder? And that's what it would be."

"Ye can bet on what Cortez has planned for the lot of ye, now ain't that so?"

"*Tres diablos!*" Maria mumbled. "Those Señor

Tarrango has sent after us. . . . *¡Dale!* We must give Johnny Cortez the money, then, *y con mucho gusto.* What good is money to us if we are dead, Victoria? Even without it, we will always make our way."

"Out o' tin, out o' beans, an' out o' bacon?" Fiddlehead asked. "Then whar would ye be?"

"What y'all tellin' us, then?" Little Sister asked. "Don't look like we got much choice."

"Well?" Vikki asked, almost demanding an answer, as though Wilson actually knew what to do and was merely being perverse.

"We bushwhack 'em or we outsmart 'em, an' that means goin' whar they don't figger women would go. Chances is real good they don't guess I'm with ye. Joe Walker an' Joe Meek an' them lads made 'er over the Sierras by midwinter, so I figger we got us as good a chance as they had. You ladies up fer a leetle rock climbin' in the snow?"

Victoria Queen glanced at her girls as if estimating the endurance of each. At length she nodded.

Then she winked at Fiddlehead and smiled a kind of honey-all-over smile.

"As a matter of fact, Chauncy," she said, "it's beginning to snow right now."

And it was.

Soon snow was spitting out of the sky, not a heavy downfall such as had blanketed the Rubies on Christmas Eve, but instead an irregular whiteness drifting through the light of their fire, snow interspersed with rain. Then the temperature rose, and after a time the snow quit altogether, becoming a thin, steady drizzle. Strange, strange for midwinter, as Fiddlehead judged things.

They ate, and he made sure the women ate well. They were going to have to make a run for it, a forced march, just as when he and Termite Joe

Hollingback and their Pawnee friends had stolen horses from the Cheyennes.

The party moved south along the Walker, but it was slow going since all the light they had was provided by a couple of pitch pine torches, and with fog streamers moving along the river bottom, not even guttering torchlight did much good.

In all likelihood, Joe Walker had come this way back in '33, and when some Paiute Indians told him about a trail over to California's Great Central Valley, he took their word and damned near starved on the backs of the Sierras. As Walker discovered, the mountains were wide, a huge ragged plateau from which sharp, treeless peaks rose up to spires. With winds and blizzards and no sense of the land, and granite canyons cutting off in all directions, Walker's men had been forced to wander about through bitter cold for a couple of weeks.

"Joe Walker never could keep his directions straight, not as long as I'd known him," Fiddlehead mused, "but anyhow, it's enough to give this child food for thought."

Cortez would find their camp come morning, and no doubt he'd deduce they were headed south to Owens River, intending to skirt the southern extremity of the Sierra, at least as far as the low pass Walker and Meek had used on their return to Snake River country, and since used by numerous parties.

But the rain was coming real good by now, Fiddlehead thought, and perhaps if it rained hard enough, they'd reach some bare, rocky area where signs of their passing would be quickly effaced. Wilson glanced westward, in the direction from which the storm was blowing.

Cortez would find the camp all right, but how

could he know for certain it had belonged to the angels?

"Them boys won't be wanting to get kotched in deep snows up in the high rocks, so chances are they won't follow a-tall, but jest keep on headin' south, supposin' they'll eventually draw up on Queen Vikki somewhar in the next two hundert miles."

A side branch flowed down into Walker River, and with a hint of dawn coming, Fiddlehead could vaguely discern the lay of the land through which they were passing. The tributary creek wasn't much, but it flowed through some broad meadows, and he guessed there would be lakes up above, perhaps even a low spot in the mountains. Anyhow, this tributary was what he'd been looking for, since it would allow a westward turn that Cortez, Wolf Mask, and Pete the Gun wouldn't be expecting.

"Ladies!" he called back over his shoulder, "I done thunk the thing through. We're headin' up country from hyar!"

Wilson and the four women crested the mountains by midmorning, and still no more than a few flakes of snow had fallen. Hell, he thought there wasn't anything to these Sierras—or else he'd discovered a pass so easy the crossing of it was child's play.

Then sunlight split through the cloud cover, and they gazed westward. That was when he realized the true extent of the problem.

There were higher mountains still ahead, domed peaks rising pure white with snows that might have been thirty feet deep, for all Wilson could tell.

He hadn't yet done any bragging about finding a low pass, so he hadn't said anything to cause Vikki and her girls to lose faith in him. He simply directed them downhill, said he'd meet up with them later at the base of a distinctively ragged bluff projecting into the canyon below.

"What are you going to do, Chauncy?" Sunshine demanded. "Don't go back and try to ambush Tarrango's men. I'd be sad for a long while if I thought anything happened to you on my account."

"Mebbe a week or two," he grinned. "Nope. This child don't start shootin' until they's no other choice. Could be we'll find us a pass up yonder, an' then she's an easy run downhill to Deer Creek Dry Diggins or Hangtown or whatever other leetle cities the gopher lads has built. But right now, I figger I ought to take a check on whar our friends be. Vikki, ye an' the gals keep yore powder dry. Two sleep an' two stand guard, then change off after a couple o' hours. It's important now, so do it like I tell ye. Hole in whar they's natural protection—jest in case something goes wrong. Move out now an' do like I tell ye."

Victoria Queen was half asleep herself, but she was also a natural leader and might have captained a fur brigade in the old days. She came fully awake now, saw the sense of what Wilson was saying, and motioned Sunshine, Little Sister, and Maria downslope toward the specified bluff.

"Don't be worrying about yore injun fighter, leetle Sunshine," Fiddlehead said by way of farewell. "A man gets to be my age, he learns caution, an' it's caution what's sending me back down yonder for a look-see. If the turnoff worked, we're shed o' the three divvils, for a time at least. Bad pennies always turn up, but later's the best we got to hope for."

Then Fiddlehead urged his mule downslope, kicked the animal's ribs, and made for some point where he could survey the land properly.

He kept watch over the long meadows at the foot

of the pass for quite a while, but nothing moved except a dozen or so deer and one fat old grizzly sow that was up and about for a midwinter stroll—probably awakened by the warm winds that were causing the rain instead of snow.

When his eyes grew heavy for a few moments, he realized he'd best get to moving. The sky was gray once again, and he knew the long-delayed snowfall was about to begin.

"Come on, mule," he said. "This hyar's no time to be standing around in no brown study. Ain't sleeping time, nuther, even if Tarrango's hired guns haven't followed our trail toward the mountains. Let's get on over the hill an' down to that bluff, make sartin Sunshine an' the others hasn't done nothin' terminal dumb while we been squatting hyar."

He found the women without difficulty—asleep, all four of them. Wilson was disappointed even though no harm had come of the lapse. Well, they needed the shut-eye. He might have expected it, he thought, of everyone except Sister, but even she dozed, rifle across her lap.

Sister came awake, though, when Wilson rode in, started to aim her rifle at him, and then broke in to a wide, sheepish smile. She nudged Sunshine, who was also apparently supposed to be on watch, and the thin blond woman got up, shook her head, and then came running over to meet the bearded mountain man.

"Chauncy! I was worried—we were all worried about you. Why'd you stay away so long?"

"See ye were," Fiddlehead grinned and then kissed her on the forehead and pinched her behind, something he enjoyed more than Sunshine did.

The blond woman smiled tolerantly and wagged her finger under his nose.

"Looks like our trail's clear for a time," he said, nodding, and then he walked over to Queen Vikki, buried under her pile of blankets with Maria beside her.

"What is it, Fiddlehead?" Vikki asked, starting up.

"Wal, nothing a-tall," he replied, "only that it's time to mosey up the real mountains."

He hoped desperately there weren't any more real mountains on the other side of what rose directly ahead of them.

No sooner had the small party commenced its upslope trek beyond the terminus of some long, narrow meadows, following a small winding creek that gushed through a rocky channel beneath dark firs and occasional aspen copses than snow began to drift down, partially obscuring their vision.

"Figgered on this," Fiddlehead thought, "an' by Gawd's own pet horned toad, inside of ten minutes or so, we won't hardly know whar we're heading."

It was difficult going, and after no more than a few miles, the horses and mules were laboring, stumbling along, and no doubt wondering why humans wished to travel under such conditions.

Wilson squinted, rubbed his nose, and glanced back at the women. Other than new-fallen whiteness, he concluded, whatever snowpack was up above ought to be fairly well compacted, owing to colder temperatures at the higher elevations. Even though the mountains around them were hardly a match for the Tetons or the Colorado Front Range, word was that the Sierra Nevada, in places at least, were a far more formidable wall than any other in western America. All known trails were both high and entailed extremely rugged terrain, nearly impassable once winter snows accumulated.

Horses and mules struggled along, and after the

ascent of three or four miles, Wilson and the angels were obliged to lead their animals along. By angling upslope and keeping to the cover of a thick stand of pines and firs, they were able to continue to make headway, avoiding the ever deeper drifts of icy snow.

When dark took them, they'd made their way to the head of a lake a half mile long. Fiddlehead, nearly asleep on his feet, was stumbling and occasionally squinting and shaking his head. He wondered if it were finally starting to happen—was he getting old?

To hell with that idee, he thought, I ain't buying it. Nope. It's jest that I've spent too much time prowling around at nights, checking things out in case Wolf Mask an' them might of come up on us. Wal, they's one other thing. Serious matin' takes a considerable out o' a man, more than's the case with a woman.

Little Sister brought in a bundle of dead limbs, and Maria got a good blaze going. The party huddled about the flames as wind began to howl down from high peaks, invisible in storm and darkness but felt as driving gales of snowflakes in a torrent nearly parallel to the ground. Sunshine and Vikki, capes flapping behind them, cut up some elk meat and set that to hissing over the fire.

Fiddlehead hardly had energy left to make coffee, and when he pushed his trailworn pot in against the coals, a long fleer of sparks whirled away into the dark forest of gnarled and deformed trees. He staggered backward, shook his head, grimaced.

"This child's wobbly as a leetle kid," he said. "It's a plumb disgusting feeling. Guess it's about time for me to hibernate fer a month or two."

No great amount of snow had fallen by morning,

only two or three inches of thin icy white dust covering bare spots beneath trees and crusted drifts from earlier storms.

But the sky was still slate-gray and ugly.

After a quick breakfast Fiddlehead and the women were mounted and ready to go. Wilson looked over his charges—something was wrong.

"Whar's the other mule?" he demanded. "One's missing."

"Don' know," Little Sister replied. "He's done gone—and taken our elk meat with 'im. Pulled loose his line an' wandered off during the night. Y'all guess we wan' go back for 'im?"

Wilson shook his head.

"Vikki, ye an' the gals keep headin' for the pass ahead—jest whar them two rims come together. This child'll see whar the flop-ears with the chow's got to."

Vikki looked doubtful, and for a moment Sunshine's expression was actually stricken, but with reassurance that Fiddlehead didn't intend to desert his charges, the women moved on upslope, toward the high defile Wilson had pointed out.

"Ain't it jest like a damned mule?" Wilson grumbled, cinching his own mount tight and trudging off on foot in search of the pack animal.

Vikki and the angels were nearly to the summit when Fiddlehead caught up with them.

"No luck," he told them. "We're subject to run mighty short o' food unless I can manage to run down some kind o' game up hyar in the high rocks. That's the bad news. Good news is, I didn't see hide nor hair of Cortez an' them, nuther. I'm guessin' the bounty hunters rode on south. Probably think they're hot on yore trail.... Tell ye what, worst that can happen is we have to sacrifice one o' the mules. Best

I don't say it too loud, though, on account mules is smart. Mebbe that's why the other'n took off the way she did."

The party pushed ahead up a last tortuous few hundred yards and emerged onto a nearly level area studded with large firs and whitebark pines. Snow was deeper here, and, heavily crusted or not, the horses and mules were floundering badly, even though they were being led along.

An hour was required to negotiate less than a mile of deep snow, and by sundown the group had not managed more than three or four miles.

They came to the head of a drainage, however, and by all appearances it was running away westward, winding down into a deep canyon between high walls of rock and ice. Ragged gray and white peaks rose to every side of them, summits vanishing into low clouds, and by this time Fiddlehead Wilson decided the various stories he'd heard about difficulties in crossing the Sierra Nevada were, if anything, understated.

The sky grew ever darker, with light vanishing almost totally as Fiddlehead and the women worked to set up camp for the night.

Then snow started to fall again and turned, within moments, into a cascade of large, damp flakes.

"It's slow going, isn't it, Chauncy?" Sunshine remarked, not really asking. "Do you think we'll be able to get through?"

"O' course we will. Ain't no mountain range ever was what could whip this coon dawg. Don't go thinking about them Donners, now, an' cannibalism, an' all that. Hellfire, lass, trouble was the damned fools didn't have me with 'em. Less'n it snows five foot afore morning, we'll find a way down."

Sunshine stared at him, and it troubled him just a

bit when he saw momentary doubt in her pale blue eyes.

"*Nieve, nieve,*" Santa Maria said, staring upward, "it will snow forever. We must be like the Eskimo, we build the *casa de helado*, an igloo."

Vikki shook her head.

"Here we are, the richest hookers in the West," she said. "Plenty of money, and by God nothing to eat—a little flour and a few dried beans. What good's money without a trading post? In the middle of all this, gold coins are no more than a hindrance, and bank notes good for nothing except to start a fire. Ladies, I think God's punishing us for our sins."

"At least we don' have to worry 'bout Tarrango's executioners any more, Miz Vikki." Little Sister shrugged. "Fiddlehead an' me, we'll find something to shoot so's we don' starve."

"Danged rights," Wilson grinned.

The mountain man had already begun work on a crude pair of snowshoes. With these, he was certain, he'd be able to negotiate the terrain and so find a deer or perhaps even a wolf if necessary—something to eat, at least.

It didn't snow five feet that night, but it did snow four. When Wilson awoke, the stuff was still coming down, though not as heavily as when he'd fallen asleep.

He built up the campfire, backlogged it with a big pitchy limb he found sticking up out of a snowbank, strapped on his snowshoes, and set off in search of game.

Wilson stumbled onward, fighting his way through one drift after another, falling through at one point into a hidden streambed and emerging wet and chilled to the bone.

But he refused to let it beat him, and within the hour he'd managed to shoot a porcupine out of its tree and a fat marmot that had come out of its den for a look around.

His hands were numb with cold, but he managed to skin both creatures without cutting his fingers off and avoided the porcupine's quills as well.

He kept the women's smoke plume in sight, difficult enough in a world of near monochrome whiteness, and at length, without further luck, he turned and began his long trek back to camp.

The snowfall had stopped by now, and sunlight split gray clouds. Blue patches of sky appeared as if by magic, and already trees were beginning to shake their limbs, sending gushes of snow downward in spirals.

Another marmot was perched atop a projecting granite ledge. Fiddlehead raised his Hawken, fired, and grinned.

"By Gawd, old man," he said, "ye ain't lost yore touch with a rifle, no sir."

His hands were too cold and stiff to skin out the creature, however. He laced the big rodent to the pair of carcasses he'd been dragging along at the end of a cord, said a short prayer of thanks to the spirits of the animals he'd shot and another for unexpected gift of sunlight, and struggled on toward that plume of smoke and its promise of warmth.

Sunshine made much of him when he arrived, and Fiddlehead felt as good as if he'd brought in a buffalo, tender and fat. The women worked on his frozen feet and hands, even made him take off his icy leathers so they might warm and partially dry them by the fire while he sat huddled beneath blankets and started feeling almost human once more.

"Not too long, now!" he growled. "Or this child

won't never be able to get 'em back on. Ain't dignified for a man to have to walk bareass nekkid down into Californy."

Little Sister skinned the remaining marmot, and Vikki herself endeavored to put together a stew, using the last of the flour and dried beans.

Never, they all agreed, had any meal ever tasted so good—and the assessment included a certain feast during frozen darkness not long before on the Humboldt River.

They slept deeply that night, and morning dawned glorious blue upon a mountain landscape glittering with reflected light.

The little party ate a quick breakfast of leftover stew and prepared to make an attempt to move ahead, down into the canyon below, out of this desert of drifted whiteness.

"Leaving so soon, ladies?" a voice snapped from close by.

Black Johnny Cortez, Pete the Gun, and Wolf Mask were standing there, a kind of unholy trinity, with guns leveled.

8 Between intervals of brilliant midwinter sunlight, spates of snowflakes came hushing down. Pinyon and juniper alike were hung with whiteness, providing the illusion, during interspersed sunny moments, of a huge, unpruned orchard of apple or pear trees in the midst of riotous spring bloom.

Shadows fell over the meadows at Ruby Dome Ranch, but at the same time running clouds were fractured westward, and the Sulphur Springs Range beyond South Branch's wide basin was suffused with brilliance, the mountains almost mirage-like in a clear and unbroken glittering whiteness.

Blue-gray smoke rose from the McLafferty chimney, and inside the house a fire blazed. Mike was cleaning and oiling his Colt Walker while Moon mended harness for the pack mules. In the corral, animals were frisking about, and then Ghost whinnied twice. Something about the sound suggested difficulties. Elizabeth Harrington put aside the muslin pillowcase she'd been embroidering and stood up.

"I'll go check the horses," she offered, reaching for a thick red jacket that hung from one of several pegs Mike had doweled into the wall in order to create a makeshift coatrack.

"Me, too!" Jacques sang out, always ready for anything that hinted at adventure. "I'll bet Ghost wants me to ride him again, like I did last week."

"No riding today, Little Bull," Mike said. "Spotted horse, he's probably angling for a bit more hay. Well, it's almost time. Toss some out."

Then Elizabeth and Jacques were through the door, which banged shut but didn't quite close.

"Wretched kids," Mike grumbled, slipping his revolver back into its holster and crossing the room to secure the entryway.

Elizabeth and Jacques, the small boy frisking, approached the corral where Gray Boy, Ghost, and the mules were kept. Whatever the disturbance, Elizabeth noted, the pack mules were apparently undisturbed, but the two horses were standing together at the enclosure's far end, as if frightened of something close at hand.

Then a short, muscular Indian, his upper torso and cheeks daubed with some kind of blue-gray substance, bolted from behind the lean-to of a barn, grabbed Jacques while still at a full run, slung the child over one shoulder, and struck off toward the high meadows, his bandy legs kicking out in either direction as he moved rapidly and surefootedly across a thin covering of snow. The kidnapping occurred so suddenly, so unexpectedly, that Elizabeth didn't even yell. For a moment she simply stood still, stunned and blinking.

Then she knew: the Shuckers, hanging close for all these weeks, almost like hungry coyotes, had finally struck. Other Indians appeared from behind pinyons and junipers, angling toward the blue-daubed man, following him. There was no shouting—there was no sound at all other than the terrified howling of young Jacques. Elizabeth turned, sprinted toward the McLafferty log cabin, her skirts flying.

"Mike! Moon! They've stolen him . . . the blue man and others . . . they've got Jacques!"

For a moment McLafferty stood blocking the entryway. Then Moon Morning Star pushed past him, grasped Elizabeth by the shoulders.

"Where?" she demanded.

Elizabeth, sucking in breath, pointed toward the high meadows, pointed to a last Te-Moak just disappearing from sight into thick growth of pinyons.

In the meadow's cover of snow, they found several footprints made by the abductors, but no sign of Jacques. Moon dismounted, scanned the area to determine the direction the Te-Moaks had taken. She attempted to quiet her shallow, rapid breathing sufficiently to listen for any possible sound that might lead in the direction of Jacques and his captors, but she heard nothing beyond the soft plop of a clump of snow falling from a pinyon branch, faint hissing of a brief gust of light wind, and the pounding of her heart.

"There," Mike said, nodding upslope. "They're not taking time today to move from one bare spot to another. Looks like they're heading north toward the rim."

Moon remounted without speaking and kicked Ghost into a gallop again, following a clear line of tracks to the upper end of the meadow. There the marks of human passage vanished once again into a grove of firs, where little snow had reached the ground. Mike and Moon were forced to dismount and search on foot for sign on the spongy, needle-covered soil. They found little—a few vague depressions that might or might not have been footprints, a few places where the layer of needles was scuffed by a careless step.

"Most likely heading the same way they were. Those Te-Moak bastards want to get over the ridge and away from our part of the country."

Moon nodded, still not speaking. Her eyes were wide, unnaturally shiny, and her mouth was set in a tight line. The man and woman rode in silence to the top of the rim, where the trees thinned. On the other side they picked up a clear trail again, one that led down into the next drainage, where the single trail they'd been following became many trails leading off in different directions.

The McLaffertys stopped, tried to determine a general course.

"They haven't killed him yet," Mike said, hoping to reassure Moon, "and that probably means they're not going to."

"Of course they haven't killed him," she snapped, turning a fierce gaze upon her husband. "That's a foolish thing to say. They didn't steal my son to kill him. This isn't the time for talking, Red Coyote. The Shuckers can't be far ahead. The trails will come together later. Let's keep moving."

They continued, cutting across a drainage and up the far slope, coming at length to a bare, rocky rim where winds had blown the snow away, and once again the trail disappeared. Mike and Moon cut back and forth in a broadening semicircle until they picked up a track, rode northward, up the spine of a ridge and onto a crest overlooking the broad desert basin.

Great, ragged holes had formed in the clouds, and now sunlight gleamed from a broad area of blue, wide bands of sunlight pouring down onto the snow and reflecting with blinding brilliance. Moon squinted into the glare, searched the vast white landscape, suddenly grabbed McLafferty's arm and pointed below.

Mike strained to see, cupped half-open hands around his eyes against the glare.

Far down on the valley floor, nearly invisible against the brilliance of reflected sun, a straggle of tiny dark forms, human not by discernible shape but almost certainly by the pattern of movement, spaced out but moving purposefully away from the mountain, heading, Mike realized as he watched, straight as an arrow flight across the flat surface of the basin toward Sulphur Springs Mountains.

"We'll catch them, Red Coyote," Moon breathed. "We can see them, can see where they're going. They won't be able to escape us once we get out onto the desert."

Her words were confident, but the voice was tremulous, like that of a little child asking for reassurance, and the eyes that had been dry and bright since the beginning of the pursuit suddenly threatened to spill tears.

"We'll catch them by nightfall, I think, don't you, Mac-lafferty?"

Mike reached across and squeezed her hand, smiled, nodded with what he hoped was a convincing show of confidence.

"You can bet on it, lady," he said. "Old Jacques will be back home plaguing us for candy or stories by bedtime—that's what this child figures."

Once they moved down off the crest, they could no longer see the desert, and their descent was a long and slow one, maddeningly complicated by rough terrain and systems of ridge and ravine. Mike determined after a time that the route they were following veered off in a southerly direction, and they had to cross into another drainage and then a third.

The progress was difficult, their horses occasionally losing footing and sliding several feet on loose rock concealed beneath the snow. The animal's breathing was more strained on every steep upslope, foam hanging in strings from their mouths and eyes rolling back in exhaustion.

"We can't push the animals any farther, Moon," McLafferty finally said, reluctance in his voice. "They've got to have a breather."

"You rest Gray Boy, then," Moon said, turning to glance at Mike, her expression wild, strange. "Ghost is a Cheyenne pony. He'll go on for as long as I wish him to."

"Maybe so, and up ahead somewhere you'll find yourself sitting on a dead horse. Look at him, Moon!"

Moon rode on a few steps, then reined Ghost in, slumping forward until she sat with her face buried in the spotted horse's mane. After a moment she dismounted and turned the animal loose to graze in the marshy canyon bottom where they'd stopped.

Mike stepped behind her, put his hands on her shoulders, squeezed gently. Suddenly she whirled to face him, her eyes bright with controlled desperation.

"You stay here with the horses," she said. "I'll go on. You can catch up with me later."

"Moon, no," Mike said as she began walking rapidly away. He caught hold of her arm, turned her around again.

"Let me go, Red Coyote," she shouted, struggling to free herself. "I can't just stay here. Every minute I'm sitting here, the Te-Moaks are moving farther away. That's my son!"

"He's my kid too, goddamn it! You're not going anywhere, Moon-Gal, not alone. Then I have to find you before I can even start looking for the Shuckers again."

He held her by both arms now, gripping tight as she tried to flail out at him, twisting and writhing like a captive animal. At length, however, he felt her losing some of the wild energy, and suddenly she collapsed against him, sobbing as he held her and stroked her hair.

"They know every gully in the desert," Mike said softly, "and we can't match them on that. But we can use our heads. If a man's going to hunt a bear, he'd best think about the bear's habits. The Te-Moaks are human, nothing more than that. They've got human needs, just like us. Furthermore, they've probably got a village over in the Sulphur Springs Range. That's why we've never come across a campsite. Moon, we made it across half a continent together, you and me, and we'll find Jacques, too. We've got horses, and the Shuckers don't. We've got guns, and they don't. We'll tail them to the gates of Hell, if we have to."

When she'd calmed somewhat, Mike brushed snow from a boulder and set her down on it in the weak January sunlight and went to scrounge for wood dry enough or pitchy enough to start a fire.

"I don't know what it would be like to live without you, Red Coyote," Moon said, her voice soft, almost like a small child's. "It's as if I can't really remember the time before you came to me, and I can't imagine living that way. We have to find Jacques. Please, Mac-lafferty."

Occasionally Mike realized that this woman he'd somehow attached to himself, his life, apparently permanently, was not really a large person, at least not physically. The present moment was such an occasion. He remembered her on the night of the final battle with Jean Laroque—she'd painted her face in the manner of a Cheyenne warrior; fierce, indomitable, she'd seemed almost supernatural. Her courage never wavered, and at the end, wounded and so weak from loss of blood that she could barely stand, she had by sheer nerves and will risen to face her husband's murderer and fired the shot that killed him.

But now, when it was her son who was in jeopardy, the extraordinary strength seemed to have failed her, and she looked small, almost frail, sitting hunched against chill sunlight, the usually proud lines of her face uncertain, frightened. McLafferty said something that he hoped sounded hearty and reassuring, and then he turned away, suddenly wanting very much to shout curses at God or Old Man Coyote or whoever might be sitting off in the distance, listening and grinning.

"Maybe four hours to sundown," Mike calculated, "no more. The damned Shuckers have a few short-cuts we don't know about. One way or another, they've got five miles on us, at least by trail. Not sure the horses are that much of an advantage in country like this, not through the damned snow anyway."

"Then we will have to be extremely lucky, Mac-lafferty," Moon replied. "When we get down to the flat ground of the desert, they will not be able to outrun our horses, never mind the snow."

'Cept that it ain't flat, it's all cut up with gullies and washes and leetle hills an' hollers, an' she knows that as well as ye do, Michael thought.

The voice in McLafferty's mind, of course, was Fiddlehead's. Somehow that irascible individual had long since been internalized as conscience and common sense commentator. Mike didn't bother to pass Fiddlehead's observation along to Moon.

Perhaps an hour later they emerged onto the desert floor. McLafferty and Moon both squinted and scanned the horizon to north and east, the ragged profile of the Sulphur Springs Range beyond an irregular line of cottonwoods that marked the course of the Humboldt's South Branch.

"I think we're pulling up on 'em," Mike said. "They were headed northeast when we saw them, making a beeline for the hills over there. If we bear north-northeast, we should cut their trail before long. Shouldn't have much trouble spotting their tracks in this white stuff, as long as more of it doesn't start coming down."

Moon glanced apprehensively at the sky, which had once again grown overcast and threatening, and then she nodded.

"We'll do as you say, Red Coyote. But let's move quickly."

The sky continued to threaten as they moved away from the foot of the mountains, but no more snow fell. The man and woman kept their tired horses at a fast walk and covered a good deal of distance in a short time, although in this desert world of vast horizons, endless repetition of low ridge and shallow basin, of ravine and sudden bare outcroppings of stone, sagebrush, and greasewood rising gray-green against the snow-dusted earth, Moon had the frustrating sense that they were crawling at an insect's pace across the terrain. She forced herself to remain calm, not to give in to the impulse to pound her heels against Ghost's sides, sending the gray-speckled Palouse pony into a wild gallop that would exhaust the beast in short order.

She tried to keep her mind silent, as Cheyenne hunters were schooled to do, in order to avoid alerting prey to the hunter's presence. She concentrated her energies upon continual and careful scrutiny of everything within her perception, from the snow-crusted ground at the horse's feet to the broad span of the landscape, watching for anything abnormal. But there was nothing, no sign of human presence. The only tracks visible were little crosshatchings of birds, a set of cloven impressions from three or four deer browsing together on the silver-leaved sage, scooped-out trenches from the hind feet of a jackrabbit in flight. And very little moved except small birds scratching busily in the snow near clumps of vegetation.

Once Moon's eye caught movement farther away, and her heart seemed to jump until she realized that it was only a coyote, no, two coyotes, one stalking something invisible on the ground, ears intently forward as it slowly lifted one foot and then the other, while the second song dog waited inconspicuously near a cluster of greasewood.

As miles dragged by and the McLaffertys still came upon no sign of the Te-Moaks, it was more and more difficult for her to keep her mind quiet, to keep at bay the cold heaviness, the ache, the increasing conviction that somehow Jacques and his abductors had simply vanished into the desert and that she would never see her son again.

The sun had not been visible for hours, not even as a silver disk through dull overcast, and yet Moon found herself glancing with increasing frequency and anxiety toward the region where the star of the daytime should be.

"It's getting late, Red Coyote," she said, breaking a long period of silence. "Perhaps we were wrong. Maybe we were already north of their path when we came out of the mountains."

"Don't think so," Mike replied. "Patience, patience. We'd have cut their path sooner if we'd headed straight north, but we've been angling east too. Takes longer to find a trail this way, but we'll catch them quicker. Don't give up, lady."

"I will not give up while they have my son," she said, a spark of the familiar warrior woman in her voice once more. "I'm only wondering if we should not be looking in a different direction. Perhaps we've crossed their path already and didn't see it. I'm afraid we'll run out of time. If we have to wait until tomorrow, they could be very far away."

"I don't have a certain answer, Moon, but I figure they've got a winter encampment not too damned far from here—back into the Sulphur Springs Mountains, some sheltered meadow. All we can do is play the odds. We could use a dose of Fiddlehead's instinct right about now, I'm thinking."

Mike scanned the mushy, snow-free sand carefully, suddenly gave a muffled whoop and climbed down from Gray Boy, going to hands and knees in the icy seep to look more closely at his discovery.

"It's them, Moon-Gal, sure as painter piss," he said. "Take a look. Figures they'd be sticking to the gullies."

"Yes," Moon said, dismounting also to inspect the depressions in the soft ground beneath its film of shallow water. A moccasin print, without question, and a few moments' searching turned up several more. Moon raised her eyes to McLafferty's, closed them in relief, and then threw her arms around his waist and clung to him for a moment.

"Now I know we'll catch them," she said. "Hurry, Red Coyote. There are not many hours of daylight left."

Both remounted, and Moon guided Ghost up out of the ravine.

"Better for the Te-Moaks in the gullies," she said, "but better for us on top, I think."

"Not so sure of that. We stand a good chance of seeing them, all right, but we also give the Shuckers a fair chance to spot us. Once they know we're close behind them, they might still be able to disappear. They've lived their whole lives out here—must know every dry wash and mesquite bush by its Christian name."

"If I see them, they won't get away," Moon insisted.

Mike shrugged, followed.

Up on more level ground, she drummed her heels against Ghost's sides until the tired animal responded with a canter, and they rode along beside the ravine until it widened out and the ground dipped to meet it and the declivity disappeared. Here the trail of the Te-Moaks became quite clear again, and they followed it at a speed both recognized as dangerous in this land of loose rock and hidden gopher or ground squirrel holes.

When they came near an upthrust of crumbling stone, however, Moon drew the spotted horse to a halt, dismounted, and scrambled to the top, standing clearly silhouetted against gray sky for a moment, her long hair and deerskin cloak blowing about her. Moon's action caught Mike by surprise, and he nearly called out to warn her back down, then shrugged, shook his head.

"She knows better than that," he thought. "The Shuckers can see her from five miles away if they're looking. God, she's beautiful, though."

Moon turned abruptly, leaped, scrambled, slid down.

"I saw them," she said breathlessly. "They're less than a mile away. We have them now, Red Coyote."

She jumped on her horse, urged him into a hard gallop, set off at breakneck speed without looking back at McLafferty.

"Moon, damn it, slow down!" he shouted, but to no effect.

Wind in her face, sucking the breath from her lips, Ghost gathering and plunging, the great play of muscles, tears blown into her eyes so that the white earth, clusters of gray brush, all blurred into streaked monochrome of speed and movement toward the child who seemed to glow in her consciousness, the spark of his need drawing her on in a heedless rush.

Movement, speed, then motion disrupted, a wild jolt and she was flying, free of any constraint, any connection with horse muscles, moving, flying, turning in air for a very long time, and through it all she heard a long wail, a voice that seemed to be Red Coyote's:

"Mo-o-o-o-n!"

Then earth re-established the connection, ground coming up fast, nothing to stop it, unbearable violence of return, crushing jolt, instantaneous blackness.

Nothing.

9

Mike fed a few sticks of greasewood into his small fire, filled a tin cup from his saddlebag with snow, and set it in beside the flames to melt. Then he pulled the saddle blanket up more tightly around Moon's chin, held his hand close under her nostrils to assure himself her faint, shallow breaths still stirred the air.

He reached a hand gently toward her forehead, then withdrew it without actually touching the skin. The right side of her face was scraped raw, and a violent purple swelling had risen on the temple. He rose abruptly, pounded his right fist hard into the palm of his left hand, strode several steps away from the fire, then turned and went back.

Gray Boy lifted his head from where he nibbled disconsolately at tips of sage, stared at McLafferty, then blew out a loud breath through his nostrils. Ghost stood a few paces beyond, front legs wide, head down but not grazing. His eyes seemed glazed, and he appeared to be still somewhat stunned from the fall, although Mike had run his hands over the animal and discerned no broken bones.

McLafferty knelt beside the motionless woman once more, put a hand lightly on silky dark hair.

The snow in the cup had melted, and he added another handful to the tepid water that only half filled the vessel now. When that melted, Mike pulled a handkerchief from his rear pocket and dipped it into the fluid, rubbed the abrasions on Moon's face, gently wiping away dirt and sand that were ground into the cuts.

She moaned feebly, tried to turn her head away from the pain, then quieted again.

"You're going to be pissed at me when you wake up, lady," he said, talking more to fill silence than for any other reason. "You're going to tell me I shouldn't have let the damned Shuckers get away when we were so close. They'll have vanished back into the rocks by now, the way they always do. No help for it, damn it. Was I supposed to run past you, let you lie there until I got Jacques and then came back to see if you were dead? Sure as hell, that's what you'll tell me I should have done. Well, sorry about that, ma'am. I'll be happy to take whatever you can dish out if you'll just wake up. No, no, I mean when you wake up."

He had carried her into the best shelter he could find, a slightly overhanging bank of a draw, partially screened by a stunted mahogany tree. He'd wrapped her in the blankets from both horses after checking carefully and determining that at least she'd sustained no broken bones.

The bump on the head was another matter. He had seen enough concussions of the sort to know that matters could go in any one of a number of completely unpredictable directions. Indeed, the previous summer it had been he himself who was thrown, and days drifted by in a haze of chaotic memories and misapprehensions. Mike McLafferty of the thick skull, and now he was hoping Moon's was thicker.

She might awaken at any time and be completely free of aftereffects except for a nasty headache. Or she could awaken, seem fine, and then lapse back into unconsciousness, could alternate between sleep and waking for days.

"Some god," he mused, "keeps whanging us on the head—and maybe that's McLafferty luck too."

Or she might never wake up. Face it, McLafferty, she might never wake up at all.

The voice of his fear had crept in without his willing it, and he suddenly had to stand, move about as if to escape the nagging whine.

He climbed out of the draw, walked rapidly some distance across the essentially featureless plain, topped an easy rise that nonetheless commanded a wide view of desert landscape. Nothing moved, no sign of life in the whole expanse. Even birds that had scratched around the brush had vanished, and there was a sense of expectancy in the air, a sense of hidden life waiting. . . .

Waiting for what, though?

Snow, he realized.

Mike passed a hand across his eyes, moved back toward the draw.

We won't stand a chance of finding them if it snows again, he thought. They've already disappeared. Probably got a gander at Moon when she climbed up on the rocks and saw them. Snow'll wipe out everything. How do I tell you, beautiful Moon, if you do come back to me? You're probably never going to see your little boy again.

The snow started before he reached the gully, a sudden releasing of tiny, hard flakes that hissed faintly when they hit earth. Mike cursed silently, broke off another chunk of dead sage, and carried it down, fed it to the fire. A tiny sound made him turn, and he saw that Moon was awake, her wide black eyes staring at him.

"Red Coyote. My head hurts. Will you bring Jacques to me? I was dreaming—I thought the Te-Moaks had taken him. I want to . . . see him. . . . Why does my head hurt so much?"

McLafferty bent as if to tend the fire, fearful she would read his features before he had a chance to compose them. Then he moved to her, knelt beside her.

"It's about time you woke up, little warrior," he said. "It's a hell of a fix you left me in, halfway to hell out here, dry camp, no grub, not even a damned coffee pot. But I've heated you some water. Thirsty?"

She didn't reply, continued to stare at him for several very long moments.

"It wasn't a dream, then, was it, Mac-lafferty?" she said at last.

"No dream, I'm afraid. You fell. Ghost stumbled in a gopher hole or something. You've been out cold for a while. We'll catch the Shuckers after you've rested some."

"No!" Moon cried out, struggling to sit up and free herself of the tangle of heavy blankets. "We have to go now! They'll get away."

"You just lie down, damn it," Mike ordered, taking her by the shoulders to keep her from rising. She fought against him, then suddenly went limp and lay back, moaning, clutching her head.

"You go, then, Mac-lafferty," she said after a moment.

"Can't do it, Moon-Gal. I'm not leaving you alone here. We might as well face it—we're not going to catch the kidnappers today. It's already starting to get dark. In another half hour there'll be no light at all. No moon tonight, not even any stars. Can't track a band of ghosts across the desert in pitch dark."

Moon pushed herself up to a sitting position again, closed her eyes, opened them.

"It's snowing," she said, her voice flat with despair. "We'll never be able to find them now."

"You're forgetting this is Pathfinder McLafferty you're talking to. We'll find the bastards, Moon, if I have to bust a gut and turn the goddamned desert upside down to do it."

The light was by now deep blue, fading quickly, and the snow showed no sign of letting up. McLafferty rose, fed more sticks to the fire. Ghost and Gray Boy drifted in and stood as close by the small warmth as they could crowd, their long faces filled with sadness.

"What will I do without him?" Moon asked into the gathering darkness. "My Little Bull, he's out there somewhere in the cold with only strangers around him. They don't even talk a language he understands. He must be very frightened."

Mike sat down beside Moon, put his arm around her shoulders, and drew her head down against him.

"If I know young Jacques, he's probably got all the wild Te-Moaks eating out of his hand by now. Fact is, he's likely a good bit more comfortable than we are. The Shuckers didn't just run out of the house like we did. They knew exactly what they were doing—spent an unholy long time planning the entire operation, in fact. They'll have food and blankets stashed along the way—probably eating a nice soup of boiled camas root and crickets or something right now. Jacques is all right. We're the ones to worry about."

Mike could tell by the shaking of her shoulders that Moon was weeping, and he gave up talking, only held her and petted her hair until she was quiet.

Darkness grew complete, the hiss of falling snow pellets audible above the crackle of the fire. They huddled together beneath saddle blankets and restlessly passed through the hours of darkness. Moon slept fitfully, waking several times with a loud cry. Cold penetrated their coverings, and eventually the frozen dampness of snow did as well. Mike rose several times to feed the fire and stare into impenetrable blackness beyond, a blackness filled with the sound of falling sleet.

At first light they rose, saddled their horses, and rode out. Moon insisted she was well enough to ride although her face, with its ugly purple contusion, appeared to Mike to be haggard, yellowish, and she had dark circles under her eyes.

I should take her home, Mike told himself. Hogtie her and rope her to Ghost and lead her back to the ranch, then go out on my own. No point in even suggesting it, though. God damn it, Moon, you stubborn bitch. We both know what the chances are of getting within fifty miles of the Shuckers now.

Up out of the draw the desert was pure white, about four inches of snow having fallen in the night. In blue-gray light of an overcast dawn, not a track marred the surface so far as the two could tell. Moon didn't speak, her face again tight, grim.

"Just head the way we were heading yesterday, I guess," Mike said. "Looked like they were making straight for the Sulphur Springs Range. Probably have their village tucked away in those hills somewhere, like I said before once or twice. If we're lucky we'll spot smoke or something."

They rode on through the morning without stopping, making wide detours to the north and south of their general track, seeking signs of the passing Te-Moak party. But they found only a blank silence of white unmarred by anything more than an occasional animal track.

The snow had stopped before dawn, and later in the morning, clouds began to break, sun dazzling their eyes so that tears formed and it became difficult to focus, particularly when looking out over the distance for a hint of movement, dark figures against the brilliant expanse.

Mike watched Moon anxiously. She was slumped in the saddle, and as they continued, detouring to search bottoms of draws for sign of passage, she occasionally swayed and caught herself. Her face was drawn, her eyes haunted. He tried to persuade her to stop, rest from time to time on some ruse or another, but she grimly insisted on continuing.

The fall took more out of her than she's admitting, he realized. She needs food, warmth, real rest. Not that far to the hills. If we haven't found sign of the Te-moaks by then, we're stopping until I can take some kind of game—if I have to tie her to a tree.

The hills were stark, barren except for a scattered growth of pinyons, ghostly gray lines of leafless aspen marking the draws, no different from a hundred other desert ranges.

They reached the foot of the mountain range near its southern extremity, then rode north along the base. Moon suddenly straightened her shoulders, squinted against the glare, and looked intently ahead.

A splash of color, bright red against the general monochrome.

Moon dismounted, stumbled and nearly fell, then

ran ahead to the object clinging to a sagebrush in the mouth of a draw coming down from the hills. She grabbed the vivid thing, turned in Mike's direction, and waved it excitedly above her head.

"It's his, Mac-lafferty, it's Jacques' mitten," she shouted.

Mike had by now gotten down from Gray Boy and ran to meet her, took the small knitted glove and rubbed it between his fingers as he examined the ground for clues.

"Snow's covered whatever tracks they left. That means they came by here yesterday. They could be thirty miles the other side of the hills by now—"

"No," Moon insisted. "They're close to us. I can feel it. Besides, we can climb to the top of these mountains. From there, we will be able to see any smoke even if it's thirty miles away. Let's go, Red Coyote. This draw seems to lead up toward a saddle. Perhaps it will lead us to them."

"Moon—"

"What? We're wasting time. Let's go!"

The draw led easily up to a high bench, and here they again dismounted, scanned across the folds of hills, searching for smoke, a moving figure, anything. When the survey turned up nothing, Moon seemed to sag at the knees, and McLafferty caught her, eased her to the ground.

"You've got to rest, miz b'ar killer," Mike said. "You can't go on like this. You're hurt. We both need something to eat. Goddamn it, act human."

"I'm all right. I was only a little weak for a moment."

"Like hell. I'm giving the orders now, Moon, and what we're going to do is go back down to that basin at the head of the draw, and you're going to sit there and rest and wait for me to hunt something."

Moon protested again, but Mike's will was stronger. Even her characteristic stubbornness was diminished with her general exhaustion.

He left her with Ghost, the horse's saddle blanket wrapped around her, and her back resting against a boulder.

"And you stay here, damn it. Don't move! Until I get back."

She stared at him, after a moment nodded, then leaned her head against the stone, closed her eyes.

It took him the better part of an hour to find game, and that no more than a scrawny jackrabbit he'd been obliged to go clear back to the desert floor to scare up.

When he returned to the basin at the head of the draw, however, he found Ghost still tethered to a pinyon but no sign of his wife.

"Moon!" he called out, not yet willing to believe she was gone. "Moon, damn it, where are you?"

The sloping walls of the basin returned his own voice to him, echoed a second time, and after that nothing, the heaviest silence imaginable.

"Most pig-headed woman alive," he muttered, tossing the dead jackrabbit onto the ground near the remains of the fire. "I should've known."

He didn't acknowledge the icy fear in the pit of his stomach, the thought that accompanioned it: What if the Shuckers came back, or were watching all along, saw me leave the woman alone . . . ?

He searched the area, so trampled by their own prints, human and equine, that it was not possible to discern anything, extended his search wider and saw what he should have noticed before and hadn't—Moon's moccasin tracks heading up to the ridge they'd come down from before, her tracks mixed in with those of the horses but headed the opposite direction. He sucked in a long breath of relief. So far as he could tell, she was alone. For the time being.

Riding Gray Boy and leading Ghost, Mike followed Moon's trail up the ridge and across a saddleback to the base of a rocky peak, wind-blasted and bare of any vegetation. Moccasin prints led toward the top, and he was forced to leave the horses in a snow-covered swale.

No tracks coming back down this way. With luck I'll catch her at the summit. With good luck, that is, not McLafferty's usual variety . . .

Wind blew hard on the high rocks and had scoured many areas free of snow so that footprints were impossible to find, but Mike felt certain Moon had headed directly for the crest. The slope was steep and covered with loose reddish stone so that he often had to employ both hands and feet in the climb. Icy wind seemed to draw the breath from his lungs. And when he emerged on the back of the mountain, he found jagged outcroppings of stone and a stunning vista—the tips of the range stretching away both north and south, folds and ridges, and far below a white desert glittering dream-like in pure, cold light.

The sky was completely clear now, flawless blue, and wind stung his face. An eagle floated in the middle distance above the desert, roughly on a level with him, and farther away other big birds turned circles—he saw all this but no trace of Moon. And she had left no clue of direction she might have taken from the peak—no footprints on the scoured stone, from this distance no trail visible in the snow lower down.

Cursing, he swung his gaze north, detected something slightly different in the quality of light, stared harder. A faint blue haze seemed to hang above a fold of the mountains some miles distant. He looked away, looked back. There was, indeed, a specific area where the haze hung.

Smoke? Could be, or nothing but haze, ice crystals forming in the air. Had Moon seen it too, was that where she was headed? Mike had no way of knowing for sure. He could only take his best shot with the cards he'd been dealt.

He made his decision, came down on the north side of the peak, leaving the horses where they were and was elated when he picked up Moon's trail again without difficulty, the moccasin prints leading northward.

He tracked her easily now, making good time, crossing from one drainage to the next. At times he lost the trail on slopes where wind or the morning sun had cleared the ground, but he was sure now of her general direction and managed to rediscover the trace quickly enough. He expected to catch up to her at any moment, but when he moved from the shoulder of one peak on the next without so much as catching a glimpse of her, he began to feel again a nagging fear.

It was when McLafferty was skirting the south face of this second peak, nearing noon, that he somehow lost the trail completely. Only patches of snow remained on the sunny slope. He didn't bother to look particularly hard for signs of Moon's passage here, confident he'd find the path again on the shadowed north side.

Instead, when he crossed to that slope, he found a blank expanse of snow, no sign of human passage whatever.

"What the hell?" he muttered. "Farther down?

Maybe she cut for a ravine when . . . Saw something and headed back for the desert . . . ?"

Vanished. Beautiful Moon. I never quite believed she was real. Gone, maybe never existed, maybe the time since I went back to the Cheyenne village to see White Bull never happened at all. Could be I'm still lying in bed in my St. Louis townhouse dreaming . . . Got to control my mind . . . Fiddlehead could pick up her sign, and by God so can I. I'm acting like a damned greenhorn.

In the silence, his solitude had taken on a disturbing sense of unreality that he found very difficult to shake. Then, a voice of intuition spoke: She clumb this mountain too, ye dung-eatin' one-eared cattymount.

"Thank you, Fiddlehead, you cantankerous old hawg." Mike laughed. "You figure she's still up there, then?"

Even as he spoke to his imaginary mentor, he heard a clatter of loose rocks, several small stones bounding down the slope and coming to rest a few yards away from him. He looked up, saw Moon running down the mountainside, sliding and kicking stones loose, losing her balance and falling more than once before she stood breathlessly before him.

McLafferty began to laugh harder as he reached to wrap his arms around her, and found himself roaring with mirth, unable to stop.

"Gawddamn it, Moon, for a while there I thought I was tracking nothing but skookums, that you'd melted into the damned desert too. I thought I told you to wait for me. I brought you a jackrabbit, but it's way back with the horses now—"

"Hush, Red Coyote. You speak like a man without sense. I am no ghost, and neither are the Te-Moaks. I saw something up there though. Now we must go.

No time for jackrabbits or horses either. Hurry, Maclafferty, hurry."

She'd already struggled out of his embrace and set off northward again, walking rapidly. McLafferty caught up to her in several long strides.

"Damn it, woman, I was so sure I remembered telling you to wait for me back there. But maybe I was wrong. So what the hell did you see?"

"I couldn't wait," she replied. "Smoke. I thought I saw it before, but now I'm certain. I know exactly where the Te-Moak village is."

10 Below stood a cluster of four brush houses, small, untidy constructions heaped with sage and mesquite and pinyon branches, barely large enough in diameter for a grown man to lie down inside. Wisps of smoke still drifted from the vent holes of these lodges, but there was no other sign of activity in the encampment at all.

"This must be their village, then," Moon said. "But they've seen us coming. They have all left."

"Got to have a scout posted." Mike nodded. "Probably not far away right now, hiding and waiting for us to leave. Might as well go down anyhow, see what we can find."

Moon pushed herself to her feet, staggered a little, and caught her balance. Mike took her arm and stared critically into her face.

"You're going to have to give in and rest soon, gal," he said. "Maybe the Shuckers left behind something to eat, at least."

"Perhaps," Moon said indifferently. "There will be time for eating and resting after we've found Jacques. He's very close now."

"Mike sighed, followed her downslope.

"Halloo the camp!" Mike shouted. "If any of you

can hear me, we don't want to hurt you. We want the child back."

Moon repeated the message in Shoshone, for they knew the language the Te-Moaks spoke was related to that tongue. But there was no answer, not even the barking of a dog. Wind rustled among sage and blew the smoke in thin plumes.

"Might as well check the lodges." McLafferty shrugged. "Not that I figure anybody's home."

Moon nodded, lifted the hide covering over the nearest hut's entryway, stooped, and peered within. They found no one in the first three they checked, and a rudimentary search also failed to turn up anything edible. The last lodge they looked into was set a little back from the others, and when Moon stepped inside and stared into darkness dimly lit by embers of a dying fire, she could at first perceive nothing. Then, just as Mike pulled back the flap and stooped to enter, she sucked in her breath and took a step backward, colliding with McLafferty.

On the far side of the lodge, eyes reflected the faint firelight.

"Who are you?" Mike demanded.

An unintelligible reply came in the cracked sibilance of someone very old, and gradually the two intruders were able to discern the features of the occupant. It was a face of a woman, brown as leather, weatherworn, and seemed like parched earth. The old squaw sat huddled in a blanket woven of strips of rabbit skin, and on the ground nearby rested a tightly woven basket containing water and another filled with some kind of meal.

"Greetings to you, mother," Moon said in her hesitant Shoshone, crouching down so that her face was on a level with the old woman's. Her voice had grown soft, respectful. "May we speak with you?"

The ancient one continued to stare blankly at Moon for a few moments, and then her lips parted in a gap-toothed smile. She spoke, but neither of the McLaffertys could make sense of what she said. The languages were too dissimilar, or possibly the woman was senile and merely babbling.

"We're looking for a little boy, my little boy," Moon persisted, switching to English. "He is about so high" —she held her hand approximately a yard from the floor. "I think someone from this village has him."

The Te-Moak woman held her own hand at the height Moon indicated, broke into a wheezing laugh.

McLafferty decided it was time to switch tactics, and rising to his full height, his head touching the ceiling in the center of the lodge, he spoke sternly in Ute dialect.

"Old woman, tell us where the others have gone," he roared. "They have stolen our little one, and we want him back. Speak, and do not pretend you have no ears!"

The pathetic creature cowered, hid her face in her hands, and whimpered.

Moon heard a slight noise outside and rose, squeezing Mike's arm in warning. Abruptly the entry flap was pulled open, and a short, powerfully built man stood for an instant outlined against daylight outside. The man launched himself with a loud shriek at Mike, skinning knife glinting in his hand.

McLafferty sidestepped the frontal attack, drew his revolver as the man turned, but held his fire.

Something in his opponent's blue-daubed features, had stayed him, a quality of desperate courage, defiance and despair mingled in the face of certain death.

The attacker remained crouched, knife still held wide, ready. For a long moment the two men stared into one another's eyes, neither moving, and then the Te-Moak warrior dropped his weapon, spreading his hands hopelessly.

"Kill me if you wish, owl-face," he said, "but allow my mother to live."

Mike and Moon glanced at one another, startled by the man's words, spoken slowly but clearly in perfectly intelligible English.

"My husband does not wish to kill anyone," Moon said. "We want our son. You're the man who stole him."

"I am called Tallchief," the squat warrior nodded. "But that which you ask is not mine to give to you. My mother is sick, she doesn't have long to live. Leave her in peace, and take my life instead."

"Where is Jacques?" Moon persisted.

"Chack. Yes, that is the name of the child. He is a fine boy, very brave, very strong for one his age."

Mike scowled, gestured threateningly with his pistol.

"Lady didn't ask you that," he said. "Where's the boy you stole from us?"

Tallchief drew himself up, stared at McLafferty with no sign of fear.

"I am ready to die," he declared.

Mike gritted his teeth in frustration, but Moon gently took his gun hand, pressed it down.

"The rest of your people, they are hiding," she said. "Jacques is with them, isn't he? You didn't take him for yourself but for someone else? I understand how someone could want a child so much that she would take another's baby. Yes, I understand that. But I'm his mother, just as that woman there is your mother. If something happened to you, and she didn't know where you were, whether you were sick or well, in pain or even dead, she might die of grief. You know this is true. Tallchief—your name is Tallchief? You gave him to someone who is dear to you, then, someone who was pining because her arms were empty. Perhaps your sister, your aunt . . . ?"

Moon's words seemed to have a magical effect on the short-legged, barrel-chested Indian, his expression of grim resolve melting, his shoulders sagging.

"It is my wife, Swimming Duck," he admitted. "She is a good woman. She works hard for me all the time, and smart, too. She knows where camas roots grow, wild onions, when to gather pinyon nuts to be ripe but squirrels don't get them, so we always have something to eat. She makes best rabbit blankets of all women. Kind like a daughter to my mother and always wanting to make me happy, but in fifteen winters she had given me no children. Makes her sad."

"What the hell is all this?" Mike growled, growing impatient with the small, long-winded Shucker's tale.

"Hush, Red Coyote," Moon said. "I want to hear Tallchief's words."

The Indian looked from one to the other, nodded, continued as if there had been no interruption.

"Now Swimming Duck grows older like me, thinking pretty soon no more time to have babies. She walks around all the time like her chin will fall off. I say, 'I do not like to see you all long-face that way. You laugh for me.' But she cannot, she thinks of nothing but babies. So one day I see your little boy up there, I think, 'Maybe if I bring Swimming Duck that fine little boy she laugh again.' And it works, too. Now she singing all the time, driving me crazy telling me everything that boy does. Lady, that Chack, he gets more love than ten little boys."

"That doesn't make him yours," Mike insisted. "Bring him back, damn it, or by God—"

"Take me to Swimming Duck, Tallchief," Moon interrupted, winking at Mike. "I wish to meet your wife. I need to see with my own eyes that my son is well. Mac-lafferty will stay here with your mother. He roars like a bear sometimes, but he will not harm an old woman."

Tallchief studied the big Irishman.

"He is good man. Mac-lafferty. Even when he shot at us couple times, he wasn't trying to kill nobody. Don't worry none, Mac-lafferty. I make sure your woman is OK."

"Like hell!" Mike exploded. "Moon, if you think I'm going to let you go off by yourself—"

"You have no choice, Red Coyote," she smiled, leaning close and kissing him on the mouth. "I'll be back directly." Then she added in a whisper, "It's our only chance. Please."

Tallchief stuck out his hand again. "She is OK. I give word."

"Better be," McLafferty grumbled, at last reaching to shake the proffered hand.

"Moon," Tallchief said. "That's your name? Pretty. Just like Chack says. Moon."

The Te-Moak turned to his mother then, smiled, held both hands above his head, fingers and thumbs touching to form a circle, then said a few words in his own language, repeated the name "Moon" and pointed at her. The old woman grinned and nodded. The bandy-legged man spoke to her a little longer, mentioned "Mac-lafferty," and then Moon and he stepped out of the brush lodge.

Mike made a move to follow them, pulled the hide covering aside, watched the two walking side by side, talking in apparent perfect good fellowship.

Slowly he dropped the covering and turned back to the old woman, who flashed her gap-toothed smile at him again.

"Mac-lafferty," she said, nodding.

"That's me, all right."

She continued watching him, grinning, and patted the earth near to where she sat. He shrugged, sat cross-legged where she indicated.

"Moon." She pointed toward the doorway.

"Yep. Moon."

"Pret-ty. Mac-lafferty pret-ty. Chack." She held up her hand at the child's height as Moon had done.

Mike nodded. "Yeah, Jacques, the little hellion."

The old one continued grinning at Mike, nodding, apparently having exhausted her supply of English. He returned the smile and the nod, began to fidget when she continued to stare at him.

The remainder of Tallchief's band had taken refuge in a large cavern formed by tumbled boulders of rimrock on a high bench beyond the next draw.

As Moon followed her guide up the final slope, feet slipping on the loose, snow-covered shale, she heard a piercing shout above, and Jacques emerged from the dark mouth of the cave and came running and sliding down to wrap his arms around his mother's legs. A small, stocky woman emerged immediately behind the boy and scrambled after him, calling out anxious words to him but coming to an abrupt halt when she saw Moon kneeling to embrace her son. A number of other Shuckers appeared, stood in a cluster at the cave mouth.

"Little Bull," Moon whispered, rubbing her cheek against his soft hair, struggling to hold back tears. "My son. I have missed you so much. We were afraid we would never see you again."

"Oh, Mom," the boy said, squirming a little in his mother's intense embrace. "I been having fun. Where's Mike? I can make a rabbit snare now. Slow Lizard showed me. Are we going home now, Mother? It's great here with Swimming Duck and Tallchief and Grasshopper, but I want to go back to Mike and Liz-beth and Fiddlehead. Did he come home yet? Did the pretty ladies come with him?"

Moon began laughing at the eager and matter-of-fact tumble of words, laughing partly in sheer delight at seeing him and partly at the irony—her son had apparently not suffered greatly by the kidnapping. Then suddenly laughter gave way to the flood of tears she'd been trying to hold back, and she hugged the boy wordlessly and laughed and cried at once. But when the fit of near-hysteria passed, she looked up and saw the woman who had followed Jacques down the slope, her round, sweet-featured face stricken as she watched this reunion between mother and son.

Moon rose and, holding Jacques by the hand, stepped toward her apparent rival.

"You are moth-er," the woman said. "You take Chack away now?"

"I am his mother, yes. And you must be Swimming Duck. You can see that he wants to go home with me. You've treated him well, and I'm grateful for that, but what you did, what your husband did and the other Te-Moak men did was wrong."

"You take Chack away."

"Yes, I'm going to take my son home."

Swimming Duck spoke a few questioning words to her husband and then looked back at Jacques and suddenly burst into tears.

"Don't cry, Swimming Duck," the child said, reaching out his small hand to pat at hers. "Mother, we can come visit Swimming Duck and Tallchief and the others, can't we?"

"Perhaps," Moon said, glancing up the slope where the other members of the band were gathered outside their temporary shelter. One man was making defiant gestures, the others watching the scene below with silent attention. None of them, she noticed, seemed to be very well-clothed for the terrible cold of winter on the high desert, and in addition, all showed signs of having too little to eat recently. From the terrible fear and anger toward these people that she had felt only a short time before, she suddenly experienced intense compassion for the brave and miserable little band, cold in their ragged furs, hungry and poorly armed, who had risked so much to get a child for a woman who could not have one of her own. And yet during their off-and-on surveillance of the ranch, they had never in fact attempted to make off with any of the animals.

It was then that Moon made her decision.

Mike sat in silence beside the old woman, who occasionally touched his red hair and giggled but otherwise seemed content to abide the companionable silence. McLafferty rose to feed sticks to the fire, thought of asking the woman by gestures to give him food, but remembered Moon and decided it would be somehow disloyal to eat while she was God-knew-where with the sawed-off Shucker named Tallchief.

"Sonofabitch has probably knocked her over the head by now and—damn it! I should have never let her go. What's the matter with me? I let her talk me into things even when I know better. Am I spineless or just stupid?"

He spoke aloud without thinking, and Tallchief's mother looked at him, nodded, grinned.

McLafferty opened the doorflap and looked out.

"Should have been back hours ago. I hope that little bastard knows I'll roast you over a slow fire and scalp you—"

"You not do that. Tallchief not do that too."

McLafferty whirled to stare at the old woman, felt his mouth drop open and stay that way. The old woman was staring at him, laughing silently as before, and for a moment he was uncertain that she'd spoken at all, that he had not imagined English words issuing forth in the cracked voice.

"You actually speak some English then?" he managed. "She-it, I'll bet you've understood most of what I've been saying."

"Little bit." She grinned, and winked at him.

"Well, I'll be—" He broke off, held his hand up for silence. He listened intently, heaved a sigh, and rose.

He definitely heard voices, Jacques' clear tones chattering happily, rising above the others.

McLafferty stepped outside the brush lodge, saw Moon in the lead. Behind her walked Tallchief and his wife and a half dozen other Te-Moaks—another couple who appeared to be in their thirties or early forties, a white-haired man perhaps a few years younger than Tallchief's mother, a girl near Elizabeth's age, a boy of perhaps eleven, and another boy near Jacques' age. All carried bundles, their earthly belongings, Mike presumed, and all appeared happy, excited.

When moon saw her husband, she broke into a run, dragging Jacques by the hand, and she hugged Mike while the boy pulled on his pants leg until McLafferty stooped and lifted him over his head.

"Mac-lafferty," Moon said, gesturing toward the ragtag group behind her, "I want you to meet the new Ruby Dome ... crew. That's the right word, isn't it?"

For the second time in the space of a few minutes, Mike found himself speechless. Tallchief strode forward, shook hands heartily, his short, sturdily built wife behind him smiling shyly.

"Moon says you need somebody help you at your place, protect you from other injuns, chase small red buffaloes, put rails around to keep 'em in, build lodges for people and animals. We tell her, 'OK, we come help out.' We got four good strong men—got Antelope Tail, got Slow Lizard, got Smoke on the Hill"—Tallchief gestured in turn to the middle-aged man, the pre-adolescent boy, and the old man—"got Tallchief. Smoke on the Hill, he's getting a little bit old, but he tells good stories. The small one is Grasshopper. He's Antelope Tail's boy. So is slow Lizard. Me, I make good foreman—tell others what to do. Used to work for Hudson's Bay trappers over on Snake River—that's how come I speak English so good."

McLafferty, still dazed, nodded vaguely to the individuals as they were introduced, each smiling broadly in turn.

"Now the women, they all make good baskets, good rabbit blankets, tan hides, cook good. Swimming Duck, she's the best, but Antelope Tail's woman, Rain, is good too. Camas Flower, she's Swimming Duck's niece. She learns fast, she's OK. You got anybody needs a wife back there, Mac-lafferty? Camas Flower, she makes somebody damn fine woman."

Tallchief seemed to be finished and stood beaming, arms crossed on his chest. Mike stared in amazement at the band that had apparently become his "crew," and he burst out laughing.

"We don't even have any cows yet!" he spluttered when the fit had subsided.

Moon stood beside him, smiling serenely.

"Swimming Duck's going to be my second mother," Jacques said. "That's what mom told her. She said I could call her Mother if I wanted to, but I think that would be too strange. Maybe I'll call her Aunt."

"Swimming Duck couldn't bear to part with Jacques," Moon said by way of explanation, drawing Mike aside and speaking in a low tone. "They're hungry, Red Coyote. Winter's a hard time for the Te-Moaks."

"How the devil are we going to feed them? And why on earth did they want to steal another kid if they don't have enough to go around already?"

Moon shrugged.

"Maybe Tallchief thought Little Bull would bring good luck. They can feed themselves, Mike. We'll teach them how to shoot. With rifles they'll be able to get their own antelope and bighorns. It will be nice to have company, too. Elizabeth and Jacques get lonely."

"What about Mike and Moon?" McLafferty asked. "Sometimes I sort of enjoy being lonely, as long as you're being lonely with me."

"That's the best part, Mac-lafferty," Moon laughed. "The Te-Moaks will build their brush lodges in a few days, and perhaps then Jacques and Elizabeth will want to sleep with their new friends."

"Maybe I'm starting to get used to the idea already," he mused.

11 "Watch out for the old sonofabitch," Johnny Cortez said. "He looks harmless enough, but he ain't. Wolf Mask, you tie him up, and make sure the damned knots is tight. Years back, he rastled Bill Williams to a draw. That's the tale, at least. Pete and I'll keep the bitches covered. You, Sister Woman. You help Wolf Mask. Nice scalp you got there, even if the hair is a mite kinky. It'll look damned good nailed up on the wall in one of Tarrango's saloons. Move, damn it, or I'll give you another hole to play games with, right now!"

Wolf Mask grinned at Little Sister, glanced at Cortez, and then turned to get a length of coiled cord hanging from the stub of a fir limb.

"First maybe you'd better loosen up the holes she's already got," Pete the Gun laughed.

"I been blindsided like a damned greenh'un," Fiddlehead growled. "Well, mebbe the hunt ain't over yet. Ye'd best put a bullet between this child's eyes, Cortez, if ye're figgerin' to harm me girls. Otherwise, I swear to Gawd, I'll kill the three o' ye."

Black Johnny cast a glance sideways at Fiddlehead, spat onto the snow.

"Tie his feet too," he said to Wolf Mask.

Victoria Queen, taken as utterly by surprise as everyone else at the sudden and unexpected appearance of Cortez, Wolf Mask, and Pete, was nonetheless quick to size up the situation. Yes, they'd been caught with their pants down, no question about it, but she'd been in difficult situations before. Whatever else they might be, the three bounty hunters weren't particularly bright. Furthermore, Tarrango's men, though they held the upper hand at the moment, were in bad shape from wandering on foot through the snow. They were exhausted, and they were probably suffering from frostbite in addition. Apparently they'd been forced to leave their horses behind when they decided (for whatever reasons) to follow a trail that led up into the snow-choked Sierras.

"Johnny," she said, her voice almost a purr, "you've got a practical mind and a lot of good sense. You boys need help, all three of you. You're going to have to get some rest, and I'll bet hot food would go well just about now, am I right? You've caught me, so the money's yours, fair and square. That's the way of things, and no one's ever said Queen Vikki's a sore loser. Haven't I always treated you boys right when you came to my place? Hell, I knew you were Sam's three best men, and I figured I owed him that much."

Cortez squinted toward the leader of the angels.

"What the hell you getting at, Vikki?" Pete the Gun demanded. "I hate long-ass speeches."

"Just that we're in this together, that's all, like it or not. Come right down to it, what are our chances of getting down out of these mountains alive? You boys have lost your horses, and ours aren't going to do us any good. The snow's too deep. Right now you're tying up Chauncy Wilson, but he's the only one with enough savvy to be able to bring in game. You kill him, and we all starve to death, just like those Donners years ago. But if we all cooperate, maybe we can make it to the goldfield towns. Then we split up the money—hell, there's enough for all of us. Johnny, what's Sam offered as a bounty? Couple thousand apiece, maybe?"

"Thousand each," Cortez said, "if we bring back four scalps and what you took from Sam's deposit box."

Victoria nodded.

"Think about what a seven-way split would mean." She smiled. "Almost eight thousand apiece. Or better yet, fifty-fifty. Twenty-six thousand for you boys, twenty-six for me and the girls. When will you ever have a chance at that much money again, Johnny Cortez?"

Black Johnny grinned.

"Looks to me like we got the whole damned fifty-two thousand right now," he said. "Maybe we just take the money an' leave you an' your whores up here to freeze. What kind of food you got? Yellowhair an' Maria, you two start cookin' some chow. Then maybe we don't torture you before we shoot you."

"Old bastard's tied to the tree yonder," Wolf Mask laughed, sauntering back to the small group, Little Sister a step or two ahead of him. "Maybe Fiddlehead Wilson he wrestle Bill Williams, I don't know. But he ain't gonna wrestle that tree off his back. Am I right, Sister woman?"

Vikki glanced across the open space. Fiddlehead was indeed lashed to a young red fir. Wilson was in a sitting position, his hands bound behind the bole.

"More clouds starting to move in." Vikki nodded, winking and stepping close to Johnny Cortez. "Probably it's going to snow again. A smart man like you, John, he'd realize we all need to keep Mr. Wilson in good condition. He's got a way of finding game, even in the midst of a blizzard.

Cortez smiled, half under Vikki's spell.

"I'll turn the old coot loose when we need him," he said. "Miss Vikki, why don't you just give me that little silver popgun you keep inside your shirt along with those nice titties of yours? I hear what you're saying, all right. You're a damned fine looking woman, Miss Vikki. I always thought so. Only just give me the damned gun. Me an' the boys, we ain't really in the mood for killin' nobody right now. Don't push me, though, you hear?"

Vikki was right about the snow.

By the time food had been prepared for Sam Tarrango's hired guns, long streamers of cloud were racing eastward, and strong winds began to howl through the upland forest, pouring across the range in blasts that drew bandings of ice particles with them, spattering tree trunks and flowing across the frozen wilderness like so many coiling torrents of thick fog.

Then, quite abruptly, even as Cortez and Vikki worked together in an attempt to heap fir boughs over a hollow in the snow at the base of a considerable granite boulder, all wind ceased. The forest grew almost deathly silent, and snow began to fall, flakes the size of two-bit pieces.

Sunshine Hobson, ignoring Pete the Gun's threats, took hot coffee to Fiddlehead and then sat in the snow close beside him, paying no attention whatsoever to Pete's demands that she return to the fire.

"Sunshine, gal, ye'd best do what the gunslinger says," Wilson suggested. "No point in riling him jest now. Not that this child wouldn't rather set hyar an' spoon with ye, ye understand, if the situ-ation was a mite different. The coffee's a life-saver, even if it ain't made jest right. The real problem's me hands, though. Tied up this way, they're startin' to go complete numb. Ye git on back, see if ye kin bring me some more coffee in about an hour. Don't want it to look like anything's afoot, which it ain't, not yet."

"What do you mean, Chauncy? The half-breed—I'm afraid of him. I'd rather stay here with you, even if we both freeze to death."

"Ain't gonna do nothin' o' the sort, leetle love. What I'm sayin' now. See if ye can get to my possibles sack—they's a straight razor inside. I was figgerin' on shaving when we got to the goldfields—wanted to surprise ye. Get the razor if ye can an' use it to hack me loose. Ain't nobody goin' nowhar so long as she's snowing this way. An' the lads is going to be needin' some shut-eye. Jest one'll stand guard, an' that changes the odds a bit. Sunshine, get the razor, an' don't be afraid to use it, nuther, if one of the sonsabitches looks like he's of a mind to hurt ye. But I'm thinking if ye jest act kind o' quiet, ain't nothing going to happen until tomorrow at the least. An' by then—"

"But without a gun, Chauncy, what can you do, even if I'm able to cut you free?"

"First things first, gal. This old hawg's been in worse scrapes many a time. I ever tell ye about when the Utes had me tied up an' was of a mind to burn me alive? Wal, ain't got leisure for the story jest now. Git on back an' wait yore time. Mebbe we can save our bacon yet."

Snow continued to fall, a fury of whiteness now, with vision dropping away to near zero. The entire world seemed to draw in close, with a heavy, almost leaden silence covering everything.

Fiddlehead could not see those at the campfire at all, and only occasional movements of his limbs prevented snow from covering the lower half of his body.

A strange sensation, he mused. His feet were just fine, and his legs were warm enough as well. But his hands and wrists were numb, almost devoid of feeling.

Several hours passed, and still Sunshine did not return.

What was going on over there?

Were Cortez, Pete, and Wolf Mask taking turns with her?

But that didn't make sense, either. More likely, Wilson suspected, two of the men were asleep while the third, fighting off drowsiness, had the four women huddled in one place, his weapon leveled at them.

Time continued to drift past, and the mountain men, unable even to work at the knots that bound his hands behind the sapling fir, found himself reliving an adventure of years past, a time when he and Termite Joe Hollingback had gone buffalo hunting with the Pawnees, catching a number of the big animals in a surround and then running up close, taking aim, firing. The sun was hot that day; he'd perspired so heavily that most of his buckskin jacket was soaked through.

"Wagh!" he grumbled. "Be good to have some of that sunlight right about now. But even a leetle Sunshine would do the job. Gal, if ye wait much longer, the old possum pounder's goin' to go beaver. Come morning, ye'll find me froze stiff as any board."

"No I won't, Chauncy. I'm right here, and I've got the razor."

"Sunshine? Gawddamn it, gal, I was startin' to lose faith. Kick the snow loose an' cut me free. Could be this child's goin' to lose a couple o' fingers no matter what."

Sunshine slipped around behind him, hardly more

than a shadow among shadows, clawed the snow, and then felt for the bonds around Wilson's wrists.

"There!" she whispered. "Can you get up now?"

Wilson pulled his arms forward, pushed numb hands together, swore softly.

"Cain't feel a thing," he said. "My ankles . . . had me tied like any hawg . . . can ye get to 'em?"

"I think so."

"How'd ye get away, Sunshine? Who's holdin' the gun over yonder? Ain't no yellin, so whoever it be ain't figgered ye're gone yet."

"Pete," she answered. "Everyone else was asleep except me, and I was pretending. Then Pete dozed off, and I slipped away, got to your robes, found the sack. We need a gun, Chauncy, but I didn't dare. They're all between Pete's legs, even your buffalo rifle."

"Sure, now. That's jest how to fetch it, only Pete fell asleep, did he? That does it, this child can move his feet again. Hands is startin' to tingle a wee bit as well. Mebbe they'll come around after all."

"Should I go back, so Pete won't notice what's happened? Here, give me your hands, Chauncy—" She pressed her mouth to them, blew on them. "They don't even feel alive," she whispered.

He laughed softly.

"Don't feel like it from here, nuther. But hell, this high shinin' coyote's ready to do something. The question's what."

"This will help," Sunshine said.

It took Fiddlehead a moment to realize what she was doing—she'd pulled open her clothing, had pressed his open palms to either of her bare breasts. It was only when he heard her gasp involuntarily that he understood.

"Gawd love ye!" he said "Now if only I could actually feel 'em."

"Is it helping?" she managed. "They're like . . . ice."

"Guess that's right, but they're comin' to life now. Another two or three hours o' this treatment an' I'll be good as new."

She leaned forward to kiss him, missed his mouth, kissed the tip of his nose instead. "My aim's bad," she laughed. "Too dark."

"Enough o' this foolin' around," Wilson grumbled. "Don't want ye goin' back thar. Let's get to movin', gal. Got to find a safe place for ye an' then see what this child can do with a straight razor. What'd ye do with it?"

Sunshine hugged him, and then he withdrew his hands, flexed the fingers.

"Might work at that," he said. "Get buttoned up now afore ye get frostbite o' the nipples. Whar's that razor?"

She fumbled about in the snow, found what she sought, handed it to him.

"Ain't as good as a skinnin' knife, by Gawd, but I reckon it'll cut a throat if it comes to that."

"You're not going to try to attack?"

"Only when the odds is runnin' my direction," he replied. "Now let's find ye a hole to hide in."

Thin grayness of dawn began to suffuse the continuing and seemingly relentless snowfall as Fiddlehead Wilson, a gnarled section of pine branch in one hand and his straight razor in the other, crawled in close to the sputtering campfire.

From back among the trees, an hour or so earlier, he'd listened to the small commotion brought about when Black Johnny Cortez awoke to find Pete the Gun crouched forward beside a bed of glowing coals, asleep at his watch.

Cortez's cursing woke everyone else, and Pete, defending himself, asserted first that he'd gladly put a .36 caliber round into Black John's hide and second that no harm had been done.

Then Wolf Mask realized one of the women was missing.

"Probably went off to take a piss, an' the wolves got her," Pete shrugged. "Ain't none of us was interested in the little blond stringbean anyhow. Shit, a man starts poking that one, mebbe he breaks her back."

"Think she turned the old man loose?" Wolf Man suggested, peering out into darkness.

"Figure Wilson's stiff as a cedar post by now," Cortez laughed. "Goddamn snow's buried him sure."

"I go look."

"Sure now," Pete growled, "jest plough on out there. Damned snow's up to your pecker, if you got one."

"He's got one, all right." Cortez grinned. "An' fifteen or twenty bastard kids scattered around the territories to prove it. Go ahead if you want, Wolf Mask, but you're wasting your time. If Wilson was loose, he'd have tried something by now. Likes to strangle gunfighters who fall asleep on the watch. Uses a rawhide cord, from what I hear."

"Go to hell, Cortez," Pete returned.

"If you bastards are intent upon waking the dead," Victoria Queen said, "the least you could do is build up the fire so we don't all freeze to death."

"*Meintras tanto,*" Rosa complained, "stop making the noise. I wish to die in peace, *por Dios!*"

Wolf Mask shrugged, hacked off a couple of fir branches and brought down a weight of snow in the process. He cursed, shook the branches, snapped them in half, and placed them over the coals.

After a bit more talking, things quieted down once again.

Cortez himself took up the watch, huddling next to the fire and rolling a cigarette as the others fell again to sleep.

In the snow-filled darkness beyond the fire's glow of light, Fiddlehead Wilson waited. When the time at last came, he crawled close, very slowly rose to one knee, and brought down the gnarled section of pine limb across the back of Black Johnny Cortez's head.

The leader of the bounty hunters slumped forward, almost as though he too had fallen asleep, and instantly Wilson had his gun.

He rose to his feet then, stepped to where Pete and Wolf Mask were sleeping, and clubbed both with the butt of Black Johnny's pistol. He stood there, nodding and grinning and wondering if he'd split open either man's skull, deciding after a moment's reflection that he didn't care one way or the other.

"Ye can sleep until doomsday for all this child's goin' to worry," he muttered. "Queen Vikki! Ye ready to get yore purty ass movin'? I figger it's time we was on our way, storm or not. The company hyar don't please me. Come on, Maria, wake up. Sister Woman, keep an eye on the lads. Tie the bastards, an I'll see if our mules is ready to go wadin' through the woods. Sunshine, she's over yonder."

Little Sister stood up, ran her hands back over her hair.

"This gal feel better now. Mr. Fiddlehead, what take you so long?"

Soon Tarrango's men were bound hand and foot, sitting next to a blazing fire. Fiddlehead and the four angels, leading their animals along, moved away westward into the continuing snowfall.

At Vikki's urging, Wilson left one pistol, complete

with twenty rounds, behind for their former captors, thus giving them at least a slim chance at survival. For his own part, he'd as happily have blown holes in each of them. But perhaps, he reflected, Queen Vikki's way was best.

In any case, there would be no more lapses in vigilance, though further danger from Cortez and his companions seemed highly unlikely. If the boys managed to get loose after a time, the simple desire to survive would doubtless take them back down to the desert where their chances were better. If they could find their horses again, then perhaps they could eat one of those.

The band of five moved ahead, making steady if grudging progress against howling winds and driving snow.

But now the drainages were slanting away westward.

They were on their way down into California.

Three days of forced march later, staggering along the boulder-strewn course of a gathering young river and into a canyon whose jagged walls rose into dense clouds several thousand feet above them, Fiddlehead and the angels made their way down out of the snow zone.

Torrential rains were falling now, and the group took shelter in a hollow beneath a huge fractured shelf of granite close by the river's raging gray-brown waters—a stream Wilson presumed to be the Mokelumne, for such was one of the names indicated on the by now badly tattered map McLafferty had given him.

For himself, the piece of paper was of scant importance, since he'd made a point of memorizing the general configuration of terrain the map represented and because he knew well enough that maps of the far lands were notoriously inaccurate. Hell, it was only few years back that the boys were all talking about Buenaventura River, and then Jed Smith found out there was no such stream—only the little Humboldt, that wandered across high desert country and got lost in a big brackish puddle.

Vikki liked to study the map, though, and since it pleased the boss lady, it was of some use. But Fiddlehead was drawing his own map in terms of memory of peak and basin and canyon and river channel.

Right now, however, they were exhausted, their clothing sodden. The horse were limping and balky, and even the mules looked sad, their big ears wilted to the sides of their heads.

Everything was wet, and it was nearly more than he could handle to hew into a fallen cedar snag and procure splinters of burnable wood. But he gritted his teeth and kept at it.

At length a fire was started, and even though smoke swirled about in their hollow beneath a granite overhang, its warmth was accounted a blessing.

Steam rose from their clothing as the man and the four women clung together, waiting for the last of Wilson's ground up coffee beans and strips of willow bark to boil into a mixture fit to drink.

When the brew was ready, they sipped, grinned, felt somewhat better. Little Sister began laughing at nothing at all, and pretty soon they were all laughing, Fiddlehead included.

Then, clinging to one another, they fell asleep.

12 Down from the high country they came, following a flooded river that rushed torrentially between massive canyon walls studded with fir and pine, finally to the first signs of human habitation, evidence of sporadic mining activity and then a wagon trail angling southward, up an offshoot canyon. The skies were clear again, and surprisingly enough, the late February sun provided generous warmth. Indeed, signs of incipient spring were everywhere, and on ridgetops with southern exposure, one or two large black oaks had begun to show some first signs of greening.

Halfway out of Mokelumne Canyon, Fiddlehead and the angels came to a mining camp. Eight men, including two Indians, were digging a gravel bank close by a swirling creek, hauling material down to the water by means of flour sacks, burlap bags, and buckets, depositing the burden at the head of a makeshift rifle box. One miner, wearing a black felt hat and homemade britches of canvas held up by wide suspenders over a stained red upper of flannel winter underwear, laid down his shovel, leaped over the creek with an agility that surprised Wilson, and clambered onto the roadway to meet the newcomers. The man carried a holstered revolver caked with red-yellow mud.

"Whole canyon's took," he said, gesturing with both hands—only at this point realizing four of the five persons before him were women. "Me an' the boys have got claims clear to the top."

"Don't want to mine," Wilson said, his Hawken held casually across the pommel of his saddle. "The ladies . . . wall, they're entertainers. We're lookin' for a town o' some size, in fact, so's to set up for business."

The miner calculated the nature of the situation, then grinned so widely it appeared his face might split open. He doffed his hat, bowed awkwardly.

"Name's Jamie Blakemore," he said, "and this here's the Prudence & Bonnie Mining Company—named after my wife and Tom's over there. Good afternoon, ladies. It's been a spell since we've seen pretty faces here in our canyon. Where you folks coming from, old-timer?"

"We come from over the hill a piece," Wilson replied. "That's how ye dig gold, is it?"

"One way. Over what hill? You down from Sutter Creek and Jackson or . . . ? Now Mokelumne Hill, that's on up the trail a few miles."

"We were in the high mountains *hace un rato*." Maria smiled. "Sierra Nevada. We came through the blizzards to get here."

Blakemore studied the faces before him, his expression one of puzzlement.

"You folks crossed the Sierra this time of year? By Jesus, there must be twenty foot of snow in the passes right about now."

"Could be at that," Wilson admitted.

"How far do you say it is to Mokelumne Hill?" Vikki asked. "As Mr. Wilson indicates, we're looking for a good place—perhaps to buy a building or to have one put up."

"By Gawd!" Blakemore laughed. "If you ladies are going into business, me and the boys, we'll all come visit you and that's a fact. Seems like there's no womenfolk around here anywhere, not until now."

The remaining miners had by this time lost heart at digging and, trooping over to the mule and wagon road, stood about, white men with hats in hand, Indians bareheaded and barechested a pace or two behind. The men stared at the angels and their grizzled companion in buckskins.

"You look like Jim Bridger. You ain't him, are you?" one miner asked.

"Name's Fiddlehead Wilson, sonny. This child knows ol' Gabe though. Me an' him, we've rid one or two trails together."

"You know Greenwood maybe?" Blakemore asked.

"Caleb or his kid, John? O' course I know 'em. Used to rendezvous together, Popo Agie an' Pierre's Hole both. Ain't seen nuther one for five y'ars, though."

"Caleb's north of here," Blakemore said, nodding. "Him and his son over near Hangtown. I drank whiskey with John just last month."

"Mebbe this child'll visit them hosses." Fiddlehead shrugged. "Caleb, he can yarn a porkypine down out o' any tree. Ye boys got rich yet, or what?"

Queen Vikki winked at Blakemore, who actually began to stammer and get red in the face.

"Gents," she said, "I'll tell you the truth. The girls and I, we're going to set up the finest whorehouse in California. Two drinks and a hot bath, and after that a man can pick any girl he wants."

"You too?" another of the miners asked.

Vikki laughed.

"The truth is," she said, "I'm actually a nun in disguise. Never been had by man or boy. Bring your gold dust with you, gentlemen, and we'll negotiate."

"She's a what?" one man whispered.

"A nun." Vikki smiled, her dark eyes glinting mischief. "And that means I play games with none who can't afford me."

The miners laughed—except Blakemore, who stared at his split-out leather boots and kicked nervously at a clump of dried thistle.

"Well," Vikki said when they'd reached Murphys, "it's not St. Louis, and it's not even Pueblo, but I think it's a good place to run a business. What do you say, Little Sister?"

The mulatto girl, one eyebrow raised, nodded silent agreement.

"Murphys is the name?" Sunshine asked. "Who the hell's Murphy? I do like the looks of it, Victoria. Chauncy, what do you think?"

Fiddlehead pulled at his beard, squinted one eye, and studied the settlement of tents and huts and a scattering of recently built wooden frame and adobe structures.

"Passable fair," he said.

"Ladies," Queen Vikki laughed, "shall we ride through our newfound city and ascertain the possibilities?"

The main street was a muddy track partially lined with boardwalks and set perhaps a hundred feet back from but following roughly the course of San Domingo Creek, crossing it once on a bridge of heavy timbers slung across a small ravine. The creek water was the color of coffee with cream, owing to gold-hungry men who dug its banks and washed the dirt by means of its flow.

Already a surprising number of frame buildings had sprung from the earth, false fronts adorned with signs: JONES & SON, APOTHECARY, CASH MERCANTILE, ANGELO'S BOARD AND LODGING, REASONABLE RATES, QUALITY LIVERY. In addition to these, there was a much larger tent city that had emerged along the dirt track, and a dozen of the larger tents were dedicated to drinking, gambling, and the provision of the charms of the fair sex—mostly Indian women whose husbands had persuaded them to gather gold dust in supine fashion. But easily the most solid, most durable, and in some ways most prominent building was the jail, which was built close by the creek on a wide, grassy margin. The structure squatted, small, tomblike, its stone walls a foot thick, with two tiny windows high up and secured by heavy iron bars. Indeed, it seemed to have grown from the earth and promised to be there still after fire, flood, and earthquake. Like all mining camps in the first heady years after the discovery of gold at Coloma, Murphy's roared. At almost any hour of day or night, as Fiddlehead learned by patronizing one of the tent saloons, the boardwalks resounded to boots of red-shirted miners, gamblers resplendent in brocaded vests and ruffled bibs, a handful of brilliantly gowned and flounced fancy ladies, black-suited merchants, and even a scattering of soberly attired gentlewomen, some of whom were rumored to be opposed to nearly everything that commonly occurred in the town.

Occasionally fist fights broke out, and these often led to knife fights, gunfights, and (often as a consequence) lynchings. Already Boot Hill had numerous residents, some as the result of cholera or the lung disease, but a surprising number had taken up lodging on the hill as the result of lead poisoning.

There was talk of building a church on the opposite hill, toward Sheep Ranch, and the gentlewomen were no doubt behind the scheme.

"Be wantin' a school an' a proper meeting hall before long, they will," the barkeep told Wilson.

Fiddlehead grunted his lack of enthusiasm, and, after two shots of bad whiskey, strolled back onto the street and looked around for Queen Vikki and her entourage. Beyond the frenzied activity of the town, on rounded hills above the little stream, he noted, blue-gray digger pines and glossy-leaved live oaks held communion, waited.

Lonesome Dan, the officially elected sheriff of Murphys, sat behind an adze-hewn desk in a small room at the front of the jail. His feet rested on the desk, and from square-headed nails driven into the rough-cut pine boards of the wall behind him hung an assortment of weapons, an old over-under, two carbines, and a double-barreled shotgun, and a half dozen pistols of various manufacture. Pinned to the sheriff's leather vest was a silver star with one broken point, and the letters stamped upon it read *Policia*, the badge apparently a hand-me-down from Spanish and Mexican days.

Victoria Queen, clothed in a bright red dress replete with a considerable bustle and numerous black ribbons, entered the office. Her dark hair was piled fashionably high, and about her throat dangled a large sapphire, the stone set in a finely worked gold and cradled in ample cleavage revealed by a low-cut bodice.

Lonesome Dan, half asleep when the door to his office opened, was at full attention by the time Miss Victoria stepped lightly across the small room.

"I'm Queen Vikki," the boss lady said, smiling so that her dimples showed to best advantage.

The sheriff stood up, the toe of his boot catching one leg of his chair and sending it sideways with a clatter. He ignored the mishap and extended his right hand.

"Pleased to meet you, Miss Vikki," he said. "Saw you and the others when you rode in yesterday, in fact, but you looked ... kind of different at the time. I'm Lonesome Dan, but you probably know that already. The boys, well, they voted me sheriff of Murphy's after my partner blew himself up with blasting powder last summer. Guess they felt sorry for me or something. Anyhow, I'm the law now."

"Mutual, I'm sure, Dan," Vikki replied. "I'm a businesswoman, and I tend to be direct and forward about things. Do you mind if we speak in that fashion?"

"Not at all," Dan said, bending over to pick up his chair. "I figured something of the sort. Well, honesty's the best policy, as they say."

Vikki smiled, nodded, then sat down carefully and primly on the edge of the sheriff's desk.

"All right, then. I'd like to open a new entertainment palace here in town. I'll run a clean operation, fair prices and no thieving, baths required, weapons checked in before anyone goes upstairs with one of my girls. Bar and cardroom downstairs, and no fighting. Can I expect your protection and that of your deputies?"

Lonesome Dan nodded. He intended to say something, but Vikki's perfume momentarily distracted him, and he forgot the words he was about to speak.

Vikki smiled again.

"I've asked around," she said, "and I'm told the town has seven other establishments of one sort or another. Is there room for an eighth?"

"More the merrier," Lonesome Dan blurted, and then wished he hadn't.

"I won't ask special favors," Vikki continued, "only that my place gets the same protection as the others. There are proper women in town, as I've observed, and I understand they wish to close down the whorehouses and saloons as well. Is that likely to happen?"

"Not unless human nature changes from what it's always been. But where . . . ?"

"Angelo's Boarding House, sheriff. I intend to do whatever remodeling's necessary."

Dan shrugged. He knew very well that Vincent Angelo wasn't interested in renting his entire hotel. The two-story building, Murphys' one and only, had been constructed the preceding autumn. Besides that, Vincent would no doubt want a small fortune for the place. Perhaps this gaudy (but beautiful) woman was simply given to outlandish ideas.

"Don't figure that, Miss Vikki. Maybe you'd best be thinking about a big tent, like the others."

"Mr. Angelo is packing his things right now," Vikki purred. "We've already signed the necessary papers—I've bought him out. The present tenants, of course, will be given sufficient notice. I'm aware that lodging's hard to come by."

Lonesome Dan stared at the sapphire suspended between Queen Vikki's ample and extremely soft-looking breasts. After a moment he forgot about the sapphire.

Storm after storm poured in from the Pacific, bringing extremely heavy rains. At times, up and down the length of the region called Mother Lode, nearly all mining operations were halted. Pits and shafts filled with water, and rampaging rivers frustrated attempts to turn their currents. Sluices and long toms were swept away. Mule-drawn wagons became mired in red mud to the axle trees, and makeshift huts and cabins leaked so badly that some simply laid in a supply of rotgut and swore they'd go seek gold in the desert. In Sacramento City, recently repaired levees gave way, and word had it that Sutter's Fort itself was knee-deep in mud.

In Murphys, however, Victoria Queen and her girls kept busy, and the project of setting up the new entertainment palace went forward without undue complications. By the time the former tenants of Angelo's Board and Lodging had removed themselves from the premises (some loath to do so, considering the weather), and one hand-painted sign had been replaced by another, The Queen's Lair was ready for business. The lower floor was significantly redecorated, complete with crystal chandeliers and a set of ornately framed mirrors behind a rough-cut but serviceable and shellacked bar. In addition, Fiddlehead actually managed to get mules and a wagon to San Jose, crossing the San Joaquin River by means of a busy rope-tow ferry, and hauled back four baize-covered card tables, and with them a roulette wheel and a craps cage.

Vikki lured several girls away from competing establishments, and when Jamie Blakemore showed up, disgruntled with the backbreaking work of running a mining operation that couldn't muster a two-bit pan and that a flooding creek threatened to wash away at any minute, she hired him on as her regular barkeep.

During a brief interval between storms, Wilson took the mule team and wagon south to Sonora, a mere twenty miles distance, but the journey complicated by the fact that the Stanislaus River was running high and brown, with a foot of water spilling over a bridge consisting of two huge ponderosa pine logs dropped parallel across the stream where it gushed between walls of slate-gray rock.

In Sonora, so Fiddlehead had been told, none other than Old Crow himself, James P. Beckwourth, was running a mercantile house and fronting a Miwok mining operation at the same time. Wilson's primary goal was acquiring a good stock of whiskey for Miss Vikki's operation, but part of the lure was meeting Beckwourth himself, one of the few legends of the beaver trade whom he'd somehow missed getting to know—that because Beckwourth had been kidnapped by the Crows and stayed on with them for ten years or so as agent for American Fur. Not even Mike McLafferty had managed to run into Beckwourth, even though Mike was pals with Bill Sublette, one of the eventual bosses of American Fur.

As things turned out, however, Beckwourth had sold his store nearly a month before Fiddlehead's arrival in Sonora, and rumor suggested the renowned mulatto and former Indian chief had departed with a heavy bag full of gold dust, bound for Sacramento and eventually for parts north, in search of new goldfields.

The present owners of the mercantile store had a cellar full of whiskey kegs, however, and so Wilson was able to return to Murphys with mission accomplished.

Finally the rains stopped, for the time being at least, and springtime hit the foothills with astonishing force. Wild lilac and buckeye were blooming everywhere, black oaks were in full leaf, and even the intransigent blue oaks were coming out. Long vees of geese streamed overhead, taking up residence in valley wetlands to the west and south of the mining towns.

The night before the grand opening of Queen Vikki's Lair, Lonesome Dan stopped by the two-story building on Main Street. He nodded politely to Santa Maria, Little Sister, and Sunshine. Without pausing, he walked directly to where Vikki and Blakemore were filling whiskey bottles and placing them on a long shelf beneath a row of mirrors. Vikki looked up, winked, and bid the sheriff a good evening.

"Got something for you," Dan said, pulling a small bandanna-wrapped object from his coat pocket and untying it. With those words he presented to the boss lady a gold nugget that weighed a pound and six ounces—a token of his esteem, he said.

Jamie Blakemore was on the spot immediately.

"Where in God's name did you find it, sheriff? If a man could discover a placer full of eggs like this one—"

"Gil picked it up, actually," Lonesome Dan said. "Gil was my partner. The nugget wasn't off our claim, Gil saw it in the water when he was crossing Cosumnes River, over near Hangtown. To tell the truth, we used it as a paperweight. Always figured if things really got bad, we could sell it."

Vikki, a tight red silk shirt tucked into equally tight denim trousers and her long hair in twin braids almost in the manner of Plains Indian women, was fascinated by Dan's offer of the gift of gold, but she shook her head.

"Too valuable, Sheriff Lonesome. If I accepted, word would be out all over Murphys before twenty-four hours were past, and that wouldn't be good for you or me either one. What you need, Daniel, is one of this town's proper womenfolk, one who'd do you proud, not a canvasback broad like me."

Lonesome Dan laughed.

"Aww hell, Miss Vikki, you're worth twenty of

them, and that's the truth. Besides, they're all married—and thank God for it."

"Nonetheless, sir sheriff, you hang onto your big piece of gold. Don't know what I'm worth, but it's not that much. If it's a roll in the hay you're thinking about, Dan, you want to find a lady who's willing to do it for nothing, that is, simply because she enjoys it."

Lonesome Dan's eyes had a wounded look.

"Didn't mean I expected anything for the gold, Miss Vikki. Thought maybe you'd like to put it on display or something, that's all."

Vikki touched her fingertips to her lips and then pressed the kiss to Dan's forehead.

"That lady I was talking about"—she smiled (her dimples showing once more)—"you're looking at her, Daniel."

The sheriff flushed, stared down at the pointed toes of his boots.

"Well," he muttered, "it's good you hired Jamie here, anyhow. You ladies have done an amazing job in fixing things up, but you're going to need at least one man around to keep the rowdies under control, if nothing else."

He wrapped the nugget once more and slipped it back into his coat pocket.

"What you mean?" Little Sister asked, one finely plucked eyebrow raised and lantern light glinting from her large brown eyes. "We got Fiddlehead—Chauncy, this girl says. He ain't goin' to go nowheres. Chauncy Wilson, he handle any trouble we cain't."

"Of course the old codger could, but—"

"Where's Chauncy?" Sunshine demanded. "Why didn't he show up for dinner tonight? Lonesome Dan, have you seen him?"

Dan was puzzled

"Why, he's on his way to Stockton, of course. Said he was off to buy cattle for his friend McLafferty. He must have told you."

"Dios mio!" Maria said, "he cannot be gone. Fiddlehead, he's on the way toward the livery stables, *dar un paseo*, that is what I thought. Not more than an hour ago."

"Gone?" Sunshine gasped. "I knew he was planning to . . . but he didn't even say good-bye. I don't understand. Sheriff Dan, are you certain?"

Dan nodded.

"Saw him heading past my office; wasn't more than an hour ago. Yep, that's what he said. Going to Stockton to buy cattle."

A full moon flooded down over the land as Sunshine Hobson rode through the balmy night, reaching Angels Camp before midnight and perfunctorily checking the half dozen saloons still open for business. Chauncy Wilson was not to be found in any of them, however, and Sunshine (dressed essentially as a man, her long blond hair rolled into a bun beneath a slough hat she'd borrowed from Jamie Blakemore) asked directions to Stockton.

Take the Copperopolis Trail an' keep on going when you get there . . .

She drove her horse on through the moonlight, through a world of shadows and bright odors of springtime, through a world filled with the calls of owls and the cries of coyotes. At length she relented and slowed her animal to a walk. She was passing down a narrow ravine now, with great-limbed live oaks spreading above and the smell of buckeye blossoms rich in the night. Ahead, away from the wagon trail and close beside a purling stream, a single campfire was burning.

Sunshine drew her horse to a stop, stared downslope. But she could see no one. Then she smelled coffee, its odor different than most, tainted by what was no doubt an addition of willow bark and perhaps something else, God knew that, since sagebrush didn't grow in this country.

"Chauncy Wilson!" she cried out. "Are you down there?"

A Hawken rifle exploded, blue-yellow flame from its muzzle leaping straight upward into the night.

"Who'd be wantin' to know?" came the familiar voice.

The mountain man and the slightly built hooker spent the remainder of the night in one another's arms, mostly just holding on to each other and talking and occasionally kissing. Wilson got out his whiskey jug, and the two of them drank and hugged and drank and fondled one another and drank some more.

At length, with the full moon long since vanished westward and the eastern sky beginning to lighten into thin grayness, Sunshine began a concerted action to rouse Wilson to passion, but despite the administration of her best professional endeavors, a mere tumescence was the best the old mountain man could muster.

"Wagh! This . . . child's done . . . drunk too much, leetle Sunshine. Got to sleep first, I swear . . . ain't yore fault . . . that damned whiskey we been guzzling. Ain't ye dead sleepy too?"

"I'll nurse on you then, Chauncy. After that I'll let you sleep."

But even as she nuzzled and worked on him with her fingers and her tongue, she had to fight back intense drowsiness. And when she herself dropped into an oblivion of sleep, her object had not been accomplished.

The morning was well advanced when sunlight found its way through shadows of black oak and buckeye at ravine bottom, and the man and woman awoke heavy-eyed and grinned at one another. Horse and mule stood by watching as human haunches joined, listened to the strange groanings and whimperings.

"Sonofabitch, woman," Wilson managed at last, "this hyar coon dog cain't take no more. Don't even move, or by Gawd I'll die on the spot."

"Chauncy," Sunshine crooned, "it was wonderful."

They parted, Sunshine Hobson mounting her horse and riding back toward Murphys, Fiddlehead Wilson on muleback heading for Stockton and the other valley towns, intent upon purchasing cattle for Mike McLafferty's spread.

The mountain man set up a trail camp a few miles from Stockton, a bustling little city with brick buildings and houses clustered close to the yellow-gray flood of San Joaquin River. Wilson began going from ranch to ranch, explaining his mission, and buying cows. Things went smoothly enough, and he hired a dozen Miwok boys (who'd been hanging around anyway) to hack down brush from along a meandering creek and drag it in to form a makeshift corral into which he could drive his ever increasing herd at night.

A couple of vaqueros from the Rancho Sanchez upon whose land Fiddlehead had gotten permission to set up his trail camp, were hired to come out and brand the animals with a running iron, a double M for Mike and Moon—an emblem that Fiddlehead himself had thought up and deemed wholly appropriate.

But at night, sitting beside his campfire alone and drinking perhaps more than was wise, Fiddlehead cursed himself for an old fool, realized the folly of his attachment to Sunshine Hobson, and conjured at least a hundred sufficient reasons why he was better off without her. Yet ultimately he found that he simply could not keep her image from drifting into his thoughts.

"Wagh!" he said to the longhorned Spanish cattle one morning when a thin, light-suffused fog was hanging over the area beside the creek, "What's this ornery old polecat goin' to do?"

13 January passed imperceptibly, but Ruby Dome Ranch remained locked hard in winter. The snows didn't grow terribly deep at the base of the range, but the peaks were high enough to draw down whatever precipitation remained in passing clouds, and sub-zero temperatures ensured that the snow stayed around.

The Te-Moaks had built their brush lodges under the shelter of firs at the upper end of the meadow, but they preferred passing their time in the log house. Most evenings found at least Smoke on the Hill and a circle of youngsters gathered around the McLafferty fireplace, and usually Tallchief and Swimming Duck as well. The remaining couple, Rain and Antelope Tail, were less frequent visitors at first, but gradually they also overcame their reserve and hovered near what had obviously become the band's main fire circle.

Old Smoke on the Hill proved to be nearly as prolific a storyteller as Fiddlehead, and, although he spoke little English and it was necessary for Tallchief to serve as interpreter, he gave his tales a full, dramatic rendition that included animal sounds, movements, roaring voices of monsters, and the acting out of battle scenes—the words became almost incidental. Jacques was mesmerized and in remarkably short time learned enough of Te-Moak dialect so that he occasionally disagreed with Tallchief on fine points of translation. Along with the Te-Moak boy, Grasshopper, he shrieked and covered his head when a saga became unbearably, deliciously scary. Then he emerged in waves of giggles at his companion's cowardice, as well as his own.

Jacques and Grasshopper were both nearly frenetic with the delight of finding an age-mate, at times whipping each other up to demonic fits of energy and noise and prodding one another to pull pranks on the older members of the newly formed group, until Moon, driven past her breaking point, would exile them to the cold to play in the snow.

Elizabeth and Camas Flower approached one another more cautiously, spending several days sizing one another up, exchanging an occasional polite smile and not much more. Then, apparently at some signal perceptible only to themselves, they decided to be friends. Each found a great deal of amusement in the other's mispronunciations, sometimes drawing pictures with charred sticks on wrapping paper and usually finding their artistic efforts sufficient cause for interminable fits of giggling.

Odd man out among the youngsters was Slow Lizard, for the eleven-year-old boy had no new companion his own age. But he didn't seem to mind terribly much. Both Jacques and Grasshopper, when they weren't too distracted with their own amusements, trailed the older boy around in great admiration, and he basked in this hero worship, kindly condescending to display for them his skill with bow and arrow or spear or tell them about his prowess in tracking antelope.

When McLafferty began to teach Slow Lizard to shoot, the lad was in heaven and the younger boys were riddled with envy. But his primary goal was to gain Elizabeth's approval, for he was fascinated by the exotically beautiful creature with flame-colored hair and eyes like summer sky. He was less than completely successful in this endeavor, but Slow Lizard never considered giving up. The monumental obstacle of Elizabeth's complete indifference only spurred him to greater efforts, and he seemed always to be popping up wherever her gaze happened to be directed, puffing out his thin chest or conspicuously drawing a bow or pretending to squeeze off a shot with an imaginary rifle.

As for the others, Tallchief's mother Sage Hen had not in fact died and, indeed, showed no inclination to do so in the near future, thriving in her new quarters in Fiddlehead's alcove and basking in Elizabeth's solicitous and affectionate attentions, for the girl remembered and missed her own grandmother who had died back in Kentucky when she was ten.

Swimming Duck, in whose behalf Tallchief and the others kidnapped Jacques in the first place, became so closely attached to Moon and her son that Tallchief found cause to complain. "Woman don't pay no attention to her own husband," the bandy-legged warrior grumbled, holding up the barrel of an old flintlock rifle to the light and peering down the length of it.

It was early afternoon, and the men had the fireside to themselves. McLafferty and Tallchief talked as they restored a rusty and long-unused firearm that had been in Tallchief's possession, he claimed, for years. Smoke on the Hill watched the proceedings with interest, although he didn't comment much. Conversation went on in English, of which his knowledge was sketchy, and he didn't interrupt to ask for a translation, apparently content merely to observe the transformation of the long-useless gun. Sage Hen was sleeping in Fiddlehead's alcove, snoring nearly as sonorously as its former inhabitant. The others were up to the Te-Moak encampment commiserating with Rain, who'd slipped and badly sprained an ankle while out gathering firewood.

"That right?" Mike asked, using an oiled rag on disassembled metal pieces, trigger and hammer and pan hinge. "Seems like she's the one always drags you back to your lodge at night, even though you'd rather stay here and continue your lying contest with Smoke on the Hill."

"Oh, that," Tallchief grinned. "Your woman been filling her head with all this Cheyenne magic for having a baby. She tried everything Sage Hen told her years back, everything any Te-Moak woman told her. Now she got new ideas, every night something else. Man can only take so much of that. No, what I mean, my moccasins. Look, falling to pieces. This old blanket's all wore out. She won't make me anything. Too busy hanging around with Moon and trying out damn fool ideas."

"Wouldn't mind that so much, myself," Mike muttered.

"What's that?"

"Nothing. How'd you come by this old squirrel gun, anyway?"

"I already tell you about that time before, many winters ago, when I worked for those other owl-faces who come through this country looking for beaver up in the mountains and along the river. That was a long time ago—I wasn't much older than Slow Lizard there. John Work, that was the bossman's name. British men. They wanted a guide, somebody who knew this country around here. Like I say, I was a young kid, thought maybe I'd like something different for a while, so I went with those owl-faces. Saw lots of things, too. I stayed with John Work and those people four, five years. Floated down that big river starts way over there where the sun rises, only I found out the sun don't rise there at all."

"Snake River?" Mike asked absently, still working on the gun parts in his hand.

"That's what they call 'im, I think, Shoshones' river, people who talk almost like we do. Down that to biggest goddamn river anybody ever saw, so big you couldn't shoot an arrow one side to the other, down that to where there ain't nothing but water at the end of the world, only the world don't end there either, because they got these big damn boats come in. That was something, I tell you. You look way, way out and you see one like a big swan or goose floating, and it comes in, gets bigger and bigger, pretty soon it's so damn big it scares you. Anyway, that boss down there, McLoughlin, he likes me pretty good, I guess."

"Old Here-Before-Christ," McLafferty grinned. "Had some dealings with some of those HBC boys back when I was working for Sublette. Good enough fellows, I guess, but we were trained not to like each other much. The bloody Brits—"

"Yep. Well, I stayed around that country for a while, then I got tired of it and I came home."

"You still haven't said how you got the gun."

Tallchief shrugged. "Those people that live down on that river, that Columbia, they don't eat nothing but fish."

Tallchief made a face, spat toward the fire. "Goddamn pink fish, smoked fish, dried fish, fish powder, fish oil, fish eggs. That ain't food for human people. Old John Work, he got tired hearing me grumble about it, I guess, so he made one of the men loan me this gun, teach me how to shoot. Then I could hunt meat. That man got stomped to death one day by a female moose with little ones, so the gun was mine. Ain't had powder or shot for fifteen winters, though, so it just been sitting around getting rusty like it is now."

"It's going to clean up just fine," Mike said, wrapping the oiled pieces in leather to soak for a time. "Not a bad gun—Kain-tuck flintlock."

Old Smoke leaned forward and made a sudden, explosive roar. Mike jumped, and Smoke broke into a laugh.

"Make a big noise," he said, nodding toward the gun barrel. "Scare rabbits. No damn good."

Mid-February brought winds, great torrents of air that came roaring out of the north, picking up what snow was on the ground and whirling it around in blinding plumes. Icy blasts continued for several days, then subsided for a time, but the sky remained leaden, threatening.

Inside the cabin all was light and warmth and noise. Flames leaped and crackled in the mud-and-wattle fireplace, while Jacques and Grasshopper engaged in mock combat, rolling about on the floor and shrieking at maximum volume, with Slow Lizard apparently acting as referee. Camas Flower stood in Fiddlehead's alcove, wearing a partly finished red calico dress Elizabeth was making for her, while the seamstress bustled about, taking tucks here and there with quick basting stitches. The girls argued good-naturedly and giggled about the whole process.

Near the fireplace Antelope Tail and Smoke on the Hill sat to one side, the younger man straightening arrow shafts by drawing them through a notched tool made for that purpose, while the elder offered advice, encouragement, and criticism.

On the other side of the fireplace Swimming Duck, Rain, and Sage Hen were patting camas-flour paste into cakes and chattering among themselves. And when Moon, Mike and Tallchief entered with a fresh haunch of mutton for immediate roasting, the noise level only increased, as all greeted them and came to see what they'd brought.

Moon spitted the haunch over the flames immediately, and while meat sizzled and filled the cabin with excruciatingly delicious odors, it was, of course, necessary for the complete account of the hunt to be rendered. Tallchief took over this task and fulfilled it admirably, detailing, Moon thought, every sagebrush, rock, and blade of grass they'd passed on the way and standing to mimic the actions and positions of the sheep in the herd as well as those of each hunter. When Tallchief had at last finished, Smoke on the Hill followed with a hunting tale of his own; when that was done, the meat was at least partially cooked, and no one was willing to wait longer to eat.

They feasted hugely and afterwards lay back, too satiated to think of moving as the wind came up again, howling like demented spirits around the corners of the cabin. Even Jacques and Grasshopper grew quiet, their eyes wide and dark as they listened to the shrieking gusts that sometimes seemed to shake the whole structure, as if unseen beings were testing the doors.

"That sounds like the cannibal woman walking tonight," Smoke on the Hill said. "Sounds like she's out walking, screaming because she's so hungry. Listen!"

The old man held up a finger, sat silent for a time, head cocked intently, and then he nodded.

"She says, 'Oh, where are all the children? Their mothers don't let them go out when it's so cold. I'm hungry! Poor me. Poor me. Who-o-o-o. Who-o-o-o. I smell two fat little boys! Who-o-o!'"

Jacques and Grasshopper shrieked and ran to hide behind Moon, half giggling and half sobbing as Smoke, hands raised and bent into claws, face twisted into the evil mask of the cannibal woman, made as if to spring at the boys on the word 'fat.'

"Shame on you, Father," Rain said, "scaring the babies that way."

"No," Sage Hen said from the shadows near the corner of the fireplace. "It is good for the children to have a grandfather or grandmother to tell them scary stories. I didn't have any grandfather or grandmother when I was a little girl, and so I wandered too far from my village looking for salmon berries, and something, maybe it was the cannibal woman, nearly got me."

She paused here, waiting for someone to urge her to go on, but Jacques and Grasshopper were beyond speech and merely watched her with round eyes, waiting for her to continue.

"Well," she said at length, "there is not much to tell. I went too far away, and it was got dark while I was still a long way from home. Pretty soon I start hearing something behind me, walking along, it get closer and closer. I could hear big feet hitting the ground, 'Whump, whump.' Then I start running and I can hear those feet start running too, 'whump-whump-whump!' Then I got where I could see the cooking fire at our village, and I was running as fast as I could, and I could hear her teeth grinding, 'r-r-r-r-r-r.' When I got little closer, I could see my mother and the other women moving around by the fire, cooking. I screamed, 'Mother, mother, something after me!' But by then I feel its breath on the back of my neck, hotter than that fire there."

Here she stopped, leaned back and folded her arms as if finished with her tale.

Jacques and Grasshopper waited, barely breathing, but the woman didn't continue. "What happened, grandmother Sage Hen?" Jacques demanded.

"Can't guess?" she asked casually. "Why, that cannibal woman catch me and throws me into her basket and eats me up. And all because I don't have no grandmother Sage Hen to tell me scary stories."

"Somehow this didn't turn out exactly the way you promised," Mike whispered to Moon later, when they lay in bed listening to the wind wail and thunder at the house.

"What do you mean, Red Coyote?" Moon murmured, moving drowsily against him.

"Don't recall you saying that when Tallchief and his people moved to the ranch, Mr. and Mrs. McLafferty would have the house to themselves because Elizabeth and Jacques would certainly want to spend time with their new friends up in the village? But I don't recollect you saying anything about how the whole gang would end up camped out in our gawddamned house most of the time. Guess I'm getting old. My mind's slipping."

"You exaggerate, Mac-lafferty. We certainly aren't going to send them out on a night like this. Anyway, they aren't here all the time. Besides, you said you wanted a family, Red Coyote."

"Did I say that?"

"Isn't that why I'm getting fat and ugly, so you can have a family?"

"Fat and ugly, is it now?" Mike demanded. "Ripe as a wild plum in late September, and just as sweet. . . .

Yep, I think I had in mind to make one the old-fashioned way. That's the part I like."

Mike slid a hand up the silky length of Moon's stomach and cupped a breast, squeezed.

"Stop that, Mac-lafferty!"

"How are we supposed to practice at family-making with fifty to a hundred Te-Moaks sprawled all over the next room?"

"You've already done the making part, Red Coyote. Have you forgotten? A good Cheyenne wife would never allow her husband to lie down with her when she's carrying a child."

"That's why Cheyenne husbands are allowed more than one wife. Besides, when I was a little shaver, my old man always told me to do a thing right, a man had to practice. What about that? By the time we take the house back from Tallchief and company, I'll have forgotten what to do altogether."

"You talk nonsense, Red Hair. But if you insist on this thing, I can be very quiet. Besides, who would hear us in this wind? We will say it was Cannibal Woman."

A long rending sound, crashing and thundering as if the world were being blown apart, split the night. A blast of icy air rushed in under the door to the bedroom. In the next instant, wild shrieks from the main room, definitely human cries and not the voice of the wind.

The McLaffertys fumbled in the blackness for their clothing. Flickering candle in hand, Mike opened the door, Moon at his shoulder, and for several moments both stood staring at the scene in the main room, uncertain what it meant. Wind snuffed out the candle, but by the dim glow of embers, now flaring and throwing off great swirls of sparks as well as smoke into the room, they could see Tallchief standing, rubbing his head and looking dazed. Swimming Duck crouched completely over, her arms up shielding the back of her head, while Antelope Tail and Rain sat side by side, staring. Only old Smoke seemed unperturbed, standing with hands on hips. Elizabeth and Jacques, with the other three children crowding behind them, were standing hesitantly in the curtained-off doorway to their bedroom, while Sage Hen leaned with one hand against the wall near her alcove.

Objects seemed to be flying and crashing into the room from above, dark, solid objects, and the air was in utter confusion, roaring and hissing, pulling Moon's hair across her face as she tried to see.

Mike cursed, steadily and stolidly.

"What is it, Mac-lafferty, what has happened?"

"Can't you see? The goddamned wind's pulled the goddamned roof off. Son of a bitch! I knew we needed nails. Should have gone to goddamned Salt Lake City and got the bastards, but—shit!"

Moon moved cautiously into the chaotic space, took a survey of the inhabitants. Tallchief had a purple swelling on his forehead where a shingle had struck him, but the injury was minor. Miraculously, no one else was hurt, only frightened and confused.

Moon groped for the coal-oil lamp in her bedroom and lit it, used it to guide the others into the sanctuary, where there was at least a door to block the wind.

Mike poured water from the drinking bucket onto the embers in the fireplace to prevent wind-driven sparks from igniting the entire house, and then he also retreated into the small room in which an even dozen human beings now huddled, waiting for daybreak.

The storm diminished well before dawn, but the occupants of the McLafferty place slept little the rest of the night. When day came, Mike, with Tallchief to assist him, went out to salvage as much of the roof as they could. The other Te-Moaks, with the exception of Sage Hen, went off to see what the night's gales had done to their lodges. The wind had quieted somewhat, and the day promised to be fair. The sun appeared in a sky that was a faultless sheet of icy blue.

Moon built up a fire to reheat some remnants of the previous night's feast, nearly choking as smoke poured back into the room through the gaping hole in the roof.

By full daylight she could see that a very large section of roof was missing—an area some eight feet long and six wide. Jacques found the whole business novel and amusing, running outside and chattering excitedly until Mike, in decidedly bad humor, roared at the child, "Go plague your mother!"

"We'll have to ride up on the hill and cut some more shakes before we can do anything," McLafferty said when he and Tallchief came in to eat. "More saplings, too. Wind scattered things to hell and back. Damned shingles are probably in Texas by now. May have to camp out here for a few days until we get it fixed. You'll be all right until we get back?"

Without waiting for a reply, he kissed Moon and started out the door, Tallchief following.

"Can I go with you, Red Coyote?" Jacques asked. "I can help."

"Not today, partner. You stay with your mother. We'll be back."

Moon straightened things as best she could, moving stores of dried meat and camas flour, other perishables, to spots where they'd be sheltered in case of snow. Elizabeth helped quietly, but there was little to be done, and in a short time Moon proposed that they go up to the Te-Moak village to see how the brush lodges had fared.

As they climbed toward the upper end of the meadow, Moon noticed suddenly how quiet Elizabeth had been all morning.

"Don't worry, little one," Moon said gently. "You'll have your home back in a few days. We won't have to sleep out in the snow, not for very long. We still have walls."

The redhaired girl shook her head, tried to smile.

"Maybe we shouldn't be trying to make a home here. I sometimes think that it was only because of me, because I bullied you into it, that you and Mike tried to settle—here or anyplace."

"Don't be silly." Moon smoothed a strand of copper-colored hair back from the girl's forehead. "We're here because we want to be here, and you're with us because you want to be, I guess, and because we love you."

"Sometimes I think you'd be happier living in a hide tent, like the Cheyennes, moving about when the buffalo move, or when the choke cherries are ripe someplace. And Mike liked to travel too. I was the only one who wanted a home, a real home. And look how hard it is for you."

"Well, maybe someday, someday when this little one"—she patted her stomach—"when he or she is old enough, we'll all go look at the ocean. I like to see new things sometimes. Don't you?"

"I—I'm not even sure. The only time I've really traveled was when . . ."

"Yes, that was a bad time for you," Moon soothed. "But it's over now. You're a beautiful young woman, and before very long you'll have your own husband, your own house. Mike and I know that. No, we didn't decide to homestead in this place because you wanted to, but because we knew that we loved it."

Perhaps there's some truth to what Elizabeth says. I think sometimes I would rather live as Leg-in-the-water's people live, to wander here and there in freedom, just as White Bull and I once did. Why are we here? I don't know. Because I love you Red Coyote, because our child grows in my belly, because . . .

The Te-Moaks were busy when Moon and Elizabeth arrived, for the windstorm had done considerable damage to the brush lodges. Moon talked briefly with Swimming Duck and Rain, but there seemed little she could do to help, and so she and Elizabeth headed back down to the house, both feeling at loose ends.

As they neared the lower end of the meadow, she saw riders approaching on the trail below—five men. Something about them, even though they were too far off for her to identify, made her uneasy. She hurried toward the cabin, herding Jacques and Elizabeth ahead of her. Before she reached the house, however, the riders were in the yard, lead man dismounting, pistol in hand, smiling at her below his thin, dapper mustache.

"Just stay where you are, Miz McLafferty. Nothing personal, but I think you and your mister lied to me last month, and I'd like to get matters straight right now, if you don't mind."

Sam Tarrango. And all the guns are in the house, the children and I outside, and only one door.

14 Moon surveyed the situation quickly. Counting Tarrango, thirteen men were deployed about the area, the hirelings moving unobtrusively into a wide semicircle.

"Elizabeth," Moon whispered, "take Jacques into the house and bar the door. Hurry!"

The girl caught Jacques by the hand and ran.

"Hold on there, missy," Tarrango began, but by the time he had spoken and brought his gun in line with the youngsters, they darted through the opening and slammed the heavy door shut.

"How nice to see you again, Mr. Tarrango," Moon said quickly, stalling, trying to think. "Did you find the women you were looking for? I don't see them with you."

"Shit!" Tarrango spat. "You know damned well I didn't."

"How would we hear of a thing like that? We're very isolated here, as you can see."

The dapper little man scowled. "Where the hell's McLafferty? You and your man sent me on a fool's errand. No one makes an ass of Sam Tarrango and gets away with it. Where is the sonofabitch?"

"I don't know. Mike rode off a week ago to buy some cattle."

"Sure he did. You lying damned half-breed. Maybe I'll just take you and the redheaded kid along with me. Vikki and the other three sluts ain't going to be much use to me when I get through with them. The two of you could make good money for me. Who knows, you might even get to liking it."

"Maybe I would." Moon shrugged. "Things are pretty dull here. Why don't you put your gun away and tell your men to back off—then we'll talk about it? I won't discuss business matters with a pistol pointed at my belly."

Sam stared at her, then began to laugh, but the gun barrel didn't waver.

"By God, I almost like you. You got more tricks than a St. Louis cathouse on Saturday night."

"Only trying to make conversation, Mr. Tarrango, but I wish you'd stop aiming that thing at me. I'm beginning to get tired of this."

"You hear what she says, Addams?" Tarrango said to a sour-faced man standing a few yards behind him. "She's beginning to get tired of it."

"Whyn't you send her over here, Sam?" called out an unshaven individual standing near the corral. "I'll show her 'tired.' "

"Me," said another, "I'd rather have a crack at that little redhead. I got a thing for the young ones."

"Shut up, you damned barbarians," Tarrango laughed. "There's a big mick card thief hanging around close here someplace. Look sharp. I want to settle matters with him first—"

"Drop your gun, Mr. Tarrango, and tell your men to drop theirs. I'll shoot if I have to."

Elizabeth stood half behind the door to the cabin, the barrel of Mike's New Haven Whitney thrust ahead of her. Her voice was high, strained, but her aim was steady enough.

"Now, missy, you ain't gonna do no such thing," Tarrango said in a silky tone. "You just put the elephant gun away so I don't have to make any holes in your friend's pretty hide. Easy, now—"

The Whitney roared, the shot zinging high and wide past Tarrango's ear and taking a chunk of bark from a cottonwood near one of his men. Jack Addams fired off a quick, wild shot in the general direction of the cabin.

Moon crouched and ran to the cabin entryway, flung herself inside, and shoved the door to as a volley of shots went off, slugs pelting door and walls.

"Hold fire, you idiots!" Tarrango yelled.

Moon quickly hugged Elizabeth.

"Thank you, Red Hair," she whispered, then knelt and pulled Jacques to her and hugged him also. "Now reload, quickly!"

She ran to the bedroom and took her revolver down from the wall, returned to the large, open-roofed main room.

Thirteen of them, two of us. Not good odds, but we've made it this far. Be careful, Michael John McLafferty, when you come back from the upper meadows.

"Don't understand why owl-faces make such damn big houses, work like sonofabitch for two, three years, and then you can't move if you want to, because you gotta spend another two, three years, make another great big house. What you need besides something to keep the rain off, someplace to sleep and build a fire when it gets cold? We build a brush lodge, takes the women three, four hours, when game runs out we go somewhere else, build another brush lodge."

"Don't ask me, pal," Mike said, tying the last bundle of shakes in place on the mule. "I figure it was the women invented houses. Guess we're ready to head home," he added, stepping back and testing his knots. He pulled a cigar from his pocket, handed it to Tallchief, lit another one for himself.

"Yes," Tallchief said, nodding. "Te-Moak women probably thought of houses first, but they are the ones who make them. Owl-face women get men to build theirs, I see that on Columbia River. Why do it? Why not say, 'Look, woman, you want a house, you build it. You want it big, you make it big.' White women got some kind of magic our women don't know about?"

"No," Mike laughed, "I guess not. Just the men are kind of slow."

He stretched, reached for the pack mule's reins, began to lead him down toward the lower meadow, Tallchief walking alongside.

"Come to think of it, probably it was the women who invented farming, too. Never heard anybody say that, but I'll bet that's how it was, all right."

"Ah. Digging holes, putting one kind of plant in the ground that don't want to grow there, killing off the other kinds that like it."

"There you go. Basis of civilization, my friend. And that's why the owl-faces are superior to your race."

Tallchief laughed. "I seen farming. McLoughlin's people did some farming out there. Work all day, hauling water, chopping out plants that want to grow there, putting animal shit in holes to trick wrong plants into growing. Work damn near as hard as we been working today instead of eating what's already around. That's so you don't have to move big-ass houses that you work like sonofabitch to build for women."

"Just as I said. Women, at least white women, don't like to move much. I guess it's because of the kids."

"Moon that way?"

"Don't know, to tell the truth. She spent most of her life moving around with the Cheyennes. Seemed to thrive on it. Maybe it's me as much as her; that's the way us owl-faces are raised, I guess. Find the right girl, get married, and settle down. That's the way the twenty-seventh commandment goes. And if we don't provide the right girl with a proper home when we find her, we're considered derelict in our duties."

They stopped briefly at the Te-Moak encampment, found repair work on the brush lodges nearly complete. Swimming Duck came forward to whisper something in Tallchief's ear. He waved her aside, then grinned and winked at Mike.

"Woman's gonna wear me out," he said, then ducked as she took a playful swing at him.

They moved ahead and came out into the open where they could see the ranch buildings several hundred yards distant. Mike stared, saw first the horses that didn't belong there, then thought he recognized a white-stockinged bay, tried to recall where he had seen it before.

"Oh, Christ!" he said, dropping the mule's reins and breaking into a run. "It's Tarrango. Moon, the kids, they're there alone."

A powerful hand caught his arm, dragged him to a halt.

"Slow down, Mac-lafferty. These men come visit you before, but now they enemies? Pretty little wagon, I remember. You want to run like fool rabbit into a net? They ain't seen us yet, or maybe they be shooting at us. I'll go tie the mule there in those trees; my

Kentuck squirrel gun is on that mule. Then we sneak up on this Tarrango. Owl-faces no sense. How you live this long?"

"Oh, hell," Mike muttered, "Fiddlehead would have let me know in a minute if you hadn't."

"Huh?" Tallchief said. "You don't make no sense."

The tense drama at the cabin had evolved into a standoff. Tarrango and his men had moved away from the house into what cover they could find, and Moon stood behind one window, only the barrel of her revolver poking through a small slit in the hide, while Elizabeth used the Whitney to cover the rear from another position. Jacques stood behind Moon, clutching his small bow and arrows bravely, but his young face was drawn.

"You gals can't hole up in there forever," Sam Tarrango was shouting. "Why don't you make it easy on yourselves and come on out? Hell, I've got nothing against you. All I want's that damned cardsharp you're sleeping with. Where the hell is he, anyway? We can camp out here for a month if we have to."

"Your lucky day, Sam old buddy," Mike called, suddenly stepping from cover directly behind Tarrango, no more than a few yards distant. "But don't you be turning around. Don't do it, Addams, you twitch and by God I'll drill you clean! Drop the gun. That's it, that's it."

Jack Addams had indeed thought about turning quickly and firing, but Big Mike McLafferty's reputation was sufficient to dissuade him from what, after all, would have been a desperate act.

Careful, Red Coyote, Moon prayed silently, peering through the slit in her window, please be careful.

She detected movement in willow brush near the stream where Mike had emerged—a dark, unshaven man turning to fire. She held the revolver carefully, squeezed, and the man stepped backward with the noise of the explosion, looked around toward her, then suddenly went limp, dropped.

"A hell of a shot, Moon!" Mike called out. "Didn't see the bastard; he could have had me blindside. Anyone else moves, Sam, and we'll be burying you along with your hired gun. Moon-Gal, hold aim on him, dead center!"

"What do you think I'm doing?" she shouted. "I would be happy to kill him now."

"Well, Sam? What do you say? You want to pick up your dead *compañero* there and call it a day, or you up for a firefight? You've got us outnumbered, so your boys'll probably win, but on the other hand, it's a dead cinch you won't be around to enjoy the victory."

"You sonofabitch, McLafferty," Tarrango snarled. "You played me for a fool! It wasn't any of your damned concern what I did with those sluts, and you went and lied to me anyway. All right, boys, that's it for today. Dewey, Blanco, get Martin there. He wasn't worth a damn, anyway. Holster your guns. Not worth it to take lead just to get even with a thieving Irish gambler."

"Careful, owl-faces, careful now," another voice said, and Tallchief stepped from cover, his restored flintlock cradled on one arm, twin triggers set. He sat down on the ground, grinning, the long rifle aimed casually above his bent knees.

With the unfortunate Martin hastily flung and tied over his own horse, Tarrango and his men mounted.

"I got other business to tend to right now," Sam said as he sat the dancing bay, "but I'll be back. You sonsofbitches! Nobody makes a fool out of Sam Tarrango twice."

"You sure 'bout that?" Tallchief laughed. "Don't look very hard."

"Count on it," Tarrango said with a mocking bow toward the cabin. "I'll be back."

"Tell you what I'd like to see," Jack Addams growled. "You and Pete the Gun, man to man. He'd ventilate your hide, McLafferty."

Mike laughed.

"When you see old scarface, tell him I'll be happy to oblige. Might be kind of fun at that."

Moon, Elizabeth, and Jacques emerged from the cabin to watch the departure of Tarrango and his men.

"You sure we shouldn't kill them all now?" Tallchief asked, squinting toward the horsemen along the barrel of his flintlock. "Easy shot, not near as hard as bighorns. Pick 'em off, bam, bam, bam. That way we know they won't be back."

"How many shots you got in that thing?" McLafferty grinned. "Could have sworn it was just one. No, Tarrango's full of wind. He won't be bothering us again."

"I'm not so sure," Moon said. "He really hates you, Mac-lafferty. He hates all of us now."

Suddenly she draped her arms around Mike's neck, almost throwing him off balance.

"I was afraid for you, Red Coyote."

"Afraid for me? Jesus. . . ."

Mike thought of the moments of sheer terror when he'd seen the horses in the meadow, had imagined her dead, captive, tortured a hundred times over while he and Tallchief worked their way down. Suddenly he began laughing, then realized that he couldn't quit. Moon laughed also, and then Jacques, looking up puzzled, first into one face and then the other, added his tentative giggle.

* * *

February passed into March, the days growing longer. At times, Moon felt as if the brutal cold of winter would never pass, but one day a moist wind blew up from the southwest, a wind with an entirely different feel than the winter blasts, and by afternoon rain began to fall, warm rain that quickly washed away frozen patches of snow from Ruby Dome Ranch and took with it the thin scum of ice that seemingly had persisted forever.

A succession of spring storms followed, interspersed with periods of damp sunlight shining between clouds, and in a matter of days the boggy meadows were showing a delicate, hazy green beneath the waterlogged stalks of last year's growth. Willows pushed forth yellow catkins, and nubby green leaves emerged from buds. High up in the mountains, the storms brought fresh snow, but on the McLafferty spread, spring made its fragile but irrevocable assertion. Certainly there would be more snow, more freezing nights, but the corner was turned.

All creatures felt the change. Horses and mules rolled in muddy grass, legs waving in the air, and frisked about in the rain, chasing and nipping at one another like colts. Squirrels emerged from winter hiding places and darted about on the ground, looking for food after the lean months, raced up into trees when disturbed, and chattered vigorously. And one day, when Moon had walked alone to the upper meadows, she saw a trio of coyote pups, eyes still hazy with infancy, poking their stubby noses out from cover of the fir grove until a warning whuff from an unseen parent sent them scampering back into hiding.

The humans had not lain idle during the cold months, however, and now when Moon stepped out for water, she saw a series of long sheds, shelters for cattle and fodder, and a skinned-pole fence that encompassed a good half of the lower meadow. It almost seemed, Moon thought sometimes, as if these, too, had sprung from the earth like yellow flowers that made patches of distilled sunshine on the slopes and the wild iris that bloomed on marshy ground.

It was not that she'd been unaware of the construction while it was going on—often enough, she worked alongside Mike and Tallchief, Antelope Tail and young Slow Lizard, Smoke on the Hill supervising and kibitzing in mixed English and Paiute—but rather she felt that she was seeing, really seeing these things for the first time in the fresh light.

Moon felt she was blooming, too, the life inside her growing with increased rapidity, even impatience. Her belly clearly swelled now, and she was beginning to feel clumsy, ungainly. At times she was annoyed with the limitations of burgeoning pregnancy, with the awkward shape of her body, but at other times she allowed herself to fall into a rather self-satisfied lethargy, a sense of vegetative oneness with the process of renewal in the world outside.

But as the season advanced, one thing gnawed increasingly at her contentment, and that was Mike's impending departure for California to meet with Fiddlehead and drive cattle back to the ranch. It was folly, she realized, even to contemplate the possibility of accompanying her husband, but the thought of his going off without her filled her with uneasiness. White men with Indian wives, she knew full well, had an alarming trend toward forgetfulness, toward finding new wives, either red or white, and neglecting to return to families left behind.

Both she and Mike avoided the subject most of the

time, but when it did come up, she found herself unable to contain an anxious irritability.

One chilly afternoon, with a fine drizzle permeating the air, Mike and the Te-Moak men put the final poles in place for a second large corral. Moon, one arm around Jacques' shoulders and Elizabeth just behind her, stood watching, pleased with the completion of the job but dreading, also, what that completion meant.

"Look pretty good, boss." Tallchief grinned, wiping his damp face with an equally damp sleeve. "All ready for them little buffalo you keep threatening us with."

"Yes," Jacques cried. "When will we get the little buffalo, Mike?"

McLafferty glanced at Moon, shrugged. "Guess we can't put it off too much longer," he said. "Snow'll be pretty well melted out in the passes in a couple months. Suppose to rendezvous with Fiddlehead on the first of May."

"Slow Lizard and I will go with you," Jacques decided. "You might need help. Wouldn't you like to go see the big water, Slow Lizard?"

"Yes," said the older boy, "I would like that. A man should have experience of many things." Here he looked at Elizabeth, to see if the assertion of adulthood had produced its desired effect.

"Will you take us, Mike?" begged Jacques.

"Sorry, pal," Mike began, but Moon was unable to contain her impatience any longer.

"So," she snapped, "now both my men wish to desert me. I don't think Red Coyote will take you, Jacques. He will not wish any encumbrances. I will go see about supper. I'm sure all you *men* are hungry after working so hard."

She turned abruptly and stalked to the house, tears burning at the corners of her eyes.

You have made a fool of yourself, Moon McLafferty, she realized instantly. McLafferty? That's not really my name, even. What hold do I have over you, Red Coyote? Nothing, nothing at all except that fragile, delicate thread, your wish to be with me. Will that survive months apart, the lure of new land, new faces?

Jacques ran after her, caught her hand. "Why are you angry with us, Mother? I didn't mean to—"

"Oh, go be with your partner, your precious Red Coyote. Who knows? It may be the last time you will see him."

"Mother . . . ?"

She felt remorse for the harsh words, knelt and hugged Jacques briefly. "Don't pay any attention to me, Little Bull. I'm not really angry with you. They say women get cross sometimes when they have a new little one in their bellies. Go talk with the men. I'll be all right in a while."

She went into the gloom of the cabin and began cutting up chunks of fresh venison for stew, unable to resist the temptation to hack the meat with savage vigor. As she worked, Swimming Duck wandered in. As always of late, Tallchief's wife wanted to feel Moon's burgeoning abdomen, the Te-moak woman's round face dimpled with smiles, eyes gleaming wonder.

"Will be strong baby. I feel him move," she said.

"Then you can feel more than I can," Moon replied, moving away to dump the meat into a cast-iron pot.

"Old One must love you," Swimming Duck said

wistfully. "Already you have a fine boy, now another coming."

"Perhaps I will kill it," Moon said.

"No! What you talking? Must not speak such things! You acting crazy, Moon woman!"

"Then I'll give it to you, Swimming Duck. What shall I do with it?"

"What's matter with you? You been sleeping with Grandmother Moon looking at you. Gone crazy. Such talk!"

Without the slightest warning, Moon burst into tears.

"You're the lucky one, Swimming Duck. You have your husband, you know where he will be tomorrow. I'll have this child, but will it have a father? What will I do with a child, and no father?"

"You talk like foolish person. Man with no eyes could see Mac-lafferty love you. Tallchief don't love Swimming Duck that big. I don't mind. Hardly anybody love anybody that big."

"But will he still love me when he's half a world away, when he doesn't even see me for months? I loved a man named White Bull once, and he . . . he was killed. I'm afraid, afraid Mike will forget."

Moon was silent during the evening meal, and the Te-Moaks, sensing unspoken tension between husband and wife, found reasons to depart early. Elizabeth and Jacques, also subdued, crept off to bed. Mike tried joking with Moon, found her unresponsive. At last, sitting near the fire, he pulled her onto his lap, ran his fingers gently over her face.

She sat stiff in his embrace.

"You don't like the idea of my going away to get cattle," he said. "God, woman, don't you know I don't want to leave you?"

"White men always say that to their squaws."

"What am I supposed to do? Fiddlehead doesn't know anything about herding cows."

"Neither do you."

"But they're my cows. I have some responsibility."

"Of course you do. I'm being foolish. Don't worry about me. I'll get over it as soon as you come back."

She remained cold, her muscles tensed away from him.

"But you don't really believe I'm coming back. How can I convince you?"

"Don't go!" she turned toward him suddenly, pleading. "Send someone else. Send Tallchief."

"You know better than that."

Silence.

Mike continued stroking at her hair, her face. She rose, stood facing him.

"All right, go then. But don't be away long. If you're still gone when the baby gets ready to come, I'll take Elizabeth and Jacques and go back to Leg-in-the-water's village, and you'll never see me again."

"Moon. . . ."

But she turned and marched into the bedroom, closing the door firmly behind her. Mike sat for a moment, staring into the fire, then sighed and followed his wife.

"Hardheaded bitch," he said, sitting down on the bed to pull off a boot while she stood with her back to him, undressing by the light of a tallow candle. "What the hell do I want with you anyway?"

She glared at him, then got into bed, turned toward the wall. He slid beneath the buffalo robes that served as blankets on the hide bed, reached for her smooth warmth in the darkness. She lay unmoving, and after a moment he realized she was weeping silently. He soothed her wordlessly, hands sliding over tight roundness of abdomen, ripe fullness of breasts, softly moving in circles over the silky skin.

Her breathing changed as his hands continued to move, and suddenly she turned and pressed her mouth to his, tongue probing between his lips with a kind of desperation, her face still wet with tears.

He continued to stroke her over and over, as her breathing quickened, and then he pulled her onto him and they rocked together slowly, moving in gentle rhythm for a long time, fire building gradually until she flung her head back and moaned, clutching him and tensing all over, eyes clenched shut, then she relaxed against him for a moment.

He quickened his own rhythm, arched into delicious spasm, then pulled her close, kissed her hair.

"God, I love you, Moon," he whispered, and then, when he managed to catch his breath, "I've made my decision. To hell with the cows! We can have a cattle ranch without any cattle, I guess. Saves time and money in the long run. No feed, don't have to round the bastards up or brand them. I like the idea better the more I think about it. Not a blessed thing to do but lie around in bed all day. By God, we'll sell the kids to Tallchief—"

Moon kissed him on the mouth, half laughed.

"No, go get your cows, Michael Mac-lafferty. Maybe I'll even be here when you get back. Who knows?"

15 He was alone again, just as he'd been alone for the greater portion of his life—riding off into wild free spaces, moving westward just as he had when he was hardly more than a boy, his parents dead, a St. Louis riverfront vagabond who'd impressed Bill Sublette, and the great man offered him a menial job and took him up river. And so he had become a participant in the last years of the fur trade, apprentice to Aloysius Benton, adept at fist fighting, knife fighting, and gun fighting—a man it was wise not to push too hard and maybe the fastest damned gun in the High Shining.

But it was cards, not the fur trade, that had gained him a small fortune, and the money led to settling down in St. Louis, which was, in retrospect, the worst decision he'd ever made. Respectability not only had thorns, it was out-and-out deadly.

So he'd headed west once more, west toward the goldfields of California, only matters turned complicated, as usual.

But here he was, out on the trail and heading for whatever kinds of adventure McLafferty's luck was certain to involve him in.

Free for a time, just a man and his horse and a

trail beside a small desert river, a campfire and stars at night, sometimes thundershowers by day, and sometimes early April sun beating down with more than a hint of summer to come.

So why wasn't he happy?

Why, in fact, had he been on the verge of turning back a half dozen times?

Why were there an ache in his gut and sometimes shortness of breath?

A simple enough answer, actually, he knew. Her name is Moon Morning Star—no, by Gawd, Moon McLafferty, and the fact is, Big Mike, you just plain don't want to be away from her. The simple fact is . . . you're lovesick. Her presence has taken over. Hell, you're not a gunfighter anymore, and you're not a gambling man either. You're a husband, a house-bound man. You went to St. Louis to settle down, and that didn't work. So what makes you think it'll work in the middle of a howling wilderness, complete with its own band of Te-Moaks and wolves and grizzlies and song dogs and a cougar or two? McLafferty, that's no place to be raising cattle.

His logical mind said yes, get on over to California and hope Fiddlehead hasn't squandered the roll and has actually converted the money into cattle, and then drive the longhorns back over the Sierra and up the Humboldt to home.

But his emotions were clearly of the opinion that Ruby Dome Ranch could get along just fine without any cattle at all.

Logic won out, but not gracefully. And McLafferty kept moving westward, sometimes riding until well after dark, rising early, pushing ahead like a man obsessed.

The sooner he got where he was going, the sooner he'd be home again. And since he'd never actually had a home before, the matter was one of importance.

Already, this early in the season, there were a few bands of emigrants along the California Trail. Mike passed them and kept moving. He had no time for conversation or other pleasantries.

In any case, most of those who were moving westward wouldn't have made the most savory of trail companions. They were men almost without exception, and they all had gold on their minds.

On the eighth day out of Ruby Dome, McLafferty reached Truckee Meadows. The place was a small city of wagons and tents—a society of irritable males, their passage westward brought to a halt by reconnaissance that the Donner Pass trail lay buried under nearly thirty feet of snow in places, and some said that no crossing was possible.

Mike was stunned by the news.

Had Fiddlehead and the women, then, been able to make it across before the snows accumulated? Or had they been obliged to ride far to the south, to the old Joe Walker Trail?

Or might they have frozen to death in the high mountains, their bodies buried until summer melted back the snowpack?

McLafferty shook his head.

If there was a way, then Fiddlehead had found it. The old bastard had a certain knack.

What about Mike McLafferty? And if he did manage to get across, how in hell was he going to drive a herd of cattle back to Ruby Dome? The absolute last thing he wanted was to get stuck in California for several months.

"There's got to be a way through the mountains," Mike told himself. "Hell, there's no place in the world where snow gets thirty feet deep. It's pure exaggeration."

He rode onward, up the Truckee River, this stream

pouring down out of the Sierra, a flood of clear blue-green water that strongly suggested heavy snows farther up.

After twenty miles or so, the steep desert canyon widened into a large alpine basin, thickly forested, and snow—snow everywhere and getting deeper the farther he rode.

Yet more mountains ahead, pure white mountains.

He met a gray-bearded scout on his way back toward Truckee Meadows, one of Fiddlehead's cousins without doubt, and the man assured him that, yes, the Donner was impassable unless one wished to try it on snowshoes, and even that was an invitation to early death.

McLafferty nodded. The old hedgehog wasn't lying. Looking ahead at the sprawl of gleaming white mountains, Mike knew it was true.

McLafferty's luck.

But he wasn't whipped yet.

He made his way back down Truckee Canyon, telling Gray Boy over and over that there was certainly an easy pass somewhere to the north, and not so far north as Lassen's Death Horn, either.

Back in desert country, he found his way to the headwaters of a small stream that was actually flowing away from the Truckee, paralleling the mountains.

Two days of riding brought him to a broad shallow lake with no apparent outlet. But another stream ran in at the north end of the body of water, a stream that flowed down from broad forested ridges to the west. There was snow here too, of course, but nothing like the Donner route. Instead, the mountains exhibited a broad discontinuity—a few high areas to the south and a considerable snowcap to the north (it would have to be Lassen's Butte, according to the map), and in between a chance, at least a slim chance of making it!

"Come on, old mule," he said to Gray Boy. "According to all the stories, it's got to be springtime in California by now, and that means grass to the withers. No matter what things look like here, the most reliable stories say snow never falls on the other side. Let's go find out. What do you say? If we can make it, then maybe we can bring a herd of longhorns back the same way."

He followed up the little river and into dense forest of fir and pine. By keeping under cover of trees, he was able to negotiate up to two feet of mushy snow—leading Gray Boy along, cursing, wishing the weather would turn cold, so cold snow would freeze and even a horse could walk on top of it.

But nothing of the sort happened.

Nonetheless, after two days of utter exasperation, McLafferty realized that the land around him was sloping westward. Soon he dropped down into an extremely rugged canyon, and then he was out of the snow altogether.

"Keep on moving, Gray Boy. Unless the Big Coyote's got a whole new range of mountains for us to cross, we're on our way to the valley of the Sacramento. Fiddlehead's out there somewhere—at least, I hope he is."

The canyon, its naked red-gray flanks studded with irregularly shaped lava formations, slashed through the ridge country toward the southwest, a coincidence that vaguely pleased McLafferty, since that was precisely the direction he wished to travel. And close by the roaring stream was a trail of sorts, perhaps merely a deer trail, but one that did not fade away into nothingness as was usual. So maybe that meant human presence, though he came across absolutely no evidence of any kind of mining operations.

Indians, then.

Where the canyon broadened into a series of meadows, Mike found evidence of former habitation—a series of stone-lined pits and one with a sagged-in brush roof still over it. The holes were generally arranged in a semicircular manner, and at the center a ring of stones defined a communal fire circle, no doubt the main cooking fire for what was apparently a seasonal encampment of no great size.

Wake up, McLafferty, or the vultures are going to be sticking their crooked beaks into your eyeballs . . .

Sweat broke out suddenly on his forehead, and he knew with intuitive certainty he was being watched.

He disturbed nothing, turned, and walked slowly back to where Gray Boy was happily munching at tufts of spring grass. Mike swung into the saddle, drew his revolver, and waved as though he were fully cognizant of the presence he felt.

He whistled softly and nudged his boot heels into the big gray's sides.

For an hour or more as he worked his way downcanyon, he continued to feel human proximity, and yet he was able to see no one and nothing, heard no sounds not accounted for by wind through the trees and the rushing of water.

Then the presence was gone.

What it amounted to, he realized, was that he'd been escorted through a particular stretch of territory. The Indians, now confident he had no designs upon staying, was merely passing through, were more than willing to let him go, perhaps preferring to keep their existence shrouded in mystery.

He slept little that night, remaining in a sitting position with his rifle over his knees and his campfire blazing brightly, its smoke trailing up into a heaven that was riddled with stars.

The following day, though he had to fight off occasional spells of drowsiness, he kept moving at a good pace and came at length into a zone of mixed forest, the oaks fully leaved out, canyon slopes occasionally spotted with digger pines and thick growth of manzanita.

The air was warm, even balmy, and McLafferty realized the Great Central Valley of California could not be far distant.

But still no traces of mining activity, not so much as a single hole in a cut bank, no prospectors, no traces of human passage whatsoever.

The rims above him were less ragged now, smoothly rounded slopes dotted with laurel and several varieties of fully leaved oaks and intervals of lush grass in between, but punctuated by nearly level tables of rimrock and open areas where countless weathered boulders of lava stone lay strewn about—the remnants, Mike presumed, of both ancient volcanic eruptions and of floods of significant proportion, though what the source of either might be he had no idea.

From a ridgecrest McLafferty could see what seemed to be half the newly founded state of California.

"By God, it is a big valley at that," he told the horse.

Off on the green oak-dotted flatlands below were several ranch houses, a barn or two, corrals. Cattle were grazing and with them significant numbers of deer or perhaps small elk. As a matter of fact, there were animals everywhere, the half domestic and the purely wild, for the moment at least in perfect harmony. In a world with such profusion of game, McLafferty wondered, what need was there for cattle at all? Well, cows would allow themselves to be herded about, but elk and deer were of a different disposition, and corral railings were no more than a moment's inconvenience.

Off to the south a little cluster of mountains rose directly from the floor of the Sacramento Valley, and these Mike took to be Sutter's Buttes. He'd head in that direction.

Somewhere, perhaps a hundred miles beyond the strange, isolated peaks, Fiddlehead Wilson was waiting, hopefully with a herd of cattle.

He and Fiddlehead had settled on a May first rendezvous. Well, it looked as though Mike McLafferty was going to make it on time. In matters of this sort, punctuality was a virtue.

"Let's make for Sacramento City," he said to the stallion. "Might even have time for a few hands of poker or a good session of monte. With luck, I can take in a bit of extra spending money."

In Marysville he won three hundred dollars, and then the game went sour. A ragged-looking individual called Pisswater Tom, whose gold poke McLafferty had systematically emptied, decided cheating was afoot, pounded his fist on the table, and then went for a gun.

Mike pushed the table over, knocking the man backward, and drew—pleased to note that he'd lost nothing of his touch during his two-year leave of absence from the card table.

"Jesus H. Christ!" someone at the bar blurted out, "did you boys see that? Ain't no normal human can pull his shooting iron that quick! Who is he?"

In the simple act of saving is own skin, McLafferty realized, he'd turned the tide of sympathy against himself. "Been a pleasure, gents," he said as he backed, revolver in hand, toward a set of swinging half-doors.

He mounted Gray Boy and proceeded out of town, availing himself of a small, ungainly ferry boat that took him across the swirling green flood of the Yuba

River. But as he looked back, he made note of a cluster of men at the landing, one or another of them pointing in his direction.

"Friends of yourn?" the boatman asked as he worked the rope tow.

"Might have been if I'd had a chance to know them," McLafferty laughed.

Once off the tow-raft, Mike rode south toward Sacramento and Sutter's Fort, continued until darkness overtook him, and then made quick camp beside a smaller river, one he'd easily be able to swim his horse across. He built a fire, cooked his evening meal, and waited.

"Bound to have company in an hour or two," he mused. "Best I don't turn in early tonight."

When he was finished with his meal, Mike put his gear back into the saddlebags, and rubbed Gray Boy behind the ears.

"Not yet," he told the horse. "Be patient, now."

He grabbed his bedroll and walked away from the fire (hardly needed on this warm night in any case), found a convenient live oak beyond the light, propped bedroll against its trunk, and sat down to wait.

He lit a cigar, puffed contentedly, and listened to trilling calls of screech owls, the sporadic but more elaborate efforts of a mockingbird that was perched, possibly, in the very tree he was leaning against.

"Some things change," he mused, "and some things never do. Seems like I've been through this little routine once or twice before. The last time was just outside of Fort Atkinson, as I recall, and that was when Michael McLafferty decided to go straight, to head downriver to St. Louis."

An' see whar that got ye, ye dung-eatin' mongrel.

"Old-timer," McLafferty laughed, "I didn't even know you yet. Keep back in the darkness until I'm ready for you to come out."

Then he heard horsemen out along the trail, and he knew who they were—no, not who they were, but what their business was.

Mike stubbed out his cigar, instinctively checked for the spare cylinder in his coat pocket, rose, and slipped silently toward sounds of horses and low, indiscernible talking.

Then he could hear the voices:

"It's the card thief's horse, all right, same as was tied up to the hitching rail."

"You fixing to string him up, Tom, or just get your dust back?"

"Ought to swing him, all right," a familiar voice answered.

"Let's just take his money and that horse and leave the bastard bareass naked. I don't guess he'll be strutting into Marysville again, and we'll be long gone anyhow."

"A dude handles a gun the way he did, maybe it's better to string him up. Or just club him across the skull and pitch him into the river. That way he drowns, and nobody's the wiser—in case the body turns up at all."

"Keep your voice down, you damned fool. We got to take him unawares."

Mike watched the shadows of men and horses. Then the human shadows moved away in the direction of the flickering glow of his campfire.

McLafferty followed, Colt Walker in hand, came up from behind them. He was no more than twenty feet distant when the four men reached the edges of firelight.

"Ain't here, they's no one here at all, for Christ's sake!"

"Don't be moving now, gentlemen," Mike said. "Hands high, or I put a slug right between Pisswater's shoulder blades. Drop the guns, boys. I swore off killing men day before yesterday, and it's too soon to break my resolution. That's it, throw down the guns. You other three don't want to end up dead because Pisswater Tom's a bad loser, now do you? Don't tempt me, gents. I can drill the four of you before you've even figured out where I am."

He left Tom and his friends with no ammunition for their weapons, no boots, and their horses scattered. Then he rode off through warm, moist darkness, picked his way upstream along the river for a couple of miles before attempting to cross.

"One of the disadvantages of winning at cards," he told Gray Boy. "Keep that in mind in case you ever start thinking about squeezing aces, old friend."

He rode slowly for an hour or more, keeping his directions by the stars, until he entered an area overlaid by heavy fog—something he'd not been expecting. Then, concerned that he might get turned around completely, McLafferty dismounted, got out of his bedroll once more, sat down with his back to a tree, and lit a cigar.

After a time he slept, but when sunlight began to filter through foggy grayness, he was back on the trail, heading south once again.

Another raft took him across the American River, and he rode on through Sacramento, made note that portions of the bustling little city showed signs of recent flooding, stopped at a saloon for one shot of whiskey, and continued southward.

The following day he met a wagon coming from the opposite direction, hailed its driver as he came abreast.

"How far to Stockton, friend?"

"Twenty mile, twenty mile. I just come from there. Well, it's turned out to be a fine day, hasn't it?"

"Thank you," Mike replied, nudging Gray Boy ahead. "Keep an eye out for polecats. . . ."

McLafferty made a tour of the saloons in Stockton, and after five drinks he managed to acquire the information he was after: the whereabouts of one Fiddlehead Wilson.

In fact, the gap-toothed old mountain reprobate apparently frequented all of the saloons Mike visited and made no secret of either his identity or his purpose. But barkeep number five was the only one who knew the general vicinity of Wilson's camp.

"Ride east up the Copperopolis trail until you come to Sanchez Rancho. The foreman of the spread told me Wilson was gathering a herd of cattle—camped about three, four miles above Sanchez's place, alongside the crick. That crazy little bastard, is he really the Fiddlehead Wilson who used to pal around with Bill Williams and Joe Hollingback in the beaver days?"

"The very man." McLafferty grinned, surprised the barkeep had actually heard of the old salt.

The barkeep nodded, ran a stained white towel over the polished wooden surface that separated him from Mike.

"A man meets the damnedest people here in California," the barkeep said. "I actually poured drinks for John Sutter and General Fremont a couple of weeks ago. Vallejo, Reading, I've run into a bunch of 'em. Truth is, I was aboard a British merchantman when Sam Brannan brought a bunch of gold down to San Francisco. The whole town went crazy, and everyone headed for Sacramento. I was one of them, but I never found gold. Doesn't make any difference, though. I like it here, and I guess I'll stay."

McLafferty nodded.

"Now, Wilson," the barkeep continued, "he says he

came cross the mountains in the dead of winter, and by heavens in the company of some prostitutes. Victoria Queen's one of them. She's opened up the fanciest whorehouse in the goldfields. It's in Murphys, if you're passing that way."

"Much obliged," McLafferty said, grinning and putting a ten-dollar gold piece down on the bar. "Guess I'll go find my friend Fiddlehead before he gets drunk and shoots all my cattle."

McLafferty rode east, passed the ranch, and continued until he caught sight of a considerable number of longhorns, some of the animals inside a brush corral, others still grazing or getting settled down as daylight diminished.

He rode toward them, made note of a campfire.

Fiddlehead was sitting beside the blaze, drinking coffee, and whittling a stick. He looked up, pulled at his beard, and spat.

"About gawddamned time ye showed up, Michael John McLafferty. Think this child ain't got nothing better to do than tend to a bunch o' bawling cows?"

Mike shrugged, dismounted. "Figured you'd have your hands full with Sunshine Hobson," he grinned. "So how many moo-cows have we got?"

Then the two old friends were pounding one another on the back, shaking hands, and laughing uproariously all at the same time.

16 Sam Tarrango, along with Jack Addams and the rest of his entourage, reached Murphys the first week in May, setting up camp about a mile to the south of the bustling little city of miners, misfits, hangers-on, merchants and their wives, 'entertainers,' and gamblers.

With him and his compatriots were Black Johnny Cortez, Wolf Mask, and Pete the Gun. Tarrango had found his three erstwhile bounty hunters, horses lost and ammunition gone, living wretchedly among a small band of Washoe Indians close by the big bend of a muddy Walker River.

Frostbite had taken the small finger of Pete's left hand, and Cortez was recovering from dysentery. Wolf Mask, as it turned out, had saved both their lives, getting them down out of Sierra snows, where McLafferty's friend Fiddlehead Wilson had mysteriously managed to overpower the three and leave them bound hand and foot in the midst of a blizzard.

Cortez tried to explain, but Tarrango refused to listen.

"Old buddies," Sam said, "I guess I shouldn't have sent three kids to do a man's job. Well, you're still alive. That's something, at least."

"Next time I see Wilson," Wolf Mask said, "going to cut off his hose an' make him eat it before I slit his damn throat."

"Probably ain't got a pecker by now." Cortez shrugged. "Them whores must of worn it off ... One old man and three hot young women that way. She-it!"

"Vikki could do the job in one night if she was of a mind to." Tarrango scowled. "Hell, they're probably dead by now, all of them. Ain't nobody can cross those mountains in the middle of winter, not from what I've heard. Well, I hate to lose the thieving little bitch. Is it possible they could have made it?"

"Injun could do it," Wolf Mask said. "So can Wilson. He found a way, all right, and that's good. I figger he's in California. We go there and I find him."

Pete the Gun stared at his left hand, said nothing.

Once Tarrango had arrived in California via Joe Walker's pass at the southern extremity of the Sierra, proceeding northward to the goldfields, it did not take him long to locate the notorious Victoria Queen, newcomer to the area though she was. Word of The Queen's Lair had long since reached even the small valley town of Modesto, and, as fate would have it, a pair of Mexican vaqueros in the first saloon Tarrango entered had just returned from Murphys. More satisfied customers, Sam noted cynically, could hardly have been found.

From the vaqueros' description of Vikki's holdings, it seemed likely she'd already invested (or simply squandered) a good part of the money stolen from the bank in Pueblo. But that didn't matter. If she was doing well with her new enterprise, all the better. Once a cathouse was profitably established, personnel could be changed slightly, a few adjustments made, and no doubt the business could be sold, perhaps at quite a tidy profit.

About those other three women, in truth, Tarrango didn't care diddly-shit. In the final analysis, the girls had no doubt done nothing more than Vikki told them to. He'd have some of his men work them over, maybe with a leather belt so as not to leave really noticeable scars. Let the boys have fun with them for a while. But it was a simple fact of business that good hookers were hard to come by, and the girls were valuable property, just like horses.

Victoria Queen, however, was another matter. Either the thieving bitch was going to repay and beg his forgiveness, or he'd have Wolf Mask cut her heart out and pitch her body into one of these confounded flooding California rivers.

Tarrango plied the vaqueros with free drinks and elicited all the information he needed.

The following morning he set off for Murphys, arriving at his destination two days later. There was malice in his heart, but (he admitted to himself) he genuinely missed Vikki. She possessed imagination. She could do things to a man that turned him every way but loose.

In any case, the long, frustrating chase was just about over.

"You feel up to visiting a high-class whorehouse, old pal?" he asked Black Johnny. "Remember, now, if Vikki's got carpets inside, you make sure you've kicked the horse dung off your boots before—"

"Tarrango," Cortez muttered, "you're a genuine pain in the ass, you know that? Kick the shit off your own boots."

"Don't get moody, John. It's enough I have to put up with Addams. Must be something about you gunmen—uncouth to a man, no style. There's still some coin in this for you, old buddy, no matter what. I've always looked out for you. I treat you fair."

"Mebbe," Cortez scowled. "I guess I'd rather of took their scalps like you said in the first place."

Little Sister stepped into Victoria Queen's office and reported that a number of unwelcome visitors had just entered the establishment.

"Lonesome Dan still down at the jail, Miss Vikki. Maybe I better go fetch him?"

"Just what we need right now. Johnny Cortez is with Sam? The three of them didn't freeze in the mountains, at least, and I suppose that's been worrying me, though I'm not sure why. Sam Tarrango's a persistent man, but I didn't figure on this. Sister, you alert Blakemore to keep his two-barrel ready. Then slip out the side door, and don't be obvious about it. I'll see if I can handle Sam. He's probably pleased with himself for having found me, and he'll want to gloat for a while. Yes, get Dan."

"Okay, Miss Vikki. I'm wishin' Mr. Fiddlehead was here."

Then Little Sister was out the door.

Queen Vikki stood and walked to a full-length mirror. She applied a tiny bit more rouge to her cheeks, straightened her hair a bit, and then removed the sapphire pendant from around her throat, placing the jewel in the wall safe and spinning the tumblers.

She checked the two-shot Derringer she kept under the band of her full skirts, nodded into the mirror, and turned toward the doorway.

She stepped out, saw Tarrango, and walked directly to him.

"Hello, Sam. Nice of you to come visit, though it's

a long way from Jefferson Territory. Hello, Johnny. See you found your way down out of the mountains. Would you gentlemen like a drink?"

"Bitch," Cortez muttered.

"Of course she is, John." Tarrango grinned. "And that's why we were obliged to track her down. Well, Victoria, it looks like you did all right with the money you borrowed from me. Too bad I had other plans for the funds. Sure, let's have a drink. We've got things to talk about."

Vikki nodded to one of her new girls, then waited for Sam to pull out a chair for her. In a moment Jamie Blakemore brought a bottle and three glasses, set them down on the table. He'd already sized up Tarrango and was of the opinion that it would be no great trouble to throw the man out on his ear. He glanced at Vikki, but she merely winked at him and shook her head.

The miner-turned-barkeep glanced at Cortez, assessed greater difficulties with this individual, an then returned to the bar and his double-barreled twelve-gauge that was kept out of sight but ready in case of difficulties.

"I understand you and your friends ambushed my three buddies." Tarrango smiled. "Left them in a bad way, as a matter of fact. Now that wasn't very nice, Victoria, but you never were much of a lady, were you?"

"You sent Black Johnny and his two friends to murder the lot of us, in fact. Fiddlehead Wilson just turned the tables, that's all."

"Ah, yes. Mike McLafferty's old sidekick. Guess I owe Big Mike and Wilson a debt, and I'll be certain to pay them off. Where is Wilson, anyway? Hiding in one of the back rooms? Probably blind drunk by this time of the evening."

"Halfway back to the Ruby Mountains by now, I imagine. Why'd you decide to run me out of Pueblo, Sam? Another lady whose charms you found more appealing, I suppose. Yes, I took your money, but only after you'd cheated me out of what was mine by rights. If you wish to settle accounts in a decent, businesslike manner, why, I'm willing. The girls and I, we've got a good thing going here. Sam, I don't hold any grudges against you. We had some good times together—now isn't that true?"

Black Johnny listened, studied the expressions on the faces. Tarrango was clever, but he wondered if Vikki Queen wasn't more clever still.

"Want me to tell the boys they can come in now?" he asked Sam.

Tarrango downed his whiskey, poured another shot.

"Sure, sure, old buddy. It's been a long trail, and I imagine Addams and the other fellas would enjoy a little free humping. It's on the house, Vikki, am I right?"

Victoria Queen shook her head. "Not until things slow down. Nearly all my girls are occupied right now. I'll stand free drinks, though, if your men will behave themselves. All guns get checked at the door."

"So your employee told me," Tarrango replied. "In any case, I didn't suppose weapons would be necessary. Not yet, at least. You see, I'm unarmed."

"Well, I'm not, Sam," Vikki said. "Best you remember that."

"Sure thing. The little silver play-pretty I gave you. Glad you still have a use for it. John, tell our boys to come on in. I suppose it's a good night for a bit of clean fun. Keep Pete the Gun under control, now. I'm holding you responsible."

Black Johnny Cortez studied Tarrango's expression to see what hidden message, if any, was implied. Then, apprehending nothing, he rose and strode toward the swinging half doors.

"Alone at last," Vikki purred, smiling so that her dimples showed.

"Vikki, you bitch, I ought to let the boys have their fun with you for an afternoon and then hang you for the scheming little split-ass thief that you are. It's just that you're so goddamned good at what you do, and I don't have the heart to give you what you deserve. You said you wanted to talk business? Where the hell's my sapphire? Figured you'd be wearing it."

"Don't know what you're talking about, Sam. Now, listen. You've got a new lady, and I can accept that. But you stole my property, and nobody's going to cheat Victoria Queen and get away with it. You agree to my original asking price, and I'll start thinking about making a—what shall we call it? A refund."

Tarrango nodded, then placed a finger to his tongue and dabbed each of his eyebrows in turn.

"Don't be blowing smoke in my ear, darlin'. You're not talking to some idiot like Cortez. I want the damn sapphire, Vikki. And as for the asking price, as you call it, I figure it's been eaten up by the expense of tracking you down. Looks like you've done a good job of setting things up for me here, though. Maybe we can work something out."

Sheriff Lonesome Dan entered the establishment within a few minutes, Little Sister right behind him.

Sensing nothing particularly amiss, Dan sat down in a corner with one of his old mining cronies, ordered a drink, and began to talk about rumors of a new strike near Sheep Ranch.

Shortly thereafter Tarrango's crew also entered, while Vikki and Sam were still in the midst of their business conference, and within an hour the predictable thing happened.

The men got drunk, and Wolf Mask in particular became extremely belligerent, demanding repeatedly to know Fiddlehead's whereabouts, in the process telling all who'd listen what he intended to do to Wilson once he caught up with him.

The local miners and three or four merchants began to sense something was up, and tension between them and the newcomers escalated by way of two or three separate arguments.

Dan never saw who threw the first punch, but within moments the saloon area of the finest whorehouse in the Mother Lode was converted into the scene of a general free-form brawl, one that the sheriff's baritone voice was unable to quell but which a single blast from Jamie Blakemore's shotgun stopped instantly.

Dan ordered the newcomers out, Sam Tarrango included, and Vikki, greatly relieved that nothing more serious had occurred, called for a round of drinks on the house.

The furniture was not seriously damaged, and the fancy mirrors behind the bar were still intact. It took Blakemore and the girls only a few minutes to straighten things up.

"Mind filling me in?" Lonesome Dan asked as he picked up a last overturned chair.

"The one in the dude suit, that's Sam Tarrango, the honcho from Pueblo," Vikki replied. "I guess he's of the opinion that I owe him some money."

"He's tracked you clear across the country? Jesus, Miss Vikki, you rob him blind, or what?"

"Nothing I can be arrested for—at least I don't think so. But yes. It's a long story, Dan, and since you're the law, I'm not sure I should be telling you about it."

"Think you'd better, at that. As you say, I'm the law. And that means I'm obliged to follow a few rules. The miners expect it, and I wouldn't have taken the job unless—"

"True-blue Dan." Vikki smiled, her dimples showing once again. "All right, then, here's what happened."

Sam Tarrango, Black Johnny Cortez, and three or four more returned to their camp to the south of town. But Wolf Mask, Pete the Gun, Jack Addams, and several others remained for a time in Murphys, proceeding from one tent saloon to another, drinking as they went.

Pete in particular was in a foul mood. He didn't like being ordered out of Queen Vikki's cathouse at gunpoint and having, in effect, to beg for the return of his weapon. For a man with seven notches on the handle of his pistol, such treatment indicated a definite lack of respect, and he was of the opinion the world would be a much finer place if a half dozen or so of the citizens of Murphys, California, were laid to rest in the local boot hill. By all rights, chief among these should be the sheriff, but gunning that man down, even in a fair fight, would bring a great deal of trouble to Sam Tarrango and possibly cause Sam to remove him from the payroll.

It simply wasn't worth it, not at the moment.

"Let's go back to camp," Wolf Mask grumbled. "Bad whiskey. I got sour stomach, an' I can't keep my damned eyes open. What do the rest of you say?"

"I'm with you, Mask old fellow."

"Give 'er hell tomorrow."

"Wait an' see what Tarrango's got up his sleeve,"

Addams said. "Sam ain't going to take this lying down, no sir."

"Worthless bastards," Pete said, gargling up phlegm and spitting. "One more drink."

The proposal met with general agreement, even from Wolf Mask.

They filed along the street and entered Red Dog Tom's, where they learned of a Miwok Indian encampment just downstream from Murphys. Living in the encampment, several locals assured Tarrango's men, were a couple of squaws who would do anything at all for two bits a throw.

Pete the Gun nodded, signaled to his cohorts to follow him.

With makeshift torches they managed to stumble down to the Miwok encampment, only to find the small village's inhabitants asleep.

Addams kicked at the entryway to one of the brush lodges.

When an old man emerged, a rock in one hand, Pete drew his Colt and fired nearly point-blank into the Indian's face.

Miwoks poured out from the half dozen or so brush and board lodges, and Pete emptied his pistol, snapped in a spare cylinder, and continued the onslaught. Addams and the other men began to fire also, and even Wolf Mask entered into the game.

In less than a minute, more than a dozen Indians lay dead. One younger woman, perhaps in her mid-twenties, was spared long enough for the men to take turns with her, and then she, too, was dispatched.

The lodges were lit afire, and when yet a few more Indians struggled out, coughing and beating their way through flames, they were also gunned down.

Two young ones darted away into the woods, both from the same lodge, a brother and sister perhaps, both apparently just entering puberty. A hail of bullets followed them, but somehow, miraculously, they were not hit and managed to disappear into a darkness of willow, manzanita, and greasewood.

"Ain't as much fun as killing white men," Pete said, "but it was better than nothing. Ain't that right, Wolf Mask?"

"You just like killin'," the half-breed snorted. "Shit, I'm sick. Drunk too goddamn much."

He bent double and began to vomit.

"Too bad that one little cunt run off," Addams said. "Didn't get a real good look, but I figure she was a hell of a lot better than the one we gangbanged. Maybe we ought to go beat the bushes."

Pete finished reloading his pistol, thrust the weapon back into the holster.

"Always save one or two for next time, Addams," he said. "The problem is, not a one of 'em even had gumption to fight back. Just target practice, that's all. The sonofabitch sheriff's the one I want. I figure him for a dog with a badge—tin star an' no balls."

Now happy and feeling more or less fulfilled, Tarrango's men made their way back through town and toward their camp, though for most of the distance, Wolf Mask had to be helped along.

"Goddamn that Wilson, wherever he is," the Apache managed after yet another spasm of vomiting. "He owes me one."

Santa Maria de la Cruz y de la Rosa found two young Indians huddled behind the jail the following morning when she brought Lonesome Dan his breakfast, courtesy of The Queen's Lair.

She ushered the Miwoks into Dan's office, and it was then that the sheriff learned for the first time why it was that smoke had lain heavily in the night air past midnight.

"You're the one they call Stanislaus Bobby, aren't you?" the sheriff asked. "Yes, I've seen you in town often, running errands and such. Is this girl your sister or . . . ?"

"She is my sister. Her name is Toyon. Our mother and father were already dead, and now our grandmother is gone also. White men came to the village, and then they began to shoot everybody. They lit fire to our lodges."

"We hid and then ran away," Toyon said. "They were shooting at us, but we ran fast, and they didn't follow."

"Sam Tarrango's men." Santa Maria spat. "*Chinga tu madre!* They were the ones, Señor Lonesome. Someday I'm gonna keel that Sam, even if he is friend to Vikki."

"Bobby, did you recognize anyone? I mean, did you get a good look at them?"

Stanislaus Bobby shook his head.

"Couldn't see nothing," he replied, glancing at his sister, "but we heard their voices. Somebody named Adam. 'Nother called Pete. They killed everybody except us."

"Yes," Maria said, "they are the ones. That's Jack Addams and Pete the Gun. Probably Black Johnny and Wolf Mask with them—Tarrango's men."

"Pete the Gun, the stage robber? The guy who's supposed to have killed twenty men? Jesus, I heard about him way over in Fort Laramie when my wagon train stopped for supplies. Great God, you're not saying he was one of the bastards I ran out of the boardinghouse last night?"

Maria nodded.

"He's crazy man. He works for Tarrango, been

with him two, maybe three years now. *Es verdad.* I saw him shoot one drunk in Pueblo, a guy that was passed out. Pete told him to move, an' he didn't."

Lonesome Dan continued to ask questions for a time but acquired no further information in the process. His intuition that the situation in Murphys was about to blow up in his face heightened, and a specter of the possibility of having to face down Pete the Gun, man to man, further clouded his mind. In truth, Dan wasn't a gunman at all—an accidental sheriff, nothing more, and not equipped by either experience or by temperament for what was likely to occur.

He swallowed hard, stared at the three faces before him, and realized whatever was going to happen, fate had pinned a star to his chest, and that meant he was honor-bound to deal with matters as well as his wits would allow.

"Powder keg with a short fuse," Dan said to Maria. "Look, you take these two to Miss Vikki. Maybe she can put 'em to work doing something, anything, to keep 'em out of harm's way. When word of the massacre gets to that gang of Miwok men who've been working claims for Freitas and Hopewell over on Esperanza Creek, some whites are going to end up dead. If it happens, there's not an Indian within thirty miles who's going to be safe. Or maybe the boys'll come after Tarrango's bunch, and before it's over, Murphys itself will get burned to the ground."

17 Vikki told Little Sister to keep her revolver close at hand and the doors locked, neither Sam nor any of his men to be allowed inside until she returned. Then she proceeded directly to Lonesome Dan's office and demanded that the sheriff call a town meeting.

Word went out, and shortly before noon the curious began to assemble in the street outside the jail—miners not working that day, hangers-on, cardsharps, drifters, and even a few of the local businessmen.

Sam Tarrango also got the word, and he and his men showed up, having taken the precaution of bribing a half dozen locals to testify, as per instructions, should he have need of their doing so. He had guessed correctly what the occasion of the impromptu meeting was.

Dan called the group into some semblance or order and made a few brief prefatory remarks about what had happened in the Miwok encampment the night before. Then Victoria Queen, all of her girls present and Jamie Blakemore as well, stood up. Even dressed in modest gray, as at the present moment, Vikki was a striking woman, and the men of Murphys let out with a sustained and enthusiastic cheer.

During her brief stay in the gold mining town, Vikki had become an immediate favorite, indeed, one of the city's leading citizens. Some were of the opinion that the boys ought to elect her mayor, and only the fact that she was so obviously a woman prevented them from making the attempt. Even the businessmen, many of them her competitors, liked her. The few proper women in town, of course, spoke of Miss Queen as though she were the whore of Babylon, but these worthies were not invited to the town meeting.

Vikki spoke of murder and torture and rape in the Indian village, and the miners cheered her eloquence as well as her striking features and well-formed bosom. She pointed out that the Miwoks were held generally to be good workers and an asset to Murphys, and the townsmen cheered again. Then she demanded that those who'd committed the crimes be punished, and at this the crowd grew quiet.

"There's the man responsible!" Vikki said, taking one or two steps forward and pointing a finger directly at Tarrango.

An angry murmur swept through the gathered throng, and then silence. The men made assessment of Tarrango and his well-armed associates. Sam pushed forward, demanded to be heard. Once he had the attention of the crowd, he proceeded to inform them that Miss Victoria Queen was none other than the notorious Queen Vikki, wanted for bank robbery in Pueblo, Jefferson Territory. He and his men, Tarrango said, had trailed her across half a continent. Furthermore, he insisted, he held a federal warrant for the woman's arrest. As if in some way to back up his claim (but producing no warrant), Tarrango called forth his local 'witnesses,' and these gentlemen, each in turn, explained how they had gone to The Queen's Lair only to be shorn of their money, clubbed over the head, and tossed out into the street. Not only Vikki, but also Sunshine, Maria, and Little Sister were indicted.

The men of Murphys grew restive, shifting their glances from one principal to the other, then to Lonesome Dan, as if to take estimate as to where the lawman stood on the matters at hand.

"Hey, Vikki!" someone near the rear of the assembly shouted. "Take off the schoolmarm's getup an' show us your boobies!"

Laughter, sporadic at first and then general.

"Hang the fancy dude!" someone else shouted.

"Let's have a goddamn trial and then hang 'em! Whores ain't supposed to rob a man, not unless they give him a good ride first!"

"Where's Little Sister? I got some proud flesh that needs tending!"

"Let Maria show us that dance again!"

"Lock up the whole bunch of 'em!"

"Strip the whores bareass nekkid and hang 'em!"

"Tar an' feather the lot. Get the rich bastard first!"

"Vikki for governor, by Gawd!"

"Aw she-it, boys, let's go get drunk."

"Put the hoors in the hoosegaw! Mebbe they'll lower their prices!"

Lonesome Dan, perceiving correctly that the miners had lost interest in the issue at hand and that Tarrango's men were, in fact, looking forward to some gunplay, fired his revolver into the air and called for quiet.

"These are serious charges," Dan said slowly. "As of right now, Victoria Queen and her girls are under arrest."

With that, he nodded to Vikki and began to usher the women toward the door of the jailhouse. Inexplicably, the men cheered Lonesome Dan and then began to saunter off, some puzzled as to why a town meeting had been called in the first place, and nearly all certain Vikki and her girls would be released well before sundown so that evening entertainments at the former boardinghouse could take place as usual.

Dan had in mind only to calm the situation down and to protect the women in the process, but events took a bad turn. Sam Tarrango held court at Red Dog Tom's, buying free drinks and demanding that either the women should be hung for the lowlife thieves they were, or else that they should be hauled out of the jail and turned over to him so that he might escort them back to Jefferson Territory, where a trial would await them.

Tarrango received some unexpected assistance, for at the same time the proper women, who hated Queen Vikki and every other harlot in town, began to work on their husbands, making angry pronouncements and threats Lysistratan in nature, so that after a time, a number of businessmen came to heel, and a group of them marched to Lonesome Dan's office and insisted that a trial be held.

Word of "Hang the bitches high!" began to make its way around Murphys, and that was when Lonesome Dan knew for certain he had serious trouble. Not knowing to whom he might reasonably turn, he deputized Jamie Blakemore and ordered him to *ride for Angels Camp—tell Sheriff Dick Hager I need him and twenty armed men—need them now.*

Blakemore went in to confer with Vikki. "Dan says go get the sheriff in Angels Camp," he told her, "so that's what I'm going to do."

"Tell him to find Chauncy!" Sunshine said, pulling Vikki's muslin sleeve.

"You think he's still there?" Vikki asked.

"I know he is. He told me he'd come back to see me before he and McLafferty drove the cattle out across the desert. Chauncy always keeps his word. He can get us out of this, and I don't think any sheriff can. Those men outside want to kill us, Victoria!"

"Jamie," Vikki said, "you get the law, just like Dan says. But then keep riding. Wilson's this side of Stockton—crazy man with a herd of cattle. It won't be too hard to find him. He'll strike fear into Black Johnny and them, no matter what. And look. Take my horse and Sister's too. Put the Indian kids on them, get them out of town. If the boys decide to string us up, Stanislaus Bobby and Toyon won't be alive an hour afterward. Tell the new girls to open up for business as usual, just as though I were still there. Two drinks for one, and tell the ladies not to be standoffish. What do you say, Sister?"

"Things is bad, Vikki, but I figger you know best. We can't do nothin' much else."

Maria turned to Blakemore.

"Good, good, Señor Jamie. Don't just stand around, go get sheriff. Then you must *seguir su camino*, keep going, find Fiddlehead!"

Mike McLafferty had some extra money in pocket, and so he decided to select a few more animals on his own.

"Don't like the ones I done bought, is that it?"

"Great looking critters," Mike laughed. "Just want to get my own two bits worth in, that's all. Between us, Chauncy, we don't know the first thing about cattle. But maybe some of my errors in judgment will offset a few of yours."

Wilson snorted, tugged at his beard, and gazed toward the foothills.

"Wagh! Call me by that handle again, sonny, an' I'll be obliged to skulp ye an' skin ye too."

"Slip of the tongue, slip of the tongue. Don't be getting touchy in your old age. Anyhow, we can't start the drive yet. Like I told you, the Donner Trail's still probably under twenty feet or so of the white stuff, and the route I followed simply won't do for cows. We'll just relax for a few days and let the animals enjoy some spring grass. Even the Walker Trail looks to be an extra three hundred miles or more, and it's under snow too, for all we know. Some things just can't be hurried, and snow in the mountains is one of them."

"I'll tell ye about snow, all right. Way me an' the angels come, the peaks was higher than the clouds, an' the snow was coming down on our topknots. If it hadn't of been for a few tricks an old injun showed me back in '22, we'd of all gone beaver, by Gawd. Now '22, that was your real year for snow. Up in the Sangre de Cristos, pine an' tamarack alike got covered so deep, when spring finally come, the trees was all dead. Drowned, they was, for a fact. This child knows about snow, McLafferty, an' don't ye forget it."

Mike shrugged, lit a cigar, puffed.

"Now a real woodsman like me, he doesn't try to climb over the highest part of the mountains. You see, Chau . . . Fiddlehead, excuse me, the idea is that the lower the pass through the mountains, the less snow a man has to put up with. Where Gray Boy and I came across, there never was more than about two feet of the stuff."

"Got an extry?"

Mike apologized, pulled out another cigar.

"So how'd ye find this hyar low pass o' yourn, if ye don't mind my asking? If she's a good one, why we might open an emigrant trail, turn 'er into a toll road. We could by Gawd get rich, Michael, an' never have to dig fer it, nuther."

"An old injun showed me a secret route, naturally. Said something about playing tricks on you back in the Sangre de Cristos in '22."

Wilson spat into the fire, held his cigar in one hand, and used the other to rub his nose.

"Ye redhaired thief, that thar Injun died in '29. 'Fess up now, did I do a good job o' buying cattle, or not? Jest tell me, one way or the other."

"An excellent job, as a matter of fact. How'd you pick them out?"

Fiddlehead grinned. "Nothin' to 'er," he replied. "Jest figgered if the varmints was movin' about spry an' eatin' good, should be they was all right. It's that way with humans, so cows ought to be about the same."

McLafferty purchased a final group of thirty-one cattle from the Sanchez Rancho itself, good healthy animals with a lean and trailwise appearance. Thirty of the creatures were cows, but number thirty-one was something else—a huge and almost completely black longhorn bull, nearly six feet from curved horn tip to curved horn tip. He was cross-eyed, if that term could be applied to a bull, but beyond this one minor flaw, he was physical perfection itself, an animal whose corded muscles fairly rippled as he walked and became a veritable symphony during those unpredictable times when he chose to run.

Fiddlehead had already acquired eleven bulls in the process of making earlier purchases, and so McLafferty had no real need for a twelfth. But as he selected out from the Sanchez herds the animals he wanted, his attention had been drawn again and again to the big black longhorn, at the moment kept captive by the Sanchez vaqueros in a small corral constructed out of digger pine logs.

"Very hard to catch that one," a cowboy had grinned, "an' even harder to keep him penned. I say shoot son'bitch, but boss says no. Hell, he'd run the whole rancho if we didn't keep 'im penned most of time."

"Why's the corral fence so tall?" Mike had asked.

"Otherwise jump over. First pen was five-foot tall. Bastard jump right out."

"You sure he's not for sale?"

The vaquero had shrugged.

"Have him in the herd, you ain't never goin' to get across the mountains, not unless he want to go that way. Your cows, they all follow the big guy. He'll honey up to your lead cow, an' then she'll go wherever he says."

"Ask Sanchez if he's for sale."

The bull wasn't. Instead, Sanchez gave him to McLafferty.

"Just take old Enfadado Negro a long way from here—Sanchez he say you gotta promise that," the vaquero grinned from under the tasseled brim of his sombrero.

"That's his name?"

The cowboy nodded.

Enfadado Negro meant black anger, Mike knew. Cross-eyed bastard'll fill the Ruby Mountains for me with more of his kind—longhorn cattle capable of eating rocks if they have to.

To the vaquero's horror, McLafferty slipped into the corral and walked directly toward the huge bull. The animal stared at him and wagged immense horns back and forth.

"He kill you!" the hired man called out.

But Mike, on sheer intuition, walked straight to

the bull, reached out, held his hand for the monster to snuffle. Enfadado Negro snorted twice and then gazed mournfully off across the valley, as if anticipating a little canter over to the Coast Mountains, sixty miles distant.

"Tame as a puppy dog!" McLafferty laughed, momentarily turning his back on the animal. At that moment the bull stretched out its neck and gave Mike a gentle nudge, sending him sprawling faceforward. Then Enfadado Negro trotted to the corral gate and stood grinning.

So thirty-one head were added to the McLafferty herd, which now numbered 331.

"Ye had to find a gawddamned bull as was part grizzly, didn't ye?" Wilson demanded. "Hellfire, that one's half bone an' half bad nature."

"Yes," Mike laughed, "and the remaining seventy-five percent is cock and balls. Unless I miss my guess, the other bulls are going to have to stand and wait."

Mike and Fiddlehead watched as Enfadado Negro slithered his way toward the males already in the herd, studied each in turn, whipped his stringy tail back and forth, and finally bellowed three times.

The cows, for their part, stared at him, sniffed the air, and went back to cropping grass or chewing their cuds.

"Ye sure he ain't part elephant?" Fiddlehead asked as he poured Mike a cup of coffee.

McLafferty and Wilson were in the midst of branding their newly acquired cattle (excepting Enfadado Negro who, by means of staring with his skewed eye directly at the men, convinced them he really didn't need a double-M burned into his hide), and Fiddlehead was grumbling that he'd promised Sunshine

Hobson he'd make a final visit to Murphys, "Unless, o' course, ye're in a great hurry, sonny."

"Guess not," Mike shrugged. "Sure, I'll babysit the cattle for a couple of days. The way I see it, we're going to have to wait another month for the damned snows in the Sierra to melt out."

"Mebbe this child'll head up the hill, then, when we're finished hyar. Ye ain't of a mind to brand the big feller?"

"You figure he'd let us?"

Fiddlehead glanced at Enfadado Negro, contentedly battering his head against a small oak.

"Might get some whitewarsh an' paint a brand on the beast."

At that moment the friends looked up and saw three riders coming in, one of whom Wilson recognized as Jamie Blakemore, Queen Vikki's miner-turned-barkeep.

"Must of been readin' this coon hound's very thoughts." Fiddlehead grinned. "It's one o' Vikki's men. Don't know the others—looks like a couple injun kids."

McLafferty stood up. From the looks on the faces of the riders, Mike guessed, their visit was not entirely social.

"Wilson!" Blakemore called out. "Lonesome Dan's got the gals in jail, and the miners are talking about a hanging!"

Blakemore pulled his horse to a halt, and the young Indians did likewise.

"What in the name o' Satan ye talking' about, Jamie, in jail? What fer?"

"A dude named Tarrango showed up—maybe a dozen men with him. He claims Vikki robbed a bank."

Trouble in Murphys, and one of the hookers was Fiddlehead Wilson's Lady Fair, at least for the time being. Don

Quixote and Sancho Panza once again called upon to save the bacon, but how to do it? And how serious, after all, was the situation?

Mike managed to get Fiddlehead calmed down. Indeed, he'd never seen the mountain man quite so riled. Wilson agreed to spend a few minutes planning a strategy, but as McLafferty spoke with Blakemore and the Indian kids, the venerable mountain man was busy sharpening his skulpin' knife and checking his pistol and his buffalo rifle.

In the original version of the tale, McLafferty recalled, it was Quixote and not Panza who felt obliged to defend the honor of his beloved. But that, after all, was a book, a tale told in jest, and the present situation might well prove to be serious indeed. Given what Mike had already observed of the temperament of men of the goldfields, he could easily imagine them hanging four prostitutes for no deeper reason than the simple joy of doing it. A miner's life was difficult and tedious at best, and anything that might pass as excitement was relished. Hangovers went away eventually, and apparently the notion of moral guilt had been jettisoned somewhere back east along with family ties, communities, wives, and children.

So, Tarrango and sour-faced Addams and the boys had found their way to California after all and had tracked down the elusive Queen Vikki and somehow managed to get her and the girls clapped into jail. Furthermore, they faced the prospect of being hung.

Black Johnny Cortez, Pete the Gun, and Wolf Mask were also along for the ride, even though Fiddlehead had been of the opinion those three had frozen to death in high Sierra snows. Wilson had told Mike the story, complete with all manner of embellishments when McLafferty had first showed up at the Sanchez Rancho cattle camp. Bad pennies, it was noted, always turned up.

Jamie Blakemore, whom Wilson knew and trusted, seemed to have a genuine fondness for Victoria Queen and the other girls. At Vikki's urging, he and the two Miwoks had ridden to Angels Camp to alert Sheriff Dick Hager, sometimes known as "Whiskey Dick," and the latter promised to form a posse in the morning and ride directly to Murphys to help out Lonesome Dan. It was the law's responsibility, Hager insisted, to see to it that no one got hung before he (or she) was supposed to. Thereafter Blakemore came in search of Fiddlehead Wilson. Indeed, the man was apparently of the opinion, just as the women were, that their erstwhile guide to California, via the trail of snows, would somehow be able to pull a rabbit out of his beaver cap. That faith, McLafferty admitted to himself, was not altogether ill-founded. Fiddlehead had saved Mike's hide more than once.

McLafferty listened attentively as Blakemore recounted the doings, and then Stanislaus Bobby and Toyon gave their versions of the massacre that had precipitated the entire difficulty, having in the process deprived the two Indian children of their last connection to family.

Would either child, in the long run, be able to survive unprotected in a world of unprincipled and gold-hungry white men? Apparently Vikki had undertaken to provide the kids with refuge, an act of kindness that McLafferty fully appreciated, but under the circumstances, perhaps it was wise to conclude that Miss Victoria wasn't even fully able to fend for herself—at least not with a determined Sam Tarrango and his company of cutthroats on her trail.

Bobby, as Mike observed, was a big, strong boy of perhaps fifteen, not tall but thick-chested in the way of his people, and certain to grow into a considerable man if fate granted him the few years necessary to do it. In an odd way, Mike saw in the Miwok lad the very picture of himself at the same age, when Bill Sublette had provided him with a chance to venture up-country and experience for himself the mysterious realm of the Rocky Mountains, the High Shining.

Toyon, not much more than a year Bobby's junior, was a girl on the verge of young womanhood—slim and delicate-featured and, as Mike surmised, sadly wise beyond her years. She was nearly the same age as Moon Morning Star had been when he first saw her in a Cheyenne village and felt the lightning-like jolt of what turned out to be a consuming and enduring love.

Already McLafferty had a distinct feeling of inevitability. He could feel Moon's eyes upon him from somewhere back in the shadows along the creek.

The more the merrier, he laughed to himself. All I have to do is build another ten or twelve houses out at Ruby Dome.

Necessary arrangements were made.

Blakemore and the two young Miwoks, exhausted from a long and frenzied day on the trail, would remain with the cattle, catching some sleep and resting their horses. The next day Blakemore would approach the foreman of the Sanchez Rancho and, with luck, hire one of the vaqueros to ride out to tend the cattle in Mike's absence. Blakemore would then return to Murphys, while the Indian kids remained with the cattle to assist the vaquero and to stay out of harm's way.

McLafferty and Wilson rode by darkness, moonlight coming in gusts through running clouds. The night was warm and humid, and a storm was coming in, hopefully a rainstorm that would cut into the snowpack up high.

But right now other matters occupied the minds

of the two men as they passed through Copperopolis and on up through the hills toward Angels Camp. They pushed their animals relentlessly, and just after dawn they reached Murphys. A soft rain began to fall as they rode into town, halted, and tethered their mounts at a hitching rail.

Red Dog Tom's was already open, but the establishment was strangely empty, with only one other customer, a man with a broken leg. McLafferty ordered breakfast; a hand-lettered sign advertised "one egg, bowl of beans, cornbread smeared with drippings, cup of coffee, our modest price just $2.75 in coin or fines."

Mike and Fiddlehead ate quickly and secured some vital information from the waiter. There had been a trial the previous afternoon. No judge was present, but the men were insistent. A dozen miners declared themselves a jury and picked one of their own to preside. Lonesome Dan was allowed in the courtroom (saloon area of The Queen's Lair), but he was not permitted to speak, owing to the fact that he was known to be Victoria Queen's friend.

Nor was Sam Tarrango permitted to testify, on the grounds that he was a greenhorn what didn't know his ass from a hole in the ground. This latter ruling had nearly brought on an inside-the-house pistol fight, but since a hundred or so miners were present to Sam's eleven men, the gentleman from Pueblo had sat down and bade his cohorts do likewise.

The trial got underway, and three proper ladies of the town denounced the oldest profession and all who practice that sinful trade.

The men of Murphys booed loudly.

When Vikki asked to speak, she was cheered, but then the judge ruled that a criminal couldn't testify in her own behalf. A matter of English common law, he insisted.

A half dozen townsmen spoke at length and in detail about various sexual things the angels had done to them, and the proper women immediately left the courtroom.

Again the miners cheered. Sam Tarrango, the barkeep reported, had nearly laughed his head off.

At this point the jury decided it had reached a verdict: guilty of horse theft, the women were to be stripped naked and hung in order that the miners could all have a show, as soon as a proper gallows could get built.

Heated discussion followed as to when this happy event should occur, and at that point five mud-bedaubed miners entered the courtroom shouting that a big strike had been made at Sheep Ranch, *more Goddamn gold than ye've ever seen*, nuggets the size of melons. A mass exodus occurred immediately, and Lonesome Dan was able to escort the four angels back to his jail.

Tarrango didn't attempt to intervene. He and his men had headed off to Sheep Ranch with everyone else.

Mike and Fiddlehead paid for their meal and walked outside. The gray stallion and the mule were tethered in the rain, impatiently stamping their hooves in a growing mire.

Fifty yards down Main Street was the jail, and across the way, beneath an overhang in front of a plank-and-lath warehouse and clothing store, stood a swarthy individual in a battered sombrero. Mike and Fiddlehead both stared at the man and then glanced at each other.

Wolf Mask. Tarrango had sent him back to town to keep an eye on the jail.

18 "A fairly substantial jail, I'd say," McLafferty remarked, nodding. "Adobe walls, and probably two feet thick. Take a bit of blasting powder to break through, and chances are we'd end up killing the women. There's got to be some way, though. Well, whatever it is we're going to do, we ought to get it done while the town's practically deserted."

"What in blazes we goin' to do about him?" Fiddlehead asked, gesturing toward Wolf Mask.

"Let him stand there, I guess. At least he's not getting wet, my friend, and that's better than we're doing. Old *compañero*, I suggest we pay a visit to the ladies in the jailhouse. See how the stick's floating, as you're fond of putting it. Ignore the sonofabitch Apache."

Fiddlehead squinted toward Wolf Mask, tugged at his beard, and withdrew his Hawken from its sheath.

"You're not planning to shoot our friend, are you?"

"Wagh! Buffler gun's getting wet, that's all. Keep care o' your equipment, sonny, an' it'll take care o' you. Ain't sartin I feel good about showin' that make-believe Injun me back, though."

"In this version, we go around the windmills, not through them. Come along now, Fiddlehead."

237

"What ye babblin' about? Michael, they's time this child genuinely worries about ye."

They crossed the muddy street and angled toward the jail, both men keeping a sharp eye on Wolf Mask. They'd reached the boardwalk on the thoroughfare's far side when the Apache realized who they were.

"Fiddlehead Wilson! Turn around an' fight, you greasy old sonofabitch!"

McLafferty took a quick sidestep, placing himself between Wolf Mask and Fiddlehead. He stood there, leather jacket pulled open and gun hand hovering above his Colt Walker, staring across the street at Tarrango's man.

"You want to play games, Wolf Mask, then let's not waste time. Go for your weapon, if that's what's on your mind."

"My business ain't with you, McLafferty. What the hell you doing here, anyhow? Get out of the way, it's Wilson owes me."

"This child can fend fer hisself . . ." Fiddlehead protested, but Mike reached back and pushed the nose of the Hawken down.

"Draw," Mike said. "I haven't killed anyone in a week or so, and you're a good one to start with."

"Have it your way," the Apache growled, staring directly at Mike and fumbling for his pistol.

McLafferty's weapon leaped up as if by magic, and Wolf Mask, stunned to discover that Big Mike's reputation was more than a lot of hot air, closed his eyes, waited for a bolt of lead to strike him.

The shot didn't come.

"You going to draw or not? Come on, dog mask, I haven't got all day. You want a second chance? All right, what the hell?"

McLafferty slipped his pistol back into its holster and stood grinning.

Wolf Mask shook his head. "You fast, okay. Too damned fast for me. Pete the Gun, maybe he wants to try."

"Get the hell out of here, then. I don't want to see your ugly face again. Next time I'll ventilate you."

Wolf Mask blinked into the ever increasing rainfall, turned, bolted around the corner of the warehouse, and was gone.

"Now see what ye done," Fiddlehead muttered. "This child could of had 'im dead center. As is, we got to worry about him all over."

"Not until he quits running," Mike chuckled.

"Been meanin' to ast. How the hell ye do that, anyway? They a spring in the holster, or what?"

"Prestidigitation, nothing more. No sense standing here in the rain. Let's go make our visit."

Lonesome Dan recognized Wilson immediately and allowed the old-timer and his companion into the office.

"Dan, this hyar's Mike McLafferty. Guess that Angels Camp sheriff's on his way," Fiddlehead drawled. "Blakemore saw 'im yesterday, then come fetched us."

"Whiskey Dan Hager," Lonesome Dan nodded. "Well, he's taking his time. Fortunately, I don't have a lynch mob, not yet anyway. Everyone's off checking out a new gold strike."

"So we hear," McLafferty said. "And you're Dan. Fiddlehead's told me about you. Suppose we might speak with the ladies in private?"

Lonesome Dan shrugged, led Mike and Fiddlehead through the office's back door, down an extremely short corridor at the end of which was a heavy plank door, cross-bolted and with a metal grating set in place as a window.

"Chauncy!" Sunshine Hobson cried out, "I knew you'd come. Jamie Blakemore found you."

"Hello, honeydew," Wilson mumbled, glancing sideways at McLafferty and hoping Big Mike hadn't actually heard him. "Gawddamn it, gal, what ye doin' in the hoosegow? Blakemore told us what happened, but this porkeypine don't figger it."

"Michael McLafferty," Vikki said, smiling so that her dimples showed up even by the dim light inside the cell, "is that you? I see you make a career of rescuing damsels in distress. One way or another, that crazy bastard of a Sam Tarrango has managed to put the noose around all our necks, not just mine. Did you catch sight of him and his boys on the way in?"

"Us chickens, we all been plucked," Little Sister said. "Fiddlehead, think y'all can help us? This girl'd rather hang than stay shut up in jail."

"Perhaps we can work something out at that," Mike said. "I've got an idea."

"En que respectos?" Santa Maria asked. "Lonesome Dan, he won't let us free."

"What if ye promise to make tracks out o' Californy? Thought Lonesome Dan kind o' had a thing for Queen Vikki hyar."

"He's honor-bound," Vikki said. "My momma told me never to trust a man with that much honor. They turn you into a saint or Satan's own whore, one of the two. Mike, we've got to get out of here before those crazy miners come back. Those bastards are more dangerous than half a dozen Tarrangos. Friendly as hell and good customers to boot, then they turn on you. Crazy as shithouse rats, all of them."

"McLafferty pulled out a cigar, lit it, puffed.

"Just might work," he mused.

"Let me have one of your cigars while you're thinking things over, then." Victoria Queen smiled. "Condemned hookers have got some rights. All we were doing was trying to make an honest living. Convicted us of horse thieving, can you believe it? Not for bank robbing, but for pilfering *los caballos!* Crazy as drunk milk cows, I tell you."

Mike slipped his cigar to Vikki between the rails of the metal grate. He winked at her.

"Like I said, this Irishman's got an idea. I need help herding my longhorns back across the goddawful desert. Well, you girls just stay put for now and behave yourselves. Fiddlehead and I'll be back after a while."

"*Si*, we can do that," Santa Maria said. "*Soy simpatica con las vacas.* When I am a girl, I have worked with cattle many times. Little Sister, she has too."

"Can you really get us out of here, Chauncy?" Sunshine asked.

"Wagh! Me an' Big Mike, we can do 'er. Might take some fireworks, if he's thinkin' what this child is thinkin'. Spring ye tonight, by Gawd."

Sitting on their haunches in the rain, in a thicket of manzanita and wild lilac beyond the Murphys cemetery, two large black bears whined and growled, complaining softly as they awaited what they conceived as the proper moment to begin their nightly scavenging foray into town for the purpose of ingesting whatever edible refuse might have been tossed into small, neat heaps behind various buildings and tents.

Most black bears have a definite sense of propriety, and in this respect, the bears of Murphys were no different. While it was true they had once attempted a daylight raid, the result was very noisy, with much human screaming and cursing and guns going off. The pair decided, under the circumstances, that wisdom lay in turning their short tails to the rowdy humans and in launching themselves down Main Street as fast as their heavy, muscular legs would allow, which is to say, essentially as fast as a galloping horse.

Miners dived for cover, and ladies in full skirts shrieked and even swooned on the spot. However dangerous humans with guns were held to be, in this particular instance neither bear was wounded. Nevertheless, a lesson was learned. At a certain point about midnight, the town became more or less quiet, and lamps in most windows went out. Then and only then was it truly safe to waddle down and indulge on bacon rinds, spoiled meat of various sorts, beans that had been inadvertently burned in the cooking, egg shells, moldy bread, gummy leftover flapjack batter, and weevily flour.

Other animals understood the ritual as well— skunks, possums, raccoons, a couple of venturous coyotes, and of course the dogs of the town. None of these competitors, however, were of any great concern to the bears of Murphys.

Warm, misty rain continued to fall, and the air was rich with odors of manzanita and lilac blossom. The town was just about ready. The place had been unusually quiet for the past couple of days, and refuse was scant. But tonight perhaps the menu would be more varied and complete.

The bears stared at one another in darkness, first one and then the other sniffing wet air, rising to all fours, and shaking their fur in ungainly, waddling fashion.

The proper time had arrived.

Then something utterly inexplicable happened: a considerable fireball rose near the creek, and a moment or so later a tremendous explosion rippled through the night. It wasn't like lightning, but rather like a cloud that came up out of the earth, yellowish-red and scattering white streaks of flame all over everything.

The bears of Murphys were not harmed, for their waiting spot in the chaparral thickets was quite a distance from the creek, yet both the noise and the strange apparition of flame were frightening. And since black bears are both more curious and more timid than their cousins the grizzlies, as befits their somewhat smaller stature and also no doubt accounts for their greater numbers, these particular black bears, concluding quickly that they didn't truly wish to go into town on a rainy night, turned immediately and began to propel themselves toward the deepest depths of the forest.

Perhaps they would snuffle for mushrooms after all.

The explosion was too great a disturbance to ignore, and the male citizens of Murphys who had not struck out for Sheep Ranch in the wake of exciting news of a new gold strike lit lamps and pulled on boots.

Among these were Lonesome Dan, Sheriff Whiskey Dick Hager from Angels Camp, and a dozen deputy recruits he'd managed to impress into the service of law and order. The latter gentlemen were lodged comfortably within the confines of The Queen's Lair, where business had picked up dramatically after a two-day slack period, and where the local girls in Miss Vikki's employ finally drifted off to sleep in contemplation of earnings they would in all likelihood not have to share with the madame.

Jamie Blakemore was also awakened. He'd arrived back in town just before sundown, pleased to find Sheriff Hager and the deputies wandering the length of Main Street and puzzled to learn that though McLafferty and Wilson were in town that morning, they were presently nowhere to be found. After a brief visit with Miss Vikki at the jail, when she'd somewhat mysteriously given him a sealed envelope and instructions not to open it until after she and the girls had either broken out of jail or been duly hung as horse thieves, he'd returned to The Queen's Lair and opened the saloon for its evening trade, working steadily until things eventually began to quiet down for the night and the last of Hager's deputies had passed out.

Lamps were lit in windows up and down the thoroughfare, and in the aftermath of the big explosion, men with torches made their way to the site of the disturbance, the former Miwok village.

What they found was a great funeral pyre whose flames were consuming hitherto unattended bodies of slain Indians. The pyre, however, was not the apparent source of the explosion.

Lonesome Dan and Whiskey Dick walked about, Blakemore following a step or two behind, and after a time the men stopped before one of the burnt-out pits over which a brush lodge had once stood. Only now it was more the shape of a small crater in the earth.

The smell of nitrate was heavy in the air, emanating from the pit.

"Dan! Come take a look!"

The voice belonged to Jamie Blakemore.

Lonesome Dan and Whiskey Dick walked quickly toward Queen Vikki's barkeep.

Sprawled on the ground beneath a pine was Sam Tarrango's man, Wolf Mask, and close about him were some unused explosives. In his half-open fist was a short length of fuse wire.

"There's your man, by golly," Whiskey Dick asserted, "though what in heaven's name he was up to, I haven't the slightest notion. The fellow's obviously dead drunk, if not dead altogether, from a dose of excessive intoxication. Looks like you might have a case of promiscuous female boy-humpery on your hands, Daniel."

"A case of *what*?"

"Well, maybe not. Perhaps it's a matter of conspicuous and wasteful utilization of gunpowder."

"Haul his ass off to jail," Dan said to a couple of the deputies. "Wolf Mask. He's supposed to have been one of the men who was in on the massacre. Maybe his conscience got to him, and he came down to give the poor devils a proper burying. He was hanging around the jail until Mike McLafferty ran him off this morning."

Dick Hager momentarily removed his felt hat and stared out into darkness and rain. "Well, what are you charging the man with, Lonesome Dan?"

"I don't know exactly."

"Drunk in a public place and disturbing the peace."

"And performing burials without a license?"

"Now you're beginning to get the idea, by golly," Whiskey Dick laughed. "Just one thing that bothers me. If Wolf Mask here was this drunk, how'd he manage to pile up all that brush? And it must have taken a couple of gallons of coal oil to get the fire going in the midst of the rain. No empty containers around, booze or coal oil either one. Dan, I'd guess this just might be a setup of some sort. Consider the circumstances. Your suspect's just lying here with a section of fuse in his hand and a half-empty powder keg beside him. Could be we've got the wrong man. That fellow McLafferty, on the other hand, any reason he'd want to get your attention? I mean, set it up so you'd come traipsing out here in the middle of the night?"

Lonesome Dan stared at Whiskey Dick and then at Jamie Blakemore.

"Or Sam Tarrango . . . Maybe we'd best get on back to the jailhouse to check on the prisoners."

"Former prisoners perhaps," Hager said. "Daniel, I believe we've been gulled."

Lonesome Dan, in fact, was beginning to feel somewhat put upon. "Blakemore," he snapped, "was McLafferty or Fiddlehead Wilson either one at The Queen's Lair tonight? I haven't seen hide or hair of them since this morning."

"Haven't caught sight of either one since yesterday, sheriff. Me, I rode on down to Stockton after I talked with Sheriff Hager, spent the night. McLafferty and Fiddlehead, they headed up this direction."

"Surely we're not talking about McLafferty the Missouri River gambler and Fiddlehead Wilson who used to pal around with old Bill Williams, are we?" Hager asked.

"The very men," Blakemore replied. "Supposed to be partners in a cattle operation or something of the sort east of here, from what Wilson told me. But that's not the problem, damn it! It's Miss Vikki and her girls convicted of something they never even thought of doing and sitting down there in Dan's jailhouse, waiting for some gallows to get built! That's why I came to get you, Hager, so's to keep the ladies from being lynched. Dan here knows it ain't right, an' if he had any sense at all, he'd just turn them loose right now. The law's a fine thing, but not this kind of law."

"Has Mr. Blakemore got a valid point or not?" Hager asked, wiping rain from his face.

"Well, the ladies sure as hell didn't steal any horses that I know of," Lonesome Dan replied. "But Tarrango says he's got a warrant for them. Supposed to have robbed a bank in Pueblo, like I told you before."

"And that's why you're holding the girls?

"Partly, and partly for their own protection. If news from Sheep Ranch hadn't come in, I don't know what would have happened. Things were out of control, and the fellas around town had turned the trial into a regular travesty. That's why I sent Blakemore down to get you."

"Travesty, that's a good word. Always been fond of that one, by Jiminy. Well, let's get on back to the jail, Dan."

The men slung Wolf Mask, still completely unconscious, over the back of one of the horses and began to move upstream toward town.

When they arrived, they found the jail quiet. Too quiet. The single deputy who'd been left on guard was slumped over the desk, crashed cold, every bit as drunk as the prisoner they'd just brought in from the former Miwok encampment.

"The plot thickens," Whiskey Dick said. "We may have a virtual epidemic on our hands. Just how badly do you want to recapture your ladies of the evening, Dan?"

"Recapture?"

"Well, they sure as blazes aren't going to be in the

cell. I'd say that McLafferty fellow and his sidekick have sprung them slick as a Fourth of July whistle. You mentioned Tarrango, and certainly he's got a sufficient motive. But he wouldn't have left one of his own men lying out in the rain for you to haul into jail, now would he? So that eliminates him as a suspect."

"Jumping the gun," Dan countered. "Let's check the cell."

The two law officers opened the back door to the office and proceeded a few steps to the imprisonment area's impressively heavy cross-bolted gate, Blakemore following.

Still closed, still locked.

Dan grabbed the heavy ring from its appointed peg in the wall, fit key to lock, and threw open the door.

The angels were gone, but the cell was not entirely vacant. Lying in the middle of the floor, his fancy clothing somewhat mud-bespattered and his ruffled Spanish-style shirt reeking of alcohol, was an unconscious Sam Tarrango.

Lonesome Dan kneeled beside the man, cradled his head under one arm.

"Drunk as a spotted skunk, just like the other two," he said.

Dick Hager nodded.

"I'd say none of the boys exactly got this way on their own account. Had a little assistance with his drinking, or so one might presume."

"We've been foxed," Lonesome Dan snorted. "Damn my soul, I'm forever making the mistake of trusting people. Blakemore, are you in on this?"

The miner-turned-barkeep gestured helplessly. "Whole damned thing's a mystery, Dan. You were right outside while I was talking to Vikki this afternoon. Must have heard everything she said to me."

"What about that envelope she gave you?"

"Told me not to open it, so I didn't."

"Where is it?" Dick Hager asked. "Blakemore, you might be guilty of aiding and abetting. I want to see the damned envelope."

"It's over at the . . . boardinghouse," Blakemore replied. "I stuck it in the safe."

"Put on some coffee," Dan said to one of the deputies. "See if you can get somebody or another sobered up. Likely to die of alcohol poisoning, all three, if we can't bring them around. Sheriff Hager and I are going to accompany Mr. Blakemore to The Queen's Lair and find out what the mysterious letter's all about."

The first light of dawn was beginning to streak the eastern sky with flecks of crimson as the two lawmen and their companion entered the former boardinghouse. Blakemore opened Vikki's safe and was astonished to find it empty, except for the single sealed envelope she had placed in his trust the previous afternoon.

"Open it," Lonesome Dan ordered, a note of testiness in his voice.

Blakemore did as he was instructed, removed the folded sheet of paper, and read:

Murphys, California
May 8, 1850

I, Victoria Madeline Aschenhauser, more commonly known as Vikki Queen, being of sound mind and judgment but probably also dead from being hung, a miscarriage of justice if ever was one, and probably my associate known as Little Sister, a fully emancipated black woman, is also hung right along with me, do solemnly bequeath my full interest and ownership in and of the place of business known as The Queen's Lair to my good and faithful friend and associate, Jamie Blakemore. But if Little Sister somehow didn't get hung and is still alive, then she is to be a full partner with John Blakemore and fifty percent owner of the business, even if she can't legally own property according to what I understand of California law. John, you have been a faithful friend & I love you. Tell Lonesome Dan I don't hold no grudges & that I love him too, even though he's the stupid sonofabitch who got us all strung up, but he didn't mean to, and that's why I forgive him. No claims outstanding on the business, Jamie, and I hope you make a pile, and maybe that will compensate for everything you lost trying to strike it rich at the Bonnie & Prudence mine.

With love,
Vikki

Whiskey Dick studied the letter, glanced first at Blakemore and then at Lonesome Dan.

"Well, by golly," he mused, "I guess John here's the official new owner of a genuine fancy establishment, unless we can track the ladies down. Dan old fellow, you got any idea where we ought to head our posse?"

"Toward Stockton, I guess. Blakemore knows where the cow camp is."

"Reading between the lines of Miss Vikki's letter," Whiskey Dick said, "I'd guess they went the other direction. McLafferty's a gambler, smart as hell from what I hear. So you know very well he's not going to do the obvious thing. That cattle camp's nothing but a ploy. Wilson probably set things up down there for the very purpose of throwing us off the trail."

Lonesome Dan studied the expression on Hager's face.

Then he grinned.

"By golly, Sheriff," he replied, "I do believe you're right. In any case, your men are going to need a few hours of sleep and a good breakfast before we head out looking for the suspects. Let's go back to the jail and see if Sam Tarrango's come around yet. Perhaps he can shed some light on things."

"Elucidate matters under investigation, so to speak," Hager chuckled, "by golly."

19 Six riders made their way through the rainy night, pounding hell for leather (as well as darkness permitted) toward the valley town of Copperopolis. But at length the rain diminished to a thin drizzle, and stars began to appear overhead in irregular patterns. Moonlight broke through the cloud cover, and occasional drifts of light revealed the faces: McLafferty, Wilson, and the four angels, the women clad in ill-fitting men's clothing.

Midmorning brought them, exhausted, to the cattle camp above Sanchez Rancho, but there was, Mike and Fiddlehead insisted, no time to catch up on desperately needed sleep.

Stanislaus Bobby and Toyon, their round brown faces gleaming in warm sunlight between continuing spates of May showers, came running out, delighted to see Vikki and her girls once again, and behind them, obviously in complete control of all operations, trotted a huge black bull with massive horns.

The vaquero from the Sanchez spread was nowhere in sight, and Bobby said the man had gone back to the rancho for midday meal and siesta, and would return toward evening.

"Fair enough," McLafferty nodded, "but I'm afraid

I won't be able to stick around to pay the fellow. Ladies, the imposing gentleman with one slant eye—he's called Enfadado Negro, though his disposition's somewhat better than his name might suggest. Big guy, it looks like you're ready for a jaunt eastward at least. Got the rest of the herd whipped into shape, do you?"

Enfadado Negro snuffled at the air and then hesitantly approached Vikki and the girls, assessed the nature of these newcomers to his realm, whipped his tail back and forth, and began to chew some wet grass.

Mike took a scrap of white canvas, wrapped a ten-dollar gold piece inside it, and looped the cloth about a branch stub a couple of paces from the campfire.

"If the divvel don't see 'er," Fiddlehead snorted, "he's plumb blind an' cain't see besides."

"So," Victoria Queen said, "Big Mike drags us out of a nice cozy jail cell in the middle of the night and in a rainstorm to boot, makes us ride like hell until we're ready to fall off our horses, tries to intimidate us with a bull that's the size of a mountain, and now he wants us to herd his damned cows, monster and all, across the snowy mountains and the ungodly desert besides. The prospect of getting hung in the buff was better."

"Don' listen to Miz Vikki," Little Sister said. "What y'all want us to do, Mike McLafferty? Better we put distance between us an' them sonofabitch white men that thinks to kill us."

"All right, then," McLafferty yelled. "Let's get the pack mules loaded, vaqueros! We're on our way north to the Rio de las Plumas!"

The sky was blue, and the days grew warm, even

hot. In places the lush green grasses of the Central Valley were already turning to brown, a transformation that surprised even Fiddlehead.

But general forage was good as they moved northward up the valley of the Sacramento River to its confluence with a major tributary, the Feather River.

At a mining town called Oroville, McLafferty took on a load of supplies sufficient to see them through to their destination, and a rattletrap buckboard as well to serve as chuck wagon, one that he and Fiddlehead and Little Sister were required to spend several days repairing in order to make the vehicle trail worthy.

Once the task was finished, Maria announced that she would be the cook for the duration of the journey, since no one else in the company possessed even the skill of boiling water.

Wilson's hackles went up at this assertion, but in the final analysis, he was happy enough for Maria to take on the responsibility.

"All right, then, but who's goin' to drive the contrapshun? Tell me that?"

"I handle heem *esta bien, el dia entero,* and Vikki too *de vez en cuando.* Somebody got to do some work around here."

From Oroville they turned eastward, entering directly into a considerable canyon whose precipitous walls were sometimes heavily forested and at other times ragged with outcroppings of red-gray stone and spattered with oak and digger pine. The gorge narrowed and then widened by turns, with a large green stream of water gushing along at the base. A wagon trail, fortunately, was already in existence, and the cattle moved up it two and three abreast, sometimes meeting groups of miners traveling the opposite direction. The trail drive slowed to a stop when

Enfadado Negro chose to rest or crop grass and forged ahead when the huge bull could be persuaded to continue the journey.

It was just as the Sanchez vaquero had told Mike. Enfadado Negro singled out the lead cow, a speckled-faced animal not significantly different in appearance from a number of others but the one to which the animals seemed instinctively to look for guidance, almost as though they'd held an election. Through Specks, as Mike called her, the bull was able to control the movements of his herd, and when subordinate bulls chose to be balky or took it into their heads to wander away on their own, Black Anger himself, rounded them up by means of a few threatening horn movements and brought them back into line.

"That thar's the damnedest beast I ever see," Fiddlehead laughed after watching one performance. "It's positively contrary to the nature of the male of the species. He's as bad as old Lonesome Dan. Got a special thing for the idea of order, he has. Best ye stay on the critter's good side, sonny, or whar will ye be?"

They merged from the maze of canyons and entered into a high, rolling area of dense pine and fir forests interspersed with lush green meadows where a few drifts of snow remained in places, but none of these caused any difficulty in moving the cattle.

The four angels, Sunshine and Vikki included, quickly adapted to the day-long drudgery of keeping cattle moving. Maria proved an adept captain of the chuck wagon, and Stanislaus Bobby and Toyon, though they'd seldom ever ridden horses before they accompanied Blakemore down to the Sanchez Rancho, mastered the arts of horseback riding and cattle droving with astonishing alacrity, almost as though they'd been blessed with an instinct for working with longhorned bovines.

When camp was secured for the nights, Fiddlehead and Sunshine rode off together to hunt, since the thin blond girl was determined to assist the hunter as much as possible. Sometimes Little Sister accompanied them as well, but after a time she took to riding with McLafferty, perhaps feeling in the way, an unwanted third party.

"Them two havin' honeymoon kind of," she told Mike. "But they bringin' in venison, so it's okay. I'll stick with y'all, maybe learn somethin'."

Directly to the north rose a series of snow capped ragged formations crowned by a big dome-like peak, Mt. Lassen (just as McLafferty had surmised a month earlier), the identification made positive in advance of actually sighting the mountain when they passed through a settlement called American Valley. The proper name for the mountain, however, they learned from some friendly Maidu Indians living close by: It was Little Tehama, since the volcanic peak was formed at some distant point in the past after a much larger Tehama blew up in a "mighty explosion that ended our world and brought sky down to the ground." Certainly the landscape in the vicinity bore sufficient evidence of some major catastrophe. Great heaps of boulders, mud flows, denuded areas, and of course the probable fragmentary remains of a huge caldera surrounded the mountain itself, blown out fragmentary formations that were themselves significant peaks.

True or not, McLafferty concluded, it was a good story and seemed to fit in with the mute testimony of the land through which they rode.

Close by the mountain they reached the Lassen Emigrant Trail, crossed it, and moved ahead into near-desert lands beyond, then encountered the same big shallow lake McLafferty had passed on his way to California, Honey Lake by name, and then on down to Truckee Meadows and the more heavily traveled California Trail.

"Time to make a decision," Mike said to Fiddlehead and Vikki. "We can likely assume that Sam Tarrango's either following us or that he and his boys have managed to cross the mountains to the south of here. As little snow as we've run into, there's a very real chance he's made it across the Donner Pass or the Carson Trail.

"You're saying that Sam might be up ahead of us somewhere?" Vikki asked.

"Right. California Trail follows the Humboldt, and that's our obvious route. But we could be running into an ambush. After all that's happened, I suspect Tarrango's patience is wearing a bit thin. He and his outlaw band could simply bushwhack us and put us all under. I'm thinking—"

"Head for Carson Sink an' cross the Desatoyas to the Reese, o' course." Fiddlehead said. "Why didn't ye say so in the first place? Hellfire, that's purty much the way me an' the ladies come last winter. Shouldn't be no particular trouble with the cattle, not while Black Anger over thar's breaking' trail for us. Like catchin' perch with a gunny sack, that's what this child thinks. Wagh! Head south an' then east. We'll be back to Ruby Dome in no time a-tall!"

The journey continued without incident as they passed through desolate basin and range country—alkali flats, treeless rims, and relatively scarce water. But wherever a stream ran, desert grasses were luxuriant. The endless gray-green stretches of sage were blooming, and bees and butterflies of assorted kinds hovered in the air.

They crossed through the high pinyon forests of the Desatoyas and down to little Reese River at the foot of the Toiyabes. At this point a series of thunderstorms struck with torrential downpours, and while the cattle lowed mournfully in the rain and Mike, Fiddlehead, and Little Sister attempted to string up some sort of protection against the lightning-illuminated heavenly onslaught, the river began to rise, transforming itself from a shallow creek thirty foot wide into a torrent of foaming brown water.

"With all this hyar water, how come she's a desert? That's what this child wants to know."

"Bes' we move the herd, ain't it?" Little Sister asked. "What if the creek keeps on risin'?"

"Good point," Mike agreed. "Roust out all hands, then. There's high ground up ahead in the junipers."

They were obliged to move on foot, Vikki and Maria in one direction, Bobby and Toyon in another, Fiddlehead and Sunshine bringing up the rear. Mike and Little Sister moved into the herd itself and eventually found Enfadado Negro and Specks lying down amidst a thicket of sage, side by side.

"A fine pair of leaders you two are," McLafferty said. "Get up, damn it! Get up unless you're of a mind to go swimming for the rest of the night."

Enfadado thrust his nose into the night and bellowed.

"Cattle don' understand English," Little Sister said. "Give'm a kick."

"This one does," Mike insisted. *"Flood, damn it! All your cows are going to drown!"*

Slowly the huge bull got to his feet, skewed eye glinting balefully by lantern light. Then he nuzzled Specks along the flank, and she too rose.

Gales of rain driven on the wind poured down, but the McLafferty herd, snorting and stamping about and lowing disconsolately into blindingly wet darkness, moved grudgingly upslope toward juniper woods that were brought into clear outline each time lightning split through the sky and was followed by long, rolling waves of sound.

When they got the animals to higher ground, Bobby and Toyon were missing.

"The kids!" Mike shouted through driving rain. "They couldn't have got caught in the river."

Then he and Fiddlehead were both stumbling along back to the campsite, the four women straggling behind them.

And there they were, the horses and mules huddled about them, sitting side by side under the snapping and popping rigged tarp that had been attached to the side of the chuck wagon before all the excitement began.

Toyon laughed.

"White people don't have sense to come in out of the rain," she said.

The group spent a long and sleepless night, and Fiddlehead's mule made repeated attempts to get into the shelter, could apparently deduce no reason at all as to why the dry spot (such as it was) should be reserved for humans.

Then the rain stopped suddenly, and stars began to appear in desert sky. With the noise of the storm gone, Reese River could be heard plainly, sputtering and hissing, and small frogs and crickets began to sing in spontaneous praise of all things damp.

When McLafferty arose at dawn, the basin floor below them shone with countless pools of water, and the river, beginning to ebb now, was a quarter-mile-wide glistening sheet, parallel green bands of cottonwoods meandering through its middle.

"Cook!" Mike roared. "Let's get the damned breakfast going!"

"*Besa me culo, Señor McLafferty, por favor.*" Santa Maria de la Cruz y de la Rosa smiled sweetly.

And Gray Boy, chewing with evident distaste at fronds of sage, made a point of glaring in Mike's direction.

Weeks drifted by as the herd moved eastward from California's Central Valley. Now the drive crossed through a pass in the high Toiyabes and then along the base of Simpson Park Mountains, across an area where water and forage were scarce as the season moved relentlessly toward summer.

Fiddlehead and Sunshine Hobson, their love affair sustaining itself against all probability and all obstacles, spent much of their time searching for springs along the eastern face of the mountains and then returning to the herd to guide the animals to evening shelter.

Temperatures rose, and sweat soaked McLafferty's cambric shirt and collected in his bushy eyebrows. But he continued to push his irregular trail crew ahead to the point where he realized he'd become a virtual bully at times, driving onward sometimes well into darkness in order to achieve a few extra miles. The cattle themselves were becoming ever more balky, more difficult either to get moving or to control once they were on the trail.

There was a reason, of course, for McLafferty's behavior.

The time was drawing near for Moon to bear their child. Indeed, as Mike fully realized, it was possible that his wife had already delivered. The passage of nine months from a presumed moment of conception was not the easiest thing in the world to calculate.

Middle portions of the days proved intolerable, and it was necessary to rest the cattle with increasing frequency. Even Enfadado Negro seemed at times on the verge of abandoning his great responsibilities and simply walking away from the entire scheme in favor of leading Specks and a few other favorites toward green pastures and cool water his clear and intuitive ungulate intelligence told him must certainly exist somewhere up in those mountains they were traveling beneath, mountains whose presence he could sense if not see well.

"Sulphur Springs Range ahead, Michael me lad!" Wilson sang out. "Two or three more days, Gawd willin', an' we be thar!"

"It's been a long haul, and seventy miles still to go, give or take a few inches. Old-timer, we couldn't have done it without you. You've got a positive genius for finding water when it looks like the last frog pond in the world has already evaporated."

Wilson winked. "Experience, lad, experience. Once a skonk's been thirsty a time or two, he starts payin' heed to the signs. Besides, any fool can smell water from five mile off. Why do ye think the varmints don't always want to go the direction we head 'em in?"

They crossed a wide sage-dotted basin and proceeded directly toward some low hills at the southern reaches of the Sulphur Springs Range, a late afternoon traverse without water.

Trail of fine dust spewed up from the hooves of the cattle as the animals plodded listlessly ahead. Even Enfadado, thumping along beside Mike on Gray Boy, wore something of a glazed expression, as though he'd followed McLafferty against his better judgment one time too many and now almost certainly was fated to die of thirst.

But Wilson returned from his scouting venture with word that he'd found a marshy swamp area back up into the hills a mile or so.

Enfadado's ears perked up, and he held out his nose to sample the air.

"Sonofabitch bull understood what this child said, didn't he?"

"Figure that's possible?" Mike grinned. "Lead on to the gawddamned swamp, Mr. Wilson."

A pair of sandhill cranes, residents at the little oasis, flew off in great outrage, their long beaks snapping air. Frogs leaped wildly from mudbanks as cattle poured in, thrust blunt pink and gray noses into the water, drank happily, and then turned to graze upon sweet grass, sedges, tules, watercress, and anything else that was colored green.

Westward the sky blazed crimson and gold through a few bandings of cloud low to a ragged horizon defined by the peaks of the Simpsons, and bats and nighthawks streamed the darkening air in search of gnats, mosquitoes, mayflies, and other crepuscular insects.

Stanislaus Bobby and Toyon set a good fire to blazing, strangely welcome now even after the blinding heat of the desert through which they'd just passed, for nights were decidedly chilly on this high desert even as the year advanced into full summer.

Victoria Queen sat down next to Mike after dinner that night as he was cleaning and oiling his Colt Walker revolver.

The women had all taken the liberty of bathing, once again frightening off the pair of resentful sandhill cranes, and Mike noted Vikki was wearing both skirt and low-cut blouse, her large sapphire pendant set in gold dangling into cleavage that firelight seemed to heighten.

She smelled good, too—had apparently put on a dab of perfume—and when she smiled, her dimples showed.

"I've grown fond of you, Sir Galahad McLafferty," she said. "Too bad you're otherwise committed. We'd make a hell of a team, you and me."

"Don't be blowing smoke in my ear, Victoria," Mike laughed, staring momentarily into her dark eyes and at the same time trying to ignore the faint but altogether pleasing odor of perfume.

"You and me, Big Mike. The Queen of Hearts and the Ace of Spades. My California venture was a failure, though it needn't have been, wouldn't have been except for that sonofabitch of a Sam. The bastard doesn't know when he's whipped. So along he comes and spoils everything. But I'm shed of him now, at least I hope so, and I've still got enough money to get started over. Perhaps a nice, compact little operation east of the Rockies, close by Fort Laramie maybe, something the girls and I can handle all by ourselves. I'll change my name to Cherry Dell—less likelihood Tarrango'll ever track me down again. The way I see it, summer business will be terrific, with all the emigrants coming through and still with money in their pockets, and during the rest of the year, why, soldier boys aren't exactly noted for their celibacy."

"True enough," Mike said, staring across the firelight. Fiddlehead and Sunshine were sitting so close together it would have been impossible to slip a three of diamonds between them. "Sounds like an excellent plan to me, Vikki."

"Yes," she said, placing her hand on his leg just

above the knee and squeezing softly. "But I need a new partner, someone to work the card table and provide a definite edge for the house. There are a thousand ways to cheat at cards, Mike, and you probably know them all, don't you? And that's why you're so good at what you do."

"You want me for a partner? What are you babbling about, lady?"

Vikki winked. "That and maybe one or two other things. Nothing that would hog-tie you, though."

Mike grinned, spun the cylinder of his revolver, and stood up. "Another time and another place, how could I have resisted?" he said softly. "But the problem is this particular card thief's gone straight. When a man falls in love, that changes him. Gambling loses its appeal, if you see what I'm getting at. And right now my wife's about due to bring another McLafferty into the world. Mike McLafferty's turned family man, you might say."

Vikki laughed. "Got you, Big Mike. I understand what you're saying, even if I don't really understand it at all. When a girl sees a man she likes, she's a fool not to make her play. You and Moon. She's got a loyal husband, and I find that remarkable, know what I mean? I keep thinking I'll eventually find a man who feels that way about me."

"Might have to change your occupation if you do." Mike nodded.

"True enough, true enough. Lonesome Dan, now, he had possibilities, but then look what happened. Maybe it's my fate to be lonely and miserable all my life."

"Vikki, somehow I can't really imagine you ever being either one of those things."

Mike walked out among the cattle, squatted down

beside a resting Enfadado, patted the huge bull alongside the neck.

"Old fellow," he said, "we're almost there. It's a beautiful spot and grass that's knee-high even to a gent your size. Couple more days and we'll be there."

Enfadado Negro grunted, wheezed softly, and wagged his head back and forth.

"Careful with those horns of yours, you damned near knocked me silly. You're one hell of a bull, big guy, and I almost feel like I ought to build you your own bedroom complete with a silver-lined chest for hay and alfalfa. I've seemingly picked up a very large family during the past year, and I guess you're part of it. Sure you're not interested in wearing a saddle sometimes?"

"Michael, if ye got something on yore mind, why not palaver with someone as can talk back?"

McLafferty stood up, momentarily startled. For an instant he'd nearly been convinced that Enfadado had indeed spoken.

"Chauncy!"

"I ain't risin' to no worm on a hook, sonny. What's botherin' ye?"

"Bothering me? Oh, yeah. Guess I've got an intuition about Moon, like something's wrong. Could be it's time for the little one to come howling into the world, and I—"

"Ye wants to be thar, is that it?" Cheyenne gals, they don't have no trouble with birthing. Ye know that."

"That's true, true enough, but—"

"Mangy card-fannin' polecat, why don't ye hop on that gray horse o' yourn an' head over to Ruby Dome? Think me an' my crew cain't get the varmints home after we've made it this far? Wagh! Ye ain't got no faith in yore foreman a-tall. Besides, the way you've been the last week or so, it's worse than having a camp-robbin' griz with a toothache around. Hit the road, Michael. Look thar, a full moon's perched in the sky. This time tomorry an' ye'll be ridin' Leetle Jacques around on your neck an' pattin' yore wife's belly. That gal's probably missin' ye powerful."

20 Night was far advanced, the house utterly silent except for small sounds that Jacques or Elizabeth made in sleep, but Moon lay wakeful. Moonlight beat so hard against the split-hide window covering that light suffused the translucent surface, while crickets sang in raspy chirps outside. Far off a number of coyotes called back and forth to one another, the long quavering notes joining sometimes, rising one after the other, trailing off together.

Summer had come to Ruby Dome Ranch. Moon's pregnancy was approaching term, and each day that passed without word from McLafferty increased her uneasiness.

She tried turning onto her side, found that her big belly made the position uncomfortable, sighed, and rolled onto her back again.

Where are you, Red Coyote? she wondered. I do not like sleeping alone. I told you that if you weren't back before our child is born that I might go find Leg-in-the-water's village, but I will do as all foolish women do—just wait here until I am old, hoping.

She had grown exceedingly clumsy in this late part of her pregnancy, much more so than she remembered being with Jacques Little Bull, and it seemed to her that she was larger as well. She remembered a story the Cheyennes had told of a woman who married a buffalo chief disguised as a human male, only learning the true nature of her husband when she gave birth to a calf.

With the advent of warm weather, the Te-Moaks resumed sleeping at their village among the trees at the upper end of the meadows, the women spending days in gathering roots and berries and greens, the men using bows, poisoned arrows and spears to hunt rabbits and antelope and bighorns.

As Moon's time drew near, Tallchief had taken it upon himself to make sure she was well supplied with meat, for he had become by far the most productive hunter in the group now that his rifle was restored. He and Swimming Duck offered to stay nights with her in case she needed help, but Moon declined with thanks, assuring them that should anything happen, Elizabeth would carry the message to them immediately.

She was glad for the solitude, but would have been happier to share it with Michael John McLafferty.

The braying of a mule broke the moonlit quiet, the other two mules and Ghost taking up the cry. When they didn't settle down but kept on making a fuss, Moon pushed herself awkwardly up from bed, pulled a dress down over her shoulders, and padded to the door, lifting down a rifle from the wall as she passed.

Wolves, she thought, or possibly emigrants wandering off from the trail and looking for mischief. More likely nothing more than a skunk or porcupine, though. Horses and mules are excitable people.

She moved across the main room, dark and silent now—no bodies sprawled across the floor to avoid stepping on. She pushed open the front door, stood on the threshold looking across toward the corral, gun barrel poking out ahead of her, glinting in moonlight that spread across the meadow, touched yellow at raw, new wood of sheds and fences, glittered on cottonwood leaves moving in a faint wind. And then something emerged from the shadows beside the door, a human figure looming directly above her; she tried to swing the gun barrel around, but it was wrenched from her grasp at the same instant that she was caught around the neck, one hard hand covering her mouth before she could even think to cry out.

The man stank of sweat and dust, and he chuckled softly when she tried to kick backwards at him and claw his hands loose.

"Got one, Pete. How many you say are in here?"

She recognized the voice, tried for a long moment to place it.

Black Johnny Cortez, Tarrango's hireling. And Pete must be the scarfaced man who was with him, Pete the Gun.

"Just her and the redhaired kid and the whelp, best I can figure."

"Ugh. You think you can give me a hand here? Bitch is trying to take me apart, an' I can't get a hand free to—"

The second man stepped into the moonlight, held a pistol two inches from Moon's face, and aimed between her eyes.

"Just quiet down, lady. Black Johnny here can vouch that I *like* to kill people."

Moon stopped struggling, allowed herself to be pushed back inside the house. Pete the Gun struck a match on his boot sole, looked around until he found a tallow candle, lighted that.

"Now," he said, still holding his gun on Moon,

"where's the kid and the little redheaded bitch? They in there?"

Elizabeth, awakened by the commotion, stumbled through her own door, gasped when she saw the situation, tried to flee across the room. Jacques started to follow, then froze.

Cortez laughed, didn't move. When the girl reached the front door, another man was waiting to catch her and dragged her back in. Pete picked up the struggling Jacques with one hand, looked around, dropped him near Moon.

"Better keep the squirt close if you don't want him shot," the gunman said.

Moon placed a reassuring hand on her child's trembling shoulder.

"Please don't hurt them," she said. "I'll do whatever you want. What do you want with us? There's no one here. Those women you were chasing, they left months ago."

"Don't want nothin' from you," Cortez snickered. "Jest gonna keep you here nice and safe for a spell is all. Sam'll tell you whatever he feels like."

"Sam?" Moon asked. "Sam Tarrango? Is he here too?"

Black Johnny only grinned at her and addressed a blond boy, not more than eighteen or nineteen at the oldest, Moon thought. "Ben, you go tell Sam we've got 'em all rounded up. I figure me an' Pete can keep 'em under control till you get back."

Ben shoved Elizabeth into Cortez's arms, reaching out to pinch at her behind as he did so. Laughing idiotically, he left.

Pete the Gun stared at Moon with his blank, pale eyes, shrugged, and turned to study Elizabeth, now crouched on the bench beside Moon, licked his lips, grinned. He appeared to be about to speak when Sam Tarrango stepped through the door.

"Evening, ladies, young fellow." Tarrango removed his concho-laden hat as he entered. "I hope the boys here haven't been too rough on you. I warned them, but sometimes they're a little hard to control. Well, Miz McLafferty, pleasure to see you again. Got one in the oven, eh? Didn't realize it last time I was here. I imagine you're wondering what this is all about."

Tarrango explained at some length, taking pleasure in his own eloquence, punctuating his discourse with reassuring winks and nods to each of the three captives. Huddled beside Moon, Elizabeth listened, tried to focus on his voice, but she found herself unable to concentrate. The words seemed to settle on the surface of her mind, but underneath she was numb, uncomprehending. She gripped Jacques' hand tightly and sat hunched in white silence.

My mind won't work. What is he saying? Mike and Fiddlehead are all right, he saw them in California—that's important. They will be home soon. What does he want, do they want? It is like the other time's happening again—Bessie, Bessie Johnson, my friend, almost my older sister. She was pregnant, happy about the baby, about starting a new life in Oregon, in a new place. And then Laroque and his men . . .

She tried to force herself to concentrate on the matter at hand, to listen to Tarrango's oily voice going on, but visions of that other time rose before her, nearly blotting out consciousness.

Bessie screaming, begging, as Laroque and his men raped her repeatedly, tore at her like wild dogs, at last left her on the desert, something not even human anymore, battered beyond recognition, her belly torn open with a knife. And Bud Johnson and my brother—Sam, his name was Sam, too—doesn't seem right—both shot through the head and left out on the desert as well. And days, then, when I was alone among them, and they took me over and over, any of them who wanted to, and laughed when I tried to fight. I begged Jesus for death. And it's going to happen all over again. Dear God, don't let it happen again.

Tarrango was still speaking, his voice hearty, reassuring, but to one side of him Black Johnny Cortez was staring at Elizabeth, and when she looked up at him, he smiled, ran his tongue around the outside of his lips in an obscenely suggestive gesture.

Elizabeth turned away quickly, her stomach knotted.

"Yes, ma'am, Miz McLafferty," Tarrango was saying. "—Mind if I call you Moon? We're gonna be sharing close quarters for a few days, seems like we don't need all that formality."

Moon didn't reply, only stared at him coldly, and he laughed, shrugged.

"Whatever pleases you," he said. "I don't want to hurt you or those youngsters, no ma'am. This is strictly business. Hell, I'm not even mad at Vikki anymore. Probably won't even kill the bitch, unless I have to. Your husband and Wilson, they played me for a fool—kidnapped me and forced me to drink so damned much whiskey I was sick for days afterward, then left me locked up in a jail. Even that doesn't matter. No, I just want to know where Vikki is. I can't let her get away scot-free and with whatever's left of my fifty thou to boot, now can I? Where would I be if word got out: you can just rob old Sam Tarrango blind, he won't do anything about it? You see what I mean?"

Here he paused again for some response, but Moon merely continued to stare at him.

"You know, this would be easier if you'd act a little bit friendly. I told you nothing's gonna happen to you three."

He sounded genuinely hurt, and suddenly, inexplicably to Elizabeth, Moon started to laugh.

"You're holding us hostage, and you expect us to be friendly?" she asked. "Doesn't that strike you as asking a little too much?"

"Hell, no. Why if it was me—"

"If it were you, you'd understand perfectly well, I'm sure. Purely business, nothing personal, old buddy. If it were you."

Moon began to laugh again, couldn't seem to stop for some time.

"Have it your way, then." Tarrango shrugged. "Like I said, I don't want to get Big Mike riled at me. So what's going to happen for the next few days is we're just all gonna sit tight here and wait for him to show up. I'm in charge, of course, and you will not be free to come and go. But otherwise, I'll see to it that you're comfortable. That way when Big Mike comes waltzing along, we've got a little something to bargain with, if you see what I mean. You for the bitches, if they're still with him. If not, then I want to know where they've gone. Simple exchange. Vikki Queen's not worth anything to him."

"I don't think you understand my husband very well, Mr. Tarrango. He won't make any trade. He'll simply find a way to kill you."

"Could be you're right, Miz McLafferty, could very well be. I hope not, because I don't want to see you hurt, I really don't. You don't like me much right now, I know that, but what the hell? I like you. You get trimmed down after you have that baby, and my offer's still open. You can come work for me anytime. I'd set you up real pretty. You too, Red. You're just a kid, but then lots of men like it better that way."

Black Johnny grinned at Elizabeth again, and Pete

the Gun stared at her with vacant eyes, seeming both impersonal and ravenous at the same time somehow, like a wolf with its prey. She didn't move physically, but inside she shrank far, far back, safe in the dark, hidden deep within.

Tarrango supervised the arrangements for quarters, moving himself into the master bedroom and assigning Moon, Elizabeth, and Jacques to the smaller sleeping quarters with a man to guard them. Others of his men guarded the house and the trail, keeping watch for McLafferty's return.

Moon lay awake in Jacques' bed until dawn, hugging her son to her and trying to think, to plan.

Where are you now, Red Coyote? she thought. The little greasy one, Tarrango, says you're alive, you and Fiddlehead on your way home with the cattle. But you're going to run into Tarrango's trap. I've got to get away somehow, warn you. Tallchief and the others, they will see what is happening. Perhaps they can take word . . . if they find Red Coyote before one of Sam's wild dogs.

Wolf Mask, who'd been assigned to guard the three of them, sat in a chair grinning at her and showed no inclination to doze off.

With morning, Tarrango called Moon and Elizabeth out and ordered them to cook breakfast for the men. Moon went about the task grudgingly, wishing very much that she had some jimson weed or foxglove to add into the stew, but Elizabeth seemed to move mechanically, her face dead white and strangely absent.

She's remembering the other time, when Laroque and his filthy crew had her, Moon realized. Stay strong, Elizabeth. We'll find a way out.

She heard the sound of a shot outside, then some

shouting, and young Ben came rushing into the house, talking excitedly.

"They's injuns all over the damn place out there, Mr. Tarrango. I took a shot at one of 'em, but I didn't hit nothin'. They launched a half a dozen arrows down at us, then they just disappeared. Jack Addams, he went to look fer 'em."

"Shuckers," Tarrango said with contempt, waving his hand as if to brush away flies. "Nothing to worry about. They're no more account than the damned Diggers. Don't fool with 'em unless they do something. We've got more important things to worry about."

"Bastards get on your nerves, popping up and disappearing that way."

"Have something to eat and get back out there," Tarrango said. "And don't go off chasing the fool Shuckers again."

"Wasn't me chased 'em, it was Jack."

Addams came in, shaking his head.

"Slippery bastards. Cain't find so much as a track. Guess they won't be back, though. They don't like white men's guns; 'heap big thunderstick,' I'll guess."

"Doubtless. Now some of you boys get the hell back out there. Who's keeping watch, anyway?"

"I'd like to keep watch on this little redhead here." Cortez leered. "What's the harm, Sam? Just give me about ten minutes with her in the other room there. What do you say?"

"Back off, Johnny. Just remember who's buying your damned whiskey for you. When we get the whores back, you can have at any or all of 'em as much as you want, except Vikki, of course. But right now just keep a handle on yourself."

Cortez made a mocking bow and settled down on his haunches to eat, keeping his eyes fixed on Elizabeth until she became so nervous she dropped a bowl of stew and burst into tears.

As the day wore on, they settled into a kind of rhythm governed by taut nerves and bickering. The men lounged around the house or outside on watch, bored and wanting something to do. Tarrango increasingly had his hands full keeping them alert and out of fights with one another.

Moon watched the developments with interest, sure that as the men's tension and boredom increased, she would be able to find a way to escape. In a detached way, she almost felt sorry for dapper Sam trying to ride herd on his essentially anarchistic crew.

The Te-Moaks made several appearances outside rifle range, and each time Tarrango had difficulty restraining his men from riding off to hunt them down, this sport seeming considerably more attractive than the monotony of watching approaches to the ranch.

Just after sunset, however, while Cortez, Pete the Gun, and a couple of other men played a halfhearted game of poker and Elizabeth dozed in the back room, the Te-Moaks launched an attack, appearing out of nowhere and lobbing off numerous rounds of arrows before they vanished, only to reappear again from other directions and shoot again.

The men outside responded with a volley of rifle and pistol fire, and those within leaped up from the table and headed for the door, Tarrango following and shouting for them to come back, to get into some form of order.

A piercing scream sounded from the other room.

Moon ran to the door and pulled it open, found Cortez trying to pin Elizabeth to the bed, while she struggled to free herself. The man was laughing drunkenly and telling the girl, "Relax, damn it. You're gonna like this."

Moon looked about, picked up a large cast-iron skillet from the table, and brought it down upon Black Johnny's skull with as much force as she could.

He turned to look at her in surprise, then crumpled.

"Hurry, Elizabeth," Moon urged. "This is our chance. Run!"

The girl only stared at her, and for a moment Moon was afraid she didn't comprehend at all, that the whole ordeal had been too much for her. Then Elizabeth nodded, rose to her feet.

Jacques hung in the doorway behind Moon, utterly silent. Elizabeth picked him up on the way, and the three ran for the front door. Tarrango had come back in, however, and stood blocking Moon's way, pistol drawn.

She looked at him, saw him primarily as an obstacle. She still held the skillet in her hand, and she swung almost blindly, feeling the shock of impact as the implement took Tarrango across the face. He staggered back, and she ran past him, not waiting to see what effect the blow had.

Outside all was still confusion. The Te-Moaks were above, shrieking and calling as if there were twenty men instead of four, and the men below were milling about, popping off shots when a target appeared, trying to find shelter from the volleys of arrows launched in bursts.

Moon, Elizabeth and Jacques headed for the shelter of dense willow brush along the stream, crouching low as they ran across the clear space. It seemed a long way to cover. The man called Dewey saw them and set up a cry, but an arrow seemed magically to bloom from his throat, and the cry turned into a gurgle as he dropped, clinging to the shaft with both hands.

Moon pressed both hands against her heavy abdomen, partly in an instinctive gesture of protection and partly for support against the jouncing run.

This is not what a woman is supposed to be doing when she's eight-and-a-half months pregnant—no, nine months, she told herself. I'm sure Mud Turtle and the other Cheyenne midwives would not approve. Help me, One Above, if you are there. Only a few steps more. Hang on, little stranger in my belly.

"Forget about the goddamned Shuckers. Get the women!"

Tarrango's voice, pitched to a near-hysterical shriek. *I should have hit him harder.*

A bullet zinged against a rock close by, and a rifle boomed. Elizabeth screamed, stumbled, then plunged forward into the willows. Another shot followed, and then Tarrango's voice once again: "No, you blasted fools! Don't shoot them! They're no good to me if they're dead!"

Moon made it to cover, lurching through tangled brush into the water of the stream.

"Elizabeth!" she hissed. "Where are you? Are you hurt?"

"We're over here, Mother," said Jacques, parting branches and stepping into her arms.

"I'm all right," Elizabeth whispered. "The bullet must have shattered a rock. Some of the splinters hit my ankle. It frightened me, that's all. I'm not seriously injured."

"Let's go, then. Upstream. Try to get to Tallchief and the others."

In rapidly failing twilight, they stayed to the bed of the small creek, pushing their way through matted blackberries that nearly closed off passage, thorns tearing their clothing and skin. Jacques clambered along behind Elizabeth on his own, not offering so much as a whimper.

They heard continued sounds of pursuit.

"Cut 'em off. They'll be heading up toward the Shuckers."

"Like hell! I ain't goin' up there."

The thunderous roar of a rifle discharged within a few yards of Moon froze her, heart racing. A drawn-out scream sounded from below, the cry dropping to rhythmic groans, another voice shouting over it: "Shit! The fuckin' injuns have got guns! That's it, Tarrango. You want McLafferty's bitches, you go after them yourself!"

"You worthless scum! Not a single set of balls among the goddamn lot. All right, there's a thousand bucks for the one that catches the breed bitch, five hundred apiece for the redhead and the cub."

While Tarrango continued haranguing his crew and the wounded man persisted in his keening, Tallchief emerged from the brush on the far side of the stream, holding his still smoking flintlock in one hand and grinning.

"You make as much noise as bull moose thrashing around in dry bear clover," he whispered, and gestured for them to follow him.

They emerged from the willow tangle on the far side and kept low, in a few moments joining Antelope Tail, Slow Lizard, and Old Smoke at the edge of a stand of firs. By now darkness was nearly upon them, but a full moon was already topping ridges to the east.

They moved north through cover of trees, emerging among craggy stone formations, keeping to shadows in the bright moonlight, although a quick survey by Antelope could discover no sign of their trackers.

"We're not going toward your village," Moon observed. "What about your women and children?"

"Nobody home," Tallchief chuckled. "Owl-faces never find 'em where they are now. Where we're going."

"No," Moon insisted. "I've got to find Mac-lafferty. You take Elizabeth and Jacques to Swimming Duck and the others. I'll go on alone."

"Crazy woman," Smoke muttered. "How you find your man? Way out there toward Big Water. Lots of desert, and you big with baby."

"I'm going, though. It's time for my husband to return. I will find him. Mike showed me his map—like a picture of the land between here and California. And I know he left that place before Sam Tarrango and his people did, so Mike could not have followed the main emigrant road, even though that would have been the best way to bring the cattle. He and Fiddlehead knew Tarrango would follow, so they came a different way, probably the same route Fiddlehead and the women took last winter. Across the basin and then to the south of Sulphur Springs Mountains, where your old village was."

"Big desert beyond those mountains," Tallchief said, "and not much water. Don't cattle need water? Sure they do. Well, there's water okay, but white men can't find it."

Moon stared at him.

"Okay, maybe Mike Mac-lafferty can find it. How fast can cows move? McLoughlin's cows, they never moved at all unless they was hungry."

Moon shrugged. "I know what I'm doing," she said. "At least I think I do. Tallchief, do you suppose you could slip back down and get my horse? I'm certainly in no condition to be walking across the desert, but I'm positive Mike and his friend Fiddlehead are out there, and not very far, either."

"Not in condition to be riding, either," Tallchief replied. "You're a crazy woman, Moon."

"I caught up with you, didn't I, when you kidnapped my son?"

"This is different problem." Tallchief scowled.

"I can do this thing," Slow Lizard said quickly, glancing at Elizabeth. "I can get Moon's horse for her. I'm very good at hiding, and very fast, too."

Antelope Tail considered for a moment and then gestured for his son to go ahead. As the boy disappeared into the shadows, Tallchief led the others back up into an inconspicuous arroyo.

"But he's only a child," Elizabeth protested. "Aren't you afraid?"

"Like he said, he's good at hiding," Tallchief shrugged. "Boys got to be men in a hurry, this country. Besides, Liz-beth, he don't want you thinkin' of him as little child. You ain't noticed?"

As soon as the others were safely secreted away, however, Antelope Tail himself slipped inconspicuously into the darkness, returning shortly before Slow Lizard. The father was grinning from ear to ear, for his son was leading not only Ghost into the arroyo but one of the pack mules as well.

Moon kissed Jacques and hugged Elizabeth. Then, with the help of Tallchief, she hoisted her bulk up onto Ghost. Of necessity, she was obliged to ride bareback, just as she had as a girl.

"I'm coming with you," Elizabeth said. "I'll ride the mule."

"Not this time, pretty one. I need you to stay with Jacques, to take him to Swimming Duck. He'll be happier if you're with him."

"I want to go with you too, Mother," Jacques protested. "If Slow Lizard would give me his bow, I could shoot the bad men."

"The bad men will not catch me, Little Bull. I'm only going to find Red Coyote so that he can help us. You must stay with Tallchief and Swimming Duck. They will need your help."

"But—"

"Hush now. The bad men will hear you and find us all. Elizabeth . . ."

The girl nodded, took Jacques' hand.

Tallchief, however, could not be dissuaded, arguing that he knew all the land to the west, and as Moon turned Ghost to ride down out of the arroyo, the bandy-legged Te-Moak warrior flung himself onto the pack mule's back. The animal, feeling such an assault was clearly a violation of his contract with humans, shook himself violently, flinging Tallchief immediately to the ground.

Moon, growing impatient with the delays, touched her heels to Ghost and moved away.

"I'll be along right behind you," Tallchief assured her as he prepared to attack his long-eared problem again.

Moon worked her way down to the desert floor, then urged Ghost into a canter across moon-washed flats along the South Fork. She abandoned caution in the need to hurry, to find McLafferty at all costs, riding in the full glare of moonlight and visible to any observer within miles. She told herself that any pursuers were still in the mountains, not looking for her out here, and so far back that they were unlikely to catch her even if they should happen to note a moving shadow on the desert floor.

Red Coyote, where are you? her mind cried. Smoke on the Hill was right, it's a very large desert. But a herd of cattle, that's also large, hard to hide. I will find you, have to find you now. I know you're out here somewhere, I can feel it.

For the moment, Moon could only think to push Ghost westward. After a time she was forced to slow her pace, however, for the horse's breathing was growing labored, and her own body as well ached fiercely, stabbing pains in her abdomen warning her that what she was doing posed a severe danger to her unborn child.

I must be careful, she realized. He will not forgive me if . . .

21 Neither Moon nor Ghost could go farther without rest, and she guided her mount into a draw where a small, muddy seep of water provided both of them with a mouthful or two. She lay with her back propped against a stone and closed her eyes for a moment, almost immediately dozed off. Ghost awoke her by snorting, and she looked up to see a figure outlined above her against sky that was now growing pale with dawn.

She sat up, her heart racing, tried to withdraw into shadows, searched the ground frantically for a large stone.

"Goddamn mule," the intruder said, moving down into the draw beside her as she sucked in a breath of relief. It was, of course, Tallchief.

"Had to let the son'bitch go back at the edge of the big flat. Got him that far by pounding on his head, but he won't go no farther. Just says, 'Go ahead and beat me to death, you two-leg fatherless dog. I'm going home.' You okay, Moon? Not so good for that baby, what you doing."

"I'm all right, Tallchief. I'm happy to see you, but I didn't mean to stay here this long. I've got to go. It's nearly morning"

"You're right. I seen all them owl-faces startin' out from the mountains. You made plenty tracks—not hard even for them to follow. Why don't we find you place to hide out around here, then I go ahead and look for Mike and his bunch of little buffalo?"

Moon shook her head, pushed herself from the ground, and approached Ghost, who rolled his eyes wearily.

"Help me into the saddle, Tallchief. I don't know how I'd have gotten mounted without you."

Ghost refused to go faster than a brisk trot, and Tallchief was able to keep pace, jogging along behind through the growing heat of morning, the Te-Moak apparently tireless—a characteristic he shared, as she and Mike had discovered the previous winter, with all the Shucker men.

The band in pursuit, however, continued to close on them. Tallchief urged Moon to caution.

"Better stick to little hills wherever we can find 'em. Hide in gullies, travel where there's rocks, not sand. Got to outsmart 'em, Moon. Maybe if I hide—shoot, kill somebody—then maybe they stop for little bit, give you time to get away."

"Then they'd shoot you, Tallchief."

The Te-Moak said nothing as he ran beside her, his short legs pumping in sure and certain rhythm.

"The mountains—if we can make it that far, then perhaps—"

"We can hide good. I know all them places. They never find us up there."

Moon agreed to this strategy, but when they rested briefly and Tallchief crept onto a rise, he reported that the gang of men on horseback had gained alarmingly.

"Somethin' else, though," the Te-Moak said. "One rider way off to southwest. Guy on a big gray horse looks like, comin' this direction. Could be Mac-laffty, but he's alone, Moon. No little buffalo, no nothin'. Coming like a whole herd of grizzlies was after him, though. Maybe another of them owl-faces, too. What we doin' here? Like poor damn jackrabbits with whole bunch of wolves after them."

"That's Red Coyote," Moon said joyfully, "it's got to be! He wants to get home before our child comes. Fiddlehead must be back on the desert somewhere with our cattle."

"You don't know such a thing," Tallchief cautioned, "just want it to be."

But Moon paid no attention to him and pounded Ghost's ribs with such insistence that the tired horse grudgingly moved into a slow gallop, leaving the Te-Moak struggling along behind. She rode recklessly, taking no further thought to concealment. She could see, from occasional higher points she crossed, the plume of dust thrown up by Tarrango's men not more than a mile behind her, but she was now keeping almost a steady distance ahead of them, and she also spotted dust from the solitary rider approaching across the featureless sage flats at the base of Sulphur Springs Range.

She looked back over her shoulder and saw Tarrango's men but no Tallchief. The Te-Moak had taken cover somewhere.

She urged Ghost to even more heroic efforts, clinging to his mane and shouting words of encouragement and love into his ear, turned him directly toward the oncoming solitary horseman. Heat waves rose from the desert floor, refractions of light in rising currents of air distorting everything, causing the rider ahead of her to vanish and then reappear. Glaring sunlight and hot air rushed past her face—small sticky fingers tugging at her long hair, almost like

Jacques when he had been eating that candy Fiddlehead brought him at Christmas.

Then a sound, an echoing rattle, almost as if there were thunder that was not very loud.

The flintlock! she recognized. Tallchief's rifle—he's lain in ambush somewhere, waited until Tarrango's men drew close. Then other reports, pistol shots, how many? And afterward silence, not silence but only rhythmic thumpings of Ghost's hooves as they dug into gray-white alkaline sand. He was dead . . . Tallchief . . . Sam Tarrango's men killed him.

One rider fled while a gang of men came on in pursuit, but at first the significance of this configuration didn't hit him. Then suddenly he knew—not McLafferty's luck this time, but simple unsubstantiated intuition, pinpoint accurate. Tarrango and company had indeed given chase, had made it across the Donner Pass and no doubt on to the Humboldt, presuming Vikki was still with him and thinking to overtake the cattle drive somewhere along the way. Sam was no fool. He'd doubtless asked questions of everyone around and had probably picked up information concerning Fiddlehead's camp on the Sanchez Rancho. Since a herd of cattle was not likely to pass by unnoticed, Tarrango most likely found out they'd gone northward and so he had taken the more direct route across Donner. And when that plan didn't work out, Sam proceeded to Ruby Dome to await their arrival.

It was Moon on the horse!

She's already had our child, then.

But something about the way the lead rider carried himself, once he'd drawn to within a quarter mile of her, told him otherwise. "Shee-it in heaven! She's pregnant. She's going to kill herself."

The two horses came together, and the riders drew up.

"Tarrango . . ." Moon said. "I knew you were out here, Red Coyote. I came to find you!"

"What in Gawd's name?"

But there was no time for conversation, and Mike drew Gray Boy about, motioned toward a tower of slabbed-off boulders at the base of the hills, and yelled, "Get up there, damn it, we've got no time to discuss the matter."

Tarrango and his gang were coming on.

Ghost responded to the presence of his old trail companion Gray Boy, and the two horses ran as they were bid, side by side nearly in the manner of a matched team.

At the foot of the rocky formation ahead, Mike leaped to his feet, grabbed for Ghost's reins, and led his horse and Moon's as well up a steep slide area of decomposed granite toward a fringe of deformed junipers, their boughs overreaching boulders on the domed summit of the tower. McLafferty tethered the horses immediately and helped Moon down from the saddle, drew her into his arms. She was crying softly, a fact that somehow amazed him even under these insane circumstances.

"We got to stop meeting like this, Mrs. M. What kind of hell have you embroiled us in now?"

"Be quiet, Red Coyote," she insisted, flinging her arms about him and locking him in a bear hug, her mouth searching for his.

"That bastard of a Sam Tarrango," she said, "his men took us prisoner, Mike, and—"

"Naturally you rode off into the desert with the whole gawddamned rat pack of them chasing you. Jacques and Bethy?"

"Safe . . . with the Te-Moaks. Tallchief's dead,

though. Tarrango killed him back there. He was with me, on foot, and then . . ."

McLafferty nodded, his lips tight.

"Where's Fiddlehead?" Moon asked. "And the cows you went to buy? What happened, Mike?"

"Southwest of here. I came on ahead. Explain the whole thing when we've got leisure. Grab one of the rifles. Jesus Christ, Moon-Gal, you're not planning to give birth in the middle of a gunfight, are you?"

McLafferty flung himself down beside the gnarled trunk of a juniper, checked the load in his New Haven Whitney, set firing hammer, fit a cap into place, took aim, and squeezed off a round. One rider spun from the saddle. His horse bolted, and the man, foot hooked in a stirrup, was dragged screaming back toward the floor of the basin.

"McLafferty? You crazy sonofabitch, stop shooting! This is Tarrango. I want to come up and talk. What in hell did you do with Vikki Queen?"

"I recognize you, old buddy. How's your hangover? Come on up, Sam! Makes my shot a lot easier."

"You bastard! I just want my woman, can't you understand that? Where the hell is she?"

"Right. You got her thrown into jail and sentenced to be hung, and then you went running off because some damned fool found gold. Next you take off after us and can't find us, so you hotfoot it on over to terrorize my wife. Tarrango, you've got no sense of decency at all. Everything's just a damned game you figure you can win by throwing your money around. Come on up here, by God, and I'll drive an oaken stake through your heart—if I can find one, and if you've got one. There's nothing this coon would like better!"

"You're pinned down, McLafferty. You haven't got the chance of a snowball in hell, get right down to it. If you want to see what your kid looks like alive, old buddy, you'd best think things over. I want straight information, not a damned thing more. Tell me what I need to know, and you and your squaw can saunter home. Lead me to Vikki Queen, and it's worth a thousand dollars to me. Buy your wife some *foofuraw*, isn't that what you call it?"

Mike glanced at Moon. He saw in her eyes that same almost demonic determination as when they, a year earlier, had relentlessly tracked down Jean Laroque, as when he and she had trailed Tallchief and his Shuckers through a world of snow in order to retrieve Jacques White Bull.

"Moon says she's not interested, Sam. Vikki and the girls took off for San Francisco right after Fiddlehead and I busted 'em out of the Murphys jail and stuck you in their place. Use your head, man. Victoria's in Frisco, doing what she's always done. Probably owns the whole damned city by now. Moon and I, we just want to mind our own business and be left alone. Go on back to Pueblo and tend to your hotels and such. Stay away much longer, and some other thief'll take over, just the way you did."

"San Francisco, huh? Why is it I don't believe you, Big Mike?"

"Damned fools wouldn't believe Jesus, either. Take my word for it, Sam. The advice is free. Head back to Pueblo while you've still got reason."

Tarrango was quiet for a long moment.

"If she's in San Francisco, then you wouldn't be acting so all-fired hostile, McLafferty. They're back out on the desert, aren't they? You rode ahead to make certain I wasn't at your shack waiting for you."

"Hoping you would be, actually. Fiddlehead says Pete the Gun's ready to find out the hard way about which one of us can pull iron the fastest. Tell you what, send Pete up here right now, and we'll settle the issue."

"Sonofabitch bastard!" Pete yelled out. "Ain't no dude gambler ever lived that I cain't outdraw!"

McLafferty laughed. "Could be, could be. Hell, I sprained my wrist climbing the rocks. Be easy shooting for you, Peter horsepizzle!"

"You killed Tallchief!" Moon shouted and then discharged her rifle at Sam Tarrango.

The Pueblo businessman saw her rise, and at that moment he leaped for cover, yet not quite soon enough. The fire ball struck him in the calf, and he screamed.

With that, a fusilade of pistol fire was directed toward the juniper-shrouded boulders where Mike and Moon had taken cover.

"Addams!" Tarrango's voice drifted up the slope. "Goddamn it, Jack, where are you? Help me, man. Get that bastard of a card thief down here and cut off one of his fingers at a time until he tells us where Vikki is."

The talking stage was over.

Desert sun poured down relentlessly throughout the afternoon, and Mike and Moon, ever watchful of those below them, drank warm water from McLafferty's canteen and waited. Their only real hope, they knew well enough, lay with moonlit darkness and their capacity to remain sufficiently alert to take advantage of whatever slight help the night might provide.

Most of the men below were sacked out, taking turns at the watch, waiting them out.

"Fiddlehead should be along tomorrow, unless some of the animals stray. If we can hold out that long, then perhaps ... The angels are with him and a couple of Indian kids as well. Sort of picked them up in California. Tarrango's butchers wiped out their village, and Vikki gave them protection. After she got tossed into jail, she sent her barkeep and the Indian kids down to find Fiddlehead."

"Two more?" Moon mused. "Well, we have plenty of room if we can get out of this trap, Red Coyote. But those women—I don't want them staying with us."

"They wouldn't make very good ranch hands, I guess, though one can never tell. Did a hell of a job helping me and Fiddlehead with the cattle on the way across. But Vikki, she's got some notion about Fort Laramie—set up business outside the post and cater to the soldiers and emigrants coming along the trail. Wouldn't be surprised if Fiddlehead went with them, tell you the truth. He and that Sunshine Hobson, they're still thicker than thieves. Or perhaps he'll convince her to stay on at the ranch. Maybe they'll want to build themselves a cabin down along the creek somewhere."

"You mean, get married?"

"Stranger things have happened," Mike replied. "Moon-Gal, maybe you'd best try to sleep for a while. When darkness comes on, it's possible we can slip off—back up into Sulphur Springs Range, make it over to the old Te-Moak village and hole in. Even if Sam posts a guard on the hill, we might make it past him once night comes on."

"What if Fiddlehead rides straight into them? What happens to him, Mike?"

"Chauncy doesn't go anywhere without scouting ahead first, not if he can help it. Don't worry about the old fox. He hasn't lived to be six hundred years old without reason. Moon, the cattle are beautiful. I can't wait to see them grazing on our high meadows.

And one of the bulls, you won't believe it when you see him. He's the biggest, most fearsome-looking bovine ever hatched, tame, and smart as a whip. One on one, I think he could hold his own with a big buffalo bull. Enfadado Negro, Black Anger, that's his name. He's going to sire a truly heroic race of cattle for us."

"My husband is obviously drunk," Moon replied as she lay down and closed her eyes. "I'm tired, very tired. The baby's going to come soon. Not yet, though. Don't get all excited like a foolish boy. There's time enough for that."

Mike watched the lines in her face disappear as she relaxed, drifted into sleep, and suddenly he felt an even more profound sense of outrage toward Tarrango and his men.

But as she slept, sometimes she made little startled movements, her body's rebellion against what it had been put through during a long, desperate ride across the desert floor.

Or was birthing, indeed, about to begin?

The sun was dropping toward the crest of Sulphur Springs Range, and Moon was awake once more. Below, Tarrango's men had a fire blazing, and smells of cooking venison and bubbling coffee drifted up to them.

"Taking an early meal," Mike said. "That means they're getting ready to try something when they're through eating. Well, they have to climb the hill to get here, and we've got plenty of ammo and three guns to work with. They might make it if they come all in a rush, but we'll take half of them in the process. Sam must have left a couple of his boys back at Ruby Dome Ranch, or else a pair of them defected and stayed in California."

"One's at the ranch," Moon replied. "Lying dead close by the creek, unless Tarrango had him buried before they started chasing me. Antelope Tail put an arrow through his throat."

Mike nodded—then appeared momentarily to freeze, listening. He drew his pistol, spun about.

"Don't shoot me, bossman. I come to help."

"Tallchief!" Moon cried out. "How . . . ?"

"Just hid, that's all. Them owl-faces, they can't find nobody. I killed one—got him good, right in the ear. Big ugly man, one they called Wolf Mask. Was aiming at Tar-angi, but ugly guy got in the way. After that the owl-faces shot at the rocks for a while, then ride off, just leave Wolf Mask lying there."

The Te-Moak leader, flintlock rifle in hand, scrambled down over the boulders.

"Got somethin' to eat?" he asked. "I smell food."

"Look!" Moon said later. "Something's going on."

McLafferty, half dozing, scrambled to his knees and moved forward to the rim of their fortress.

"Two of 'em," Tallchief grunted. "Gettin' set to come up."

Mike studied the situation.

"Jack Addams. Think the other one's called Blanco. Looks like the damned fools are going to try it. Don't fire until they're most of the way up and out of breath. Then blast away."

Addams and Blanco made their dash, threw themselves flat behind a scrub of greasewood, and opened up with their pistols.

"Something fishy," Mike said. "Diversionary tactic, that's what. Moon, put a round or two down there with the rifle. Unless I miss my guess, we've got visitors slipping up on us from the rear."

McLafferty turned, crouched, and moved the length

of the long, sandy fracture between slabs of stone, past the scrubby pinyon where Gray Boy and Ghost were tethered. He heard Moon's rifle go off, nodded, and surveyed the area below. Nothing. He dropped over the rocks on the side away from the route by which he'd led the horses to the summit of the boulder heap in the first place, kept tight to a rock face, and moved upslope.

Tracks, slide marks in loose decomposed granite.

Mike scanned the slope above him, heard noise.

They're into the rocks already.

He scrambled upward, pistol in hand, toward the opening of the wide, sandy trench that led across to Moon and Tallchief.

"Cortez!" he called out. "Don't move."

Black Johnny, revolver in hand, stood up straight.

"Big Mike! Okay, old *companyero*, ye've got me dead to rights. For a man with no real stake in this mess, you're sure taking a lot of dumb chances. I mean, your wife being about ready to pop a kid, and all."

"Not in a mood for conversation, Black John. Throw down the gun."

"Just didn't want to do 'er too quick. Afraid you'd go trigger happy on me."

Cortez suddenly hurled himself to one side, rolled, and fired, the shot singing wide of its mark.

But McLafferty didn't miss. Black Johnny's body convulsed, his mouth wide open to suck in a final breath. Mike holstered his weapon, stood over Cortez, stared down at him.

"Shit, John, there wasn't any need to pull that. Don't know how God feels about a man killing fellows who are trying to kill him, but I don't suppose He likes it much. Had to make me do it, didn't you? Goddamn it."

"Good shootin, Mac-laffty."

Mike spun, the pistol leaping once more from its holster.

Downslope a few yards stood Antelope Tail and Smoke on the Hill, the old Te-Moak carrying two bows and two quivers stuffed with arrows, the younger a lance and a rawhide bag bulging, as it turned out, with food and an old whiskey jug corked with a pine stub and filled with water.

Moon fired several more rounds at Addams and Blanco. One shot missed by inches, striking sand directly in front of the greasewood thicket behind which the two men lay.

"Sonofabitch! My goddam eyes!"

Blanco was thrashing about, half blinded, and at that moment, Addams grabbed him by the shirt and pulled him downslope at a run, guiding his companion.

"Missed 'im an' still hit 'im!" Tallchief grinned.

McLafferty, Antelope Tail, and Smoke on the Hill came up through the wide trench between boulders. Moon, astonished, tapped Tallchief on the shoulder.

"We've got company, all right," she said.

"And the company's brought dinner." McLafferty grinned.

But there was little time for congeniality. At the foot of the granite formation, an enraged Sam Tarrango was shouting orders, screaming and cursing at his men.

"Set the fucking sagebrush on fire, you dumb bastards! We'll smoke their asses out!"

A dozen or so small fires were set, sputtering through sage and greasewood and tufts of desert grasses, while wind, blowing upslope toward the Sulphur Springs Range at this hour shortly before sundown, increased the flames and sent gray smoke coiling upward and over the crest of the hundred-foot-high rock formation. Moving behind cover of smoke, Tarrango's remaining men attempted to charge the boulders en masse, with Mike, Moon, and Tallchief firing down at them, pistol and rifle fire as well, while Antelope Tail and Smoke on the Hill launched arrows dipped in fresh rattlesnake venom.

"I am what my name says!" The old man grinned as he fit another arrow to the twisted gut string of his bow. "Stupid owls never make it up this hill!"

The advance was momentarily stopped, but now Mike glanced at Moon and then turned to stare toward the shadowed arroyos of Sulphur Springs Range westward, sky above the mountains beginning to burn with a yellow-crimson hue.

A muffled, rumbling sound, and soon thereafter the bleating and bawling of cattle . . .

The McLafferty herd, at a full run, appeared over the rim of an alluvial rise and began to pour down into the area where Sam Tarrango still stood and where his men had cooked their early supper. Enfadado Negro was at the front of the formation of galloping cattle, and Little Sister was astride her pinto no more than a few yards behind.

Wilson's Hawken rifle echoed across the intervening space, the mountain man pounding heels to his mule's sides. Stanislaus Bobby was shooting as well, Mike's loaned pistol in his hand as he rode, and Vikki, Sunshine, and Santa Maria also were in on the attack, coming on in the vanguard, with little Toyon trailing behind the cattle.

"Small buffalos!" Tallchief shouted as the cattle swarmed through the area at the foot of the boulders.

"Goddamn it now, Moon, you stay here. Don't you dare go charging down that hill . . ."

But it was too late. She was already past him, moving with awkward determination over the rim and toward the utter chaos of shouting and shooting below.

"Strong-headed woman," Smoke on the Hill laughed as he followed Mike, Tallchief, and Antelope Tail into the midst of the battle.

Fiddlehead Wilson was filled with demonic frenzy. He'd driven the herd hard all day, made early camp, and then went out scouting. When he saw smoke, he knew trouble was afoot, and he returned to the camp, rousted out both crew and animals. A word to Enfadado had been sufficient. And now, with the battle fairly joined, Fiddlehead was back in his proper element. It was like that time when he and Bill Williams's boys fought it out with the Kiowas back in '29. He fired, reloaded, fired again. And when he saw Blanco wandering about half-dazed, Fiddlehead leaped from his mule and took the paid gunman about the throat, thrust a blade into his stomach.

Dust and smoke everywhere, but after an astonishingly short time, the gunfire ceased. Dead men were lying all about. The cattle were nowhere in sight—headed eastward, Enfadado leading, toward Humboldt's little South Branch. After a run of several miles and the smell of water sweet in the air, temptation had been simply too great.

Mike stood next to Moon in the waning light of sundown. He surveyed the devastation that had been brought about so quickly, taking note that all his own people were all still on their feet. Antelope Tail had a gash across his forehead, slash wound from a knife, and Little Sister was pressing a kerchief to the Te-Moak's brow to stanch the bleeding. Victoria Queen was pacing from one body to another, apparently searching for the mortal remains of Sam Tarrango, her enemy but also her onetime lover.

Miraculously, everyone in the strange alliance had

survived. There were not even any downed cattle, accidental victims of gunfire, though it was possible one or two had been hit. Well, they wouldn't know until tomorrow. Enfadado Negro would keep his tribe close by the waters of the Humboldt Branch—no great task, since cattle, Mike reflected, were not known to be keen on exploring desert lands.

Then a voice cut through the air.

"All right, McLafferty, it's one-on-one. Tell the others to get the hell out of the way."

A lone figure emerged from behind a double-boled juniper, took half a dozen steps forward, stopped.

Pete the Gun.

Mike pushed Moon out of harm's way and then waved the others away.

"Let's call it a day, Pete. There's been more than enough killing. I've got no heart for it."

"A good day to die, Big Mike. That's what Wolf Mask used to say. Well, he's turned in his chips, and that's what you're going to do, too. A fair draw, McLafferty."

"If you do manage to kill me, Pete, Fiddlehead'll drop you on the spot. It's over, man. Get on your horse and ride off. I've got no fight with you now, and we've both got better things to do than—"

At that instant Pete went to one knee, pulling his weapon in the process and raising it to fire.

The revolver dropped from his hand as Mike McLafferty's gun went off, and Pete flopped backward, one leg beneath him and the other kicking.

In the silence that followed, Fiddlehead strode over to the dead man, stared at him.

Mike's shot had struck Pete the Gun in the center of the forehead.

"Sonny," Wilson grinned, "ye got to show this child

how ye do it. Ain't no real human can pull a popgun that quick."

"Jesus H. Christ!" Mike said, holstering his weapon. "This is no damned way to raise cattle."

"Pretty good shootin', though," Tallchief said. "You pay me for work, Mac-laffty, I'm going to buy gun like yours. Practice a lot, maybe."

Vikki Queen stood beside Fiddlehead, glanced at the mortal remains of the once-feared gunfighter, shrugged.

"I've checked all the bodies," she said. "Sam's not one of them. Maybe he hopped a ride with one of the cows."

Moon put her arms around Mike's middle, clung to him.

"Did you and Fiddlehead bring any whiskey from California?" she asked. "One or two drinks, and maybe I'll be ready to have a baby."

Fiddlehead laughed, winked at Sunshine—the blond girl standing there as if in shock, a pistol still in her hand, and the hand trembling.

"Jug's in the chuck wagon," Wilson replied. "Moon gal, since it's ye, by Gawd this spineless porkypine'll ride back an' get 'er. Could use a swig meself, come to think upon it."

22 Late June sun burned out of a deep blue sky over Ruby Dome Ranch, but Moon sat comfortably in the shade of a shake-roofed porch along the front of the cabin, working with her needle, adding a few embellishments of dyed porcupine quills to the deerskin covering over a cradle board that had essentially been finished months ago in anticipation of the new arrival. Elizabeth sat near, watching her deft stitchery with fascination, but Mike and Tallchief and Fiddlehead labored in the sun's full heat, perspiration glistening on stripped torsos as they set skinned poles into place for an addition to the house in order to accommodate their greatly increased "family" and to include proper sleeping quarters for Elizabeth, Toyon, Stanislaus Bobby, and Fiddlehead. "And maybe half a hundred more," as McLafferty said with a resigned grin.

The meadows beyond were dotted with groups of cattle moving about slowly as they grazed, making up generously for skipped meals on the trail.

Stanislaus Bobby and Toyon leaned against a railing along with Slow Lizard, Grasshopper, and Jacques, the Miwoks talking and pointing to various animals, obviously taking great proprietary pride as they explained the fine points of cattle husbandry to these boys who had never before even seen such fabulous beasts.

In the brief interval since the showdown with Tarrango's men, Moon had rested, feeling deliciously and luxuriously lazy as she waited out the final few days before the baby's birth. She leaned back, rested her hands on her taut belly, and closed her eyes for a moment. Inside the house she could hear the angels talking, their voices cheerful and their conversation punctuated by bursts of laughter as they made preparations for their departure eastward, destination apparently Fort Laramie, where they planned to develop a regular clientele among the soldiers as well as the more transient patronage of passing emigrant trains.

Of the four, only Sunshine Hobson seemed less than wildly enthusiastic about the move, her pretty features despondent when she thought herself unobserved, and at such times she let down the mask of cheerfulness that she tried to maintain.

Jacques drifted over from the fence, gulped a dipperful of water from the bucket that stood on a little table in the shade.

"You okay, Mom?" he asked anxiously. "Is my new sister coming yet?"

Moon opened her eyes, laughed.

"How many times have you asked that today? You'll be the first to know, Little Bull, I promise."

"We aren't even sure if it's a sister or a brother, Jacques," Elizabeth added. "Do you think she—he—might have red hair like Mike's?"

"Or like big sister?" Moon teased.

"Well, I guess that would be nice," Elizabeth admitted, blushing. "But I really don't care. Will you teach me to do that sometime?"

"What?" Moon asked, somewhat startled.

"That. With the quills. It's beautiful. My mother taught me to crochet, but we don't have any thread or needles for crocheting. I love to sew."

"Of course. It's not hard. It just takes patience."

"Like ever'thin' else that's worth a piss in the wind," Fiddlehead said, stepping to the water bucket himself.

"What do you know about patience, Fiddlehead?" Moon laughed. "All you mountain men move around so fast you don't even put down footprints, let alone roots."

"Wagh! Tell that to some green'un who ain't waded in beaver streams where ye got to bust the ice with a hand axe fore ye can even reach the trap. Patience! I ever tell ye about the time I hid out from the Rees? Stark nekkid in the middle o' January in a beaver's house, ice water up to the breechclout if I'd had one, an' I stood that way fer three days whilst the danged savages was whoopin' an' chasin' around like a pack o' wolves? Back in '15, that were—less it was ought-nine—"

"Strange thing, when you come to think of it," Mike commented, walking over and dropping to the ground, "how many experiences these old-timers had in common. I heard almost the exact same thing happened to Colter."

"Colter was a powerful liar, an' that's a fact. Who ye think taught that child his tricks, I ast ye?"

"You did, didn't you, Uncle Fiddlehead?" Jacques nodded.

Wilson merely smiled modestly, drew his pipe from a pocket, and began tamping tobacco into it.

"No-good crew quit on me again," Tallchief complained, joining Mike on the ground in the shade. "That it for the day, or what, boss?"

"Too damned hot to work in the sun anymore," Mike said. "Do a little bit more when it cools down this evening."

"Not this evening," Tallchief reminded him. "This evening you got to come up to the village. Women been all day long cooking that beef you give us. Big party tonight. Big celebration. Everybody come."

"What are we celebrating?" Moon asked.

"Everything. Every damned thing. Mac-laffty comes back, got cows, got two new children. Good-bye party for the pretty white women. One or two other things to celebrate, too."

"You keep saying that. What other things? You're being mysterious about this, Tallchief."

"You see tonight," the Te-Moak said and then grinned broadly. "Not working anymore today, maybe I go home and get ready, dress up fancy. Put on blue face paint."

Moon and Mike stared at one another, shrugged, and the barrel-chested Te-Moak strolled away up toward his village, humming a complicated tune.

With the angels decked out in full finery for the occasion, black lace, red satin, and plummeting decolletage predominating, the contingent from McLafferty's ranch made its way at sundown to the brush lodges of the Te-Moaks. Already a huge fire was blazing in the center of the village, and on an area spread with fresh cedar boughs, Swimming Duck, Rain, and Camas Flower were setting out flat baskets heaped with chunks of pit-roasted beef as well as rabbit stew, camas cakes, wild honey, berry soup, and other delicacies.

The Te-Moaks greeted their guests enthusiastically. Swimming Duck in particular hugged Moon and Elizabeth and made a great fuss over Jacques, as if it had been months rather than the previous day since she had seen them last, Moon observed with some puzzlement that the woman seemed to be on the verge of tears at times.

Mike contributed to the general gaiety a few bottles of whiskey that he'd brought back from the settlements and, caught up in the general celebration that prevailed, immediately began proposing toasts, insisting that everyone, including even Jacques and Grasshopper, take at least a taste from the bottles as they were passed.

"First off, a toast to my old friend Enfadado Negro and to the cows in general, without whom none of this would be possible."

"How ye figgerin' that one, Michael?" Fiddlehead growled.

"Man'd be a damned fool to put a ranch out here without any cows."

"Red Coyote is right. If we didn't have a ranch, we would not have met Tallchief and our other friends, and if Fiddlehead and Michael had not gone for cows, we would not have Stanislaus Bobby and Toyon with us. We toast the cows, then."

McLafferty decorously passed the first bottle to Moon, who sipped and handed it along to Swimming Duck. Tallchief's wife grimaced as she tasted the unfamiliar firewater and handed it quickly to her husband. With the exception of Tallchief, who'd drunk the fierce bootleg liquor of Hudson's Bay traders, none of the Te-Moaks appreciated "owl-face firewater," although all followed the ritual gamely.

"Our first toast, though," Elizabeth said, eyes shining in firelight, "should have been to us, to all of us being together, and safe after everything. Perhaps I should be saying grace instead, but maybe this means the same thing. Oh, I sound foolish. God bless us!"

"I'll drink to that, Liz-beth, whether the Old Feller's got pointy ears and a coyote snout or a set o' grizzled whiskers like this hawg," Fiddlehead agreed, "we could damn sure use somebody's blessin'. An' while we're at it, how's about we drink to these here angels? By Gawd, a man couldn't ask fer a beter set o' female *compañeros*. This old porkypine"—he stopped, glanced sadly at Sunshine, truly angelic-looking in a fluffy, off-the-shoulder gown of lavender organdy, cleared his throat—"this old porkypine's gonna miss ye, all of ye."

"Okay," shouted Tallchief, rising and looking around until the gathering grew quiet, "okay, we drink to all that, but before everybody get too damn drunk to hear, I got something to drink to."

He paused dramatically, and the others waited, silent, for him to continue.

"Get on with it, then, ye sawed-off thief," Fiddlehead finally said. "We got serious guzzlin' to do, an' ye're holdin' up the process."

Tallchief smiled widely. "All right, then, by goddamn, we drink to—to Moon and big Morning Star medicine."

The others looked puzzled, but Moon suddenly understood and laughed in happy disbelief.

"Is it true? Swimming Duck?"

Tallchief's wife, sitting modestly behind her husband, glanced up, her round face suddenly crinkling, teeth gleaming in firelight as she broke into smiles.

"Is true," she said, looking down in sudden shyness. "I have baby too after while."

The gathering sat in stunned silence for an instant

longer, then broke into loud whoops and shouts of congratulations, and the bottle was passed again. Moon rose to embrace Swimming Duck, and in a short time all the women had drifted into a group to themselves, discussing this momentous news, offering advice and anecdotes about childbearing and rearing. Swimming Duck beamed happily in the midst of them, and the men passed the bottle freely among themselves, belaboring Tallchief on the back and making broad jokes.

As this point a terrible and yet mournful sound issued from the willowbrush thickets just below the Te-Moak encampment.

"For Christ's sake!" Mike laughed. "I do believe the King of California has come to visit."

He walked toward the sound, disappeared into darkness, and re-emerged a moment later, Enfadado Negro in tow, the huge longhorn bull thumping along beside him.

Mike shrugged helplessly. "Guess he got lonely."

Enfadado rolled his eyes, lifted his nose to heaven, and bellowed.

The people moved about, some cautiously, but all making much of the huge beast whose responsibility it was to maintain order among the cattle of Ruby Dome.

In the general regrouping, however, Fiddlehead and Sunshine Hobson slipped off together, a fact that none noticed until sometime later.

The Te-Moaks slept late in their brush lodges the next day, but those in the McLafferty household rose shortly after sunrise, many red-eyed and looking the worse for the previous night's celebration, but Queen Vikki was adamant that she and her girls get an early start on their trail. When it was discovered that Sunshine and Fiddlehead had not returned to the cabin during the night, Vikki at first cursed loudly, impatient with the delay, but then she shrugged and laughed.

"What the hell," she said, "I guess I can find another girl somewhere if she's decided to shack up permanently with old Chauncy Whiskers. Guess we owe him that much."

But just then the grizzled veteran of the mountains and the thin blond girl rode up, sitting double on Fiddlehead's mule, Sunshine looking exceptionally frazzled and unkempt, and both man and woman wearing wistful expressions.

"Looks like yore outfit's jest about set to pull out," Wilson said, glancing at Vikki and the others as they stood near the corral, horses saddled and pack animals loaded.

"You coming with us or not, Sunshine?" Vikki asked bluntly.

"I'm coming," she said. "Just give me a few moments."

"I done packed yore outfit," Little Sister said. "I knowed y'all'd be along directly."

"Well, then . . . Chauncy, I . . ." Sunshine looked at Fiddlehead, tried to smile.

"Aw, hell, I know, sweetpea."

He helped her down from the mule, letting his hands linger on her for several moments after she stood on the ground, as if reluctant to let her go, but he cleared his throat and tried to speak heartily.

"Well, Vikki, Maria, Sister, you gals got a long trail ahead of you. This hoss ain't never been keen on sayin' good-bye. You keep yore damn guns loaded and stick to the trails. She's a long way to Salt Lake, and I ain't shore I'd trust the blamed saints too far, nuther. Ye head fer Bridger's Fort, and be shore ye tell ol' Gabe I blowed up that glass mountain o' his'n an' sold the pieces for ladies' makeup mirrors."

"We'll miss you Chauncy," Vikki said, leaning forward and kissing him on the cheek. "You too, Mike."

She winked at McLafferty and held out her hand.

"You got quite a fellow, Moon" she added. "Hang onto him."

"You're still welcome to stay," Moon said. "Any or all of you. Little Sister, if you ever change your mind..."

"Don't reckon I will, Miz Moon, but I thanks you for askin'. This girl gonna be jest fine, don't y'all worry none."

"*Es verdad.*" Santa Maria de la Cruz y de la Rosa smiled. "We be better than fine, we be rich, *de seguro. Vaya con dios,* Chauncy and Mike. We miss you."

"Fiddlehead," Moon said abruptly, watching the old trapper and Sunshine staring sadly at one another, "I really don't think it's such a good idea for these women to head out for Fort Laramie without a guide. That's a bad desert, hard to find water. They'll need someone to hunt for them as well. And we don't really know what happened to Sam Tarrango, do we? He could be out there somewhere. Do you think it's safe, Mac-lafferty?"

"You may be right," Mike said, rubbing his chin. "We're going to need help, now that we've got all those cows, but we can probably manage with Stanislaus Bobby and Toyon and Tallchief and the others, for a while at least. What do you say, Chaunce?"

Fiddlehead glared at Mike, and muttered, "Don't think ye're pullin' the wool over this child's eyes, sonny. I know what ye're up to."

"We would appreciate the escort, Mr. Wilson," Vikki urged, and Sunshine merely stared at him, blue eyes soft and smiling.

"All right, then. I guess thar's somethin' to what ye're sayin' at that. But don't ye go givin' that Shucker runt, that Smallchief or what the hell ever his handle is, don't be givin' him my foreman's job. I'll be back afore the snow flies, an' ye can count on that."

"Country sho look different this time o' year than it did last winter when we come this way," Little Sister remarked, lifting her wide-brimmed man's hat and wiping beads of perspiration from her face, letting the air cool her damp hair for a few minutes before replacing the sombrero as protection against fierce desert sun. It was nearing noon of the second day of their journey, one that had taken them south for some distance along the Hastings Trail, only turning eastward when they reached the southern end of the range.

The distance shimmered with heat, brown hills wavering in a yellow glare of light. The only sound beyond the creaking of saddles and the slow plodding of the animals' hooves was a clicking whir of grasshoppers occasionally leaping, brilliant red or green or yellow underwings displayed as they coasted to new perches out of the way of the intruders on horseback.

"I'd just about settle for a few inches of snow right now," Queen Vikki agreed.

"This is *el rancho del diablo*," Maria complained, waving a black lace fan in front of her face, the dainty implement most incongruous in context with the men's jeans and shirt that she as well as the rest of the angels wore.

Only Fiddlehead and Sunshine seemed oblivious to discomfort, riding a little distance ahead of the others and talking in low tones.

They rested for a time in such shade as they could find during the hours of fiercest heat, then continued, turning north once they'd reached the east face of the Rubies along this trail that would take them across the Bonneville Desert to Salt Lake and Bridger's Fort far beyond.

As the sun was dropping toward the tops of the peaks to the west, they came to a long, narrow lake, its shallow water ruffled by a slight afternoon breeze, and cottonwoods rustling their leaves beside the shore.

The tired animals picked up their pace and moved excitedly to the shore to dip their muzzles into cool liquid.

The angels dismounted quickly, all kneeling to splash arms and faces, and Santa Maria stripped completely and waded out, cupping handfuls over slender shoulders and exquisitely formed breasts.

Fiddlehead coughed and turned away grinning, while Vikki winked at him, said, "What the hell?" and followed Maria's lead. Sunshine ducked into the water fully clothed, pulling playfully at Fiddlehead's hand to draw him in after her. Little Sister, however, contented herself by filling her hat with water and clapping it back on her head, and then set off walking up the shore, exploring.

In a moment she returned, eyes large and voice hushed.

"Miss Vikki, I think you better come take a look," she said.

"What is it?" Vikki asked, wading to shore and pulling her clothes on without bothering to dry herself. Something in the mulatto girl's tone had already alerted her to the fact that whatever this was, it was a matter of importance.

"I think you better come see for yo'self. You too, Chauncy."

Fiddlehead, Sunshine, and Vikki followed the girl up the shore, Maria scrambling out of the water then as well and calling *"Esperad para mi!"* She ran to catch up to the others, not bothering to dress, reaching her companions just as Little Sister stopped, pointing ahead.

Close by the water, curled nearly into fetal position and with his head pillowed on one arm, lay Sam Tarrango, dressed only in torn, filthy remnants of slacks and ruffled shirt, arms and face bruised and bloody, cheeks sunken and blackened by sun and several days growth of beard. His eyes were closed, and he didn't move.

The angels and Fiddlehead stood frozen for a moment, silently watching.

"Is he even *alive?*" Sunshine half-whispered.

Bloodshot eyes flickered open, rested on the four women and one man without any particular sign of recognition.

"Vikki?" he croaked at last. "Is that you, darlin'? Damn it, I've missed you, gal."

"What we gon' do with him?" Little Sister asked. "Looks to me like he's about done—half-starved an' near beat to death with by sun an' whatnot. Leg's shot up, don' look good."

Santa Maria, standing naked with hands on hips, suddenly threw back her head and broke into an insane laugh.

"Fix him like *un castrado*—what you call that bull without *cojones*—like a steer, then cut his throat and throw him into the lake for *los pezes* to eat."

"Let's be civil-ize," Fiddlehead suggested. "This child says hang the damned polecat like he wanted to do to ye gals. Either that or jest leave 'im. He'll go under right purty on his own, I figger. Vultures has got to eat, too."

The subject of this debate, however, seemed oblivious to what was being said. Tarrango tried to sit up, holding a hand out toward Vikki, and then fell back.

"You got something to eat, old buddy?" he whispered. "Seem to be awful hungry. Can't think why. Just finished that big dinner at the Emporium."

"Shit!" Vikki said after some minutes of silent contemplation of her onetime lover. "I can't do it. Wish I could, but I can't. The rest of you go on without me, if you want. I got to take care of this worthless son of a bitch."

"Wha-a-a-t?" Little Sister asked incredulously, and Santa Maria exploded into a torrent of Spanish invective.

"After what he done to the four of ye?" Fiddlehead asked.

"We won't leave you, Vikki," Sunshine said, "but I think you're making a mistake. It's like keeping a pet rattlesnake."

"As I said, I wish it wasn't so, but I've got to do it. Sam and I had something going once. Hell, maybe we can use him as a bouncer in the place in Laramie."

"Cut yer throat when ye're sleepin', that 'un will," Fiddlehead warned.

"Maybe he's learned his lesson," Vikki mused. "How about it, Sammy? You going to kill Vikki in her sleep?"

"Vikki, darlin'? What do you say we go down the street for a beefsteak and a couple drinks for old times?" Tarrango mumbled through swollen lips.

"See what I mean?" Vikki asked. "Like a damned hurt hound. How could I leave him like this way?"

Fiddlehead considered the situation, lifted his beaver cap, and scratched his scalp.

"Seems easy enough to this hawg, but ye have yore own way, Vikki. Ain't never been nobody, since Old Man Gawd drug the world up from the muck, as has understood the ways of the fee-male mind, nohow."

"Ain't that the truth though?" Vikki laughed, then grabbed Fiddlehead's chin whiskers and kissed him on the cheek.

Epilogue

For the time being, all operations at the Ruby Dome spread were suspended, not by decree but by unspoken consenuss. The partially completed new quarters gaped at hot, blue sky, and a stack of peeled fir poles lay warping in the sun.

Rangy brown cattle clustered in the meadows, Enfadado Negro moving from group to group, hooking with a horn here and there or merely snorting and making threatening jumps at those cows which, for whatever reason, did not conform to his idea of proper order within the herd. For their part, the cows blinked at him, stepped quietly out of his path when he became belligerent, and went on with their grazing, apparently little concerned with his philosophical notions of ideal hierarchical rankings.

The humans also gathered in clusters, these near the ranch house and predominantly male, talking among themselves, moving about, but always with an eye to whatever activity was taking place within.

Women occasionally stepped outdoors on some errand and were quickly surrounded, questioned eagerly, allowed to return.

Mike McLafferty, Jacques riding on his shoulders, seemed an inexhaustible spring of nervous energy, unable to stand or sit but walking restlessly from corral to sheds to the front of the house, making his circuit over and over.

"Put me down, Mike," Jacques said suddenly. "I'm tired of riding. I want to see my new sister."

"I keep telling you, pard, your sister isn't here yet," Mike replied, a trace of impatience creeping into his voice.

"She's *got* to be here by now. It's been *hours*."

"Babies are that way. They have their own notion of time."

"Why can't I go into the house where mother is? All the girls are in there, even Toyon. That's not fair."

"Birthing is a strictly female business, son. At least that's the way they feel about it. We'd cause a rout in the henhouse if any of us went in there."

"Well, let me down anyway. Bobby and Slow Lizard are playing that game where they throw knives into the ground. I want to play too."

"Don't think they'll let you, but you can go watch. There's old Grasshopper. Maybe the two of you can think up something to get into."

"Yes," Jacques said, scrambling away as Mike lifted him down from his shoulders.

Tallchief approached, grinning, slapping Mike on the shoulders.

"Settle down, boss," he said. "You gonna wear out the ground. Moon be okay, everything be just fine. Women do this all the time."

"I tell you, Tallchief," Mike said, half laughing, "I don't know why they let us get them into a family way. I don't think I'd put up with it if I'd been born female."

Tallchief had a conspiratorial gleam in his eyes.

"Women like it," he said. "You see how happy

Swimming Duck is now? She sing all the time again, just like she use to, now, we got a baby comin'. Owl-faces worry too much."

Mike didn't reply, walked distractedly to the corral gate again, leaned on the railing. Gray Boy came over and nuzzled hopefully at his shirt pocket, looking for sugar lumps that his human sometimes carried. Mike scratched absently between the horse's ears.

Tallchief had followed, pounded Mike on the back once again, and laughed wordlessly.

"It's taking too damn long," McLafferty fretted. "Something's wrong."

Tallchief chuckled.

"You come over, have a drink of whiskey with me and Antelope and Smoke. Antelope been through this three times, and nobody remembers how many times old Smoke even been married, let alone how many babies."

"Where are they all now?" Mike asked, not really curious but wishing to pass the dragging seconds.

"Oh, here, there. Some dead, some married and gone off with other people. That's how it is with us. Come on over. He tell you all about it."

Mike shrugged, approached Antelope Tail and Smoke on the Hill, the men sitting on a corner of the porch, passing a bottle back and forth.

Mike accepted the container, took a long pull, and then found that he couldn't concentrate on what the others were saying. He turned to pace toward the outbuildings once more.

The door to the house opened, and he pivoted at the sound eagerly. Elizabeth stood on the porch, eyes wide and glistening with tears.

"Mike," she said, voice hushed, choking, "come in here. Moon wants you."

Suddenly McLafferty wanted to run away, terrible fear racing through his innards.

She's dying, she wants to say good-bye, he thought. Don't think that, stupid thing to think. Elizabeth's choked up, it's an emotional experience for women. Moon, beautiful Moon, don't leave me now.

"Come on!" Elizabeth said, motioning impatiently, and disappeared inside.

Mike followed, his impulse to hurry to his wife's side at war with that other impulse to flee to the corral, mount Gray Boy, and ride as fast and as far as he could so that he would never have to know.

In the main room Elizabeth, Rain, Camas Flower, and Toyon stood watching him expectantly, Camas Flower and Toyon glancing at one another and giggling. He felt an insane, momentary flare of anger at them: How can they laugh when Moon may be . . . Then he realized their laughter could only mean that Moon was not, in fact, dying, and his knees threatened to buckle from sheer relief.

"She's . . . It's . . . ?"

"Go in and see, silly," Toyon replied.

At first the one thing he saw was Moon, her face shining with perspiration in the dim light of the room, her hair clinging in damp strands about her forehead and neck. She looked tired, circles under her eyes, but she was smiling in a way that he'd never seen before.

Mike dropped to his knees beside the bed, wrapped his arms around her, clung. She touched his face, then pushed at him.

"Aren't you even going to look at your son?" she asked.

"Moon . . ."

"Look, foolish Coyote!"

He glanced up then, saw Swimming Duck standing beside him, round face beaming as she exchanged a glance with Moon, almost as if the two shared some secret.

"Your son, Mc-laffty," she said, holding out a tiny, red-faced bundle for him to inspect.

The newborn's cloudy eyes came open as Mike took the infant cautiously into his arms, and immediately the little male human began wailing, quite a lusty howl for a creature his size.

Uncertain what to do, McLafferty held his noisy bundle of nothing, felt himself beginning to smile.

"Don't just stand there, Red Coyote," Moon whispered. "Give your son back to Swimming Duck so you can see your daughter."

"My what . . . ?"

Then he realized there was, indeed, another source of noise, and old Sage Hen rose from a chair in one corner of the room. She grinned a gap-toothed smile and held out another fur-wrapped bundle.

Mike pulled back the covering from this second wizened red face, touched at it with a finger, looked back at Moon, realized his wife was now laughing softly at him. He felt a sudden urge to weep like a five-year-old. He swallowed hard, knelt again beside the bed.

"We finally did it, Mac-lafferty," Moon said. "I think we've got a real family now."

Out in the meadow, Enfadado Negro tossed his head and snorted indignantly. Definitely, something was askew concerning activities near the house. He had authorized no loud noises such as the prolonged *WHOOP!* that resounded from inside the walls, nor the great banging of the door and the ridiculous human laughter that followed.

The big bull stared coldly at the sudden whirl of movement among the two-legged members of his herd, considered leaping the fence to chastize these unruly individuals. At that moment, however, he noticed a group of cows who clearly had been grazing in the same area of particularly lush grass for too long a time, and so he trotted away to deal with this more urgent problem, forgetting for the time about the growing chorus of laughter and happy shouts coming from the lesser beings clustered near the log cabin across the way.